Rave reviews for Jacey Bedford's Psi-Tech novels:

"A well-defined and intriguing tale set in the not-too-distant future.... Everything is undeniably creative and colorful, from the technology to foreign planets to the human (and humanoid) characters. Author Bedford's world-building feels very complete and believable, with excellent descriptions bringing it all to life." —*RT Book Reviews*

"Bedford mixes romance and intrigue in this promising debut, which opens the Psi-Tech space opera series.... Readers who crave high adventure and tense plots will enjoy this voyage into the future." —*Publishers Weekly*

"A nostalgic space opera.... Bedford's prose is brisk and carries the reader quite sufficiently along." —Tor.com

"I'm very, very excited to see where this series goes next. The foundation that Bedford has laid has so much potential and promise. This is an author I will watch" —Bookworm Blues

"Space opera isn't dead; instead, delightfully, it has grown up.... A fine example of a novel which has its roots in the subgenre but grows beyond it." —Jaine Fenn, author of *Principles of Angels*

"The first of a new space opera series that delivers the goods and holds lots of promise of things to come." —SF Signal at kirkus.com

"Bedford packs a high-interest punch into each paragraph. Characters, plot and technology, plus way-out-there stuff: *Crossways* has it all." —Kings River Life Magazine

DAW Books proudly presents
the novels of Jacey Bedford:

The Psi-Tech Novels
EMPIRE OF DUST
CROSSWAYS
NIMBUS

Rowankind
WINTERWOOD
SILVERWOLF

JACEY BEDFORD

NIMBUS

A PSI-TECH NOVEL

DAW BOOKS, INC.
DONALD A. WOLLHEIM, FOUNDER
375 Hudson Street, New York, NY 10014

ELIZABETH R. WOLLHEIM
SHEILA E. GILBERT
PUBLISHERS
www.dawbooks.com

First Printing, October 2017
1 2 3 4 5 6 7 8 9

Acknowledgments

When you pick up a book from a shelf and look inside, you are not simply seeing the work of an author, but that of a team. I would especially like to thank all at DAW: my lovely (Hugo-winning) editor, Sheila Gilbert, Josh Starr and all the publication staff, copyeditor, proofreader, and publicists. I'd also like to thank Stephan Martiniere for another great cover. Thanks also to my (then) agent Amy Boggs and to my new agent Don Maass, and all at Donald Maass Literary Agency, for enthusiasm, expertise and guidance.

I am especially grateful to my beta readers, those who dismember my manuscripts to find all my mistakes, especially Jaine Fenn for critiques above and beyond. I am also indebted to writers in the Northwrite SF writers' group: John Moran, Terry Jackman, Gus Smith, Liz Sourbutt, Tina Anghelatos, Tony Ballantyne, C. J. Jessop, Sue Oke, and Kari Sperring (without whom this book, and others, might never have happened).

In addition I'd like to thank those not already thanked who attended Milford and wrestled with my first and last chapters in 2015 and 2016: Ben Jeapes, Liz Williams, Dave Clements, David Turnbull, Val Nolan, Jackie Hatton, Tiffani Angus, Chris Butler, Matt Colborn, Heather Lindsley, Dave Gullen, David Allan, Guy T. Martland, Jim Anderson, Glen Mehn, Elizabeth Counihan, Lizzy Priest, Sue Thomason, Amy Tibbetts, Pauline Morgan and Siobhan McVeigh.

Thanks also to my bandmate in Artisan and regular cinebuddy, Hilary Spencer, who turns seek-the-typo into a game, and attacks my manuscripts mercilessly with a metaphorical red pen.

An extra-special thank you and much love to my husband, Brian, offspring, Ghillan and Joe, and my mum, Joan

Lockyer, for tolerating my obsessive, post-midnight keyboard pounding and other writerly foibles.

And lastly, thanks to you for buying, reading, talking about, reviewing and recommending not just my books, but all books. Without readers there would be no writers. You rock! Keep turning the pages.

Jacey Bedford
Yorkshire, June 2017
www.jaceybedford.co.uk

Chapter One

SWITCH

IF THIS WAS WINNING, CARA CARLINNI WAS sure as hell glad they hadn't lost. It had been a tough year since the combined fleets of five megacorporations had tried to pound Crossways into submission.

Tried and failed.

Cara threaded her way through what had been a piazza, if that didn't sound too pretentious on a space station. It was an area wide enough for an assortment of shops, booths, and pavement cafes. Enterprising merchants had cleared away enough rubble to set up their stalls again within a few days of the bombardment, and since there were other, more urgent repairs, they'd been allowed to get on with it. They'd reused the rubble, incorporated it into new walls or carted it off, bucket by bucket, to be disposed of—probably illegally— via an airlock, overseen by someone's uncle's third cousin with a blind eye suitable for turning.

She came here most days, ostensibly to get her coffee fix, but largely to take the temperature of the feelings on the station. Empathy cranked up to eleven, she wandered between the stalls, chatting with some vendors, nodding politely to others. She gave the impression of being relaxed, but she glanced left and right, cataloging the faces, noting anything out of place in the organized chaos.

The wounded space station spun in high orbit above Olyanda, a planet with significant deposits of precious platinum, vital for the jump gate system. A platinum bonanza was both a blessing and a curse—a blessing only if you could hold on to it.

Sadly, all the platinum in the galaxy couldn't bring back the dead. They might never know how many they'd lost. A station like Crossways didn't keep tabs on its inhabitants.

Whether you called Crossways a free port or a rogue depended on which side of the corporate fence you stood on. Cara might once have called it rogue, but she'd crossed that line when the good guys proved to be anything but and Crossways' criminal community—most of them, anyway— turned out to be not so bad once you got to know them.

She stood in line at Java Joe's. The woman in front of her had thinning gray hair. There was the ridge of a scar running diagonally across her scalp, leaving an odd spiky tuft sticking up at an angle. The woman ran her fingers over her head, combing the tuft back into place. It lasted about five seconds and then, strand by strand, sprang to attention again. Cara was suddenly curious to run her fingers through her own short locks to see if there was anything out of place. No, she'd combed it this morning; it was fine.

Joe wasn't the fastest barista on station, but he gave each customer his full attention, served great coffee from his little handcart, and picked up the best gossip. The thin-haired woman took her cup and wandered away, leaving Cara at the front of the line.

"Hey, headspace lady." Joe grinned at her. "How are you doing this morning?" He'd quickly worked out that she was a Telepath. The Free Company flash on her buddysuit identified her as a psi-tech of one sort or another, but she could have been a Finder or a Navigator or even a Psi-Mech.

"Hey, Joe. Usual please."

"Coming right up." He hit the grinder, filled the filter basket, and tamped the coffee grounds. While the water jetted through, he half-turned his head. "You tell all the Free Company to come here for their morning coffee. I could do with the business."

Cara glanced round. "It looks busy enough."

"Yeah, now it is, but Captain Syke put a temporary curfew on us. Close at nine sharp and don't open again until seven the following morning. I used to stay open until midnight for the shift change workers."

"Curfew? Has there been trouble?"

"A few locals getting excited. You know how it is."

"I know."

There were still tensions, of course. Nearly fourteen months after the battle, and some sections of Crossways were still sealed off, leaking air like an old sieve. Fifty thousand displaced inhabitants from the station's rim had migrated toward the illusion of safety at the central core, crowding the established residents. Tempers flared and trouble erupted on a regular basis.

"I think you should go and look at Flash Harry's stall. There's something there you might be interested in." Joe took a scan of her handpad in payment and winked at her before he turned to the next customer in line.

Cara knew where Flash Harry displayed his wares. He was a purveyor of collectibles, or so he said. In practice, that meant he sold items he'd scavenged from the wreckage. One way or another, there was a plethora of abandoned stuff that had once belonged to the dead or the displaced. She suspected he had a stash somewhere, and was gradually filtering it out via this and other stalls he ran.

Harry saw her coming, but not soon enough to hide the one item that drew her attention. Among a selection of bags was a battered satchel with a recognizable scar where a logo had been. It was a Psi-Mech's satchel, normally filled with small spider bots used for cutting, drilling, riveting, and welding. All mind-controlled.

"Where did you get this, Harry?" She opened it and checked. No bots. "And where's the tech that was inside it?"

"I swear it's genuine, Miss Carlinni."

"I can see it's genuine. I know exactly what it is. I want to know how you came by it and, more importantly, what happened to the Psi-Mech who owned it."

Harry's face took on a scrunched-up look that told her he was going to start whining.

"Or should I call the militia?" she asked.

"No need for that. One o' my urchins found it close to where the Saturn Arm sheared when the ring broke away.

This side of the big blast doors. No bots in it. Reckon whoever owned it was about his business when whatever happened happened. Know what I mean?"

She did. They'd lost psi-techs in the bombardment, some
accounted for, some not. If they could figure out who this
had belonged to, they'd at least know where he—or she—
had died.

"I'll take it." She tucked the satchel under her arm.
"Anytime you find something you think belongs to the Free
Company, you bring it to us. Understand? And don't hide it
away for so long next time, or I'll ask Captain Syke to find
an excuse to search your stash."

"Sure, Miss Carlinni."

"You won't be out of pocket." She flipped a small credit
chip over the stall, and Harry caught it with practiced ease.
A greasy smile replaced his hangdog expression.

Sipping her coffee slowly, she passed the antigrav tube
and made her way to a stairwell with medonite walls and
foam-metal steps in a mesh pattern that let her see down to
the dizzying depths. Antigrav tubes and hot coffee didn't
mix, and she'd forgotten to ask Joe for a lid for the cup. She
skipped up three flights of steps, light in the half-gravity,
regaining weight when she emerged close to Blue Seven
where the Free Company had made their home.

The duty guard waved Cara through with a nod and a
smile.

She walked along the dimly lit barbican, hearing the
doors at one end lock behind her before the doors at the
other end opened.

She headed straight for the main office where Morwenna
Phipps worked her organizational magic. Wenna professed
she could run the place with one hand tied behind her back,
which was probably just as well since she'd lost her right
arm above the elbow several years before, when pirates
raided Hera-3. The prosthetic was good, but she still com-
plained that they hadn't got the nerve grafts right.

Cara put the satchel on Wenna's desk. "Found by the
blast doors near the Saturn Arm," she said.

Wenna reached out and then drew her hand away without touching. "Max might be able to tell us who it belonged to."

"Is he in yet?"

"I'm not sure he ever goes home. It must be lonely without Gen and the baby."

"The station's over the worst. Surely, it's time for them to come back. Ben could collect them if they couldn't hitch a ride on a shuttle. I'm sure he wouldn't mind. A trip to Olyanda would be as good as a holiday. It would get him away from Garrick for a while. He's been working sixteen hours a day for the last—"

"Are you talking about me again?"

"Ben!" Cara spun to face him, feeling a flush of pleasure. "Only saying what anyone with half an eye can see. You've been working too hard. I didn't even hear you get up this morning. What time did you leave?"

He shrugged. "I was awake, so—" He noticed the satchel. "Is that what I think it is?"

Cara repeated the story about finding it on Flash Harry's stall in the bazaar.

"Kinan Odell would be the best one to ask," Ben said. "Max is a better Finder, but Odell knows the crew better."

Cara sent out a narrow strand of thought and mentally located Odell working in the equipment repair room. She invited him to take a break and join them. He was at the door in less than five minutes, wearing a greasy coverall and pushing his ginger hair out of his eyes with oil-stained fingers.

"You wanted me?" he asked.

"We wondered if you could identify who this belonged to," Cara said.

"Where was it . . . ?"

"Near the blast doors by the Saturn Arm. It was on Flash Harry's stall this morning."

"Damn. I searched that area myself. Did I miss something?" Odell reached out and took the satchel.

"You were looking for people, not equipment," Ben said. "Whoever this belonged to was probably long gone, but at least we'll know who it was and where they died."

"I can probably figure it out if no one's been using it in the meantime." Odell closed his eyes. His face took on a dreamy expression.

Cara cranked up her Empathy to coast along the mental path he took. She could feel his thoughts as he absorbed the—for want of a better word—aura of the satchel.

"It's been through a few hands." Odell stroked the fabric of the bag. "Some I don't recognize. Not all ours, I mean. Maybe whoever found it. There's a hint of Serafin West, but he's obviously still with us. The only one I can identify from the missing list is Greg Tilney," Odell said. "Was he on the wrong side when the Saturn Ring ripped free and opened the Arm to vacuum?"

"It's likely," Cara said.

"Well, at least we know." Odell's face softened. "I owed him a beer. I guess I always hoped he'd found an escape pod." He cleared his throat. "He was a good man."

"He was," Ben said.

"Do you need me for anything e—" Odell's eyes grew wide. He staggered as if he'd forgotten how to use his feet. "No!" His pupils rolled upward and he fell to the floor as limp as a discarded child's toy.

Cara, still empathically linked, felt a mental presence she didn't recognize. She snapped off all contact and jammed her shields down. She leaned heavily on Wenna's desk, breathing as if she'd run a marathon. Ben knelt by Odell while Wenna called for a medic.

Cara knew instantly what had caused Odell's collapse. Ben wasn't going to like it.

No one was going to like it.

✦ ✦ ✦

Ben Benjamin saw Odell go down and Cara reel back. His first instinct was to help Cara—that would always be his default—but she wasn't unconscious, and Odell was. He dropped to his knees and checked the obvious. Pulse: fast but present. Breathing: ragged. Pupils: reduced to pinpricks.

He sent out a call for a medic at the same time as Wenna.

Odell started to squirm without regaining consciousness. His head rocked from side to side. Ben rolled him into recovery position and steadied him so he didn't hurt himself.

"Coming through." Ronan Wolfe arrived with two med-techs and a well-equipped gurney.

Ben stepped away to give Ronan room, and turned to Cara. "Are you all right?"

She stared at him, hollow-eyed.

"What happened?" Ronan asked as he clipped a portable heart and blood pressure monitor onto the fallen psi-tech.

"He simply keeled over," Wenna said.

"Uh-huh." Cara shook her head. "I felt it happen. Someone got to him. The Trust—one of their Telepaths—found him and . . . and . . . switched off his implant. He'll be going all kinds of crazy inside."

Ben saw realization dawn on Ronan's face.

"Oh, shit!"

Any registered psi-tech could theoretically be traced by their implant. And if they could be traced, they could be damaged.

"It would take a psi-tech equally qualified as a Telepath, a Finder, and an Empath to be able to do it at this distance," Cara said. "And someone with those kind of qualifications—a triple-threat—is as rare as hen's teeth. Why would any megacorporation, even the Trust, waste a triple-threat psi-tech on destroying a middle grade Finder?"

"It's always been a possibility they'd come after us," Ben said.

"Yes, but why now? It's almost a year and a half since we defected. Is it worth the expense?"

Ben rubbed his hand across his forehead and swallowed hard, trying to get rid of the knot in his throat. "If Crowder's behind it, it means he's back on his feet. He'll find the budget from somewhere. It's personal with him now."

The Trust's psi-tech—Ben hoped there was only one—couldn't get to either himself, Cara, Jussaro, or Max because they'd had new implants fitted on Crossways, but the rest of the Free Company was horribly vulnerable.

Cara had turned pale. As Ronan floated Odell away on the gurney, she sank into a spare chair.

"Can I get you anything?" Ben asked.

"Brain bleach, please. That felt . . . awful."

"Did you get an impression of the Telepath on the other end?"

"Not exactly, but I'd recognize them again. Him. I'd recognize him again. I'm pretty sure it was a man. Young, but not new to this kind of work. Bastard!" Her cheeks began to flush pink as Ben felt her anger bubbling around her shields.

Wenna shoved a cup of water into Cara's trembling

hand, and she looked up. "Thanks. I haven't felt anything like that since Donida McLellan."

McLellan was dead, but there could be others like her. It wasn't only the skill they needed, but the will to use that skill to hurt other psi-techs. Cara shuddered and took a sip of water, then a deep breath. "Whoever it was used up a hell of a lot of energy. He'll not be going after anyone else today. Maybe not even for the next week."

"But you think he might try again? Someone else?" Ben asked. "Or was it maybe a warning shot—something to keep us metaphorically looking over our shoulder."

She shrugged and shook her head.

"Why Odell?" Wenna asked.

"He was using his talent to the full," Cara said. "It would have been a stronger signal for the psi-tech at the other end to follow."

"Random." Ben thumped the flat of his hand down on Wenna's desk. "It could be anyone. It could be you next, Wenna, and then where would the Free Company be?"

"I don't do anything that can't be done by someone else."

"Yes, you do. You're a prime target," Ben said. "So are all of the original section heads from the Olyanda mission. They'll be at the top of Crowder's list."

"You're sure it's Crowder?" Wenna asked. "Just because you think it is doesn't mean we can ignore other possibilities."

"Damping pins," Cara said. "We should concentrate on protecting everyone. You should all be wearing damping pins."

"Stop using our implants and hide?" Now it was Wenna's turn to shudder.

"Only until we can find a solution."

The way Cara said it, Ben knew she had something in mind, and the fact she wasn't sharing proved it would be something he wouldn't like.

"I need to see Jussaro," she said.

"Slow down. What are you planning?" Ben asked.

"The Trust doesn't like what it can't control, and it can't control us. We need a way to make ourselves safe. I think Jussaro might be able to help."

"You're talking about Sanctuary, aren't you?" Ben said.

"Isn't that a myth?" Wenna asked.

"Not entirely." Cara shook her head. "At least it did exist. I'm not sure how much of it still does."

"And Jussaro would know?" Ben asked.

"If anyone knows, he does. He used to be part of the Sanctuary network. It's what they nixed his implant for. There aren't many who survive that kind of treatment—at least not and stay sane. He might even be able to help Odell."

"It's worth a try," Ben said. "In the meantime, I'll organize some dampers for here and our people on Jamundi."

Chapter Two

SEARCH

CARA HAD FIRST ENCOUNTERED EMIL JUS-saro when she was on the run. He wasn't officially a member of the Free Company, but they'd adopted him. He had an office on the far side of Blue Seven, tucked behind the storage bays. It was fitted with a switchable damper to prevent thought spillage in either direction, for when he gave classes and one-to-one refresher sessions. He'd been particularly successful in upgrading psionic skills. Four class three Telepaths had advanced to class two, and Laurie Gilmartin, previously a class two, was on the cusp of reaching class one status, which was a good thing since they only had Cara on Crossways and Saedi Sugrue on Jamundi with the settlers.

No matter how good your use of an implant, there was always something more you could learn. Cara had acquired skills she didn't particularly want, and Jussaro had helped her to rationalize them. Like any good therapist, he'd nudged her in the right direction although he hadn't provided easy answers to hard questions. She hadn't found all the answers yet, but at least she was asking the right questions now.

She didn't get as far as Jussaro's office. He was hurrying

toward her in the slightly uncoordinated way he had, as if everything that was going on in his head didn't leave much room for the nuts and bolts of working his body.

People tended to notice Jussaro. He was squat, with the scaly purple-black skin associated with the genetically engineered inhabitants of the Hollands System, designed to survive in a high-radiation environment. Hollanders didn't tend to travel much.

"What's happened, Carlinni? I felt something."

She gave him the rundown on Odell.

"Bastards." Jussaro's monobrow creased into a frown. "Has Wolfe sedated him?"

"I heard screaming. Then it stopped."

"Let's take that as a yes. We need to be there when he wakes."

"Can you do anything?"

"I don't know."

Ronan's small infirmary had a front office, a treatment room, a recovery room, and two wards. A young med-tech looked up as they entered, saw who it was, and nodded them through.

Odell was still on the gurney, lying still and quiet, a fluid drip in his left arm.

Ronan turned. "I've done all I can for now. I don't know what will happen when he wakes. Either he'll be all right, or he'll be in a psych ward for the rest of his not-very-long life." He glanced at Jussaro. "Do you think you can help?"

"It depends on how much natural psi talent he had before they fitted his implant as to how much I have to work with. Do you have his files?"

"Only what was on the records we brought with us to Olyanda. I don't think they go as far back as pre-implant testing."

"When will he wake?"

"Without another dose of sedative, about half an hour."

It was a long half hour. Ronan's med-techs transferred Odell to a bed with safety rails and a full set of biomonitors. Jussaro and Cara sat on one side and Ronan on the other.

"Why do people always look so young when they're unconscious?" Cara asked.

"It's because they're vulnerable." Ronan leaned over and brushed a stray lock of ginger hair from Odell's forehead. "It makes them look younger. And their expressions are blank. It smooths out wrinkles."

"How old is Odell?" Cara asked.

"Forty-three, but he's lost six years in cryo, so thirty-seven personal elapsed time."

"He looks about twenty. Family?"

"None on his records."

"He's like most of us," Cara said. "The Free Company is his family."

"Isn't that always the way of it?" Jussaro said. "Implants separate us from the people who share our DNA and link us to each other."

Odell's eyelids fluttered. The biomonitor beeped. This was it.

Join with me, Jussaro said. *We need to keep him calm, give him a sense that he's still connected. Tell him it's a temporary glitch.*

Everyone knew Ben, Cara, and Jussaro had received second-chance implants. It was possible that it was temporary for Odell, though not everyone was suitable for reimplantation.

Here goes . . . Jussaro said. *Gently, gently into his mind. A warm bath of reassurance rather than a cold squirt of reality.*

They were all three Empaths, not the Free Company's only Empaths, but probably the strongest. Cara locked on to the feelings coming from Odell as he surfaced from the sedative. She couldn't hear individual thoughts, just a wash of emotion—mostly terror. She joined with Jussaro and Ronan, projecting reassurance, but it didn't make any difference.

Odell began to scream for his mother.

Jussaro pulled away. *There's nothing there,* he said. *Nothing to get hold of. Poor bastard. I'm sorry.*

Ronan stepped forward to administer another sedative, but Odell began to flail his arms around. He yanked the tubes out of his arm, spraying an arc of blood droplets across the white wall.

Two med-techs moved to secure him, but before Ronan

could get a blast pack to the side of his neck. Odell went rigid, and then began to shake. His eyes rolled back.

Cara and Jussaro stepped away to let the med-techs work. It didn't look good, but Ronan was good at miracles. Knowing they weren't needed, they escaped into the reception room where Ben and Wenna were waiting. Wenna wore a damping pin, which dulled her aura and left her mind unreachable.

"I can't do anything." Jussaro's voice broke. He pressed his lips together on whatever else he'd been going to say.

Cara tried to look on the hopeful side, but her feelings were in limbo. On the Schrödinger's Cat principle, until they heard otherwise, Odell was going to make it.

"Call it," they heard Ronan say.

Damn. Damn. Damn. Cara felt as though her stomach had hit the floor.

A few minutes later Ronan emerged from the room, his face set. "I'll need to do an autopsy, but I'd say he's had a massive brain hemorrhage."

Ben handed him a damper. Ronan looked at it. "I can't work with this. Healing is what I do. I need my Empathy— all my skills."

"Take it off when you need to," Ben said, "But you don't need your implant when you're eating lunch, or sleeping, or out dancing the night away with Jon."

"Jon . . ." Ronan said. "I never thought to check. Is everyone else all right?"

"As far as we know. And hopefully with these pins they'll stay that way, at least until we find a way to neutralize this threat."

"How the hell do we do that?" Ronan asked.

"Sanctuary," Cara said. She turned to Jussaro. "They had a way of protecting people, didn't they? Otherwise, how could they ensure psi-techs got clean away?"

Jussaro looked uncomfortable. "They did, but I never had that particular secret. All I know is there's a way to change the programming of an implant so that it can't be traced or accessed by anyone."

"How do we get hold of the information?" Ben asked.

Jussaro shrugged. "When Alphacorp broke our cell, they did it pretty thoroughly. There may be some cells left, but I don't know how to contact them. I may have a few leads, but it's six years ago. I am pretty sure, however, that Zandra Hartwell escaped. If anyone has the codes, it's her."

"Then we find Zandra Hartwell," Cara said.

"If we do," Jussaro said. "If we get the unlock codes, does that mean we recreate Sanctuary on Crossways?"

"One step at a time," Ben said. "Find her first."

Chapter Three

TRAVEL

BEN HAD COUNTED EACH DAY WITHOUT Cara. She'd been away for a month, following leads around the inner systems with Jussaro, traveling by commercial transport links from hub to hub, hub to planet, and planet to hub. She contacted him whenever she could and gave him a rundown of the search so far, but it wasn't a substitute for sleeping next to her at night or working with her during the day.

He worried about her, but she'd been right. Jussaro's contacts wouldn't talk to him. She'd been the victim of one of Alphacorp's best—or worst—mindbenders, and she could prove it to anyone who mattered. That was her ticket. Between them, Jussaro and Cara could go where he couldn't. Mother Ramona had provided them both with a string of false identities, all of which kept them out of jail as they progressed from one lead to another.

Meanwhile, hampered by damping pins, the Free Company was getting cranky. Some people were starting to take risks, switching off their dampers briefly for essential jobs. Without their implants, most of the Free Company psi-techs were unable to work, or at least unable to work effectively.

So far, no one had run away screaming, but each person had to deal with the loss in their own way, some quietly determined, others angry. Ronan reported an increase in the use of antidepressants and mild sedatives. Tempers flared.

No one knew whether there were attempted attacks on people protected by damping pins, but two more attacks had succeeded, though only one more death. One of Ada Levenson's cooks had had a fatal accident with a fryer, and they discovered she'd not been wearing her damper. Since she'd begun to scream and tear at her head before she'd fallen into the hot oil, the accident had probably been secondary to losing her implant. After that, everyone had started to take their pins much more seriously, resorting to using communicators while on station.

The second attack had been on Jon Moon, Ronan's partner, when the two of them had been in the bedroom. Most people who slept naked had taken to pinning the damper on their pillow, but that only worked while pillow and head were in close proximity. Luckily, Jon had felt the "handshake" from an unknown Telepath's implant and had flung himself toward the pillow, nearly causing, according to Ronan, an interesting and unusual physical problem. Thereafter he recommended unclothed sleepers should wear their pins on a lightweight choker around their neck, even during sex.

Jon, luckily, had suffered no more ill-effects than a raging migraine for three days, which Ronan had ministered to sympathetically, and with a certain amount of admitted guilt. While Ronan always displayed an even temper outwardly, he'd confided to Ben that the thought of losing Jon had almost paralyzed him with fear.

Ben had told Cara and Jussaro what had happened. He hadn't wanted to load any more pressure on them, but he was pretty sure that's what he'd done.

Cara called him most nights from wherever she was.

Hey. Cara popped into Ben's head as he was clearing his desk for the evening.

Hey, yourself. How are you? Where are you?

Athabasca Terminus. We're coming home.

You found something?

Not exactly, but we have a lead. We need a jumpship to get us to a planet called Dounreay. It's an ex-prison planet, now colonized. It's four months' travel from the nearest jump gate, so we need a shortcut.*

I'll take you.

She did the mental equivalent of a sigh. *I knew you'd offer, but I don't know how long we'll need to be there. We only have a slim lead, but it's our last one, so we have to follow it.*

And you want the jumpship to be in orbit in case you need to make a fast getaway.

That's the idea. Can we borrow Jake and the Bellatkin?

He's gone to Butterstone to pick up a consignment of spelt flour for Ada Levenson, but you can borrow him when he gets back. Four days at most. How long before you're home?

We can get a freighter outbound to Cotille. Journey time, two days.

I'll come and pick you up there.

Do you have the time?

It's been a month. I have a hard-on just thinking about you coming home. I'll make time.

She giggled. *You know what Jussaro will say.*

Get a room! they both said together.

Anything I should know? Cara asked.

Not since Jon Moon.

Is he all right now?

Ronan says so, but they're both jumpy as hell.

I'm not surprised.

Close call.

We're on the clock, aren't we? Cara asked. *The longer it takes us to find Hartwell, the more likely it is that someone else will slip up. It's Crowder, isn't it?*

Without evidence to the contrary, that would be my best guess.

Cara let out a string of obscenities that were no less effective for being purely mind-to-mind. *Maybe there's a way to lure the attacker to me,* she said. *I'm probably the only one who could follow the link to its source. Maybe I could—*

No, you'd have to meld with the person being attacked—even presuming we knew who was next. If you weren't fast enough, or if you tried and failed, the consequences could be fatal to both of you.

Yeah. I get it, but it's hard to sit by and—

You're not sitting by. Find Hartwell. See if there are unlock codes that will free the implants.

Ben signed off with, *Love you. See you soon,* and Cara replied with something warm and fuzzy, not unlike a kiss.

Two days later, as promised, Ben was waiting as she walked down the freighter ramp in the commercial dock to the east of Cymbalom, Cotille Colony's capital city. Instead of her usual buddysuit, she'd dressed to blend in, wearing layers of impractical, but decidedly fetching, skirts and a form-fitting top. Cara began to run as she saw him, past the cargomeister and his antigrav cart, skirts flying. She flung herself at Ben and wrapped her legs around the leathery hide of his buddysuit.

"Get a room, Carlinni," Jussaro said as he sauntered past.

Ben and Cara surfaced for air from their kiss, to laugh at Jussaro's retreating back.

"Was he sniggering?" Cara asked.

"I don't care." Ben kissed her again and set Cara's feet gently on the dock. "Since we have a perfectly good room waiting for us on Crossways, I suppose we should go. Jussaro's already halfway to *Solar Wind*. If we give him enough of a head start, he'll be trying to persuade Yan Gwenn to raise the ramp to embarrass us."

"Yan knows better than to try," Cara said. "Are you ready to go now? Did you have any business with President Lake?"

"I arrived early and delivered a neatly unobtrusive package of platinum wrapped with gracious and diplomatic words. Both the platinum and the words supplied by Norton Garrick. We arranged for Anstruther and Daughters to take another consignment of bots for repair and to supply us with some of the machine tools and cutters that we need to reestablish a bot repair shop on Crossways."

"So that was your reason for being so eager to meet me here."

He put one arm around her shoulder and hugged her. "You know it wasn't. Let's get your bag out of the hold and be on our way."

Much as he would have liked to take Cara straight to their cabin, Ben followed her up the access tube to *Solar*

Wind's flight deck. She looked out of place in her calf-length layered skirts.

She slid straight into the comms station as if she'd never been away. Ben let his gaze linger on her a moment longer than was necessary. The colors suited her, a riot of blues and greens. He was so unused to seeing her in a skirt. He had a sudden vision of it lying in folds on the floor and Cara stepping naked out of it.

Damn, that would have to wait. He needed all his concentration to get them safely through the Folds. He was always on edge, always expecting the worst. The worst was not the void dragon. That was strange enough, and unsettling. The worst was the Nimbus.

Ben blinked slowly, settling his pre-flight nerves. He had the usual belly full of butterflies at the thought of what waited in the Folds. Even veterans of foldspace cracked sometimes.

Been there. Done that.

Recovered.

Or maybe: still recovering.

Flying the Folds engendered equal amounts of fear and exhilaration. There were things in the liminal space between realities that defied explanation. He'd seen them and survived to tell the tale.

He shoved that thought behind him and mentally connected with the ship's systems. Safely away from Cotille, Ben brought the jump drive online and, with a rush, they entered foldspace.

The flight deck lights dip, flicker, and then resume normality. That's not always the case in foldspace. You can never tell in advance what it's going to be like. Sometimes it's pitch-dark, other times there's a strange phenomenon which shows everything up as a visual negative, either in shades of gray, or—more disconcertingly—in full color.

Ben wonders whether they'll get a visitation on this trip, but Yan Gwenn marks elapsed time in fifteen-second bursts and nothing untoward happens. A good passage, then.

Ben finds the line to Olyanda space. With a ping he doesn't quite hear, they emerge into realspace again a hundred klicks out from Crossways, spot on target. He smiles.

*   *   *

The first time Ben saw Crossways, a vast man-made habitat hanging in space, it looked as if it had been cobbled together by a lunatic using parts from several mismatched giant construction kits. Its solid central spindle supported a core of concentric rings resembling a child's spinning top. From that, it had sprouted additions and extensions—excrescences which had expanded organically in a way which owed little to long-term planning and much to necessity.

The recent bombardment had scarred and reshaped the station.

Now in orbit above Olyanda, Crossways was protected not only by the planetary defense grid, but also by its own fleet and armaments. Attacking Crossways had cost the megacorps dearly. They wouldn't try again—at least not until they'd finished licking their wounds.

Ben docked *Solar Wind* in Port 22, Garrick and Mother Ramona's private dock. Gwala and Hilde, their bodyguards, were there to meet them. They made their way to Blue Seven in one of the garish tub cabs that buzzed around the station's traffic system like part of a demented fairground ride.

Jussaro excused himself and headed toward his office. Ben would have hustled Cara through Blue Seven and straight into their apartment if he could, but she'd been away a long time and couldn't avoid friends and well-wishers even if she'd wanted to. Ben let them get on with it. It felt like an age before he got Cara alone in their apartment with the door safely locked.

"How long before Jake gets back with the *Bellatkin*?" she asked.

"Two days."

She grinned at him. "I hope you weren't planning on being too busy."

"Funny you should say that—I cleared my schedule."

No one disturbed them for the rest of the day and for one glorious night, but Ben should have known that only a miracle would have given him two whole days off. He tried not to disturb Cara as he slid out of bed the following morning, but she raised herself up on one elbow and blinked at him.

"Go back to sleep," he told her, planting a kiss on her disheveled hair.

"Whassup?"

"Wenna beeped me. Saedi Sugrue's calling me in ten minutes."

"I must have been sound asleep. I never herd the beep. Saedi wouldn't be calling about something routine. She should be wearing her damping pin and keeping her head down."

"That's what I figured."

"I'm awake now, anyway." Cara swung her legs out of bed, picked up the skirt they'd discarded on the floor and draped it over a chair. Her buddysuit hung in the wardrobe. "I've missed this," she said, drawing on the softsuit liner and shrugging into the trousers.

"I liked the skirt, especially when it fell around your ankles."

She thumped his arm gently, trying to hide a smile.

"You can't pull it off."

"What? The skirt?"

"Looking serious after a night of blistering sex."

They walked over to the office together. Wenna was already there.

"Sorry to disturb you both, but this sounded urgent. Saedi didn't want to hang around waiting for you to wake up."

"She could have woken me."

"That's what I told her."

Ben felt Saedi's mental handshake, implant to implant.

What's wrong, Saedi?

Kayla Mundi. We found her dead this morning. No sign of external trauma, but she looked as though she died pretty hard. She'd bitten through her own tongue and almost clawed the skin off her forehead.

Was she wearing her damper?

We found it on the floor under her bed.

You'll have to get—

Mel Hoffner to do an autopsy. I know. Mel's here now, and Gupta.

Don't risk yourselves more than you have already, Ben said. *Fix your damper again. I'll come myself.*

Signing off.

Ben looked at Cara. She had no trouble with a serious face now. "You don't mind, do you?"

"Hell, no, of course not. As soon as Jake gets back with the *Bellatkin*, Jussaro and I will be off to Dounreay. It's our last chance to find Hartwell."

"Good luck."

Chapter Four

DOUNREAY

DOUNREAY WAS A BASTARD OF A WORLD. IT had sounded dismal from the description and Cara liked it no better now she was slogging across its vast northern continent toward a small settlement called Wonnick. Her mount, a lumbering crestedina, a saurian riding beast twice her height at the shoulder, rumbled and grumbled quietly to itself as it plodded across the endless baked mud, head low and crest undulating.

She reached down and patted its thick hide. It was time to give the beasts a short break and some protein.

She glanced at her companion.

Jussaro surreptitiously shuffled to ease his backside in the saddle. He returned her look, his eyebrows raised in a question. That always looked slightly strange on Jussaro because he had a huge brow ridge to shade his eyes with their nictitating third eyelids.

What? He asked her mind-to-mind since his mouth and nose, like hers, were swathed in a scarf to keep out the blowing dust.

Your friend has a knack for picking particularly lovely planets. I have grit in places I barely knew existed.

He shrugged. *She's been in hiding for six years, one step*

ahead of the megacorporations. I guess she's run out of pretty places.

I thought Vortigern was bad enough with its heat and humidity . . . Cara pulled a face. *And the leeches. I hate leeches, especially ones the size of my fist.*

You're not wishing we were still on Vortigern.

Not exactly. I'd like a nice temperate planet with modest precipitation and green foliage. I'd settle for a comfortable hotel with clean sheets on the bed, running water in the washroom, and a competent chef in the kitchen.

She leaned back and the crestie obligingly slowed and stopped, giving her the opportunity to grasp the balance strap and slither the three meters to the ground. Jussaro pulled up his beast alongside and, with a groan, did the same.

Cara's crestie snorted through its nostril flaps and took the opportunity to lower its head to whiffle its prehensile lips for sand-spiders, crest now resting flat against its neck.

"You'll be lucky." The scarf muffled her words, but the big saurian raised its head and rippled its crest hopefully.

"Okay, big guy, lunch."

She released the pulley strap and let down one of the packs secured to the saddle. Inside, there was a selection of small cloth sacks.

Make sure you get them the right way around, Jussaro said.

She curled up her nose. The beasts' food, shiny brown-and-black husks of dried mixed insects, almost looked more appetizing than the pouches of osteena pulp that were all they had to last them until Wonnick, where, no doubt, they could get dried osteena, osteena pottage, osteena juice, and if they were very lucky, pickled or roasted osteena. Somewhere around the third day on this planet, she'd begun to dream of field ration packs and Ada Levenson's bland coffee. She'd even be prepared to try the *Don't Ask:* the stew with no definable ingredients, except for *genuine vitamin supplements,* that Dido Kennedy served up to all the feral kids she'd unofficially adopted in Red One.

Cara scattered a double handful of insect mix on the ground for each of the cresties. While she waited for them to chase down every last morsel, she popped a pouch, sucking the wet osteena, now reduced to baby-food consistency.

She never thought she'd miss Crossways, never thought

she could make her home on a chunk of metal and ceramic spinning in space. It was the people not the place, she told herself. One person, in particular.

The brief break with Ben had been spectacular, but it had been weeks ago.

She mentally inserted his lean brown body between the clean sheets on the bed in the comfortable hotel with running water in the washrooms and a competent chef in the kitchen.

Perfect.

Instead, she had one more day of travel across the baked mud flats to look forward to, with only Jussaro's company. She liked the guy, but he wasn't Ben.

She saw Jussaro smirk and checked her shields, hoping she hadn't broadcast that thought inadvertently. Her shields were good, but Jussaro's mental skills were off the scale. He'd been training psi-techs while she'd still been chasing her first promotion, in her Alphacorp days. He'd not only been training them, but encouraging them toward independence; pointing out ways they could take the first steps toward Sanctuary should they ever need to bail on their megacorp contract. It was an activity that earned him two bouts of Neural Readjustment before they finally nixed his implant completely.

The megacorps had shattered Sanctuary. Zandra Hartwell had escaped, others had gone to ground, but many died. Cara fervently hoped Hartwell was still alive and still in possession of the unlock codes for the Trust's implants. They needed Hartwell right now. Every day that passed increased the likelihood that someone would get careless and another psi-tech would fall to the Trust's killer Telepath.

Cara looked about her. This part of the planet—the equatorial band—had only two seasons: hot and dry, and hot and wet, following each other in cycles close to two Earth months long. Cara and Jussaro had been here since the end of the last wet season when lush vegetation had waved shoulder-high and the harvest, a three-day frenzy, had occupied every man, woman, and child old enough to gather the spongy osteena. The ubiquitous native fruit resembled a squash and held moisture and sustenance— enough to live on if you had to—but it tasted like mud. Everything on this world tasted like mud.

What's that?

Cara looked around at Jussaro's sharp question. A shimmer of dark cloud, barely a suggestion of something approaching, hung on the distant horizon. In the clear violet sky, it was as good as a giant red flashing light. Cara's first thought was rain, but they were less than eight days into the dry season, long enough for all the wet season's rains to soak in, run off, or evaporate to a distant memory.

It's either a skimmer, in which case it's the law and we're screwed, or it's a Lifer band, in which case we're screwed unless we can outrun them.

Jussaro's thought translated into something close to: *Shit!*

Yeah, right. Let's go. Whichever one it is, hanging around here will get us into a heap of trouble.

Lifers were the remnants of Dounreay's troubled past as a prison colony, descendants of those individuals who had not accepted the amnesty when the planet's status had been changed, fifty years after the last offenders had been dumped to live or die by their wits. They were the children and grandchildren of the original inmates serving life sentences. The Lifer bands embraced their heritage and continued to live by their wits. They were the main reason that neither private skimmers nor airborne craft were allowed west of the GID, the Great Irrigation Duct. The authorities figured that if anyone took mechanized transport into the waste, the Lifer gangs would soon acquire it, and then they would encroach into the more civilized areas of the continent.

Anyone living out here, including the Lifer gangs, relied on crestedinas. Hence Cara and Jussaro's choice of transport. She was beginning to regret trying to blend in with the locals, even though they didn't have much choice. Landing a spaceship would have been a bit obvious, but so much easier.

We might have a situation developing down here. Cara tapped her crestie behind its left foreleg while opening up a communication to the *Bellatkin*, skulking beyond Dounreay's moon where the planetary defense systems wouldn't pick up traces of the craft.

Her crestie obligingly braced its leg in a forward position and curved its head around toward her, flattening its crest against its neck. Tucking up her skirt—another disadvantage of trying to look like a local—she grabbed on to the balance strap dangling from the saddle, put her left foot on the crestie's outstretched leg, gripped the top of its neck and sprang for the mounting rung. She threw her right leg across the saddle and pulled herself upright, tugging the skirt out of the way.

Jussaro, wearing a shorter tunic and trousers, wasn't quite as hampered. He settled into his own saddle and shortened the balance strap. *Let's go, Carlinni. What's keeping you?*

If the dust cloud was a fast-moving Monitor skimmer, it would be a short race, but if it was a Lifer band, they stood a fair chance of staying ahead. The Lifers might not even have seen them yet. It might be a family band, in which case they wouldn't move any faster than their slowest rider. If it was a raiding party, however, all bets were off. And they'd be easy to follow. Their own cresties would kick up even more of a dust cloud once they began to pound the ground. There was a chance, if they simply stayed put, that the Lifer band might not spot the gentle dust cloud they'd already stirred up, but it wasn't a chance worth taking.

How far away do you reckon they are? Jussaro had lived on space stations for most of his adult life and had poor long-distance perception.

Hard to tell. Fifteen klicks, maybe. Cara pushed her crestie into a run which was half lope, half bound. Cresties had an unsettling two-by-two gait: front legs, with toes splayed like fingers, hitting the ground in a leap and hind legs, with short, clawed toes overreaching, to whump down to either side and ahead of the front feet. The net result was that the balance strap was essential to staying on board. At that height and speed, falling off was not an option.

Cara? Whassup? Jake Lowenbrun responded mind-to-mind from the *Bellatkin*. The connection was weak. Jake was a first-class pilot and strong on Navigation, thanks to his neural implant, but his Telepathy skills sucked.

Cara clutched the balance strap, trusting her crestie would follow Jussaro's while her mind wasn't fully on riding. *We've picked up a tail, Jake,* she said. *It's either a Monitor skimmer or a Lifer band. What's your estimated time to a rendezvous?*

About six hours if I come in nice and slow and legal.

Maybe three hours if you don't mind me lighting up every air traffic warning on the planet.

We'd lose any chance we had of finding Zandra, Jussaro said with obvious reluctance.

Come in slow, Cara said. *If we need you sooner, we'll yell. If it's a skimmer, you can't get here in time, anyway.*

I've been watching traffic at the jump gate since I dropped you, Jake said. *No Monitor vessels in the area. It could be the local law, but my guess is you've picked up a Lifer band.*

In which case, if we can beat them to Wonnick, we won't blow our cover.

Good call, Jussaro said.

The only possible call under the circumstances. I hope Zandra Hartwell is worth it.

She's the very embodiment of Sanctuary, Jussaro said.

Cara disengaged mentally and gave all her attention to the crestedina's uncomfortable stride. How far and how fast could she push the beast before it succumbed to exhaustion?

♦   ♦   ♦

Ben returned from Jamundi no wiser than when he'd gone out there. The autopsy on Kayla Mundi had shown no underlying cause of death, so with lack of other evidence and the fact that she'd not been wearing her damping pin, they could only assume she'd been the third victim of the Trust's triple-threat Telepath. Gods, Ben hoped there was only one of them out there.

Missing Cara more than he could articulate, even to himself, he'd hardly slept last night. He'd had two distinct dreams, one of the Nimbus, from which he'd woken, sweating even though he should be used to Nimbus dreams by now, and the other in which the Free Company were all actors on a stage in a complex whodunit mystery, with a new corpse turning up every five minutes. The Great Detective, who wore a deerstalker hat on top of her space helmet and smoked a pipe inside it, knew exactly who'd done it, but confessed she couldn't bring the culprit to justice because he was too well-protected.

Blinking grit out of his eyes, Ben set off to take a tub cab from Blue Seven to Garrick's office at the Hub. Crossways should have a better transport system. The tub cabs were ridiculous; their garish paint grated on his eyeballs, and the squeaks and clatters from the jolts and scrapes were sandpaper to his ears.

Apart from being hard on the eyes, the cabs were also open.

Of course, no one needed sealed cabs when there was no wind, rain, or sun on a space station. Whoever had designed this system, in the days when Crossways had been a company spaceport, no doubt intended it to be egalitarian—which it was by its very nature. They had not considered the possibility passengers might wish to ward off potential assassins.

Ben took the first cab that came his way. The very randomness of grabbing a cab made the old method of assassination—a bomb under your personal vehicle—impractical, but it still left the way open for someone taking a pot shot into your open cab.

Why was he even thinking about that? He had security up the wazoo though he still didn't feel important enough for an entourage of babysitters. After all, he was simply a farm boy who'd proved to be good at flying, and by a series of coincidences ended up as caretaker for the Free Company.

Gwala and Hildstrom had drawn bodyguard duty again. As minders went, they were the best in the business, and he had hired Tengue and his mercs to run security for the Free Company on Crossways, so he had only himself to blame if sometimes their presence felt smothering. There was little point in employing an expert and then not letting him do his job. Tengue was right, on a station like Crossways with over half a million people, any number of assassins could be lining up to take a shot at him, literally or figuratively.

Maybe even today. Maybe even in this tub cab.

Crowder still wanted a piece of him, preferably cold and on a slab; he was on the Monitors' most wanted list; half the criminals on Crossways blamed him for Garrick trying to clean up the station, even though the idea had been Garrick's own.

It was nice to be popular.

Hilde Hildstrom gave him a sideways look as she dropped into the seat beside him. Had he actually sighed?

Emmanuel Gwala punched in their destination and sat on the other side. They made an interesting looking trio, all dressed in severely practical buddysuits with only their faces and hands showing. Gwala's skin was the deep brown of his African ancestors; Hildstrom's Nordic skin was so pale it was almost cream. Ben was somewhere in the middle, mid-brown from his mixed ancestry.

"Seen the results of the grapple quarterfinals?" Gwala asked.

"No," Hilde said. "And don't tell me, Manny, I don't want to know. I'm going to watch the replay when I get off shift."

As far as Ben knew, Hilde was the only person who could get away with calling Emmanuel Gwala *Manny*. They'd obviously worked together for some time. Ben wondered whether they kept the same professional distance when they were off duty. Sometimes they bickered like an old married couple. Were they more than good friends? If it made them happy, he hoped so.

The little tub cab shuddered for a few moments, as if undecided which way to go, then with a jerk it hurtled into the traffic stream, bouncing haphazardly off the fenders of other cabs as it pushed its way into the throng of similar vehicles.

Whirling into the denser stream of the main arterial traffic, another tub ricocheted off the sidewall and bounced right into them. A man drove, while his passenger knelt leaning against the cab's side. Ben's first thought was that anyone trying to drive in this traffic was crazy. His second thought—always worth taking notice of—said something was wrong with this picture.

Was it because he'd been thinking of assassins?

Shit!

He hit the floor of the tub with Hilde on top of him as something whined overhead. Gwala's foot was in his face as the big man crouched on the seat to return fire. A dart had lodged itself in what passed for upholstery on the inside door panel.

Ben pulled a derri out of his thigh pocket and thumbed off the safety. Ordinary citizens were not supposed to carry weapons, especially ballistic projectiles, but this wasn't the first attempt on his life. Hilde sprang for the cab's board and took over manual control, crouching down to make a smaller target.

"There they are." Gwala indicated a red-and-yellow tub, mercilessly bumping through traffic.

"Quick! After them." Ben raised his lobstered helmet and flipped down the face shield, leaving only a very small vulnerable gap under his chin. An assassin would have to be lying almost at his feet to make that shot. His buddysuit was armored and would turn a dart, but the assassin had obviously been aiming for his unprotected head. Damn, he didn't want to have to travel everywhere fully helmed.

"We're supposed to be getting you to safety," Hilde said. "It's the job. Tengue will pick up the chase."

"Once they dump the cab, he doesn't stand a chance. Move it! At least get close enough to ID them." His own helmet cam was already recording. "That red and yellow is pretty distinctive. Cotto's colors, I think."

Gwala grunted assent. Hilde smacked her hand down on the control board and they shot forward, rebounded from the same two tubs the would-be assassins had bumped so hard, and zoomed through into a gap, barely twenty meters behind the red-and-yellow tub.

Ben heard a soft whoosh and turned to see a dart quivering.

"Air filters. Pull over. Now!" He snapped out.

Hilde didn't falter. She swept into a pull-in and jumped out of the cab. Ben held his breath and scrambled out after her.

Ben's suit was now blowing filtered air into the face mask. He breathed again.

The pull-in was a standard platform with a single foam fire extinguisher hanging on the wall. Ben grabbed it, pointed the nozzle at the dart, and released a stream of foam which immediately hardened and formed a shell to seal it in.

"Gas dart," Ben said. "Did you activate your air filters?"

Gwala and Hilde both nodded.

"They didn't need to get a direct hit on a body. They could have killed all three of us with that."

Thankfully, there was no damage done.

Hilde and Gwala covered the entrance and exit and the traffic stream. The red-and-yellow cab was long gone, but there was also a chance the attack had been designed to trick them into pulling in to a waiting trap.

Gwala spoke briefly into his comms unit and then looked up. "Tengue will have a crew here in five minutes."

Hilde waved away a couple of curious bystanders.

"Are you all right?" she asked Ben.

"Yes, fine." And he was—at least if you didn't count the adrenaline pounding through his system. "Did we get close enough for an ID?"

"I've uploaded my helmet cam to the matrix, but I doubt we were close enough to identify faces. However, we did ID the cab, so we can get footage from other security cams. We might be able to identify them."

Minutes passed.

Nothing happened.

Ben didn't interfere. He'd leave it to the security team. No use butting in on their territory. Besides, it wasn't the shooters he had to worry about, it was whoever had employed them. He huffed out a breath.

"Do you think it was Crowder?" Hilde said.

"Could be. Could be Crowder, the Trust, Alphacorp or any number of small-time crooks who blame me for Garrick's decision to legitimize Crossways and put them out of business. Crowder can take a ticket and stand in line."

"Crowder's going to come after you one day."

"I know."

Tengue arrived with six buddysuited figures in three tub cabs. All had their helms up, face masks down, and breathing tubes at the ready. After the usual are-you-all-right exchanges, Tengue set two of his guards to block the entrance and exit to this quiet throughway.

"We should go back to Blue Seven while we're so close," Hilde said, indicating the tub Tengue had brought for their use.

"No point," Ben said. "They're not likely to try again now we're on to them, at least not today and not from a tub cab. Let's get on with living."

Chapter Five

LIFERS

IT WAS A LIFER GANG—NO DOUBT. A MONITOR skimmer would have had them by now.

Cara eased back, and her crestie slowed to a walk. Jussaro caught up and matched her pace. Both beasts plodded on, sides heaving, heads down, crests rippling.

Jussaro swiveled in his saddle. *Can you tell if they're any closer?*

Not really. They're no farther away, though.

He grunted. *How far to Wonnick?*

Cara checked her handpad. *Fifty-three klicks.*

If they're no closer, they're not going to be able to close the gap before Wonnick.

Unless they're a raiding party, in which case they'll have spare cresties and can make much better time.

I was trying not to dwell on that possibility.

They walked the cresties for ten minutes before setting off at a lope again. Cara thought the Lifers might be closer now, but pushing the cresties any faster would see them both on foot sooner rather than later.

Fourteen klicks farther on, they pulled up to give the cresties another brief breather.

Even with my eyesight I can tell they're closer now. Jussaro squinted into the distance.

Cara pushed her scarf aside and took a few sips of water from the skin anchored to the saddle. *Yeah. I didn't want to worry you. How are you holding up?*

Ask my arse. I never want to see another crestedina as long as I live.

Hey, they're from your home planet.

Why do you think we export them?

Point.

They set off again. Cara's beast stumbled, its pace more sluggish. Cresties were biddable and would keep going for as long as they had breath in their bodies, but because of that, it was possible to run them to a standstill. If that happened, they'd be on foot in this unforgiving landscape. She checked her handpad at regular intervals: twenty klicks to Wonnick. Seventeen. Fourteen. Thirteen. Her crestie stumbled. She halted and slithered off.

I'm going to walk for five. Give the big guy a chance to catch his breath.

Jussaro joined her on the ground. *How much lead do you figure we have on them now?*

Not enough.

Five minutes later they both scrambled for their saddles again.

Can we make it? Jussaro asked.

If we don't kill the cresties trying.

Nine klicks out from Wonnick, Cara checked the dust cloud behind them. It was closer. She couldn't make out detail, but by the density of the dust it was a sizable band.

Last push, she told Jussaro. *Let's go.*

Both cresties leaped forward.

A rocket flew over their heads and landed barely a hundred meters in front of them with a dull bang, throwing up a large dust cloud.

What the hell was that? Jussaro said.

Ordnance.

Looked more like a firework.

May have started out life as one. Not exactly high tech, but it packs a bang.

A second rocket landed about a hundred meters behind them. The cresties bounded forward, startled.

A third showered them with chunks of baked mud from close by their left.

Damn, they've found our range, Cara said.

How far now? Jussaro asked.

Three klicks, maybe. Cara urged her crestie even faster.

The last few klicks, were pure slog across baked mud riven with cracks and craters.

Cara heard the rocket but couldn't judge its trajectory until an explosion knocked her crestie to its knees. She lurched toward its neck, saved only by its crest jabbing hard into her stomach.

"Come on!"

It staggered to its feet and galloped on, but its pace was uneven.

"Can't stop now." She urged it on.

From the top of a slight incline, Cara saw the town of Wonnick spread below them. Relief and consternation vied with each other. It was a collection of mud huts—okay, adobe or maybe cob houses: stone foundations topped with mud bricks and then plastered with more mud. The roofs were thatched with osteena stems and overhung the walls to keep the rain from washing away the whole structure.

But at least it had a wooden palisade. Would that be enough?

Outside the town walls a large osteena processing shed hunkered down low. Every town had them. Wonnick's was powered by a pair of helical wind turbines on the roof.

Not much to look at, is it? Jussaro echoed Cara's first impression.

It doesn't look like I expected Sanctuary to look.

I said Zandra Hartwell embodied Sanctuary. I didn't promise you'd find it right here, fully formed, but she has the network key. Trust me, if we find Zandra, we're one step closer.

If I didn't trust you, I wouldn't be here.

Yeah, you would. Lives are at stake.

She looked over her shoulder. She could make out individual figures in the dust cloud now. They were close, but Wonnick was closer.

Her crestie slithered down the hill and raced for the town with Jussaro's beast barely a pace behind.

✦ ✦ ✦

Ben took the antigrav tube from the Mansion House up through the levels to Crossways Control. Garrick and

Mother Ramona had set up house there after the battle, opening the Mansion House for refugees, a move that had won them many friends, especially since, more than a year later, they were still living in two rooms next to their respective offices.

To get to Garrick's office, Ben had to pass through the operations room where the flight controllers worked. He stepped inside, retracting his buddysuit helm.

"Hey, it's Benjamin," Roebuck said. "Going off-station anytime soon?"

"Why, have you got another bet on me?"

"Sure have," she said.

"Save your credits. I'll be sticking strictly to the standoff limits."

"That's what you always say," Troop joined in. "And then you finish off by saying 'except in an emergency.'"

"You don't want any more emergencies, do you?"

"Not exactly, but—"

"I can't win. Come in hot with someone dying in my sick bay and I'm the worst pilot in the history of Crossways. Stick to the rules and I spoil your sweepstake."

Roebuck laughed. "Life's a bitch, Benjamin. At least you've never twisted a docking bay door or busted a ship-cradle."

"I'll bear that in mind."

"Say, did you hear that the *Ashington* didn't make it through the Folds?" Troop gestured toward a board at one side of the room. Most of the ship names on there were old, but *Ashington* and the date had been scrawled in bold capitals.

"*Ashington*?" Ben hadn't heard. An icy shiver found its way down his spine.

"Freighter belonging to Lomax trading. Small outfit based on the Saturn Ring. Outward bound with a cargo of spare parts." He emphasized *spare parts*, which probably meant the freighter was carrying smuggled weaponry. "Bound for Burnish. It made it through the Folds from our gate to Pinch Point Hub, but took Gate Three from Pinch Point and never came out again at the other side."

"How many on board?"

"Five. You thinking of going into the Folds to get 'em?"

Was he?

He'd done it twice before. Once for the ark with thirty thousand settlers on board in cryo. The second time for Garrick's shuttle. That second time was not an experience he wanted to repeat. There was a limit, and he'd reached it.

"It's not as simple as that. If it was, everyone would be doing it."

His days of hanging around in the Folds looking for waifs and strays were over. When he had to, he'd go through, but as quickly as possible with no sightseeing en route. In, through, and out was his new motto. There were enough ways to die in space without adding to them.

Gwala and Hilde headed for central control to pull the surveillance images for the attempted hit.

Ully, Mother Ramona's personal Telepath, ushered Ben through to Garrick's office. He felt he should be holding the door for her. She was a tiny woman, stick-thin, with dandelion clock hair. She must be at least ninety by the look of her lined face, though you'd never guess from her strong telepathic touch and the twinkle in her gray-blue eyes. Ully approved of having the Free Company on-station and always went out of her way to be helpful.

Mother Ramona, handsome in her strangeness, flashed Ben a smile and continued to check off something on her handpad display.

Garrick stood and shook his hand. "My friend, come in. I heard you had trouble." He was a little more effusive than usual. Ben felt a slight tremor in the man's handshake. Garrick's badger-striped beard was trimmed to perfection. His eyes were bright, but his pupils were pinprick small. Ben hoped he wasn't on something. Garrick was the rock at the dead center of the station. Crossways would soon be plunged into chaos if the old coalition of crimelords tried to take over again. They'd never been able to agree on anything among themselves.

If Garrick was using, he wouldn't be the first to need a little chemical help in a crisis. Garrick had accomplished miracles, pulling Crossways together after the megacorps attack and directing the rebuild. He'd persuaded the station's great and good, that is, its richest criminals, to partially finance the restoration, and the rest came from the platinum profits. It reduced the dividend paid out to investors, but at least they weren't sucking on vacuum, so most of them didn't squeal too loudly.

"A seat. Please . . . sit." Garrick's voice was slightly louder than it needed to be in the confines of this room.

He led Ben to a group of four comfortable chairs. Garrick flopped down against the cushions in one, and Mother Ramona took up a perch opposite Ben, crossing her long legs which still looked elegant despite being encased in a buddysuit—practical, comfortable and, more importantly, providing a layer of body armor. Garrick had eschewed the safety of a buddysuit and instead had gone for an open-necked, deep-red silk shirt and black trousers. It was as if attack wasn't a real and present danger. Assassination was, after all, the way Garrick had taken over from Chaliss.

Since Crossways' original bid for independence over a century ago, political backstabbings—and sometimes literal ones—determined who was at the top at any given time. Temporary alliances lasted only as long as it benefited one or the other party. Truces sprang up and broke down again. So far, Garrick had managed to stay on top for close to five years, something of a record.

"So what happened on the way over?" Garrick asked.

"News travels fast."

"Having to flush toxic nerve gas from a minor pull-in is a dead giveaway. Your friend Crowder, do you think?"

"That would be everyone's best guess, but speculation without information is pointless. Now that Crowder has moved to Earth, I have someone keeping tabs on him."

"Someone you can trust?"

"In this particular case, someone I can trust implicitly though I've never met him. A family connection." Cara had contacted Nan; Nan had made a suggestion to a very old friend.

"Heh, that's good."

Ben smiled. "As to this morning's unfortunate incident, Hilde and Gwala are checking the security recordings right now to see if we can work out who it was or—better still—who sent them."

"Save yourself the trouble." Mother Ramona said. "The perps were on our contractors list, a pair of twins who use a variety of names. We know them as Kurt and Marie La-

mond. They're independent. They'll take any assignment
that pays well enough."

"They were on your list? Past tense?"

"We removed them from the protection of the list as of
five minutes ago. When we find them, and we will, we'll remind them of the severe penalties for breaking the rules.
They're allowed to base themselves here as long as they
work anywhere but Crossways. We'll let you have any information they offer before we ask them to leave the station."

Her voice told Ben all he needed to know about the two
assassins' method of departure. It would be out of an airlock, and there wouldn't be a ship waiting on the other side.

Ben had known Mother Ramona since his days in the
Monitors. He'd come to Crossways looking for someone
who could supply forged papers for a bunch of Burnish refugees he was trying to resettle while the frontier war raged.
The someone Ben had found was Mother Ramona, a star-
tlingly beautiful woman of indeterminate age, white skin
with silver-gray marbling, and cerulean hair. She'd driven a
hard bargain, but she'd delivered as promised, and insisted
on sealing their bargain physically on the overstuffed couch
in her den.

That was before she'd risen to prominence, joined the
ruling council, and partnered up with Norton Garrick. Between the two of them, they outgunned every other council
member—literally.

Unlike other alliances in the history of Crossways,
Mother Ramona and Garrick had not only retained their
business partnership, but they'd formed a personal one as
well. Maybe they'd sealed their bargain on the couch, too.

"So . . ." Garrick leaned forward. "How many jumpship
pilots do you have for me?"

Now that Crossways had a retrofit jump drive available,
it made sense to convert their fleet, but jumpship pilots
were rare. Ben had agreed the Free Company would train
suitable individuals. So far, they'd recruited twelve pilots
with potential, but not all of them were ready to face the
Folds alone.

"Seven, possibly eight."

"Is that all?"

Mother Ramona touched Garrick's arm. He jumped visibly, but lowered his voice. "I'd hoped for more."

"I know. Me, too," Ben said. "But it's no use putting pilots into the field who are going to snap. Just because they can see the void dragon doesn't make them good pilots. Not all of them are going to make the grade. Being able to see the void dragon also makes them vulnerable to the terrors of foldspace. Seven are ready, one is almost there, but I'd like to keep her in the training program for another month. Three are simply not ready, and might never be. We've only lost one, so far, out of the original dozen."

"Lost?"

"Not literally. James Suli cracked. You know what it's like out there."

Garrick swallowed hard. "I wish I didn't."

"If you look into foldspace for long enough, sometimes it looks back. It could happen to anyone at any time."

"Suli—will he recover?"

Ben shook his head. "He'll never fly the Folds again, but he's not having conversations with angels or trying to harm himself. I've put him on light duties, and he's thinking of retraining as a flight controller."

"You flew again when it happened to you."

"Yes." Ben lowered his voice. "But don't think the Folds don't look into my soul every time I go out there. I've forced myself to accept it and fly anyway, but it's like being a recovering addict. I doubt I'll ever be able to say I'm cured, only that I'm all right so far. Suli wasn't so lucky."

Chapter Six

NIGHTMARES

GARRICK LOOKED UP AT THE SOUND OF A commotion. The door shushed open, allowing the last few phrases of a heated argument to boil through from outside: Ully's voice and a man's.

"Let him in." Garrick recognized the voice and nodded to Ully.

"As if she could stop me." Henry Roxburgh, self-styled Lord Roxburgh, purveyor of entertainment to the masses via casinos, strip joints, whorehouses, and fight arenas, stood in the doorway, powerful shoulders almost filling the space, handsome face scowling.

Garrick sighed. Roxburgh was such an arse. But a dangerous arse. There was never a good time to see him, but this was as good a time as any, and better than most with both Mona and Benjamin here. Garrick wasn't exactly surprised at his intrusion.

Garrick noted Ben's hand close to the thigh pocket where he doubtless carried a weapon. Roxburgh would be a fool to start anything other than a battle of words here in Garrick's heartland. Sadly, Roxburgh was no fool. Pity. It would be worth the risk to be able to put him down right here and now. The man was dangerous. Not only that, but he stood in the way of Garrick's plans for Crossways.

Roxburgh hadn't objected when Garrick ousted Chaliss with extreme prejudice and took over Crossways, but Garrick knew he wasn't happy about it. Some said the only reason Garrick had the top job was because Roxburgh didn't want to take time off from making money to put any effort into governance. It was always easier to let someone else do the hard work and then complain. Garrick knew it was only a matter of time before he made his move.

Ully ducked around Roxburgh and glared at his back as she made a hasty retreat. Roxburgh, being a deadhead, didn't pick up anything from her disregard, but he muttered something under his breath. It didn't sound complimentary.

"Treat that lady with respect, Roxburgh," Mona said. "She's not only my personal Telepath, but she worked the clock around to keep communications open after the battle. You can be thankful that the banking houses kept their interest in Crossways. Where would you be without them?"

Garrick fingered the small diamond in his earlobe and casually waved Roxburgh to a seat, trying to appear relaxed. "What can I do for you this time?"

Mona uncrossed her legs, rose from her chair, and brought a tray with a decanter and four glasses. She placed it on the low table between Garrick and Roxburgh and then retreated to lean casually against the wall. Almost too casually. Garrick could tell she was tight as a coiled spring beneath the languid exterior.

What weapons might Roxburgh be carrying? It was a safe bet that, despite station regulations, he was armed to the teeth.

"You know Ben Benjamin, Henry," Garrick said.

"That's Lord Roxburgh to you."

Garrick kept his tone light. "Henry, I've known you since you arrived on this station calling yourself Hank; don't expect any deference from me."

"I never expect anything from you, Garrick. That's why I take what I want."

"Just be careful who you take it from." Garrick glanced sideways at Ben.

Ben merely cocked his head to the side and raised one eyebrow.

"I've had this notice." Roxburgh waived a flimsy.

Of course, he had. Garrick had wondered how long it

would take for the communication to pass through several administrative layers and land on Roxburgh's desk. He'd expected Roxburgh to start yelling yesterday.

"Yes, that's right. We need to reroute some power conduits that pass under Roxburgh Heights. It's part of the post-battle restructuring, a proper refit instead of a temporary fix. We're going to need you to shut down operations for a day or two."

"Like hell I will! Not without compensation. Do you know how much we lose for every hour of closure?"

Garrick leaned against his cushions. He laughed, but the sound was entirely without mirth. "Are your establishments still standing? Did you lose any staff in the battle?"

"Compensation, or we're not closing for one second."

Garrick raised both hands, palms out. "No compensation. We'll figure something else out."

"The power's fine. Never better."

"Take care, Henry, I might even consider that to be an endorsement. Go away now. Count your blessings. Look after your own power supply. Don't come whining to me if it fails."

"Why, you—"

At the unmistakable whir of a bolt gun charging, Roxburgh froze in the act of leaning into a lunge toward Garrick.

Mother Ramona said, "Henry Roxburgh, don't give me an excuse. I would love to paint the wall with your brains. I always said this place needed a little imaginative decoration."

Garrick saw Ben sit up, his hand barely an inch away from his weapon. Mona had the situation under control.

Roxburgh didn't raise his hands, but his whole body stiffened.

Mona stepped forward. Her eyes narrowed as she sighted along her outstretched arm to the barrel of the lethal bolt gun. Her hand was rock steady.

"Mona, my love, Lord Roxburgh was about to leave," Garrick said. "Henry, I'll send you a waiver to sign regarding the electrical work."

Roxburgh glared at Garrick, turned smartly, and walked out, ignoring the fact that Mona's weapon never wavered.

"That one's dangerous." She clicked on the safety and

deposited the bolt gun on top of the cupboard she'd taken the drinks from. "You'll have to deal with him sooner or later."

"When the time is right," Garrick said.

"You played him," Ben said. "You never expected him to close down so that you could run cables under Roxburgh Heights."

Garrick's eyes crinkled at the corners. "I've primed him for his power to fail. When the electricians are running new cables past his front door, they'll install an isolator. If I need to, I can turn off his power. As Mona says, I'll have to deal with him one day, so I'm planning ahead. I like to give myself an edge."

✦ ✦ ✦

Cara yanked her crestie to a ragged halt outside Wonnick's defensive palisade. The timbers didn't form a straight wall, but were shaped like a tilted letter Y. The outer timber stake was sharpened to a point at crestedina height, and the inner one vertical and enmeshed in a spaghetti of razor wire. It wouldn't keep determined attackers out, but it would give the residents some time to prepare.

The gate was the weakest point in the perimeter, tall enough for a crestie and rider, and wide enough to take a single wagon and outriders. Right now, it stood wide open. Outside the gate a pod of crestedinas gathered in the lee of the osteena shed, some dozing quietly, others whiffling along the dried-up mud looking for sand-spiders. Cara glanced over her shoulder.

"Who goes?" The kid on the gate looked about eighteen. A crossbow pistol dangled from a tie on his belt, neither cocked nor loaded. Obviously, they didn't look very threatening. Perhaps the whole blending-in thing had worked.

"Let us in and close the gate!" Cara dismounted.

"Not from around here, are you?" the kid said, staring at the narrow strip of purple skin around Jussaro's eyes, all that was showing between the head-wrap and the scarf.

Cara led her crestie past him, turned, and pointed. "Close the bloody gate!"

Jussaro slithered off his own beast and followed her through.

"Oh, shit! You might have said. Stay right there. I guess

the mayor will come to you soon enough." The kid was babbling now. "Don't move." He scrambled for a bell rope and
yanked on it three times.

"What's your business here? I'm supposed to ask you
before I let you in."

Cara didn't like to say they were in already and he could
hardy stop them when all he was carrying was an unloaded
crossbow. Her own pulse pistol was a solid presence
strapped firmly to her middle under the surface layer of
clothing. Smuggling it through the perimeter hadn't been a
problem since it was fabricated from ossio, a man-made
substance that registered as human bone on all scanners but
was as strong as steel.

People ran out into the street, some carrying crossbows,
others implements that had some heft to them, right down
to one rotund middle-aged woman wearing an apron and
wielding a heavy skillet.

There were questions and exclamations, mostly repeating a pattern of *what, where,* and *oh, shit!* A scruffy dog ran
in circles barking until someone aimed a kick at it, whereupon a boy grabbed its collar and pulled it close to his leg.

Three women stepped outside the gate and called in the
cresties who plodded obligingly toward town, entering in a
slow procession that delayed the closing of the gate for long
enough that Cara could see the Lifer gang approaching
through the dwindling gap.

*Looks like the whole town's here, Jussaro. Anyone fa-
miliar?*

I said I'd find her and I will.

Cara felt Jussaro psyching himself up to contact Zandra
Hartwell mentally, though he'd been trying without success
ever since he'd had his implant restored. Since Hartwell was
on the run from every megacorporation in the galaxy, that
was hardly surprising. She would either be wearing a
damper, powered down, as Cara herself had once been, or
she'd have one hell of a mental shield.

But if they'd come to the right place, and if she wasn't
powered down, or dead, the proximity should help. Cara
hoped she hadn't been taken by the authorities and had her
implant decommissioned, in which case she was probably
half-mad with shock.

Ready, Carlinni?

Now?

Have you anything better to do?

Yes. There's a Lifer gang at the gate, or hadn't you noticed?

Get your arse into gear.

My arse is at your disposal, metaphorically speaking.

He didn't waste any time. He connected mentally and Cara lent him her considerable psionic energy. Jussaro was the most powerful Telepath she knew, and he had the advantage of knowing Zandra Hartwell personally, or he had known her when they both guided runaway psi-techs to Sanctuary.

He took Cara's power, wrapped it in his own, and sent out a searching call for Hartwell. If she was alive and sane and still had an implant, she should be able to pick up that call from the other side of the galaxy. Theoretically, there was no limit to the distance a class one Telepath could cover, and two class ones in tandem should be unstoppable.

But they stopped.

They'd bounced off something solid.

Shit! Are you all right? Cara asked.

Jussaro gave her the mental equivalent of a giggle. *I'm fine. Success!*

You call that success?

We hit a shield. That means she's here, somewhere, and she's still a functioning Telepath. Nothing else could have generated that kind of shield.

Here, as in here in this town or as in somewhere on this planet?

She's close.

How close?

Jussaro simply smirked.

◆ ◆ ◆

"Our last day in temporary accommodation." Garrick sat back from his desk screen and glanced around. They'd sent most of their things to the Mansion House already, only keeping one small bag each—enough luggage for one last night. "It doesn't look like we've lived here for more than a year, does it?"

"You're not going to miss it, are you?" Mona asked. "You sound almost mournful."

"I've become used to it. Habituated, you might say. The

Mansion House is going to feel very grand after this. I've had times in my life when accommodation was much less grand than a couple of well-protected rooms. I don't need grand—though I won't say I don't like it."

"Grand works for me. I get why you didn't want to be seen living the high life in the Mansion House while people were still struggling with the aftermath of the battle, but I think you've made your point. No need to wear a hair shirt any longer."

"I still feel guilty. We as good as invited the megacorps to attack."

"They were looking for an excuse."

"Did we do the right thing?"

"What is wrong with you, Garrick? I think I liked you better when you were a crook." Mona crossed over and put her arms around him, leaned forward, and flipped off his screen. "Come to bed."

Was that an invitation to do more than sleep? He patted the slim hand resting on his shoulder and sighed.

She touched the waist seam of his buddysuit which separated the top from the trousers and deactivated the medical readout and the temperature stabilizing circuits. He let her undress him like a child, his mind still dwelling on the dead and missing. He would never know the numbers. Finally, he stood before her, not only unclothed, but naked, the tiny pinprick bruises on his stomach from the detanine shots exposed. He saw her notice them, but she made no comment.

"Come on." She drew him down to the bed and snuggled with him, covering them both with an airquilt. Did she want sex? If so, she was out of luck. He was limp and cool. Detanine did that to a man. He could have a few hours of dreamless sleep or sex, but not both.

When she touched his prick, it wasn't demanding. She covered his soft flesh with her warm hand. "Some people can take it when they need it and stop when they like."

"What?"

"Detanine. It is detanine, isn't it? You're not one of them, Garrick. It'll get its hooks into you if it hasn't already."

"It hasn't."

"As long as you're sure."

"Sure, I'm sure."

He would have touched her shoulder in reassurance, but his hand was trembling.

Mona corkscrewed round and rested her back against his chest and her delightful arse against his useless junk. He couldn't help but put his arm over her then. "I love you, Ramona Delgath."

Even with his prick in sleep-mode, he could appreciate her lean rib cage topped by the sudden bounty of her generous breasts. He rubbed the nub of her nipple with the exact center of his palm.

"Quite right, too." She snuggled closer in, her voice heavy with sleep. "Hmm, I'll give you just four hours to stop doing that."

He felt himself drifting off. The detanine was working, thank goodness. He let it take him. The station whirled inside his head. He saw it whole, as it had been, and then broken as the combined fleet left it.

He must have slept because he dreamed there was a conversation—something about electrical supply lines. He wasn't even sure who he was supposed to be talking to. He almost knew it was a dream, but he tried to hang onto it as he passed into wakefulness.

"Don't try and tell me it wasn't bad," he mumbled into the quilt. He blinked. It might have been a few seconds, or maybe minutes, or even hours.

"I won't." Mona was obviously still awake and answered his random dream-comment. "But we're coming out of it now, mostly thanks to you."

He took a couple of breaths, drawing his thoughts into the waking world and hanging on to the conversation with his fingernails. "Kennedy and Benjamin between them saved all of our asses. I'm surprised Crossways held together. She's been living on borrowed time for the last century. Systems jury-rigged. Incompatible components made to fit by persuasive engineering or simple brute force. Patches like that are tenuously serviceable under stable conditions, but fitting a jump drive to the station and flying it through the Folds . . . Reckless in the extreme. Impossible."

"Impossible problems demand impossible solutions," Mona said. "You gave them the opening they needed to do it. Turn over." He did, relinquishing his hold on her breast reluctantly, and this time Mona curled herself around him, her own hand over his heart. She had his back in more ways than one. "And now we're building something here."

He clutched the hand that snaked around his chest and held it close. "Did I tell you I love you?"

"More than once."

"I love that you're an optimist."

He lay in Mona's arms, willing his last detanine shot to kick in, longing to feel it forming the buffer between him and his memories. At last he realized he didn't have to hold his chest so tightly. He sighed, relaxed, and patted Mona's hand.

He sank into a black pit of exhausted sleep . . .

And woke again, screaming.

"Hush, love, you're safe. Safe."

Mona held him, her voice reassuring in his ear.

He wrenched himself away and sat up, sweat running down his forehead and between his shoulder blades.

Safe. He wasn't safe. None of them were safe while that thing lurked in the Folds.

"Nightmares?" Mona asked.

"Yes. Maybe. I think so. I don't know." Whatever had troubled him had slipped away, detail dissolving like mist, but the terror remained. There was something dark and powerful out there: ineffable, numinous.

"The station?" she asked.

He shook his head. "Not this time."

"Foldspace."

He nodded. "You didn't see it. It was . . ." What? Big? Black? Cloudlike? Alien? Sentient? He couldn't begin to describe it.

He'd been closer to it than anyone except Kitty Keely. Closer even than Ben and Cara. He'd felt it alive with purpose. For a moment, it had sucked all the life from his body and then returned it, somehow jumbled. He'd heard it sing.

If the Nimbus ever found its way into realspace, everything else was for nothing.

Chapter Seven

CROWDER

CROWDER WAS DUE UPSTAIRS FOR A MEETING with Malusi Duma. The outgoing Pan-African president might not wield the power he had before stepping down at the last election, but until Samuel Ajibola took over on the first of January, he was still the president, and even after that he would retain massive influence.

The Trust needed African platinum, and the present agreement was in its final year. Alphacorp would be trying to muscle in, so Crowder had to keep Mr. Duma sweet. Yolanda Chang had almost ruined the negotiations. She'd been so puppy-dog eager that she'd come close to giving away their negotiating advantage. Crowder had been able to step in and reverse the damage, but Duma was a wily old fox, a worthy opponent at the negotiating table.

Stefan entered the office quietly and placed a blast pack of painkiller, a blister pack of his daily meds, a glass of water, and two dataslides on his desk. "Is there anything else I can get you, sir?" he asked.

Crowder waved him away without making eye contact, and then thought better of it. "I have everything I need, Stefan, thank you."

The young man's half smile didn't reach his eyes. Crowder made a mental note to be nicer to him. The neural

conditioning would hold, but winning goodwill with kind
words was a cheap option. He'd make sure Stefan was rewarded with a substantial end-of-year bonus as well.

"How are you settling in, Stefan? Feeling more comfortable on Earth? It's a bit different from Chenon."

"I like it, sir, though twenty-four-hour days take a bit of
getting used to. I thought, since it's the homeworld, that my
body would adjust naturally, but darkness comes so fast,
and so often."

Crowder chuckled. People making the move in the opposite direction often had a hard time getting used to Chenon's fifty-hour day. "Did you manage to shop for local
clothes?"

"I did. A very nice young lady in reception took pity on
me and took me to the mall. I even have clothes for the
beach. Though they were extraordinarily expensive for
something so small. We're going on Sunday; that's if you
don't need me here."

"Take Sunday off. I believe that's the local custom."

"Thank you, sir."

Crowder slapped the blast pack to the side of his neck,
popped the pills, then levered himself up out of his float
chair and reached for his cane. "I'll be in a meeting for the
rest of the afternoon."

"Yes, sir. Do you want me to hold calls or put them
through?"

"Hold them—unless it's one of my daughters."

It wouldn't be, of course. He'd tried to tell the girls that
there had never been any danger to their mother on Norro.
Benjamin wouldn't hesitate to kill Crowder or any one of
his phalanx of bodyguards, but he was too principled to let
any harm come to innocent bystanders, and that included
Agnetha.

Principled. That was Ben Benjamin all over.

Crowder could barely stop his mouth turning down at
the thought. If Benjamin had been less principled and more
flexible, then the Trust would have had Olyanda, lock, stock,
and platinum. His last assassins had failed spectacularly and
had ceased all communication, which was a bad sign, but
this time he'd sent an expert. Swanson—his best hope—had
found himself a place with the station militia.

Crowder click-clacked along the corridor to the elevator,

a bit of an oddity at this sublevel, but it came into its own once it rose into the light. It was completely invisible, made of transparent glass-steel so clear that you couldn't see the walls even when you were standing inside it. They'd had to place a mat on the floor so people would travel in it. Stepping onto an invisible floor was against most people's instincts for self-preservation. Even so, Crowder tapped the glass floor with his cane before stepping in. For luck, he told himself.

By the time Crowder's elevator reached the eighteenth floor, he'd fixed a smile on his face.

"President Duma, how good to see you again."

"Just mister will do, Mr. Crowder. I'll be out of office soon, and my successor is already growing into the title. It's a time of transition, and I plan to slide gracefully into obscurity once we've concluded our negotiations. You're looking well. Are you fully recovered?" Duma glanced at the cane.

"Almost. The cane is a minor irritant but no great inconvenience."

"Excellent. I brought you a gift of wine, one of our excellent Cape reds. There's a case being delivered to your suite right now."

"Thank you. It's only a little something, but I brought you a terrarium of Chenon plants, some of our most exotic. My secretary is having it delivered to your office."

"How lovely. My late wife used to scold me for my plant collection, but I have nothing from Chenon. It will take pride of place. I only traveled there once, to visit family, but I thought it a lovely planet."

"You have family on Chenon?"

"I had, but not anymore."

The way he said it made Crowder think he'd probably outlived his family—one of the problems of the rejuv treatments. He didn't want to inquire too deeply. Duma's personal life held no interest. He knew from the company file that there had been several wives, a gaggle of children, and an army of grandchildren. He changed the subject.

"I thought we could have our meeting on the terrace where it's comfortable."

"A lovely idea. After you."

Crowder led the way to the terrace which overlooked

sculpted gardens. Duma put both hands on the balcony rail
and looked over. "Did you know my ancestors used to live
here?"

"South Africa?"

"I'm a Zulu, Mr. Crowder, so I mean here in KwaZulu
Natal. In fact, right here on this very spot. The Trust Tower
stands on the site of Umlazi Township where my not-so-
well-off ancestors scratched out a living. That was before
the meteorites, of course, and before the Trust moved its
headquarters from the ruins of New York to an O'Neill colony in space and then finally here when they saw Africa's
potential."

"Long before my time, of course, but my ancestor, Anne
DiDoren, was chair of the board for fifty years through the
difficult time of reconstruction. My family has always been
deeply involved with the Trust."

"And mine has always produced rabble-rousing troublemakers and politicians. Sometimes both in one package."

"So which are you?" Crowder asked.

Duma cracked out laughing. "I like to think I'm a little
of both, though at my age I leave most of the rabble-rousing
to my grandchildren. Do you have children, Mr. Crowder?"

"Two daughters and two grandchildren here on Earth, in
Europe."

"You must miss them."

"More than you know."

"I have twenty-eight grandchildren, and I love them all
though two of them are long-distance ones. I confess I've
never met them as adults, though I saw them both as very
small children. I get news regularly, though, from their
grandmother. We never married, but we've always shared a
fondness for each other. Family is so important, don't you
think?"

Crowder agreed with him in an effort to move the conversation along. He wondered if Duma knew his own family situation and was using it to needle him.

Pleasantries over, they moved on to discussing the platinum trade deal in general terms, Crowder trying to find out
if Alphacorp was in the running for approval to negotiate,
and Duma trying to ascertain what side benefits might ac-
crue from renewal of contracts. It was all very amicable on
the surface, but they were like two contestants in a boxing

ring, using fancy footwork to keep out of the reach of the other and keeping their guard up at all times until they could make a sudden jab at vulnerable flesh.

At the end of this round, the score was pretty much even, but Crowder sensed they were heading for a renewal of contracts even though they hadn't been able to resolve certain taxation issues which Crowder thought he'd skirted quite nicely for the moment. It would doubtless crop up again in future negotiations.

Feeling fairly confident, he slid sideways into a question about the Five Power Alliance, which Pan-Africa supported wholeheartedly. Essentially, it was a whole-Earth government, and though Earth's economy had diminished compared to the megacorporations, its influence was still disproportionately high. Plus, they had a top-class space fleet, untouched by the Crossways debacle, and massive influence with the Monitors who largely adopted the London Accord on human rights.

"I will, of course, be giving up my seat on the FPA as a voting member," Duma said. "That's for Mr. Ajibola to claim. I will still have my seat in an advisory capacity for the next two years, however."

"I wondered about your thoughts on the breakaway colonies and colony independence."

"Ha! As an African, I thoroughly recommend it! Self-government is good, Mr. Crowder. It allows creativity and innovation to flourish alongside ambition and self-determination. You may, of course, get a completely different answer from the Europeans in the FPA. Their history of colonialism takes a somewhat diametrically opposed view."

Crowder knew when to retreat gracefully. There would be other days, other discussions.

✦ ✦ ✦

We've reached Wonnick, Cara told Ben. *Jussaro is convinced we'll find Hartwell this time. It's not a very big town.*

I hope he's right. I miss you.

Miss you, too. Anything interesting happening?

Ben told her about the way Garrick had played Roxburgh.

I hope Garrick's not being too clever for his own good,

she said. *When you find a reptan under a rock, it's better not to poke it with a sharp stick.*

When Garrick decides to do something about Roxburgh, I'm pretty sure it will be sudden, swift, and conclusive.

What if Roxburgh does something about Garrick first?

Yes. I'd thought of that. Garrick has a lot on his mind. He might have taken his eye off that particular ball.

After Cara had signed off, that thought echoed around Ben's brain for the rest of the day.

At 1700 station time, he headed hubward to where Captain Arran Syke, formerly captain of Mother Ramona's private guard, now head of Crossways Militia, had his office. Close to the Mansion House, this was, in all but name, the central police station for Crossways. There were five smaller offices spread about the station plus an eighth office on the Saturn Ring, now separate.

Three young men, dressed in buddysuits marked with a shoulder flash which represented the scales of justice, chatted in a corner. A woman stood before a holographic screen, arranging images, mostly mugshots. The desk sergeant in the outer office looked up as he entered, recognized him, and smiled.

"Come to see Captain Syke, sir?" She inclined her head toward his office door, which stood slightly ajar.

"Yes." He searched his memory for her name. "Heator, isn't it?"

"That's right, sir."

"You've made sergeant?"

"Yes." She grinned at him. "Got my stripes a month ago."

"Well done, Sergeant."

"Thank you."

"Commander Benjamin." Syke opened his door. "I thought I heard your voice. You three . . ." He glowered at the young men. "If you can't find something to do, I'll assign you to guard duty at the public docks."

The three idlers jumped up immediately and separated to their individual desks.

"Sorry, Commander Benjamin, come right in."

No matter how many times Ben circumvented formality, Syke remained proper to the point of stiffness. Ben had lost the title of commander when he deserted the Trust, but it had stuck anyway. His own people at the Free Company usually addressed him by name, or called him boss, but Syke championed etiquette with the zeal of the newly converted. Ben was bound, therefore, to address him as Captain Syke.

That was all right. He could ignore the idiosyncrasies because Syke was conscientious and diligent. Unfortunately, he wasn't a trained police officer. His new role as head of the militia had evolved over the past year. Now, instead of having a unit of fifty, his staff had grown exponentially. The job was getting away from him. Crossways was a big place to police, and the population was law-averse. A significant number of inhabitants were on Crossways to avoid the attention of the Monitors.

Garrick's directive was to ignore the petty criminals, for now, and to target the ones who were causing real harm, both on-station and off. In the last month alone, Syke had shut down two piracy operations and ended a very nasty kidnapping with the victim still alive, though missing three fingers. None of the kidnappers had survived the smackdown.

That was one way of avoiding an expensive court case, though not necessarily one Ben liked. There was enough of his Monitor training left in him to still believe everyone deserved a fair trial, however guilty they appeared to be.

He accepted the offer of tea, brought in by one of the young men.

"What can I do for you, Commander?"

"I wanted to congratulate you on solving the kidnap case. It's rare to rescue the victim alive after more than three days."

"We got lucky—an informer—otherwise . . ."

"I'd like to offer my help."

"Your Monitor experience?"

"Not particularly, no, though there's a retired officer I know of who practically wrote the book on criminology and social theory in closed habitats. In fact, she wrote several books and taught classes. She lives alone, no family, and might well be interested in a consultancy on Crossways. I imagine she could get a good book out of it, and her expertise would be invaluable."

Ben held his breath, wondering whether he should have

made that suggestion in advance of the next one he was about to make.

"Thank you." Syke looked thoughtful. "You came all this way to recommend a consultant?"

"Not exactly. I'm setting up a new training program for the Free Company. Morton Tengue is supervising. His crew is sharp—sharper than mine when it comes to the physical stuff. I want to give my guys an edge."

"You're expecting more trouble?"

"Always. Though I live in hopes of being disappointed."

Syke laughed at that. "I know what you mean."

"I came to offer you the option of sending some of your officers to train with us."

"You think we need sharpening up, as well as hiring in a consultant?"

"No offense, Captain. You don't have an easy job here, and good as you are, you've had to take on new officers and put them in the field with little training. Garrick's trying to bring law to the lawless, and I'm sure as hell glad I'm not in your shoes right now."

"So you're only offering combat training?"

Ben nodded. "Generally, yes, but specifically, I'm offering to train the detail that you set aside to protect Garrick and Mother Ramona. If something happens to them, this station slips into chaos. Tengue's mercs have many skills. They are particularly effective bodyguards. Garrick had a set-to with Roxburgh recently—"

"Another?"

"I don't trust Roxburgh—particularly where Garrick's concerned, and prevention, in this case, is certainly better than the alternative."

Syke nodded. "Happy to accept your offer, Commander. When do you propose to start?"

Ben relaxed. He'd worried Syke would take offense.

"Pick your men. Twenty initially. We'll fix up a time and meet in the training gym in Blue Seven."

Chapter Eight

SIEGE

SOMEONE WAS COMING. A RIPPLE RAN through the assembling crowd. Cara felt their expectation and their faith in their mayor as if they were shouting it from the treetops.

She heard the woman before she saw her.

"Jordan, you and Ives take six men and watch the north gate. Emma, plasma rifle, second-story window. Treat it gentle. Don't go popping off for no reason, but if you need to use it, make it count. Arlette, Jonno, Dow, Walters, up on the rooftops. Make sure you've plenty of bolts." A short, slender woman, possibly fiftyish, strode through the crowd snapping out orders. She wore a slouch hat pulled down low over her forehead and an assemblage of clothing layers indistinguishable from any of the other inhabitants. In one hand she carried a crossbow, in the other a coffee cup. Cara liked a woman who got her priorities right.

"Are you the folks who brought trouble to our door?"

Her lack of height didn't diminish her obvious authority.

"What should we have done?" Cara asked. "Didn't fancy hanging around to meet those guys on their own ground."

The woman grunted, handed her coffee to the gate boy, and cocked her crossbow with a lever. It took strength to make it look that easy. Then she waggled her fingers in a give-me gesture, and the kid handed back the coffee cup. She took a sip.

"You can let your cresties go, they won't go far. What's your business in Wonnick?"

"Looking for an old friend." Jussaro pulled the scarf from his face and grinned. "Guess we came to the right place."

"Emil Jussaro! Son of a—"

"Hello, Zandra."

Cara took another look at the town mayor. Now she had the opportunity to study her up close, Zandra Hartwell was probably closer to sixty. The ramrod-straight posture belonged to a younger woman, but the tightly scraped-back gray hair—what could be seen of it under her hat—and the fine mesh of lines around her eyes gave her away.

"What in all seven hells are you doing here?" Hartwell said.

"I just said." Jussaro grinned at her.

"If that old friend is me, you should have saved yourself the effort."

"You need to hear what I have to say."

"After I've dealt with them." She jerked her head toward the gate, which was now closed. A pair of stout bars reinforced it from the inside.

"I didn't think they'd follow us right to town," Cara said. "Are they dangerous?"

"We trade sometimes. Mostly we don't bother them and they don't bother us, unless there's something they want without paying for it. Something you two aren't telling me?"

"We spotted them about fifty klicks out, but I suppose it's possible they've been tracking us since we crossed the border."

"Hmm, could be. We don't see too many tourists, but the ones who do come often smuggle in weapons that are hard to come by this side of the Ditch. Are you carrying?"

Jussaro shook his head. "You know me and weapons. We don't get on."

Cara patted her side. "I'm carrying for both of us—a derri and an ossio pulse pistol."

"Can you use them?"

"If I have to."

Hartwell shrugged.

"I don't recall you ever showed a liking for firearms," Jussaro said.

"People change. This place makes you change. It's a hardscrabble life here. Some of us choose one way, some another." She nodded to the kid who'd been on the gate. "Open the slider, let's see what they want."

He opened a head-height panel that gave a letterbox window onto the world outside.

The dust cloud resolved itself as the gang approached. In the center was a team of six crestedinas harnessed in pairs to an antigrav sled. A dozen mounted men flanked the sled, all dressed in local style, their heads swathed and faces masked against the dust. The sled wasn't a sled at all, but a bastardized armored groundcar with the top sliced off. How had that crossed the Ditch? It was painted blood-red and decorated with bones. The woman who drove it rose from the cockpit and leaned across the top of the front roll bar, her bare arms corded with muscle and burned brown by sun and wind.

Hartwell planted her feet slightly apart and held her crossbow in plain sight. "State your business."

"We're here for a neighborly visit. No need to get spiky." She looked up to the first-floor window. "That you up there, Emma Swithington? Put the rifle down. I can see the muzzle from here. It's a Tesla 120. You might take one of us, or even two, but not before I'd cut through the gate with this." She patted the plasma gun at her side, still holstered. "And my boys have you in their sights. Nice try, but not today."

"Stay where you are, Emma," Hartwell called, "but take a step back. I asked what you want, Lizzie Rhodes."

"Travelers crossed my patch without paying tolls."

"I know what your tolls are like. One hundred percent of everything they own is a touch excessive. We found the last traveler you caught up with. Leaving him without clothing and water in the dry season was a death sentence. You went too far. Besides, these are under my protection. Old friends."

She scowled sideways at Jussaro and lowered her voice. "Who is your friend, anyway?" She jerked her head at Cara.

"Someone I would have sent your way a couple of years ago," Jussaro said. "But you'd gone to ground."

Hartwell put a finger on the center of her forehead where it was likely her small implant scar rested. She raised one eyebrow. Cara placed a finger on her own implant scar, a tiny knot, and nodded.

"All right." Hartwell acknowledged the nod. She turned to the gate and shouted, "We don't want any trouble. I'm sorry for your inconvenience. Go home."

"It ain't no inconvenience. We'll catch 'em on the way back if you ain't going to send 'em out."

"She's right about that," Hartwell said. "The minute you step outside these gates she's going to be on your trail. Trouble follows that one like a long shadow. We can't stop her and her boys from roaming the Big Dusty, and like them or not, they're our neighbors. We don't pay them off, though. It gives 'em big ideas."

"We have a way out," Cara said. "A safe way out for two of us, or possibly more."

"Is that an invitation?"

"It could be," Jussaro said.

"I've done enough jumping around the galaxy. I've found a place here where I'm needed."

"Should I ask how you've been?" Jussaro said.

"No need. You can guess. Step under the porch, here. It's a touch more private." She stepped up into the shade of an overhanging front porch and glared at the nearest of the townsfolk. "Private, I said." She watched them slink off out of earshot. "I've been busy staying one jump ahead of the megacorps—sometimes only half a jump. I lost Bronnie on Logan's World. She went down fighting."

"I'm sorry. I know Bronnie was—"

"She was everything." Hartwell held up her hand to chop off that line of talk. "I heard you'd lost your implant."

"I did."

"Yet here you are."

"Someone had a dirty job that needed doing. It suited them to give me a second chance."

"So you traded with the establishment."

"Wouldn't you?"

She didn't answer.

"It came with a price."

"You paid it."

"Not like they expected. It's a long story."

"I've got time."

Cara watched Hartwell's face while Jussaro told how

Crowder had set him to spy on them for the Trust, and how he'd managed to twist the situation his own way. She'd not asked him to tell her mind-to-mind, which was one way of making sure he was telling the truth. Lying by Telepathy was damned difficult, even for someone with Jussaro's level of skill. No, it was obvious Hartwell trusted Jussaro's word. Cara wondered if theirs had been a simple working relationship or if there had been more to it.

Gods! She missed Ben.

"So Emil found you on Mirimmar-14." Hartwell turned to Cara.

"I like to think I found him."

"She was powered down—on the run from Alphacorp," Jussaro said.

"I was looking for Sanctuary. I found something else. I'm part of the Free Company now. We're independent. Over two hundred psi-techs."

Hartwell turned to Jussaro. "Looks like you can build Sanctuary right there."

"Not like the old days. You took them in, gave them new IDs, a quick lesson in camouflage, and sent them off to who knows where. Only you had the key to the whole network."

"And the Monitors nearly busted me for it. Bronnie, Elf, and I slipped out minutes ahead of a raid that took thirty of our people and turned them into morons. Blasted their implants so badly they barely had two brain cells to rub together. You should know. You got caught in the backlash."

"I don't blame you for that."

"I blamed me. I left the Sanctuary business for good. After Bronnie died, Elf gave up. Breathed vacuum somewhere on the run from Kokassec to Leira. No one saw her go. I traveled on my own for a bit, ended up here. This side of the Ditch there's no law to speak of. No one to turn me in."

"We have a situation," Cara said. "Two hundred psi-techs who are forced to wear dampers because the Trust has started to send a mindbender to cull them one at a time. We need Sanctuary, again, Zandra."

"You won't find it here. I've got my own to protect, see . . ." *Jonti.*

One of the men who'd rounded up the loose crestedinas turned. *Yes, Ma?*

He was younger than Cara expected, maybe fifteen or sixteen at most.

"You have a son?" Jussaro asked.

"I kept him hidden, even from you. Sent for him after I settled here. He likes it. He's made friends."

Come here and meet Emil Jussaro. You've heard me talk about him.

The boy came over, a cautious smile on his face.

"Don't worry, Emil, he's not yours."

That much was obvious from the boy's skin. Beneath the tan he was Caucasian, and the hair that peeped out from his head-covering was straw-fair.

*Hello, Mr. Jussaro. Ma has told me about you. I thought you'd be . . . *

Taller? Jussaro's laugh was like a bark. *I just talk that way.*

Cara was trying to pin something down. *You don't have an implant,* she blurted to the boy.

Hartwell gave her a sideways look. "You're good, lady. No, he doesn't have an implant. I've been training him since he was a baby, since before he was born, in fact. External influences and environmental factors can affect an embryo *in utero.* We've known that for years. Those of us who have implants have them because we already have an underlying natural talent. Enhance that talent with an implant, and it not only changes us, but it affects our offspring." She looked smug. "The megacorporations take advantage of that. They recruit the children of their psi-techs because they already have a predisposition toward psionics, but once they're implanted, it masks any natural talent. None of us knows what talent we would have had if it had been nurtured from birth instead of subsumed into an implant. Jonti's a natural."

"What's his range?" Cara asked.

"If we were going on the old psi-tech scoring system, he'd be a class three."

"Impressive."

I am here, you know. Jonti scowled.

Sorry, love, his mother said.

"My apologies, Mr. Hartwell," Cara said. "Have you ever thought about getting an implant? If you can throw a thought over a hundred klicks without one, then with one, you'd be able to throw a thought across the galaxy."

"We've discussed it." Jonti looked to his mother, as if for approval. "I don't know anyone on the other side of the galaxy, and having that kind of talent makes me a commodity for the megacorporations to bicker over. I'd rather run my own life."

"Good for you." Jussaro shook the boy's hand vigorously. "You're giving me ideas, young man. Cara, we should talk to Gen and Max's little girl."

"She's not fifteen months old yet."

"I know. Exciting, isn't it?" The enthusiastic smile on Jussaro's face faded as he turned to Hartwell. "So you don't want to return to the Sanctuary business?"

She shook her head. "I'm settled now. I look after my town . . ." She waved at her people. "They look after me. We're family. I'm too old to change again."

"But Sanctuary . . ."

"It's yours."

"How can it be? I don't have the unlock codes or the key to the network."

"I can fix that."

She leaned forward and touched her forehead to Jussaro's. He stiffened and jerked backward, eyes wide.

"There. I bequeath it to you, Jussaro, the name, the idea, the codes, the key, the contacts—everything. That's all you need. The Free Company has the resources. You know what to do and how it works. Be the change you want to be in the universe." She laughed. "Better sit down before you fall down."

Jussaro had that typical wide-eyed look of someone who'd recently received a huge infodump and needed time for his brain to process it. Hartwell sat him on the step. "Jonti," she called to her son who was chatting up a teen girl and looking a little awkward. "Some water for our friend, here."

She looked toward the gate. Lizzie Rhodes was still standing in the sled, hands on hips, watching from a distance. "I hope you weren't kidding about a way out. She's cranky today."

"We have a ride," Cara said, glancing up at the sky. "A few hours at most. But will you be okay with them out there?"

"Once you're out of reach, they have nothing to gain by

coming at us. They know we've nothing except osteena, and that's not worth bleeding for. It's not like they haven't got stockpiles of their own. It's hardly rare during wet season. Of course, if they could get their hands on a flyer, it might push them into being reckless."

"It's a bit more than a flyer, but unless they have any Navigators, they won't get very far."

"I wouldn't put it past them to try for it, or maybe try for you, and use you as hostages to get access to your crew. You got a plan?"

"The beginnings of one."

"I'll wish you success, then." She bent and kissed Jussaro on the cheek and handed him the water Jonti had brought. "For old times' sake."

He blew her a kiss in return. "For old times' sake. Luck go with you, Zandra Hartwell."

"And with you, Emil Jussaro. Stick it to the corporations. I know you can do it." She turned to the gate.

Cara didn't mind if Jake Lowenbrun lit up every warning light on Dounreay's air traffic system as long as he arrived before the Lifers ran out of patience.

Two hours, maximum, he said.

Can you make it one? You'll have a reception committee, Cara told him. *This Lifer gang would probably like a nice ship for a bit of upward mobility. Might need a plan.*

Oh, yeah. I'm sure we can come up with something. Cara could practically hear him grinning.

A little more than an hour later the air vibrated with energy as the *Bellatkin* dropped out of the sky, skimming the baked ground and throwing up a massive dust cloud. She was only a small freighter with a boxy belly, like a cube rounded at the corners, and a long skinny tail. Her atmospheric maneuverability was assisted by extendable rotors on a pair of stubby upper wings. She wallowed on her antigravs and came to rest farther from Wonnick's town wall than Cara would have liked.

Is that the best you can do, Lowenbrun? she asked.

You're lucky I hit the damn planet. This heap of junk is designed for space docking. She doesn't like atmospheres, and gravity sets off her arthritis. I see you've got company.

Yes, that's the Lifer gang under the leadership of Lizzie Rhodes.

A party of Lifers peeled away from the main band and circled the *Bellatkin* at a safe distance.

"That ship's not for the likes of you, Lizzie," Zandra hollered. "Call off your boys and skedaddle, and we'll say no more about this."

"Yeah, right. To make use of anything those guys are bringing in, they've gotta get their cargo from the ship to the town. I reckon we should have a percentage of that. Call it taxation or call it a toll. Hell, call it whatever you like."

"I don't suppose she'll believe us if we tell her the *Bellatkin* isn't carrying cargo?" Cara asked.

"Would you?"

"Probably not, but it's the truth."

"Your ship armed?"

"Ship-to-ship anti-piracy guns. It's likely they'd take out the Lifers and the whole of Wonnick if we used them in the atmosphere. I presume you don't want anyone dead."

Hartwell shook her head. "The Lifers are a nuisance, but we're not at all-out war with them, most of the time, anyway. And we'd rather keep it that way."

Cara nodded. "I have an idea."

The *Bellatkin* sat on the baked ground, stabilizer legs extended, but cargo- and crew-doors sealed. After ten minutes of zero activity, the Lifers crept toward her. When nothing else happened, they crept closer still. They found the cargo hatch lock and yanked on it. Slowly, the cargo ramp extended from a maw big enough to accommodate a lift-loader, or an exoskeleton. During the Battle for Crossways, the *Bellatkin* had even carried a pair of hornets, two-man space fighters, all thrust, and bristling with weapons. But right now, she was empty, her hold nothing more than a sealed box.

Weapons extended, but with little caution for the true danger, the Lifers slid from their cresties. While two stayed with the saurians, six of them charged the ramp in pairs, firing off a few warning rounds into the blackness of the hold.

With barely a creak of her hydraulics the ramp rose behind them.

The two riders and all the cresties bolted toward the town walls as the *Bellatkin* rose on antigravs and shot away.

Easiest pickup I ever made, Lowenbrun said. *Can you*

believe it? The numpties started firing at the walls. How far do you want me to drop them?

Fifty klicks should do it. Take them due north. Drop a smoke beacon with them. I guess they aren't carrying much water.

Lizzie Rhodes had her plasma rifle leveled, but with her band cut in half, she didn't have the numbers.

"Put the weapon, down, Lizzie," Hartwell yelled.

"You bring my boys back. Don't think I won't use this."

"May I?" Cara asked Hartwell.

"Go ahead."

"Ms. Rhodes," Cara called. "My pilot will be giving your boys a choice right about now: either leave my ship peacefully or get taken into orbit to chew on vacuum. I'm guessing they'll choose the nonfatal outcome. They'll be fifty klicks north and will be given a beacon that will burn for about four hours. If you set off now, you can find them in daylight before they get too thirsty. I understand you sometimes come here to trade peacefully. Next time you come, leave your weapons at home. We'll give the mayor, here, some basic medical supplies. Some for the town and some for trade. I guess those are even harder to come by than weapons. Call it a sign of good faith, payment for our safe passage."

Lizzie Rhodes' eyes narrowed, but she holstered the rifle, sat down in the sled, and gathered the reins. "You'd better be speaking the truth, girl."

She didn't wait for an answer.

Chapter Nine

LEAVING

BEN WAS THE FIRST TO ADMIT THAT NEWS OF the training sessions with Morton Tengue hadn't been universally popular. The psi-tech crews had always trained according to their specialty. No one expected the catering staff to be up front in a firefight, and the Psi-Mechs had specialized in using their engineering bots as weapons, and had never gone beyond basic training in hand-to-hand.

This time Ben insisted on everyone training.

Ada Levenson had been the first to express her displeasure. At the age of forty, Ada had not been in the training ring since her early days with the Trust as a new recruit. She was a large, muscular woman, tall as well as broad, but tending to heaviness with a generous bosom. She probably had a buddysuit tucked away somewhere, but she rarely wore anything other than short-sleeved kitchen whites which contrasted with her florid complexion.

"You don't seriously expect me to sweat it out on that mat, Benjamin, do you?" She confronted Ben in the dinner queue. He knew he was in trouble as soon as she called him Benjamin instead of boss.

"You and all your staff, Ada," he said. "No one gets out of this. We need to be ready for anything that might go down. It makes sense."

"I've enough to do already. I guess you let Wenna off, huh?"

Ben shook his head. "Wenna's in the first rotation."

"What about you?"

"I'm in the second."

She huffed out through her nose, snatched his coffee cup away from him, and pushed another into his hands. He sipped it on his way to the office and grimaced. She'd deliberately given him the good stuff, which he hated. Cara would love it, but it was too bitter for his palate. He put it down on the corner of Wenna's desk.

"You brought me coffee?" she said.

"I intended to bring me coffee, but Ada Levenson's not happy with me."

Wenna picked it up and poured it into her own empty mug. She sniffed appreciatively. "It's the stuff from Blue Mountain. She should be this displeased with me."

"I told Ada I'd put you in the first rotation for the new training program."

Wenna laughed. "It's as good a place as any. No one gets off, right?"

"Right."

"What about you?"

"I'm going in the second rotation. Each class has a mixture of Free Company, Tengue's mercs and Syke's militia. I'll come and watch yours, though."

A couple of hours later Ben eased himself into the training gym. The first class had drawn a small audience. Ben suspected most of them simply wanted to see what was in store for them later. Thirty individuals, dressed in softsuits, feet bare, were running through stretches followed by practice moves and, finally, some pairs work.

Wenna, gray hair pulled into a tight band, kept up with the younger participants. Ben knew that even though she appeared to be welded to her desk, she made time for gym sessions, usually early morning or late at night when no one else was around.

Ada Levenson was in the audience, frowning.

Tengue, all muscle himself, in a singlet and loose trousers, knew his business. He was hard on those he thought could do better and encouraging with those who were trying. He'd paired Wenna against Franny Fowler, the smart-mouthed mercenary. They were fairly evenly matched for height and reach, though Wenna maybe had ten pounds on Fowler, and Fowler was young enough to be her daughter.

"You want me to go easy, Ms. Phipps?" Fowler asked as they squared up to each other.

"Why?" Wenna raised one eyebrow. "You think an attacker will go easy on me because I have a prosthetic arm? Or is it that you think I'm too old for this kind of shit?"

"Yeah, whichever."

"Come on, girl. Give it your best shot."

"Right. You asked for it."

Fowler closed quickly, but Wenna twisted away. Ben watched and smiled. The best defense was not to be there when someone was trying to hurt you. He watched the two women whirling together briefly and breaking apart again. Wenna had been a strong fighter in her youth and had become a canny one as she gained years and experience. She held off the younger woman, finally putting her on the mat as Fowler went for a chop and Wenna blocked it with her prosthetic arm. Wenna ended up on top.

"Good use of that arm," Fowler said as they stood up and grinned at each other. "Though I might have had you if you hadn't used it to block me."

"You might, but you didn't. You have to learn to twist disadvantages to advantages."

"That wasn't too bad," Wenna said to Ben as she passed Ben on her way to the showers. "Score one for the seniors."

"You're hardly a senior."

"I'm twice that girl's age."

"Well, you don't look it."

"It's good to have a boss who knows the right things to say. You'd better think up a few good lines for when it's Ada Levenson's turn." She laughed as she sashayed past him.

✦ ✦ ✦

Jake brought the *Bellatkin* down on the edge of town, within a hundred meters of the north gate.

"You're sure about this, Zandra?" Jussaro gave her one more chance to change her mind. "What about Jonti? Do you want to bring him up in Wonnick?"

"Can you guarantee any place safer?"

"Maybe not safer, but certainly more interesting."

She laughed. "I've seen plenty of interesting places. Most of them came with a health warning."

"And Wonnick doesn't?"

"Comparatively?" She shook her head. "I'll be sharing a beer with Lizzie Rhodes next time she passes through."

"Would that be osteena beer?"

She smiled. "You get used to it. Wonnick has its advantages. We're building something here, something good. Give it another couple of generations and the Lifer gangs will integrate. It's already starting to happen. You see the girl with the rifle?"

Cara looked to where Hartwell pointed.

"That's Emma Swithington," Hartwell said. "Lizzie Rhodes' niece. We tried an exchange program. Emma came here for some schooling, met Matt Swithington, and stayed. They visit to and fro with their kids.

"A couple of seasons ago we had the biggest damn osteena harvest in living memory. More than we could cope with, but it goes against the grain to waste it. Rhodes' gang and three others negotiated to use our processing plant and worked with us on the harvest for three weeks with no trouble at all. Occasionally they overstep the mark, like today, but mostly we get on okay in spite of the fact that we're interlopers in their territory."

Jake carried a box of medical supplies from the main cabin. "Ma'am." He nodded politely to Hartwell. "Antivirals, antibacterials, one-shot antibiotics, analgesics, and anesthetics — a veritable A-list. How's that?"

"Very welcome, Mr. Lowenbrun. You're sure you can spare them?"

"We brought them for trade, ma'am, and since our next stop is our home base, we can afford to leave them."

Cara and Jussaro hefted their saddle packs onto their shoulders.

"Hey, off-worlders, you got plenty of room in that ship?" a young woman, swathed from head to toe in multiple skirts and tunics called out as Jake dropped the boarding ramp.

"Not for passengers," Cara said.

"Lady, do I look as if I want to go anywhere but here? I'm not looking for passage, but I have a fine cargo of dried osteena. Sell it anywhere in the known universe and it'll double its value. To you, only fifteen hundred creds. You'll make a fortune."

Cara shook her head.

"Osteena. Very nutritious. Very tasty."

Hey, doesn't Crossways need supplies? Jake said. *Spend fifteen hundred to make three thousand. Sounds like a good deal to me.*

It's osteena, Cara said.

Very tasty, according to the young lady.

If you like mud, Jussaro said. *I still have a pouch in my pack. You're welcome to try it.*

They boarded the *Bellatkin*, and Cara raised the ramp before anyone could make them any more irresistible offers. Once in the main cabin, Jussaro handed Jake a sealed pouch of osteena pulp.

"Here, suck on that before you spend fifteen hundred creds."

"Thanks, man. Always willing to try something new." Jake took a swallow.

"Well, how do you like it?" Jussaro asked.

Jake cleared his throat. "Tastes like mud . . . maybe with a little . . . organic matter mixed in."

"As in . . ."

"Yeah, all right. It tastes like shit. You guys have been living on this?"

"Pulped osteena, stewed osteena, osteena cubes and, for a special treat, osteena jerky. They even make osteena wine."

"There are ration packs in the galley."

"I never thought I'd say this, but that sounds wonderful." Cara helped herself and handed a pack to Jussaro, then flopped into the copilot's chair and spooned down every last salty, savory mouthful before starting on something sweet and fruity.

"Did you get what you wanted?" Jake asked.

"I think we did," Jussaro said. "Though Zandra couldn't be persuaded back."

"Sorry to hear that. It's been a long haul."

It certainly had. Cara had missed Ben so much. "How long do you reckon it will take us to get to Crossways?"

"About twelve hours, plus another two hours to dock if there's a tailback. Fourteen hours maximum."

"I'm going to talk to Ben. Is it all right to tell him about Zandra, Jussaro?"

"Sure. I'm going to write it all up anyway. I may need some help if I'm going to create Sanctuary again."

"You're going to do like she said." Cara felt excitement bubble up inside her. Psi-techs had a raw deal with the megacorps. Providing them with a way out would have double benefits. Crossways' gain was the megacorps' loss.

"I'm thinking about it. It's . . . important."

"Yes, it is."

"If I do, will the Free Company back me? We need to discuss it with Ben."

"I can't see any reason why they wouldn't."

Cara dropped the empty ration packs in the recycler and strapped into her chair for takeoff. Though there were systems and comms stations on the *Bellatkin*, she was designed so one person could fly and navigate. The retrofitted jump drive made things slightly more complicated, but they had to be a considerable distance from the planet before they activated it, hence the journey time. The trip through the Folds would take minutes, though it always felt longer. Most of the journey time was acceleration away from Dounreay and deceleration from the jump point inward to Crossways.

Hey, Ben. She reached out across several billion klicks of space and found him drowsy.

Cara. The warmth he put into that one word made her shiver in parts of her anatomy she'd been ignoring as best she could. *We're coming home.*

I've missed you.

She shivered. *Jake says about fourteen hours.*

I'll take the afternoon off. Boss' privilege.

She laughed, anticipating the homecoming. *How's it going?*

Remarkably well. Garrick is having the power grid strengthened. It's a miracle how fast contractors can work when they're paid in pure platinum. Wenna says hello, and to get your arse into the comms chair.

I will, very soon, though maybe not this afternoon.

Quite right, too.

How is Garrick?

*Mother Ramona says he's fine. He says he's fine, but I'm not sure. He went through a lot. I'd be surprised if he was *over it completely. Hell, I'm still having bad dreams about foldspace and I've been trained to deal with it.*

Are he and Mother Ramona still planning—

To tie the knot. Yes. They think it will show the good folks of Crossways that the worst is over. We're all invited, of course.

That's a good thing, don't you think?

That we're invited?

That they're committing to each other. I mean, we all thought that it was a union of convenience, but it's obvious they're dotty about each other.

Dotty?

You know what I mean.

She felt him smile. *Of course I do. I'm dotty about you. We could—*

Let's think about it later.

Sure.

Did she want to make their relationship official? Would it make a difference?

He accepted her put-off without missing a beat. Cara had never been all that good at reading Ben Benjamin despite being an Empath. Maybe he was offering because he thought she expected it. Maybe he was relieved she'd said no. Or maybe he was all chewed up inside because he thought she didn't want to commit.

I'm dotty about you just the way you·are, she said.

Dotty?

Totally.

She thought she felt him smiling.

See you soon. Travel safe.

You can sack Jake Lowenbrun if he loses us in the Folds.

Don't even think about it. She felt his smile evaporate. Disappearing into the Folds and not coming out the other side was the way his parents had died. She shouldn't have made a joke about it, not after discovering there was life of sorts in that other dimension—that the visions of strange creatures were not hallucinations.

We'll be fine. Jake's a good Navigator.

One of the best.

She thought about saying: "What could possibly go wrong?" but decided against it. Instead, she sent him the equivalent of a kiss and signed off, then sank into her chair, suddenly weary. Too much dust, too much osteena, and not even time to spend a single night in a real bed.

"Wake me when we get home," she said, tilting her seat into the recline position.

"You want me to warn you when we're about to make the jump to foldspace?" Jake asked.

"Not unless you need me to do anything."

"You can warn me," Jussaro said from the other crew chair. "Carlinni might be blasé about jumping through the hereafter, but I'd rather go into it with my eyes open."

Cara closed her eyes and let her mind wander. Talking to Ben had reminded her that she'd soon be getting back to station duties, taking turns manning long-range comms and generally filling a go-anywhere-do-anything brief.

She heard Jake telling Jussaro to prepare himself for foldspace in three . . . two . . . one. She was taking a breath to tell him she'd wanted to sleep through it when reality changed with a lurch.

Time doesn't behave itself in foldspace. It isn't like real objective time, it's more like an elastic band that stretches and stretches and stretches . . . then snaps with a twang and curls round itself. Yes, Cara knows there's no such thing as time if you ask a physicist, but humans are used to the subjective passing of seconds, minutes, and hours. In this strange dimension, however, it doesn't flow straight. It whirls and eddies. She can't even hear her own heartbeat or find her pulse. The handpad that registers her lifespan in subjective time doesn't always register elapsed time in foldspace even though sequences of events happen or are perceived to happen.

Cara couldn't see void dragons at first, but she can see them now. They aren't dragons, of course; they are creatures from another dimension. They must have rifled through a human mind, once, and stolen the most fearsome image they could find from some dark recess. There's no telling what their true form is—or if they even have one.

She looks around the cabin. Foldspace is never the same twice. Sometimes it's like something you might see while under the influence of a mind-altering drug. This time she sees it as a negative image, but instead of black and white, it's blood-red and silver.

The bulkhead shimmers and two sleek shapes, maybe each as long as a man is tall, swim through the bulkhead. Ben calls them *otter-kind* because that's the closest reference for their shape. Are they young void dragons? Ben used to think so, but now he's not so sure. One nudges Jake's shoulder, and he brushes it away, batting it gently on the nose as if it's a too-eager puppy. Jussaro isn't reacting. She doesn't think he can see them. One otter-kind does a barrel-roll across the cabin, noses Jake's ear, and flips over backward before heading out through the far bulkhead. The other opens its jaws wide, unhinging them, curls round Jussaro, and lunges for his head, biting it clean off. Jussaro doesn't notice and his head is still on his shoulders as the otter-kind follows its partner. There's a sense of amusement in the air.

Yeah, bastards, I suppose you think that's funny. Jake doesn't need to say it out loud.

A feeling of agreement floats back to him.

Great! Void creatures with a sense of humor. At least it's only the otter-kind and not the void dragon. After several meetings with it or possibly them (it's hard to tell), she's no more comfortable than she was the first time. But at least the void dragons appear to be benign—curious, but not actively malevolent.

The Nimbus is something else altogether. She's seen it kill.

Twang!

The elastic snapped and they were out of foldspace.

"Everyone all right?" Jake asked.

The words grated on her ear after the weird sensations in the Folds.

"Smooth ride," Jussaro said, oblivious to the visitation.

"You saw them, Jake, right?" Cara asked.

"The snakes? Yeah I saw them."

"Ben calls them otter-kind."

"Yeah, whatever. I saw one of them chow down on Jussaro's head."

"Huh?" Jussaro rubbed his temples.

"It was joking—at least I think it was joking. Maybe it was a warning."

Chapter Ten

OSSIO

NORTON GARRICK AND MOTHER RAMONA stood on the threshold of the main door of the Mansion House and peered in.

"It doesn't look too bad," Mona said. "The cleanup crew has done a good job."

Garrick shrugged, almost nervous to see what the last year had wrought. He could have found places for the refugees in the makeshift dormitories and reclaimed his home at any time, but it had been a point of pride, and a message to the rest of Crossways, to sacrifice comfort for the sake of those left destitute after the battle.

Situated at Crossways' hub, the residence had been protected, which was why the refugees had gathered here, and it had been only logical to take in all he could house, close to fifty of them, with the big reception room turned into a dormitory and four to each bedroom. Almost a year of living between the converted ready-room next to his office, and Ramona's small but secluded den in Yellow Five, had served to lead by example. Returning home marked a significant step forward on the road to normality.

Mona ran her fingertips over the table in the hallway and examined them.

Stepping from room to room, Garrick reassured himself

that there was remarkably little damage. How strange to see something so normal again when this last year had been anything but. Perhaps living in the Mansion House once more would help him to reclaim the time before the Nimbus had taken Kitty Keely and then almost swallowed him whole. The battle and all the dead of Crossways hadn't given him the nightmares that those few moments of proximity to the Nimbus had.

"There's a little wear and tear on the fixtures and fittings," Mona said, "but it's all cosmetic damage. There's nothing that can't be mended, replaced, or refurbished."

He should have felt relieved, but he found he was numb.

"Oh, look." Mona tapped him on his arm and drew him into the present.

Someone had left a huge bunch of flowers on the dresser in the bedroom. Garrick was startled. Fresh flowers were the last thing he'd expected to see. Alongside them was a pair of carnival masks, one silver and one gold, studded with sequins and bling.

"Artificial," Mona said.

"The masks?"

"The flowers. Good quality ones, though. You can't tell until you touch them. Even then . . ."

"Thoughtful."

"The people appreciate you."

"Most of them don't know I exist, or what I do."

"Does that worry you?"

"No. I shall remain a benevolent dictator until such time as I slip quietly into obscurity."

Mona snorted. "Obscurity? Hardly. It's not in your nature. What are the masks for?"

"A reminder. When Crossways fought for its independence the first time, the citizens wore masks so they stayed anonymous on the surveillance recordings as they pushed the megacorps personnel back to the docks. After they won, the Independence Day celebrations were characterized by masks. It fell out of fashion, but maybe we should revive it. Have our own Independence Day again."

"Let's do it. Our wedding and a general celebration—with masks. The people deserve it." She opened a cupboard. "We deserve it. The flowers were a neat touch, maybe some thanks for cleaning us out of my not so secret stash of

imported single malt. I'm going in search of a new bottle.
Let's see if some of the locks held. I believe Gibney may
have squirreled the booze away. I hope so, anyway. It could
be a while before we get any luxury supplies."

She dropped her bag on the floor and sauntered down in
the direction of the kitchens, the domain of the ever-reliable
Gibney and Mrs. Gibney, who had taken the refugees into
their care.

Garrick watched her leave and then bent to his own bag.
Swiftly, he pulled out a small packet and stepped into the
bathroom. The packet contained six bulbs, barely half as
long as his little finger. He snapped off the end of one to
reveal a short stub of hollow needle. Pulling up his shirt, he
gently pressed the needle to the skin of his flat belly. A
small resistance, a sharp but not desperately painful prick,
and the needle slid into flesh. He squeezed the bulb steadily
and felt a sting followed by a warm glow spreading outward, buffering the anxieties of the day as it would surely
drive away the terrors of the night.

He wasn't sure how long the effects would last. The detanine had given him six hours of dreamless sleep when
he'd first used it; now he was lucky to get five. Still, five was
better than waking up screaming eight or nine times a night.
Mona might not approve of the drug, but she wouldn't be-
grudge it if she knew what the nightmares were like.

He heard her footsteps in the bedroom and hastily
dropped the empty bulb down the pan and vaporized it.

"Give Gibney a raise," she called. "He's preserved all my
single malt. Not a bottle cracked. Want some?"

"No tha—" How would it mix with the detanine? Only
one way to find out. "Yes, all right. Just a drop."

She poured him a very generous drop as well as one for
herself. "Here's to the cleanup crews, the engineers, the psi-
techs, and the guards, plus all the volunteers who've fixed
what could be fixed and made do with what couldn't. And
to the shuttle pilots who've delivered two hundred thousand refugees safely to the planet, whether they wanted to
go or not."

"There'll be a few folks down there cursing my name."

"I didn't hear them grumbling when they took first pick
of the crops ready for harvesting."

He took a sip of the whisky and felt its warmth spreading

down his throat while the detanine tingled through his nerve endings.

"Ah, Mona, love. I honestly thought we were done for, but I'm beginning to think we might survive this. The station's not going to fall apart and the ships have been coming in steadily with relief supplies. We've more friends out there among the colonies than we knew."

"They're all thankful we took the hit and not them, but they're beginning to see the benefits of an alliance."

"Indeed, they are."

✦ ✦ ✦

Max Constant slipped inside the crowded room and nodded briefly to Ronan Wolfe and Archie Tatum. They'd got a better view than he had, but he wasn't going to miss this training session for anyone. He'd argued against being put in the rotation—argued and lost—so he wasn't going to miss the opportunity of seeing Ben Benjamin pulverized by Morton Tengue. Oh, no. Benjamin was good; no one would argue with that. Everyone in the Free Company had, at one time or another, experienced Ben Benjamin's training, either at first hand, or watching him in matches against other members of the company. He was good. Maybe it was his inbuilt talent as a psi-tech Navigator. It wasn't simple geography, but spatial awareness. Ben Benjamin always knew which way was up which, considering the time he spent in space where there was neither up nor down, was impressive.

But it wasn't simply Ben's skill in the training ring. Max had seen him in action. When the chips were down, there was no one Max would rather have by his side—or preferably between him and danger—than Ben, but today wasn't a chips-down kind of day. Today was the chance to see Benjamin pasted to the floor by the unstoppable Morton Tengue.

Oh, yeah, this was going to be good.

Plenty of other people had the same idea. The training ring—not a ring at all, but an oblong mat in the center of the gym—was surrounded by a sea of spectators. Max spotted Ada Levenson, who'd come with exactly the same idea as himself, no doubt. Wenna was on the sidelines. Max didn't know how old Wenna was, but he suspected she'd never see the low side of fifty again. She'd done well in her own session yesterday by all accounts.

Neither man wore a buddysuit. Tengue, all hard muscle, was dressed in loose trousers and singlet. Ben was similarly dressed and, though not as muscular as Tengue, was lean and fit, his mid-brown skin looking darker than usual against the white of his singlet, his hair pulled severely into a single stubby plait.

It wasn't the two of them, of course; this was a class of thirty or so drawn at random: some Free Company, a few of Tengue's mercs, and half a dozen of Syke's militia.

Tengue ran the group through a series of stretches and warm-up exercises, correcting some members of the group on posture and form, giving others an acknowledgment of good work with a nod or a soft-spoken word. Everyone appeared to be trying their best. Max hoped he could do as well in his own session tomorrow. He wasn't exactly unfit, but he'd ended up in the Free Company almost by chance, previously enjoying a soft lifestyle behind a desk until he fell in love with Gen Marling.

He glanced around to see if Gen had turned up to watch. She'd expressed an interest, but these days she hardly did anything that didn't include baby Liv. He would have never guessed she was going to be so infatuated with the baby that she'd instantly rejected any idea of leaving Liv in a nursery and returning to work. Liv was at that restless, curious stage and very vocal with it. Gen wouldn't be likely to bring her to such a crowded event. Perhaps that was no bad thing.

Uh-oh, he'd missed something while woolgathering about his wife and child. Tengue was having quiet words with one of Syke's crew. Max couldn't hear what was going on, but the man had evidently made some kind of complaint about the training routine. Bad move. Catching the instructor's attention could lead to all kinds of extra grief as Max had discovered on first joining the Free Company.

The troublemaker was unremarkable except for his mouth: average height, average weight, pale skin-tone, mid-brown hair, the kind of regular face that was easy to forget. He was dressed in a beige softsuit with loose trousers and a sleeved top tied with a belt.

They'd barely returned to their exercises when the man must have made a joke at Tengue's expense. Max winced. If he were going to pick someone to be the butt of a joke, it wouldn't be Morton Tengue. The man was great at his job, but possibly needed a sense-of-humor transplant.

Tengue didn't stop the class, but Max caught a glance between Tengue and Benjamin. Ha, the poor sod's fate was sealed. Tengue wouldn't take him down personally, but Max guessed the guy would find himself up against Benjamin. Ah, well, that meant the anticipated match of Ben against Tengue wouldn't happen today, but this one might still prove interesting.

Just as Max figured, when the time came to pair off combatants, Ben drew the mouthy white guy. Max prepared to be entertained.

Now that it came to the crunch, the guy didn't have much to say. The screen high on the gym wall showed two names, Benjamin and Swanson, with zero points each. Max would never call himself an aficionado of combat matches, but he had a basic appreciation of the moves and an expectation of how the match would go. The two combatants would each show respect for the other; this was, after all, a friendly match. Then there would be some sparring followed by what looked to an outsider like nothing more than a scuffle. Max didn't expect it to get beyond the scuffle stage. Benjamin would doubtless put his opponent on the mat pretty quickly. He didn't like to play with his food.

Ben nodded to his opponent, but instead of returning the nod, Swanson launched himself at Ben. He'd obviously heard Ben's reputation and wasn't giving him any leeway. Ben gave as good as he got. Swanson rocked, gathered himself together, and went in low and hard. It didn't look like a training match; it looked like a street-fight, and an ugly one at that. Ben jerked his head away, and a spray of blood painted itself across his singlet. Swanson stepped back. Ben tried to lunge forward, but his move was, for Ben, uncoordinated. His legs had turned to rubber and he went down. There was a cheer from the coppers on the side of the mat and they pounded Swanson's shoulder as he returned to their ranks. To their ranks and through them.

Something was wrong. Ben had hit the floor and not moved. Ronan was running forward, med-kit in his hand, and Swanson was not turning around to see what had happened to his opponent. He was walking through his colleagues and out behind them, heading for the door.

Oh, shit!

Max was close enough to grab Swanson's sleeve as he headed for the door. Something clattered to the floor. Swanson shrugged him off and was gone. Max looked down. On the floor was a bone knife, or rather, Max thought, an ossio one. It would have been undetectable on the security scanners. He bent and picked it up carefully with two fingertips and turned to where Ben was sprawled, surrounded by friends.

"Ronan," he called. "I think Swanson stabbed him with this."

Ronan turned to take the knife, and Max saw Ben was lying as still as death.

Tengue appeared at Max's elbow. "You're a tracker, right?"

"I'm a Finder."

"Can you find Swanson?"

"I touched him. Yeah, I'm pretty sure I can."

"With me."

Tengue took Max by the arm and thrust him out into the wide concourse that ran through Blue Seven. "Which way?"

Max heard running feet and turned as a squad of ten arrived with Gwala, Hilde Hildstrom, and Franny Fowler in the lead.

"This way." Max felt the tug that told him where Swanson was. He'd expected the man to head for the main exit, but instead he was going deeper into Blue Seven. The area enclosed by security walls was big, but not big enough to hide in forever. Max broke into a run, following the pull.

"Up there!" Tengue directed his squad and they overtook Max. He was about to caution them to wait, but then he realized they were heading for the antigrav tube to the upper docking cradle. That only made sense if . . .

If there was a ship waiting there for Swanson.

Max's brain caught up to what his gut had been trying to tell him since he saw Benjamin lying still on the mat. This was not a scared man trying to put some distance between himself and a crazy accident.

The security squad all beat Max to the antigrav tube and thrust themselves up into it, pulling themselves hand over hand, quick and slick. Except for Tengue, they all wore buddysuits, while Max was in civvies, a casual tunic over trousers. He could see they were all extending their lobstered helms and adjusting full faceplates as they reached the top of the tube. A buddysuit wasn't a full space suit, but it would give some protection for maybe five minutes in an emergency, such as grabbing a fleeing assassin as he tried to get to a waiting ship.

Max steadied himself at the top of the tube. All of Tengue's squad, minus Tengue, who wasn't equipped, had gone through the airlock. All Max could do was wait for it to cycle and see who returned. He counted the minutes. At two and a half, Franny Fowler and three guards staggered through.

"What's happening out there?" Tengue asked.

"Small flyer." She wheezed and bent over, hands on knees.

Tengue rubbed her back. "You all right?"

"Will be. Lungs."

Max remembered that Fowler had undergone reconstructive surgery the previous year for chest burns. "You need to sit?" he asked.

"Gimme a minute. How long has it been?"

"Since they went through the airlock? Four minutes."

"Shit and double shit. Come on, guys." She straightened and pressed her face up against the thick window into the airlock.

At four and a half minutes the airlock light turned red, then began to flash red, then red and green and finally turned green. Hilde, Gwala, and three others crowded together with Swanson dangling between them.

"You got him. Well done," Max said.

"We got him," Gwala said. "But it would only have been well done if we'd got him alive."

Chapter Eleven

HOMECOMING

ON SOME LEVEL BEN UNDERSTOOD HE WAS dying. It didn't worry him. Death was what it was. Always harder for those left behind. That wouldn't be him this time.

Of course, there were things in life he still had to do. He'd never found time to take Cara away somewhere to have fun. Since the day they met, they'd been on the run, or fighting off attacks, or keeping their heads down, or sorting out the aftermath of a battle. Always doing things for the good of others, never for themselves. The Free Company and Crossways could have managed without him for a little while. They were going to have to manage without him now.

Was that a regret? Maybe. He had few regrets.

There were things he could have, should have done that would have made a difference. Killing Crowder would have been one of them. He'd had the opportunity once and rejected it. The second time he'd not hesitated, but Crowder had survived. He should have made sure. One more dart would have done the trick.

And though Crowder was no psi-tech, himself, he had the Trust's resources. He must be the one behind the Telepath attacks. No one else would have access to a triple-threat specialist like that.

What a stupid way to die. A gym exercise.

His family would mourn, of course: his brother Rion, farming on Jamundi with his elder son, Kai; Nan, who had been both mother and father to Ben and Rion after their parents were lost in a ship transiting the Folds; Ricky, Rion's younger son, who was currently with Nan. The boy would never settle down to be a farmer, but he was bright and talented. He could do anything with his life.

Leaving Cara would be hard, though he suspected he wouldn't know much about it once he'd passed over that final threshold. She was resourceful. She'd find some meaning to her life. She'd probably already found it: Sanctuary. Wenna would run the Free Company and Cara and Jussaro would save the psi-techs—their own first and then as many others as could be saved. He felt an upsurge of pride. That was his Cara, an indomitable spirit. With or without him, she had a goal and would achieve it.

From a distance, he heard Ronan's voice. "We're going to put you under now, Ben. Hold on. We've got you."

Not for much longer.

It was the image of Cara that he took with him into the blackness.

✦ ✦ ✦

The *Bellatkin* emerged from foldspace one hundred klicks out from the station. Cara enlarged the view on her screen. Despite all the repairs that had been carried out since the battle, it still looked fragile to her. Buried beneath the surface of her memory was the pounding of ordnance, the tearing of metal, and the shatter of ceramic layered upon the shrieks of the people and the pressure of fear that threatened to overwhelm her mind. No matter how good her shields, she was an Empath. That amount of fear and panic would leak through even the best defenses.

Ben? She reached out mentally but couldn't find Ben.

Wenna? Looking for Ben. He's not off-station, is he?

Cara, good timing. He's in sick bay. Ronan's with him. Looks like an assassination attempt nearly succeeded.

Nearly?

Better get here fast, girl.

With Cara's urging, Jake clipped a little time off his

estimated two hours by circumventing the docking tailback.
He hooked onto one of the external docking cradles one
level up from Blue Seven. A small flyer on a long tether
caused a slight delay, but Jake maneuvered around it and
clamped the *Bellatkin* onto the docking ring.

Cara hit the tube ahead of Jake and Jussaro and raced
through Blue Seven to the med-center. She slammed
through the outer door. "Where's Ben?"

Max caught her with an arm across her shoulders before
she could burst into the treatment room. "In there. Ronan's
given him an antidote."

"What? Start from the beginning."

Max told her what he knew, what he'd seen from the
sidelines and then how Tengue had caught Swanson, unfortunately dead.

"It turns out the ossio knife had a toxin on it," Max said.
"Ronan said they wouldn't have found the antidote without
having the knife."

"But they found it in time, right?"

"Ronan thinks so."

"Thinks so!" She stood up and peeped through the clear
pane in the door. She couldn't see much. Ronan had his
back toward her, and she could see a couple of med-techs
and a tall, thin woman whom she didn't recognize. She
tapped on the window. One of the nurses said something
and Ronan turned, saw her, and beckoned her in.

Wenna was sitting in a corner. She stood up as Cara entered, but Cara only had eyes for Ben.

"He's unconscious, but he's stable, so far," Ronan said,
inserting himself between her and Ben. "Thanks to Dr.
Grant, Dockside Medical's best toxicologist."

"Actually, their only one," the thin woman said. "Glad I
could help."

"So far?" Cara touched Ben's arm. It felt reassuringly
normal.

"The next couple of hours may be crucial. You can stay
with him if you like. We need to wait for him to wake up."

"But he will recover. Yes?"

"I hope so. If it hadn't been for Max getting hold of the
knife, we'd have been stuck, but I think we gave him the
antidote in time."

"When I said you and Ben should get a room, Carlinni, I didn't mean one like this." Jussaro stuck his head around the door. "Is he okay?"

"Ronan hopes so."

"I'm going to get some real sleep, but you know where I am if you need me."

"I'm going, too," Wenna said.

"Wenna." Cara turned. "You were here all the time."

"I didn't do much except get in the way and worry." She stepped forward and hugged Cara briefly. "You can get in the way and worry for a while."

"Is he . . . ?" Max appeared in the doorway.

"Away with all of you," Ronan said. "You're making the place untidy. Cara and medical staff only. Speaking of untidy . . ." Ronan eyed Cara's clothes. "Don't think much of the new uniform. Desert dress, is it?"

"Dustbowl chic." Cara patted her skirt layers. "Complete with added dust and Eau de Crestedina. I'm starting a new trend."

"Can someone bring Cara some clean clothes, please," he called after Wenna's retreating back.

Wenna brought clean clothes.

Ada Levenson delivered coffee personally, and a bowl of risotto.

"Whatever you hear, I didn't really laugh when he hit the deck," Ada said. "Though if it sounded like I did, I'm sorry. Tell him I'm sorry for the coffee, too. From now on he gets it exactly as he likes it."

"I'll tell him. I'm sure he didn't take offense."

"Well, as long as he knows. . . ."

"He knows."

Ronan came to check his vitals.

Cara asked, "How's he doing?"

"No change."

"That's good, right?"

"It's not bad."

Every quarter hour, Ronan checked and Cara asked. The answer was always the same, "No change."

At last, sometime late in the evening, Ronan's answer came with a smile. "He's doing a little better."

"He's going to be all right?" Cara asked.

"We'll know for certain when he wakes up."

"I've been away for too long. I should never have left."

"You had something to do that needed doing." Ronan was in on what she and Jussaro had been searching for. "Did you find Hartwell? Did you get what we needed?"

"Yes, and yes. Hartwell's not coming back, but Jussaro has the unlock codes. All that time away. I missed Ben so much."

"You both had responsibilities. It happens. All his readings are edging toward normal. He's strong. Don't worry."

But, of course, she did.

She sat by Ben as evening turned to night. The bedside chair was a recliner, and Ronan must have dropped a blanket over her when he found her dozing because she awoke feeling unexpectedly cozy.

Ten minutes later, Ronan himself arrived for a final check. "I'm going to get some sleep, but I'm only in the next room if I'm needed. Tilda Duncan will be doing Ben's vitals throughout the night, so call me if you need anything."

"I will. Thanks, Ronan."

✦ ✦ ✦

Crowder rode the glass elevator upward. This was his fourth meeting with outgoing president Duma, but they were still no closer to signing an agreement over platinum, and there was always the question of tax. Crowder was beginning to think he might not be able to resolve the one without addressing the other. He'd spoken to Tori LeBon and had set the tax division working on the problem of how to give Duma the concessions he required without it costing them more.

If LeBon had taken more of an active interest in renegotiating this deal three years ago, before Olyanda became an issue, he wouldn't have to try and put things right now. LeBon was too cautious to lead the Trust board. It needed someone with more vision—himself.

The elevator slid to rest at the eighteenth floor.

"Mr. Duma, I'm sorry. Have I kept you waiting?" He knew he had. He'd done it deliberately.

"Not at all. I only arrived a few minutes ago."

They shook hands, Crowder's fleshy pale one against Duma's wrinkled brown.

Crowder offered refreshment. Duma accepted. They exchanged the usual pleasantries.

"And how are your grandchildren, Mr. Crowder?"

"They are well, and yours?" With a multitude of them, Malusi Duma's answer might be protracted, but asking after family was the polite thing to do.

"They are all well except for my next to oldest. He's in some kind of scrape on the far side of the Galaxy. I'm sure he'll manage to get himself out of it."

"Ah, one of your troublemakers and rabble-rousers, is he?"

"I rather think he is. They say the apple doesn't fall far from the tree." Malusi Duma grinned, which suddenly made him look twenty years younger.

"Now, about the platinum," Crowder said.

"You still want it?"

"Why wouldn't we?"

"There are cheaper sources now. Olyanda for instance. I hear they've come in at twenty percent below current market prices."

Crowder knew when he was being played. What did the bastard know about Olyanda? He covered his thoughts with a polite smile. "We wouldn't dream of abandoning a trusted supplier in favor of one which didn't have a track record."

"How refreshing to hear that attitude. Now, if we may move on to more pressing issues of taxation . . ."

The Trust was officially registered as a corporation on Burnett, a small but economically sound planet with extremely low rates of taxation. They had, in effect, created their own tax haven, nominally independent, but owing everything to the Trust. It made their South African tax liability ridiculously low. Duma had been after them for years. Now that he was about to leave office, he'd redoubled his efforts. Their meetings were always very cordial, but Duma was relentless. Crowder had offered to bring Tori LeBon into the dialog, but while she left it up to Crowder to negotiate, she had the element of plausible deniability.

Also, if negotiations all went to shit, Crowder was under no illusions that he would get the blame. She would throw him under the bus without a second thought. The higher he climbed, the more unsteady the corporate ladder became. The last few rungs were the worst. If he could keep his grip and his head and make it to the top, he'd be able to rest. That top job was meant for him.

He smiled at Duma as the talks began, but the smile didn't reach his eyes.

◆ ◆ ◆

The image of Cara brought Ben back.

She was by his side, in a recliner chair, covered by a gray blanket and snoring gently. Maybe snoring was too coarse a word for the heavy breathing that comes with exhausted sleep.

"Am I dreaming?" He coaxed words out of a dry throat.

No. If he was dreaming, he wouldn't be seeing Cara asleep. She'd be lying next to him, naked, eyes bright and eager. He felt himself stirring at the thought. Maybe he wasn't dead, after all, or maybe this was some strange sort of afterlife, certainly one he'd never expected. He weighed the two possibilities and decided on balance that he was probably still alive.

"If you're dreaming, so am I." Cara tilted the chair upright, dropped the blanket on the floor, and swung toward the bed so her face was on a level with his. "I've called Ronan. Don't move. You're attached to so many tubes and wires you're like the center of a giant cat's cradle."

She leaned forward and kissed him lightly on the lips. "Can you feel that?"

"Yes."

"Good."

"Do it again."

She did. This time he responded.

"Get a room, you two," Ronan said from somewhere out of Ben's line of vision.

"I thought we had," Ben said. "Did you knock before entering?"

"I didn't need to. This is my domain."

"I suppose it is."

"How are you feeling?"

"I don't know. Numb. Groggy. What happened?"

"You don't remember?"

Ben closed his eyes and drew his eyebrows together in a frown. "Something happened at the gym. There was a training session. . . ."

"You almost got taken out by an assassin with an ossio knife doused in neurotoxin. Luckily for you, Max grabbed the knife, and we figured out what the toxin was and gave you the antidote before your brain checked out and shut down your vital organs."

"Max? I owe my life to Max?" Ben groaned. "He's not going to let me forget it, is he?"

"I doubt it." Ronan grinned. "He says he's already ordered the I-saved-Ben-Benjamin T-shirt."

"It could be worse," Cara said. "At least it wasn't Ada Levenson."

"When can I get out of here?" Ben said.

"Don't be in such a hurry. There are tests. You knew there'd be tests, didn't you? We don't even know if you can walk yet, though you can obviously talk. A couple of days if everything is all right."

"Two days?"

"If you cooperate."

Ben sighed. "I always cooperate."

"Yeah, right!" Cara pushed back her chair. "Well, if you're going to be busy cooperating, I'm going to go and have a shower. I still have grit from Dounreay lodged in places where grit shouldn't be. I'll see you later."

Chapter Twelve

TOGETHER

CARA LEFT THE INFIRMARY, TRYING TO HIDE the trembling in her knees and the tears prickling her eyes. Something must have shown on her face, though, because none of the people she passed on her way to their apartment tried to stop her to ask questions. She closed the door and leaned against it, smothering a great gulping sob. He was alive, and if he was alive, he was going to be all right.

She stripped off her clothes and went to stand in the shower for much longer than the regulation four minutes, letting her tears flow until she was all cried out.

It wasn't quite two days later when Ronan pronounced Ben fit and told him to get out of the infirmary while Ronan still had a shred of sanity left. "I'm not saying he's a bad patient," Ronan said to Cara as they waited for Ben to dress, "but if ever there was a case for running before you can walk, Ben personifies it. But please try to make him take it easy for a few days. Two days of bed rest, preferably."

"Is that doctor's orders for two days of wild sex?" Ben came out of his room dressed in the singlet and soft trousers he'd been wearing when he was brought in.

"I was thinking of two days of you staring at the ceiling. At most, I recommend a little gentle snuggling, though if you can manage a two-day marathon in your condition, good luck to you." Ronan mock-fanned his face with his fingertips. "But please remember to shield."

Cara gave him a wide-eyed look. "We always shield when—"

"You think so? Huh?"

She turned to give him a mouthful of good-natured abuse, but Ben leaned across and kissed her. *He's teasing.*

I know—only he's pretty perceptive, and wouldn't it be awful if we shared—

We don't. We won't. I'm not sharing any part of you.

They walked the fifty meters to their apartment hand in hand, returning acknowledgments and greetings before letting the door close behind them. The apartment's clean lines and functional furniture spoke of a couple who'd never quite turned the place into a home. It was somewhere to fall asleep, or pass a few free hours reading, or watching a mindless drama on one of Crossways' entertainment channels, all simply a prelude to falling into bed.

It backed on to a shared central quadrangle that had been planted over a year ago and was now a lush garden.

Cara opened the double doors.

"You got a bench." Ben halted on the threshold and looked around.

"I persuaded the workshop guys. They didn't even make me put in a requisition in triplicate."

"Your powers of persuasion—"

She shook her head. "It was all for you. The Free Company loves you."

He harrumphed, but all the same he sat down.

Cara made tea, glad to be doing something normal and domestic.

She set a mug down on the bench beside him, then sat down herself.

"I've missed you," he said at length.

"I've missed you, too."

"When I was . . . dying . . . I suddenly realized we'd never taken time to do anything fun."

"Fun?"

"You know, a tourist trip, maybe to somewhere like the ice fields of Venezuela—the planet not the country. They say the frozen Klemiss Falls are spectacular. Two thousand meters of ice as bright as diamonds. Or maybe you prefer an urban vacation. The Golden City of Akhbar on Timon Two has everything city life can offer. I've never even asked what you like to do for fun."

"The Klemiss Falls sound good, or Akhbar, but right now . . ."

She glanced inside to the bedroom door.

He smiled. "I thought you'd never ask."

"Ronan recommended gentle snuggling." She took the mug of tea from him and set it down, then leaned into him. She could smell the faint antiseptic aroma of the infirmary on his skin. His lips tasted of tea; his tongue was hot.

"I think Ronan's forgotten how long we've been apart." He sighed. "How about we compromise? I'll let you do all the work. Well—maybe not quite all the work, but—"

"I get the idea. Come on, mister. If I'm in charge, better not keep me waiting."

"I'd forgotten how bossy you were."

"Yeah, right." She took one of his hands and pulled him to his feet.

He caught her by the waist. "I love you, Cara Carlinni, even if you boss me about."

All of a sudden, she was hot and needed to get out of her buddysuit fast.

"I'm glad I have my uses." She led the way to their bedroom where the utilitarian gray was broken by a nonstandard burnt-orange coverlet. She pointed and then placed her fists on her hips and did her best drill sergeant's voice. "Okay, mister, strip and onto the bed. Let's start as we mean to go on."

"I thought you were going to do all the work."

"You want me to . . . All right. Arms up." He did as he was told, and she grasped his singlet and pulled it off in one quick movement, helped by him bending forward. He grinned at her. His brush with death didn't show in his body, lean and hard. She wanted to run her hands over his brown skin, but stepped back, pressing her lips together.

He looked down at his trousers, then at her, then down at his trousers again.

"Oh, all right. Big kid, or what?"

"Ronan said—"

"Ronan said you were a pain in the backside, and he wanted you out of his infirmary."

Ben's mouth twitched up at the corners.

She mock-scowled at him, debating the best way to tackle the trousers. From the front and her face would be on a level with . . . and there was already a bulge forming there. From the back and . . . well . . . he had a delightful arse, of course. She needed radical action. Yes, he was close enough to the bed.

She stepped up and ran her hands around the inside of his waistband. Chuckling at his gasp, she slid her hands lower, twanged the soft band, pulled it quickly over the bulge, and tangled his trousers around his knees.

"Ha! Got you right where I want you." She toppled him onto the bed and pulled the trousers off, throwing them across the room.

"Be gentle with me. I'm a fragile flower." He clasped both hands behind his head, trying not to grin and failing.

"More like a tree."

How quickly could she tear off her own buddysuit? Or maybe she should slow down. She unclasped the top half of the suit from the bottom and began to unfasten it. She heard him draw a sharp breath and took her time. "Should I have music for this?"

"I'd sing, but I can't hold a tune in a bucket."

The waist fastenings on the trousers made a soft ripping sound as she pulled apart the hook and loop fastening.

"Music to my ears. Come over here." He wriggled to the far side of the bed and made room.

"I thought I was in charge this time."

"Oh, yes. You can be in charge of me any time."

She stretched beside him. "Gods, you're hot."

"Thank you, ma'am."

"Not that kind of hot." She play-punched him lightly on the arm. "Temperature hot. Are you sure you're all right?"

"I will be soon."

"Well, maybe that kind of hot, too." She straddled him, hovering on knees and hands, and leaned forward to kiss him, forehead, eyes, nose, and finally mouth.

Ben ran his hands down her back, his fingers eliciting shivers along her spine and down to the cheeks of her arse.

"I've missed you so much," he whispered, his breath landing on her chin in hot puffs. "Missed this." His touch became more intimate. She sagged against his chest.

I love you, Ben Benjamin. She opened up her thoughts to his thoughts and sank onto him.

It was like coming home.

✦ ✦ ✦

In the afterglow of lovemaking, lying with Cara in his arms, Ben's world turned around right again.

Now she was with him, and there was so much to do.

"You're doing it again." Cara snuggled closer into his side.

"What?"

"Thinking, planning."

"You're an Empath. You know I am."

She sighed. "Sometimes it would be nice not to be an Empath or a Telepath. Do you ever wish you'd never become a Navigator? If you'd tested negative for talent, or maybe refused an implant?"

He took two long breaths. "No. I am what I am. I'm pretty sure Nan knew I was going to leave Chenon, just as she knew Rion was going to stay on the farm."

"Your Nan is very perceptive."

"Yes, she is. We could never slip anything past her when we were growing up."

"It must have been hard, losing her son and daughter-in-law and having to give up a job she loved to take on two grief-stricken boys."

"I used to daydream I'd gate into the Folds and find Mom and Dad's liner, and they'd still be alive."

"Do you ever wonder . . . ?"

"How my parents died?"

"Maybe I wasn't going to put it quite so bluntly."

"I used to think ships that disappeared in the Folds kept on going until their supplies ran out or their systems failed. Now I wonder how many of them were swallowed by the Nimbus." His voice broke on the last word. "I'm sorry. Didn't mean to get all emotional."

"Does flying the Folds still trouble you?"

"All the time, but it's not going to stop me."

"Can't live with it; can't live without it?"

"Something like that."

He hugged her to him and kissed the top of her head. She took the hint and stopped asking questions.

◆ ◆ ◆

Cara woke in a cold sweat, heart pounding, convinced a klaxon was sounding somewhere.

It wasn't.

She listened to the silence.

Not silence. Crossways was never silent. The great space station thrummed with energy at a pitch somewhere below the level of human hearing. Her ears might not recognize it, but her bones did.

She turned over to see if Ben was awake, and blinked twice, surprised to find him sitting on the edge of the bed, a black shape in the darkness.

"Light."

The whispered word brought a gentle glow to their room, softening the utilitarian edges.

Ben hadn't moved. He sat, bent forward, hands on knees, head hanging, breathing silently only by the greatest of effort.

Cara watched his ribs moving under the well-muscled back, not touching him in case he was still locked in a dream.

Before she left with Jussaro, Ben had been getting on top of the nightmares, and though she'd suffered from flashbacks herself, they'd eased off while she'd been away. Lying next to Ben, she remembered how bad it had been. And being an Empath meant that Cara had shared a lot of other people's trauma.

Ben sighed and shuddered, sitting up straight and scrunching up his shoulders, then relaxing them.

"Bad dreams?" she asked.

"The usual."

"Ah, that one again. You ought to be old friends with it by now."

"It's as if I know I'm dreaming, but I can't wake up. The Nimbus is clawing toward us—you're there, too, you know—and Garrick and Kitty Keely. Kitty steps into it. We grab Garrick and push off for the *Solar Wind*. That's how it happened, or how I remember it, anyway."

"Yes. Me, too."

"But this time it follows us, tendrils reaching out, black, but still outlined against the blackness of foldspace. And I know whichever one of us it reaches first will be lost forever, subsumed into whatever it is."

"You attribute human emotions? See it as a vengeful killer?"

"No." He ran a hand through his hair. "It doesn't have human emotions. It's so alien that we have no common ground."

"Yet in foldspace we're the aliens."

"Yes, we are. We travel through foldspace, but we don't understand it."

Cara knelt behind Ben on the bed and began to massage his shoulders. He stretched his neck first to one side and then the other. "Mmm, that's good."

"I had a dream as well," she said.

"Did you?"

"But I can't remember what it was." She worked on the knots in his neck. "All I remember is I thought there was a klaxon sounding. I woke up in a panic, surprised to find everything quiet."

"Klaxon. There might have been a klaxon in my dream, too. I'm sorry if I projected anything."

"I don't think I picked it up from you."

He might not be a strong long-distance Telepath, but Ben had the tightest natural shield of anyone she knew. She could rarely sense what he was thinking. Maybe that was one of his attractions. One among many. She pressed herself against him, skin to skin and put her arms round his shoulders.

He leaned into her. "Is that an invitation?"

"Do you need one?"

He chuckled and rolled into the bed.

◆ ◆ ◆

Ben tried to stick to what Ronan had told him to do, but two days of bed rest was ridiculous when he was perfectly fit to sit behind his desk for an hour or two. Well, maybe three or four.

Wenna gave him the hard stare. Cara threw up her hands in mock disgust and said if he dropped dead at her feet, she wanted everyone to know she'd tried her best to make him rest.

Jussaro had announced he was open for business and had already used the unlock codes on Wenna, Ronan, and Marta Mansoro, who were full of relieved smiles. A trickle of people had wandered by the office to ask if it was true that Cara and Jussaro had found a way of reprogramming their implants.

Ben called in Jussaro, Cara, Wenna, and Ronan. "We're going to have to find a way to bottle up this story or everyone on Crossways will know. If it gets back to the megacorps, they'll start to reprogram all their new implants and we won't be able to do a thing to help future deserters."

"When Zandra was using this to unlock implants, it was only on one or two grateful individuals at a time," Jussaro said. "Then they were quickly sent on to a new life somewhere in the colonies. I don't believe she ever used it widely like we're attempting to do."

"Did anyone else have the codes, or was it only Zandra?" Ben asked.

"Only Zandra as far as I know."

"So if you hadn't found her, the secret would have died with her?"

"I'm afraid it would."

"Do you intend that to be the case in future?"

There was a long silence. At last, Jussaro said, "Are you asking me to give you the codes?"

Ben shook his head. "Not me. I'm asking you to consider what happens if something happens to you. You should make a plan."

"You're right, of course. It has to be someone with both Telepathy and Empathy." He looked at both Cara and Ronan. "And someone with a delicate touch."

Cara leaned back as if removing herself from the potential list. Ben thought he might know the reason for that.

"Also," Jussaro said, "I could use some help. It's an exacting procedure. I can probably only manage four per day. It makes sense to have a few people with the capability."

"That's up to you," Ben said. "I'm not pressuring you one way or the other. But each person whose implant you unlock has to keep the secret."

"Does it mean the Free Company is supporting Sanctuary Mark II?" Jussaro asked.

Did it? Ben had to think about that.

"Maybe. For now."

He saw Cara and Jussaro share a knowing smile. Oh, hell, what had he agreed to?

✦ ✦ ✦

After Jussaro left without asking her to share the secret of the unlock codes, Cara relaxed. She didn't want anything to do with them. The trauma of Donida McLellan was still there, beneath the surface. Was she over it? In a sense, yes, she could function again and bury the memories, but she'd not only gone through Neural Readjustment herself, but while Donida McLellan had been inside her head, she'd learned far more than she wanted to know about how to twist someone's mind.

It was wrong, and she hated the very idea, but at the same time it gave her a feeling of safety, knowing that if she met any mindbending monsters, she had the potential to fight back. In fact, if she let herself, she had the potential to be the biggest mindbending monster on the block. But because she could, it didn't mean she would.

The difference between her and McLellan was that McLellan had enjoyed the job.

So, free from the knowledge of the unlock codes, she slipped into the routine of Crossways as if she'd never been away. Thankfully the post-battle repairs and restoration had moved on in the time she'd been out searching for Hartwell. Though it might be some years before the station ceased to show its scars, it was now safe and secure for the survivors. Life went on.

It was good to see her friends again, and catch up with what she'd missed. She took herself off to Java Joe's and collected two extra-large coffees, with lids, and carried them up to the office, placing one on Wenna's desk.

"What have I missed?"

"Well . . ." Wenna leaned back in her chair. "We lost one of the local crimelords about a month ago."

"Lost?"

"Literally. Joe Keen disappeared. No corpse found, but

there are plenty of ways to get rid of a body on a space station."

"Any suspects?"

"Yes, but no proof. His right-hand man, Newmark, took over his smuggling racket. Guess who took over his money laundering?"

"Roxburgh."

"Right first time."

"I guess Garrick had something to say about that."

"Nothing public, but he wasn't pleased."

"Roxburgh's organization is too big for Garrick to take on without the kind of firefight you don't want to see on a space station."

Wenna shuddered. "Roxburgh's a bastard, but it's probably better to get the station back to normal before trying to tackle him."

"What else?" Cara asked.

"Serafin's lung transplant went well, but he had an infection, so Ronan isn't prepared to discharge him from care yet. Serafin says the medics on Jamundi can take care of him, but Suzi Ruka says he has to stay put until Ronan's absolutely sure he's fully recovered. He says Suzi's trying to keep him out of her hair while she gets the harvest in on Jamundi, but she says she's built a new house for the old man's twilight years so he can retire in peace."

Cara smiled at the thought. Serafin West was a Psi-Mech of extraordinary ability and even at his age—a well-kept secret, but she guessed he was top side of seventy—he was unlikely to retire. Suzi, maybe twenty years his junior, was on Jamundi helping the Ecolibrian settlers break ground on the virgin planet. Serafin had promised to join her permanently once he was fit.

"Anything else?" Cara asked, "How are Gen and little Olivia now they're home from Olyanda?"

"They're calling her Liv. She's very forward. Steady on her feet, and already talking in complete sentences."

"Is that normal?"

"What's normal? It's not normal to be born in foldspace with a void dragon looking on." Wenna shrugged. "Max is having sleepless nights. He doesn't say anything, but you can see it written in his face." She jerked her head toward his office. "He's late again this morning."

"I owe him. Ben owes him. Is there anything we could do to help?"

"Not unless you want to volunteer to babysit and give him some time alone with Gen. I suspect the lack of sleep is putting a strain on their relationship."

"I can do that. How hard can it be?"

Wenna laughed. "Try it and find out."

"Any juicy scandal?"

"Surprisingly little, or maybe not much shocks us these days."

"Garrick and Mother Ramona?"

"Personally, never better. You know they're planning a big celebration at New Year, right?"

"Their wedding. Yes."

"A joint celebration. Their wedding and Olyanda's first platinum dividend. It's going to be a masked shindig. Apparently, the station used to celebrate its original Independence Day with masks, so they're reviving the tradition."

"And how is Garrick really?"

"You know how he was before you left?"

"He looked like death warmed up half the time. Lack of sleep, stress. And I'd be surprised if he wasn't having nightmares about the Nimbus."

"That's a fair assessment, but he looks fine now."

"Huh?"

"I'd have said he was heading for a breakdown, but he appears to have turned himself around."

"Good for Garrick. I'm glad he's doing so well."

"Of course, I don't know if that means he's on something."

"Ah, I see."

Chapter Thirteen

VISIT

GARRICK RAN OVER THE CATERING AR-rangement for the evening to take his mind off the wedding the following afternoon, and then had a small glass of Mona's best single malt before retiring. The bedroom was too big for one. Mona had insisted on sleeping at her old place tonight. Why should he be so nervous? He'd been living with Mona for eighteen months. Why should the thought of marrying her have his stomach tying itself in knots? He knew he wanted to do it. She'd become the most important person in his life.

When he'd first seen her, he'd been a little shaken by her marbled skin, so white and fine, but broken up with what looked like scars. Then he'd seen her close up and realized the marbling was nothing like scars. It sparkled softly, like a vein of quartzite. He'd touched her hand, finding her skin silky and unblemished. He'd been totally fascinated.

She was an expert forger of identities, and he'd needed her to provide a couple of his couriers with credentials to get into the Greek Embassy in Johannesburg. She'd agreed to do it and insisted they seal their deal on her couch. That had been the start of it.

She was a miracle on two legs.

Now they were going to seal the deal for real with marriage vows. They'd invited half the station—or at least any-body who was anybody. They'd even invited Roxburgh, though mainly because it was better to know where he was.

Garrick felt shaky all over. He'd never get any sleep at this rate. He'd already taken one detanine shot, but it hadn't done much to settle him. How long ago was that? He checked the time on his handpad. Two hours. He shouldn't take them this close together, but . . .

He took the small bulb from the pack in his pocket, broke off the top to reveal the needle and popped the skin on his stomach with it. The needle was so fine that he hardly felt it, but he felt warm as soon as the detanine began to seep into his system. He sighed and began to relax.

That was better.

Mona wouldn't like it, of course, but once they were married, he could ease off the drug. After all, it was nice, but he didn't need it. He could give it up any time he liked.

◆ ◆ ◆

Cara and Gen had been friends on Olyanda in the first days of the Ecolibrian colony, before the discovery of platinum had started a chain of events that ended with the Ecolibrians fleeing the planet and Crossways taking it over.

There had been a few rough patches. Gen falling for set-tler Max Constant, getting pregnant, and trying to hide the fact had not helped their relationship, but they'd survived it. Max had even turned out to be one of the good guys.

Gen and Max's baby, Olivia May Marling, was the fold-space baby.

Since the birth, Cara had seen more of Max than of Gen. Visits to Gen were full of talk about nappies and feeding.

Cara felt her jaw drop slightly as the door to Gen and Max's apartment swung open. The tiny dot of a baby had turned into a sturdy toddler, walking and talking.

"You look well," Cara said to Gen. "She must be letting you get some sleep at last."

"Amazingly, yes," Gen said.

When she'd seen Max in the office an hour ago, he'd had dark circles beneath his eyes. Better not to say anything about his state of rest.

"It's Cawa, Mummy," the little girl said.

"Cara," Gen corrected her.

"Ca-ra," Liv said very carefully.

"Good girl." Gen swept up her daughter on to one hip and put her other arm around Cara. "Glad to see you home. Some success, I gather."

"Well, we found Zandra Hartwell, but we couldn't persuade her out of retirement. Jussaro's still trying to work out the value of the information she gave him. Altogether, though, I think we did well."

"You're going to recreate Sanctuary."

"Don't ask and I won't tell."

Gen raised one eyebrow.

"Have you had a call to see Jussaro yet?" Cara asked.

"Not formally, but there are rumors." Gen tapped the damping pin stuck in her own collar. "I'd like to get rid of this."

Cara nodded. "I'm sure it will be your turn soon. When you get the call, don't put it off."

"Help Ca-ra," Liv said, as if she'd followed the conversation.

"Very possibly, sweetheart," Gen said.

"That's right, Liv," Cara said. "You tell Mummy."

"Oh, she does. All the time." Gen glanced down at Liv. "I don't want the whole megacorp thing for her when she grows up." She put Liv down on the floor and the toddler immediately sat and began pulling toys out of a basket.

"Quite right. No one should have to worry that the Trust or whichever megacorp paid for their implant will come after them mind-to mind."

"How's Ben?" Gen asked. "We were all worried." She crossed to the kitchen corner. "Tea or coffee. It's only CFB, I'm afraid, and decaff at that."

"Tea, please. He says he's recovered, but I think he tires more easily. Garrick and the Free Company between them keep him on the hop constantly. With his background in the Monitors, he's advising Garrick on policing, which means he often gets called on to sort out station problems that Syke's militia can't deal with."

"And how is he about foldspace?" Gen handed Cara a mug and flopped on to one end of the couch. Cara took the other end, half-turned to Gen.

Gen was also a psi-tech Navigator, good enough to fly a jumpship. If anyone knew the perils of the Folds, and Ben's reactions to them, it was Gen.

"Oh, you know, he does the man thing and doesn't talk about it in case he shows weakness, but after the business with the void dragons last year, and then the Nimbus, I reckon he has more reason than most to run away screaming. He won't let himself, though. And no matter how he feels about it, he's still damn good at what he does. Sometimes I think he keeps going on willpower, but however he does it, he's still flying."

Gen pressed her lips together and shook her head. "If foldspace hasn't broken him by now, it's not going to."

"Have you ever spoken to void dragons?"

"I've seen them, and I may have muttered obscenities at them a few times, but I've never had a meaningful conversation with one. I mostly saw the little things, the ones Ben calls otter-kind and Jake calls snakes."

"What did you call them?"

Gen laughed. "Pests, mostly."

"Want to see the dragon." Liv swiveled round on the floor and looked up at her mother. Her eyes shone. "Want to fly to the dragon."

"No, you don't, sweetheart, not yet," Gen said. "When you're older, a big girl."

Liv pulled herself up on a chair and tried to stand on tiptoes to make herself taller. She wobbled and would have fallen, but Gen steadied her. "Much taller than that, sweetie."

"When are you likely to want to return to foldspace?" Cara asked.

"I don't know if I will. I couldn't leave Liv behind."

"Not even with Max?"

Gen gave her a look that said more than words could express. There was something wrong there.

"Want to see the dragon." This time Liv spoke directly to Cara. "Want to fly with Unca Ben."

"Sorry, Cara, I don't know where she gets these ideas from. Liv, honey, you're too young to fly into foldspace."

"I'm old now."

"No, you're not."

Liv's little mouth compressed to a sphincter and she managed a pretty good scowl for a child of her age.

"Do you need some time off?" Cara asked. "I could babysit for you. Let you and Max have a bit of together time."

Gen shrugged. "Thanks anyway, but that's probably not a good idea."

"Okay, but the offer's open."

"Thanks."

Cara couldn't quite interpret the look in Gen's eyes. She supposed she might feel differently if she had children of her own, but surely it was all right to leave a child with a babysitter occasionally. Maybe Gen didn't think Cara could be trusted, but it wasn't as if she would be out of contact.

That set Cara off on another train of thought as she left Gen and Liv a short while later. Contact between mother and baby was natural, but what if it was more than that. Had she sensed something in Liv? Was the baby a natural telepath? With two psi parents, it was quite possible Liv would be predisposed to having that kind of talent.

Cara made a detour to visit Jussaro.

"Hey, can I come in?" Cara hovered in the doorway of what had become Jussaro's training school. "You're not fixing any implants or giving any lessons today?"

Jussaro shook his head. "I unlocked two more implants this morning: Yan Gwenn and Archie Tatum."

"How are you doing?"

"I'm tired if you must know. Zandra delivered a load of information that I'm still trying to process. Right now, if the megacorps caught me, I'd provide them with the biggest birthday present they ever had."

Cara raised one eyebrow. "A good reason for staying here, then."

"It sure is. I could do with some help, though."

"You haven't decided who to ask yet?"

"I was going to ask you, but I saw how you backed off. I know you've got . . . issues."

The way he hesitated and then emphasized the word made it Issues with a capital I.

"You know why I don't want to get too deep inside anyone's head."

"You're worried you might like it."

"No—well—yes, probably."

"You're allowed to like helping them. Besides, if you haven't gone psycho by now, you're not going to. The very fact that you don't want to do it is one of the reasons I think you'd be perfect."

She laughed. "You're more trusting than I am."

He shrugged. "I've had more experience."

"I'd like to help with Sanctuary, though not the actual unlocking part."

"There was a complex network of people involved, but most of them only knew their immediate contacts. That's why, when Alphacorp caught up with us, our cell was taken, but a lot of the others escaped."

"Would it help to talk it through? You have all the cells, right? You know who to contact to get Sanctuary up and running again."

"Before you start doing a happy dance, there are problems. It will take more time than I thought. I will, of course, unlock all the Free Company implants first, both here and on Jamundi."

"What about all the other psi-techs out there?"

"I always thought that if I had the codes, I would pass them on, but that won't work, will it? As Benjamin pointed out, if the megacorps know we have a way of freeing their psi-techs, the first thing they'll do is change the way all new implants are coded from now on. Once they do that, we're stuck. If we keep the codes secret and only unlock the implants of those who find Sanctuary, we free fewer, but we can continue to free them for the foreseeable future. It's a conundrum. What's the most beneficial thing to do? This is going to take some thinking through."

"Well, I'm here if you want to bounce ideas off me."

"I know, thanks."

"Only don't call on me tonight, I'm going to a party."

"Mother Ramona and Garrick's wedding. I hope their security is tight," Jussaro said. "It would be a perfect opportunity for the megacorps to get everyone who mattered in the same place at the same time."

"Tengue's been working with Syke. Their security net is so tight I doubt if anything could slip through."

"I hope those aren't famous last words."

She grinned at him. "We aren't going to let the megacorps spoil tonight."

Chapter Fourteen

CELEBRATE

"OKAY, LET'S SEE WHAT TODAY HAS IN STORE for us."

Stefan took Crowder's cane from him and placed it into the stand, within reach, but not in the way. Crowder dropped into his float chair and stretched his bad leg. Ah, that was better.

"Coffee, sir?"

"Sure, Stefan. I'll take the usual."

Crowder waved his thumb over the message command. The holographic screen flickered into being, and more than twenty messages flashed up, ordered by what his messaging system judged to be the most important first. There was one real-time message flashing. He hit receive.

Akiko Yamada's face appeared on his screen. CEO of Alphacorp; priority number one.

"Akiko, good to see you. How are you? How are Yoshiko and Etsuko?"

"My girls are fine, Gabrius, as am I."

Her plain features were immaculately groomed, her smart business suit tailored by the best fashion house in Japan. She might not be a true beauty, but power lent grace and Yamada had that in abundance. She'd inherited her shares in Alphacorp, but had worked hard to rise to CEO and was fiercely protective of the corporation and her place in it.

"Are you at home?" Crowder asked.

"The girls are. I'm flying to Tokyo later today. I'm in Sandnomore."

Ah, that was Alphacorp HQ, one of the new towns—though maybe not so new, now—in the Saharan rainforest.

"So what can I do for you?"

"How much do you know about this retrofit jump drive that Crossways has developed?"

"Only as much as my techs can tell me. It's damned inconvenient for us, but apparently it eats platinum for breakfast, so it's not much use commercially. They'll never be able to sell it, not as it stands."

"Except Crossways has Olyanda's platinum production to rely on."

She didn't need to remind him of that. Crowder immediately felt on the defensive. "Sure, they can retrofit jump drive vessels for their own use, until the platinum runs out."

"Which it isn't going to do for years."

Crowder bit back a snappy retort and forced himself to shrug as if it was no big deal. The muscles across his ribs pulled, so he relaxed his shoulders and shook his head instead.

Yamada's exquisitely shaped eyebrows drew close together. "We still have a third of the Alphacorp fleet locked into Amarelo space. Are you considering another strike force against Crossways?"

"They've developed a planetary net to protect both Olyanda and Crossways. It would take another combined fleet to—"

"My board has rejected the idea of joining another frontal attack. They believe we've wasted enough resources. We still haven't buried the Ari van Blaiden scandal deep enough."

"I understand."

"I hope you do. Your loyalty to the Trust is nothing short of monumental, Gabrius, but I think you've turned Crossways and Olyanda into a personal vendetta."

"Me? I'm the one who almost died if you recall."

"I haven't forgotten, but my board members have

authorized me to make Crossways an offer for their retrofit drive."

"You're going to deal with criminals?"

"There's every indication they're cleaning up their act."

He felt anger welling up. How could she? "Don't trust them, Akiko."

"Any deal would be dependent upon them assisting our stranded ships out of Amarelo space. Arquavisa is assembling a temporary jump gate. We're going to delay until we see whether they succeed. I wanted to give you some advance warning. I owe you that."

"Thanks. I think you're making a huge mistake, but your warning is much appreciated."

As Akiko Yamada's image faded, Crowder's bland expression turned to a scowl. "Dammit all to hell." His fists clenched so much that his knuckles turned white. "Stefan, you heard that."

"I did, sir."

"Get a message through to Arquavisa's CEO. Offer our unreserved assistance with his jump gate project."

"The budget, sir?"

"Contingency fund."

Stefan cleared his throat. "You might want to take a look at the state of that, sir."

"Get on to Finance; see what they can come up with."

"Yes, sir." Stefan turned to leave the room, and then hesitated. "I don't wish to interfere, sir, but I noticed there was a message from Swanson, prioritized at number nineteen. I thought you might want to look at it straightaway."

"Yes, thank you, Stefan."

Crowder waved his hand over the controller. "Play number nineteen."

It would be a recorded message, of course. Hope began to bubble up in his chest. If Swanson had taken care of Benjamin, he could relax. Yamada was right; he was treating this as a personal vendetta. The sooner it was over, the better for all concerned.

Swanson's instantly forgettable face appeared on the screen. "If you're watching this, then I'm probably dead or in detention and not able to do my weekly check-in. I thought I should let you know and remind you that I don't give refunds."

That was all. Crowder stared at the screen. Nothing on his lexicon of swear words would suffice on this occasion.

"Well, damn." The words tasted bitter on his tongue.

✦ ✦ ✦

Cara accepted a narrow glass from the uniformed waiter whom she recognized as being one of Syke's militia officers. She sniffed it. The bubbles went up her nose and her eyes watered behind her carnival mask, a confection of gold and black which covered the top half of her face. The smell was almost entirely like champagne, though she suspected it had never seen a grape in its life.

"To Crossways and all who fly in her." Norton Garrick, his own mask in his hand, gave the toast from the podium.

"Let's hope her flying days are over," Ben muttered at Cara's side while raising his own glass in response. His own mask covered three-quarters of his face, but his mouth and firm chin were exposed.

"That's probably up to you." Cara squeezed his hand.

"I'll settle for a nice stable orbit around Olyanda and no incoming missiles."

"No incoming missiles tonight."

"It would be a perfect time to attack, when we're all partying like it's 2547."

"It is—"

"2547," they said together, and laughed.

"Friends," Garrick commanded the room, looking relaxed, but Cara wasn't a hundred percent convinced. Garrick always kept up a front, no matter how he felt. It was a good act, though. He didn't need the formal suit or Mother Ramona on his arm to command the attention of the assembly. Garrick had earned their respect. He'd held the station together at Crossways' darkest hour and cajoled, bullied, blackmailed, and sweet-talked the rival factions into contributing to the rebuilding program.

Crossways was supposedly run by a loose coalition of crimelords, but both Indigo and Sharputra had abdicated responsibility in favor of consolidating their own resources after the attack. Once Garrick and Mother Ramona amalgamated their organizations, the smaller outfits were frozen out. That left only Roxburgh. Garrick had earned his place in the Mansion House. Roxburgh could go hang.

"Friends, thank you for coming here this evening." Garrick turned and smiled at Mother Ramona who looked particularly lovely in a flowing silver dress shot through with a titanium rainbow, echoing the colors of her fashionably spiked hair and white marbled skin. "It's a double celebration: our wedding and Crossways' own Independence Day. One hundred and twenty-five years ago today, by the Station Clock, Crossways fought for and won its independence from a succession of megacorporations who saw us as nothing more than a jump gate nexus, a refueling stop on the way from one profitable colony world to another. They denied the station resources, reassigned personnel regardless of family attachments, and considered it nothing more than an asset to be used and discarded. You all know your history. Crossways prevailed. Those in charge took control instead of decommissioning, and we became a successful free-trade port . . ."

There was a gentle sweep of laughter around the room. Free trade was a euphemism for a variety of criminal activities from smuggling to outright piracy, and the best-connected fences had lined up to open a Crossways office.

Garrick supported the laughter with his own grin, boyish despite the silver at his temples. "I know, I know. But it's time we took our legitimate place in the economic system of the settled galaxy. We knew the megacorps had a long memory and that sooner or later they'd try and put us in our place."

There were low mutterings from the room.

"Well, they tried and failed."

The room erupted into cheers.

"I needn't remind you of what we've overcome—you've all lived through it—but I would like to thank you for your support and hard work. Not much more than a year ago we were fighting five megacorporations. We had a station that was barely functioning, leaking air like an old sieve, and threatening to break apart. Now we have a viable home in space, stronger and better than before."

Another round of applause.

"I have two special people to thank—"

"Oh, no, that had better not be—" Ben tried to step into the shadows, but Cara kept hold of his hand.

"Ben Benjamin and Dido Kennedy."

Kennedy, with unerring instinct, was a no-show. People swiveled round to where Ben was standing. He wasn't one for public accolades, but he offered a polite nod of acknowledgment.

"We're masked. How do they even know it's me?"

"You're tall and brown."

"So's Gwala . . . and Tengue's not much lighter than me. . . ."

Didn't he realize what an imposing presence he was?

"And you're here at Garrick and Mother Ramona's wedding with the great and the good. Or maybe the great and the bad because I can see quite a few heads of criminal organizations. Not hard to spot if you know who you're looking for."

"Roxburgh?"

"Not him—at least, not that I've spotted, but there's Nathalie Beauvais of House Indigo. You can tell her by the coterie of young men, though I'm not sure how many are lovers and how many are bodyguards."

"I think the roles are interchangeable." Ben raised one eyebrow.

Cara slapped him lightly on the arm and tried not to laugh. "I'm pretty sure the one in red is Fynan Sharputra," she said.

"Yes, it looks like him."

"And that long streak of nothing is Civility Jamieson. I'm surprised to see him here. I didn't think he took much notice of anything except the latest implant technology."

"He has to qualify as the doc with the worst bedside manner in the galaxy."

"Knows what he's doing, though."

"He does, indeed." Ben fingered his own tiny implant scar.

Garrick was in full flow now. "Dido Kennedy modified the jump drive so it could be retrofitted to the station, and Ben Benjamin flew us safely through the Folds. Without them, we'd have been a shower of space junk orbiting Amarelo. Gentlefem and Gentlemen, a toast to Kennedy and Benjamin."

"I'll drink to that!" Cara winked at Ben over the rim of her glass.

"Did you know about this?" Ben asked.

"At least I talked Garrick out of giving you a medal. You can thank me later."

Ben pressed his lips together.

"Relax, that's it. He's moving on."

Garrick thanked all those who'd given time and credits or contributed resources. He congratulated specific individuals for achievements: a maintenance engineer for rescuing twenty-three souls trapped when the Saturn Ring had separated; a medical orderly who had stayed with three high-dependency cribs to make sure their tiny occupants weren't left behind in the panic of a mass evacuation; Jake Lowenbrun for putting himself and his ship between attacking forces and Crossways, and giving them time to get the new jump drive online.

And then it was time to honor the dead. It was a role of honor too long to read in its entirety and acknowledging individual names would devalue the names not mentioned, so Garrick simply called a minute's silence for all those who had lost their lives. The wall behind him coalesced into a patchwork of all known names, thousands of them, though they might never know the full extent of the losses, since a station like Crossways, operating outside of whatever laws could be enforced in the vastness of space, didn't ask for details of the crews when vessels sought a landing pad. Cara still had hold of Ben's hand and felt his fingers tighten on hers.

"Gone but not forgotten," Cara said along with everyone else as the minute ended.

"And now a toast to the bride and groom," Ben said, raising his glass once again. "Norton Garrick and Ramona Delgath, we wish you happy."

Happy echoed around the room.

"Thank you, my friends." Garrick pulled Mother Ramona to him. "Let's party!"

Cara gulped the rest of her champagne. "Happy couple toasted, duty done, do you want to stay and get blasted or shall we retreat in a semidignified manner?"

"Retreat." Ben hid his answer behind a smile as the band struck up a tune. "Before anyone asks me to dance and I lose whatever credibility I have. Quick. I can see the Magena twins heading in this direction. If I dance with one, I have to dance with both."

"Evasive action." Cara turned into him and wrapped her arm around his neck. "Looks like we're dancing."

They began to shuffle toward the exit in time to the music. Out of her peripheral vision Cara saw Chilaili and Tama Magena veer off in search of other victims.

"Okay, it's safe," she said, but Ben continued to hold her close and she followed his steps. "I thought you said you couldn't dance."

"Mmm? Is this dancing? I can manage this much."

She relaxed into him as they twirled together.

The Mansion House, Garrick's Palladian-style residence in the very center of Crossways, glittered with light from extravagant chandeliers, simply because it could. If it hadn't been for the faint buzz beneath her feet Cara might not have known she was on a station of three quarters of a million people in high orbit around Olyanda.

"Not thinking of leaving us so soon, are you?" Mother Ramona's deep voice startled her.

"Too much fun is bad for my image," Ben said, smiling. "Besides, you and Garrick are the stars of the show tonight."

"I bet Garrick you'd vanish before the speeches."

"If Cara had warned me, I would have."

She laughed. "We're honored you're still here. You need to relax more, Benjamin. Tell him, Cara. Oh, it's no use telling you, you're as bad as him. Both workaholics." She looked over her shoulder to see who was close. "Well, come on, Benjamin, don't you want to kiss the bride?"

Cara relinquished her hold on Ben and he swept Mother Ramona into his arms. They'd known each other a long time, since he'd been a Monitor stationed on the Rim, and she a small-time crook involved in smuggling goods and people across the galaxy quietly and quickly. Mother Ramona whispered into Ben's ear before their lips locked.

What was that all about? Cara asked Ben mind-to-mind as he surfaced and released the bride to her duties.

We have to go right now. I'll tell you on the way.

Chapter Fifteen

ROXBURGH

BEN AND CARA PICKED UP THEIR TWO BODY-guards, Lumb and Peckett, in the entrance hall where someone had supplied them with a plate of fancy cakes and a jug of juice. They all exited the building, down the flight of steps to Hub Square where a small crowd had gathered to catch a glimpse of the happy couple. There were picnickers in Hub Park, and a general holiday mood, a far cry from the wreck the station had been. Many people sported masks. The idea of picking up the old Independence Day celebrations had caught on.

Ben snagged a tub cab that ran in the shallow laneway to one side of the square. "Roxburgh Heights," he told the cab and the little vehicle whirled out into the traffic. He pulled off his mask and wiped his forehead, then fixed it firmly in place.

"Roxburgh's casino?" Cara asked.

"He should be at the reception, but he isn't, and neither are any of his most trusted. Garrick thinks something's going down. It's been building for a while—Roxburgh pushing his luck. I don't like it." He looked at their two guards. "I presume you're fully armed."

"Everything except a tactical warhead," Peckett said.

"Let's hope we don't need the one thing you've left at home."

Peckett's lips twitched into a smile. Lumb either had no sense of humor, or she simply didn't find it funny.

"Can you pull in Tengue's security team?" Ben asked Cara.

Cara quickly connected with Morton Tengue, at Blue Seven, and brought Ben in on the communication.

Tengue, Ben said, *Garrick thinks Roxburgh's up to something. Is there any word on the street?*

There was a slight pause as Tengue checked his sources.

Big party at Roxburgh's casino tonight. It's masked, but that's no surprise. Tickets are expensive.

"So he's chosen to make money instead of attend Garrick's celebration," Cara said. "He has managers, so his casinos could still be fleecing the public while Roxburgh did his civic duty."

"Then there has to be a better reason for not attending. Mother Ramona's right. Roxburgh is at the center of whatever's happening." *Tengue, how much backup can you send to the casino? Cara and I are going straight there with Peckett and Lumb. Get your people into position and wait for further instructions.*

Will do. I'll send ten with Gwala in charge.

Have we got anyone at the docks?

Fowler.

Ask her to see if Roxburgh's moving anything in or out. Tell her not to make it too obvious.

This is Fowler we're talking about. She doesn't do subtle.

Well, tell her not to get herself killed. That new skin she's wearing cost too much to throw away. If you need backup at the docks contact Syke. Mother Ramona has the militia on standby.

"It looks like we're going to gatecrash Roxburgh's party," Cara said.

"You don't have to come. You're not dressed for it."

"I think I'm dressed perfectly for it." She ran her hands down the close-fitting dress in a way entirely too distracting.

"I mean you're not wearing armor."

"I doubt they'd let us into the party if we turned up in buddysuits. Anyway, you're not wearing armor either. I bet you're not even armed."

"You'd lose that one."

"Derri?" she asked.

He nodded. "You?"

"Derri. Calf holster."

This was Crossways. Even peace and prosperity held danger.

Their tub cab pulled up alongside a brightly lit plaza, filled with holiday crowds and lined with booths taking advantage of the footfall Roxburgh's casino inevitably created.

"Wait here for Gwala," Ben told Peckett and Lumb.

Lumb nodded. "Please don't get yourselves killed on our watch."

"We'll try not to."

The largest gambling establishment on the station, Roxburgh Heights was the epitome of decadence. The entrance was a blaze of light, sparkling pillars, seductive music, and the swish of cool scented air. Beautiful, androgynous youngsters, oozing sexuality, drummed up business, flaunting themselves in exotic costumes and cajoling potential customers inside. Despite their apparent youth, if they worked for Roxburgh, they would have lethal skills and an arsenal tucked away in their glittering outfits or even grafted into their flesh.

Ben took Cara's hand and they sauntered through the plaza crowd and allowed themselves to be persuaded inside. Negotiating the entrance with its row upon row of machines of chance, they passed into the body of the building, an open central floor three stories high with a succession of shaded balconies. Cara looked over the crowd, everyone masked, dressed in their finery, drinks and gambling chips in their hands, some alone, some with partners, some with house escorts, rented by the hour. Staff, easily identified by their various styles of house turquoise, had masks painted on. That didn't, of course, mean all the masked customers were actually customers. Roxburgh would have security seeded throughout the revelers, and they were as likely to be female as male, slight as butch.

What are you getting? Ben asked.

Cara had been scanning with eyes and ears only, but now she opened up her talent for Empathy and checked the mood of the room.

Excitement, elation, pensiveness—all the usual emotions I'd expect to find around a gaming wheel. Whatever they're

*serving, it's pretty potent stuff. There's more than a little ine-
briation, but people are having a good time. Ah, someone
dropped a pot on the wrong number—definitely a surge of
disappointment.* She looked round. *Yes, over there. He's
lost a fortune, but the woman moving in on him is a house
girl about to make up for his loss and keep him sweet.*

*Good business. Cuts down on trouble and for what the
house has won, her cost has been covered a hundred times
over.*

*I'm getting a sense of anticipation as well. Some, not all,
are looking forward to something happening later tonight
and—oh—*

Something wrong?

*Someone's angry, more than nervous, and a little bit
drunk. Bad combination.*

Gambled and lost?

I don't think so.

"Drinks, sir, gentlefem?" A turquoise-bedecked waitress
with cleavage she could have hidden a laser cannon inside
sashayed up to them. "May I direct you to a table or find
you a booth? Or are you here for the floor show?"

There was something in the way she said floor show that
emphasized it. Given that the stage curtains were closed,
Cara figured she wasn't talking about a regular entertainment.

"Floor show." Ben didn't hesitate.

"Entrance is five thou. Four thou off your first purchase.
Price includes delivery anywhere on-station this side of the
docks. There's an additional fee of two thou on your bid if
you require delivery past the exit barriers direct to your
ship."

"Understood."

The waitress held up the payment meter on her left
wrist. Ben hesitated and without looking at Cara, said, *Do
you still have your anonymous line of credit?*

She'd arranged untraceable funds for the trip with Jussaro.

"I'll get that," she said, and pinged the reader with her
handpad.

The waitress held out a wristband embedded with a chip
and Cara took it before Ben could.

Did we just spend five thousand credits? she asked.

The floor show is where it's at.

I thought I was supposed to be the Empath.

Call it a hunch. Garrick will reimburse us.

"What the heck are you two doing here?" A small, stout woman confronted them, wearing a bright red, sequined dress that stretched alarmingly over her generous proportions, and a matching mask that covered her eyes, but failed to disguise her double chin.

Oh, great. That's all we needed, Ben said.

The source of the anger and nervousness, Cara warned Ben. *Drunk, definitely drunk.*

"Dido—"

"Shut up, Benjamin, I'm here in disguise. How did you know it was me?"

"I'd recognize your voice anywhere."

He saw Cara biting her lip, trying not to smile.

"The bastard's taken one of my kids, and I can't even get in there without sodding five thousand. I haven't even got five hundred. What am I supposed to do next?" Dido shoved a hand beneath her mask and swiped it across her eye.

"Hold on. Which bastard? What kid?" Ben asked.

"You know which bastard. Roxburgh."

"Okay, we're halfway there. What kid?"

Ben had rarely seen Dido's den in Red One without a pack of feral kids from the neighborhood.

"Efra. Not much to look at but hella talented. Had to chase off one of Roxburgh's scouts a few months ago, but they musta tagged her. She disappeared the day she turned legal. Sixteenth birthday."

"Are you sure they took her against her will?"

She scowled. "Not entirely. They mighta 'ticed her away. Life's pretty tough down on the lower levels, 'specially this year. Folks barely get by. They mighta sold her. Sometimes families'll sacrifice one kid to feed the rest."

It wasn't an unfamiliar story, even out in space. People slipped through the cracks, and a station the size of Crossways had its underclass barely scraping a living.

"So Roxburgh's taken one of the kids from Red One and he's doing what, pimping her out?"

"Nah. Benjamin, listen, willya? She's not much to look at, but she's talented." She whirled her index finger around her temple. "Talented. Get it?"

"Implant talented?" Cara butted in.

"Maybe talented enough without an implant. She's empathic, a natural. Roxburgh and the other casino owners can't employ psi-techs—no one would play the tables—but there's nothing against employing someone naturally talented. I mean, how could you tell? You could put an implant in this girl and she'd be worth a small fortune on the black market, but someone with that kind of talent without an implant would be worth a large fortune."

"He'll sell her rather than keep her himself?"

"Too close to home, here. Someone might recognize her. He'll sell her off-station and buy in from outside. Probably get his pick of the merchandise for facilitating the auction. It starts in less than half an hour."

Auction. Ben felt his guts turn over. Cara was talking about Sanctuary for psi-techs, yet they hadn't considered that naturals needed protection, too.

Ben swore. "I presume you want your girl back."

"What do you think?"

"For what it's worth, we're here because Garrick thought something was going down tonight. What do you know?"

"Not much."

"Anything at all might help."

"You have to pay to get in."

"We know that."

"Word is that there are ten lots for sale, all of them talented, none of them fitted with an implant."

"All of them from the station?"

She shook her head. "Some from on-station, others from outside. This is a specialist sale. These kids are from all over the settled galaxy."

"Are they all kids?"

"I'm not sure about that. All I know is they're all natural telepaths or empaths or whatever, and the merchandise can't go back to the planet, or station of origin, in case they're recognized. It's part of the deal that they ship out within six hours of the sale being finalized."

"Who are the buyers?"

"No names, no ID. That's why tonight being masked is a huge advantage."

"So they have to move the—oh, hell, we can't call them merchandise, let's call them slaves because that's what they are—they have to move the slaves away from the casino and to the docks after the event."

"Yeah, I suppose. Your guess is as good as mine."

Better to intercept them on their way to the docks rather than try to raid the auction and start a turf war, Ben said to Cara. *We'd need a lot more planning to take Roxburgh down in his own lair, especially with so many civilians.* He glanced around at the happy customers. *The collateral damage would be brutal. We'll have teams to stake out the possible exits. If we can catch them en route, so much the better. We probably need an Empath with each team to identify the naturals.*

I'll tell Mother Ramona, Cara said. *Any we miss on the road we can catch at the docks. Station control can hold up any vessels launching from private bays.*

Dido scrunched up her forehead. "You guys making plans?"

"Made," Ben said.

"What are you going to do now?"

Cara pulled the wristband from Ben's fingers. "I'm going shopping."

"Why you?"

"Because you're big and brown, and even with your mask, Roxburgh's thugs might recognize you once they only have a few people to focus on. I'll blend in better: not too tall, mask, hair with temporary colors on top of the blonde, party dress—shall I go on? Besides I can identify the naturals and flash descriptions to the teams, and you can coordinate from out here."

Damn, she was right.

Stay in touch.

You know I always do.

He watched her sashay into the crowd with a sinking feeling.

"Come on, Dido, into this booth and keep your head down until Cara calls for backup." He hustled her toward an empty corner.

"What now?" she asked.

"We watch and we wait."

Chapter Sixteen

AUCTION

CARA SETTLED HER MASK FIRMLY AND WAVED her chipped wristband at the security hulk on the door. "One for the floor show."

He drew aside the curtain and invited her into a short corridor leading to a room with tables and chairs set around a small raised dais.

She accepted a glass from a circulating waiter, but noted with relief a carafe of water on the table as she took a seat.

I'm in, she told Ben on a very tight communication. *Eight people here already, all masked. No one I recognize. They all appear to be individual buyers except for one couple, both female, who have their heads together talking quietly. I think I'm early. Ah, another party arriving now, six together, obviously know each other. Another three individuals, all male.* She detailed arrivals until the room filled up, thirty-seven people in all.

The lights dipped and the platform lights brightened.

It's starting. Stand by.

Roxburgh put in a personal appearance and welcomed everyone. That man could sure wear a formal suit. It hung from his powerful shoulders and fit in all the right places. Roxburgh's fair hair reminded her of Ari van Blaiden, but luckily that's where the comparison ended. Ari had been impossibly handsome. Roxburgh was striking but not gorgeous. She knew he didn't have an implant, but at this distance she should have been able to pick up underlying emotions, even from a deadhead. Unfortunately, he had a kind of emotional fog around him which meant he must be wearing a damper to protect himself from empathic snooping.

"On the tables in front of you, you'll find bidding numbers, gentlefem and gentlemen. Raise them to place your bid. At the end of the auction you may pay by credit chip or by house chip. Names and contact details will not be required. You are assured discretion."

Until station security picked them up on their way to the docks. Cara stifled a smile and passed the information in to Ben.

Without wasting any more time, Roxburgh brought in twelve individuals and lined them up in front of the stage, as diverse a bunch as it was possible to get.

There are twelve of them, not ten, she told Ben. *Two boys look like twins. I doubt they're more than fourteen years old.*

Can you see Efra?

Cara quickly identified Kennedy's kid from Red One. Apart from the twins she was the youngest and was obviously scared out of her wits, but she wasn't running or weeping. Roxburgh had probably explained what would happen if she didn't cooperate. The other nine ranged in ages from roughly fortyish down to perhaps early twenties, and in color from deepest black to someone who was pearl-white with a tattooed design on his skin in grays and blacks.

"You may examine the merchandise," Roxburgh said.

Some of the potential bidders moved in immediately; others hung back, perhaps because they'd had a private viewing earlier.

Cara, Dido Kennedy's about to burst. Is the kid there?

Yes. She projected what she could see to Ben.

Dido says can you get her out?

Not from here. She's right under the spotlight.

Find some way to tag her, so we can follow her with a Finder if we have to. I'll get Max.

If you can pry him away from Gen and the kid. Max was wrapped firmly around his daughter's little finger.

Little finger—that might work. Cara plucked three hairs

from the crown of her head where she'd let it grow a little longer than usual. Good job she'd missed her last haircut. Quickly she twisted them round each other and tied them in a loop.

She left her table and walked down the line, trying not to lock glances with anyone. A fair proportion of the buyers, whether they were the actual buyers themselves or proxies, would be implanted psi-techs trying to test the potential of the naturals. Cara kept her mental shields firmly locked in place and didn't open herself up to the possibility of psionic attack. Just because he wasn't allowed to have implanted psi-techs operate in his casino, didn't mean Roxburgh only employed deadheads behind the scenes.

She took the hand of the first young man in line, as if examining it. She wanted to say help is on the way, but she daren't let anything slip mentally. The next was an older woman dressed in traditional Japanese costume. Again, Cara took her hand and when the woman made a slight bow, she returned it. The third had glistening scaly silver-black skin and gills on the side of his neck so was most likely an adapted human from a water world, maybe from Aqua Neriffe like Marta Mansoro, the Free Company's stores and supply specialist. He snatched his hand away and gave her a look that said he'd like to dismember her slowly with a blunt spoon. Even with all her shields in place, he was uncomfortable to be around. His face, which should have been silver, was flushed a strange shade of bronze, and his gill slits undulated, indicating discomfort. It was hot in here and he was drying out.

Next was a man she'd taken to be in his forties, but on closer inspection he could be twice that age, not a sound investment for anyone looking for a long-term return for their credits unless he was exceptionally talented. She regarded him with new appreciation.

By the time she reached Efra, close to the middle of the line, Cara had established a pattern. As she took the girl's hand, she slipped the loop of hair over her little finger and squeezed, glancing up to meet her eyes. Efra frowned briefly and then closed her hand into a fist to keep the loop in place. Good. Cara hoped that was enough. A good Finder, someone as good as Max, would be able to locate the hair.

Should I bid? Cara asked Ben. She settled in her seat

as Roxburgh bowed out and a professional auctioneer stepped forward.

Only if you're sure you're not going to win, or if not bidding would make you stand out from the crowd. Roxburgh will have someone watching and is probably recording the whole thing from several different angles.

Or maybe not recording if he doesn't want evidence of this. The station's convention says no human trafficking.

You've always been able to buy anything on Crossways. Garrick's trying to alter the old ways, but it's slow going.

I get four thousand off my first purchase, right?

That's what your ticket entitles you to. Cara . . . don't . . .

If I buy, then I get to see what happens afterward, and I can let you know which exits to watch.

There was Ben's mental equivalent of a harrumph followed by, *Take care. Roxburgh's not above dumping a body out of an airlock to protect himself.*

Noted.

Cara watched the bidding intently. They took the lots in reverse order to the way she'd viewed them. The first two went for eighteen and twenty-four thousand each. The twins went for sixty thousand as a pair.

Efra sold for twenty-six thousand to two women who nudged each other, obviously pleased with themselves. Cara bid, but was forced to drop out while there were still five bidders.

She gritted her teeth as the auction carried on. She bid on the little old man, surprised to see him go for thirteen thousand. The bidding on the water world man was slow, however. Cara hadn't opened herself up to sense his feelings, but if he was projecting trouble like he was dishing out hate-filled looks, he'd no doubt scared off some of the customers, which was probably his intent. The bidding went past six but stalled at seven.

"Seven, am I bid seven?" The auctioneer called out. "Seven, no? Six, five hundred. Six, two-fifty, then. No takers? The bid's with table six at six thousand credits."

Cara realized that was her.

"Six thousand it is, to table six."

She nodded an acknowledgment. She'd make the best of it. She hoped the man didn't put up a physical struggle. She was fairly sure he wouldn't be expecting her to be able to floor him in three seconds, but she didn't want to overplay her hand.

With a snap, the auctioneer closed the deal on the last lot and invited the buyers to remain behind while three stewards politely but firmly cleared the room of all the unsuccessful bidders.

Cara's purchase, easily as tall as Ben, but not as well-muscled, glared at her from beneath a scowl.

"Do you want a receipt?" A clerk slapped a pair of ferraflex manacles onto her purchase and handed her a leash and a key.

"If I said yes, would I get one?"

He laughed and moved down the line.

Conscious that anything she said could be caught on a recording, she had to play this straight, which meant dealing with her charge quickly before he did something brave or stupid. Or brave and stupid.

"Wait there," she told him and dropped the leash, turning to the table to retrieve the carafe of water.

As she moved, she felt rather than saw him step forward. Good, she'd been expecting something like this. She whirled, grabbed one hand and twisted, knocking him off balance and sweeping her foot behind his knees. He went down like a felled tree and she dropped with one knee across his solar plexus, trying to judge it so she didn't leave him too breathless to walk. Quickly, she leaned over him and touched her forehead to his, putting everything she had into one flash of communication. *This isn't what you think it is. Play along if you want to be free.*

Then she poured the carafe out over his throat, letting the water trickle over his dried-out gill slits, watching his color subside to silver.

"I'd ask if you need any help, but it looks like you've got it covered," the clerk said.

"A little misunderstanding, nothing more." She looked at her scaly charge. "Right?"

He nodded.

"What's your name?"

"Lev. Lev Reznik."

"Come on, Lev."

She let him rise, taking his leash. The others were already leaving. She tagged onto the end of the line, keeping an eye on Efra and her masked purchasers.

We're in a service elevator heading up two, no—three levels. All of us together, so far. Four being led away at this level, not Efra. She kept up a running commentary to Ben. *One more level up. Efra and her handler are among those getting out here. Damn, they've held us back. Her handlers are female, about my height, but one stocky and one skinny, dressed in plain browns. Make sure you get Efra. We'll be okay.*

The elevator rose again and jerked to a stop. The clerk in charge let the rest of them out and told them to follow the waiting guide. Cara glanced around. There was the white youth with the tattoos, the elderly man, and a young woman, all being led by purchasers wearing nondescript clothing. *They all dressed ready for this exit,* Cara said. *You wouldn't pick any of them out in a crowd. I stand out in my party dress.*

Gwala's on your level. You should see him as soon as you lose Roxburgh's guide.

Cara pushed the key to the shackles into Lev's hand. "When the rumpus starts, keep out of it. If we get split up, make your way to Blue Seven."

"Why should I—"

She silenced him with a look. "Or don't. I don't care. Stay out of trouble. Have a nice life."

Ben was wrong, Gwala didn't wait for the guide to depart. His team moved in while they were still in a narrow service corridor. Cara recognized the big African behind his full-face helmet by his height, and that was most likely Hilde Hildstrom behind and to his left. One of the purchasers produced a bolt gun, illegal in half the galaxy and required equipment in the other half. Gwala took him down with a neat shot to his thigh before he could do any damage while the other members of the team fanned out and covered the whole party.

Lev melted out of sight; Cara let him go. Maybe he had a bolt-hole, which was fine by her—one less traumatized human being to deal with.

She waved to Gwala and Hilde and sprinted down the corridor to the main roadway ahead, one with a channel for tub cabs. No cabs—damn! It looked like this part of the business sector had closed down for the holiday. She followed the guide on the wall. White Five, not a part of the station she was familiar with. Any large station, particularly one as large as Crossways, fully ten kilometers in diameter measured across the outer rings, had sections that looked very like each other. The color coding and segment labeling helped, but it was easy to get turned around.

Ben?

White Four, Hubward.

She headed for an antigrav shaft, pushed off into it, her dress billowing around her hips, and swung out a level below, feeling the pull as weight returned.

I'm on your level. I'm—

There you are!

Ben appeared at the far end of the corridor, still dressed in his smart evening suit. Beside him was Max Constant, buddysuited and ready for action, with three of Tengue's security guys, uniformed and helmeted. Dido Kennedy followed a few paces behind, mask now removed and her wispy hair fuzzing around her pink, flushed face.

"Have you got something for me?" Max asked.

Cara plucked another three hairs from her crown. "I hope you don't need more than that or I'll be bald."

"Hair? You seriously want me to find a hair?"

"Three hairs, actually, twisted into a ring."

He snorted. "You realize I could find your shed hairs all over the station, not to mention the water reclamation units where your shower drains to."

"Do your best. She can't be far."

"Yeah, Constant, come on. Find my girl." Dido's breath came in snatches. Cara hoped she wasn't going to have a heart attack from all the unaccustomed exercise.

Max grunted and scowled but slipped into an almost trancelike state while he searched for Efra via Cara's ring of hair. Cara locked glances with Ben, the only acknowledgment they allowed each other while the chase was on.

✦ ✦ ✦

"This way." Max led the way purposefully to a cab pull-in. "They're on the move, heading rimward."

"Public docks?" Ben asked as they all piled into one

tub—seven in a tub meant for four, and one of those seven was Kennedy, who was almost sitting on his knee.

It looks like we're heading for the main terminus, Cara opened a channel to Mother Ramona via Ully.

I'll have Syke meet you there with breathers.

The main public docks worked on a low pressure, low oxygen system designed to discourage problems before they kicked off. All the workers had grafted breathing tubes, but visitors had to pass through the immigration queues while trying to breathe and fighting off headache and nausea. Too much exertion could bring on altitude sickness within minutes. Max and Tengue's three security guards would be fine, as they all had emergency breathers in their buddysuits, but Ben, Cara, and Dido's party clothes were woefully inadequate for running around the docks following people traffickers.

"Freight docks," Max said, and their little tub cab veered left.

Cara relayed the information, keeping them all in the loop.

We're shutting down all departures, Mother Ramona said. *Better make this quick, or we'll have half the merchants on Crossways suing us for unreasonable delays.*

Tell them it's a safety drill, Ben said. *Have you shut down the private docks as well?*

We have now, but at least five ships squeezed out ahead of the order. We don't know what or who they were carrying.

Our girl's still on-station, Max said. *I'm sure of it. Either that, or I'm chasing the garbage from the last time Cara cleaned her hairbrush.*

"Not at the docks," Cara said.

There was one main dock for passenger transport and another for freight, each with twenty bays. Between them, they handled ninety percent of traffic. They were policed by a unit under an individual called Lloyd Dow, who reported directly to Garrick. Mother Ramona warned them that although Garrick hadn't been able to prove anything, he suspected Dow was "'old school Crossways,"—that is, not above taking bribes to look the other way. It was one of the reasons Tengue had one of his crew stationed here with a watching brief. Today it was Franny Fowler.

Syke met them on the concourse with a team of ten

militiamen and a spare set of protective vests with built-in breathers. The vests were small versions of the ubiquitous buddysuits, in this case only covering the torso from throat to crotch, providing body armor, basic status monitoring, and emergency medication.

"Oh, yeah, like you're going to get me into one of those things," Dido said as Syke held out the vest. Ben was already in his, and he left Cara to explain how to put it on and seal it up.

"Come on, woman. You can invent a jump drive, but you can't put on a vest?" Cara grabbed the vest and thrust it at Dido.

Ben tried not to smirk.

Cara pulled on her own vest and sealed it at the throat and down the side. Then she pulled the knife out of the tool pouch and slit her dress from crotch to hem and pulled the safety strap between her legs and secured it.

Ah, pity about the dress. Ben had liked her in it, but he appreciated even more her no-nonsense approach to not getting her arse shot off.

"You're kidding me, right?" Dido pulled a face. "It'll do like this." She fastened the vest at the throat and would have left it gaping at the side, but Cara yanked on the fabric and sealed it.

"How on earth do you wear these things? It's like a blasted corset." Dido wriggled and the fastenings strained.

Ben left them arguing. Max was already loping toward the entrance to Dock 16, and he sprinted to catch up, the militia close behind. Syke's regulars and Tengue's mercenaries had spent the months since the Battle of Crossways working together on search and rescue and keeping public order. They fell in together quite naturally.

Somewhere behind them, he could hear Dido telling Cara to slow down and wait and Cara urging her onward. Good luck to them.

Chapter Seventeen

EFRA

"JUST GIVE THE VEST A MINUTE," CARA SAID. "It will adjust itself to fit. You're sure you don't want the crotch strap?"

"Hell, no."

"Then keep your arse tucked out of the way if anyone starts shooting."

"If anyone starts shooting, I'll be running for the exit."

Max was already loping toward the entrance to Dock 16 with Ben and the security team, Syke's regulars and Tengue's mercenaries following closely. Cara hauled Dido along by one elbow, running to catch up.

"You sure you don't want to wait for us here?" Cara asked, aware of the older woman's ragged breathing even with the extra supply of oxygen that the suit gave.

"That's my girl out there. She'll be scared."

"Fair enough. Run faster."

"Here." A sharp female voice grabbed their attention, and Cara yanked Dido into a space between two transit containers. Franny Fowler was waiting, pulse pistol drawn. "Your guys have spread out. Your Finder says the kid's on the *Lian-X*, but she's all sealed up—prepped for departure and not answering hails. They're looking for a way in, but it might need a Psi-Mech. Archie Tatum's on his way."

"He'd better be good," Dido said.

"He is," Cara said.

It took less than five minutes for Archie to arrive, buddy-suited and ready for business, though the lingering warmth of alcohol on his breath said he'd been out partying until called.

"Where's the fire?" he asked.

"There." Ben joined them and pointed to the *Lian-X*.

The ship wasn't huge: a fast cruiser shaped like a flattened oval with docking struts extended. Depending on her internal configuration, she'd carry a maximum of twenty passengers and probably fewer if they wanted to travel in any kind of comfort.

Cara opened up a channel to the port's traffic control and brought Ben into it.

Has she answered any hails? Ben asked.

Is that you, Benjamin?

Briggs?

Yeah. Briggs had been one of the flight controllers constantly berating Ben for materializing from the Folds too close to the station. He'd obviously got a promotion. *No answer to hails. The port's locked down. She's not going anywhere.*

What data can you give us?

She's registered as an independent trader with Eridani.

A substantial company, but not one of the megacorporations.

Captain? Crew?

You know we don't ask questions like that.

If Garrick got his way, they would in future.

I was hoping they might have volunteered the information.

"Hey, Benjamin. I'm not here for the good of my health, you know." Fowler flicked on her handpad; a small holographic playback showed a party of six, all cloaked in anonymous brown, crossing the concourse toward Dock 16. One figure was smaller than the rest. "I reckon that's your girl, and from what I saw there were no more than three on the ship. Pilot and two crew at most. Though they could be heavies rather than techs. A ship like that wouldn't take more than one pilot-Navigator to fly her through a jump gate."

"The buyers were a pair of women," Cara said. Which, of course, didn't make them any less deadly than the men if it came to a showdown.

Hail them again, Briggs, Ben said. *Put it on the open comm network and give us a line.*

"*Lian-X*, this is Port Authority, Commander Orvis Briggs. Your vessel is surrounded and grounded. Please open your hatch for inspection."

"His name is Orvis?" Cara whispered.

"No wonder he likes to be called Briggs," Ben said.

"I like the name Orvis," Fowler waggled her head from side to side. "I might even use it for my firstborn."

"You're not . . ." Cara twisted her head around, but saw only a wide grin on Fowler's face.

"'Course not, but could you imagine it? Orvis Fowler-Tengue. Or perhaps I should add in a few middle names: Orvis Francis Morton Fowler-Tengue. Poor little sod would have to grow up strong to carry a name like that."

"Any child of Morton Tengue would have to grow up strong."

"Like father, like son, you mean? Nah, I'd raise him to be an artist or a musician."

"*Lian-X*, please open your hatch for inspection." Briggs voice cut through Fowler's conversation.

"*Lian-X*," Ben broadcast over the comms channel. "I've got direct authority from Norton Garrick. We're not interested in you, only your newly acquired cargo. Send the girl out and you can go."

"Why should we do that?" The reply that came across the comms channel was a female voice. "We're in the strongest position here if you want your girl in one piece. We paid good money. We're entitled to compensation. We'll take thirty thou in platinum for our trouble and you get the girl back without a mark on her. Otherwise—"

There was a sound which was unmistakably a young female voice squealing in surprise. "Oww, ya bastard, what was that for?"

"That's her, Benjamin," Kennedy said. "Just pay the money."

"My grandmother was a negotiator," Ben said, off-channel. "You never give in to the first threat, or they know they have you by the short hairs. Options?" he asked Archie Tatum.

"Drill bots, cutters, spider bots," Archie said. "I can take the ship apart on the dockside if you want me to, but it won't be quick. If they decide to do something to their prisoner, I can't get through the ship's skin fast enough for you to save her."

"Just pay the money," Kennedy said.

"Pay the money, and Crossways will become the soft-touch of the galaxy," Ben said.

"Pay up, or we'll be going now," the female voice said. The ship's engines hummed. "Clear the port and open the outer doors, or our thrusters are going to make a mess of your bay and your people as well."

"Cara, they must have a psi-tech on there. Most likely a Navigator at the controls. Can you reach him or her?"

"If I can?"

"I want you to put him out."

Cara stared at him, hardly letting herself believe what she heard. "You're asking me to—"

"You've done it before. You can do it again."

"When my life depended on it. When yours did."

"Hey, my girl's life depends on it," Kennedy butted in.

"You don't understand what he's asking."

Cara's guts churned at the thought of using her talent to bully and hurt. Yes, she could do it, but that didn't mean she had to. She'd learned the hard way, as a victim, and the thought of doing it to someone else gave her cold shivers down her spine.

Kennedy looked sideways at Ben. "He's not asking more than you can give."

"Taking over someone's mind . . . it's not right . . ." Cara pushed down a wave of nausea.

"Neither is slavery," Kennedy said. "Get over it."

I wouldn't have put it quite as bluntly as that, Ben said.

Cara stared at Kennedy. Did the end justify the means? If she did it now, on request, would Ben ask again? Would she seek an excuse to do it again? And again? But if she didn't do it, they might spirit Efra away or kill her and dump her out of the *Lian-X*'s hatch on the dockside. She saw the hope and fear in Dido's eyes.

It's okay. She's right. I'll get over it.

She hoped the psi-tech would. Having your mind invaded was as bad as having your body invaded. Worse in some ways. It would be better if she could do it quickly and render him—she was fairly sure it was a man—unconscious.

"Everybody shield," Cara called. She sent a thought, short-range but powerful toward the ship, trying to pick up emotions from individuals, sorting out one from another. She initially searched for anyone with an implant.

"Dammit, there are three of them."

"All Navigators?" Ben asked.

She'd been so locked inside her head that she'd never felt him put a supportive arm around her, but there he was.

She shook her head. "One Navigator, one Telepath and one Empath."

"Can you put the Navigator out first?"

"I can try." She shut herself off from her physical surroundings and concentrated on the mental plane where she saw other psi-techs in shades of color and shapes of light. She knew Ben was there, but he had a tight natural shield. Syke had powered down his receiving implant, as had Tengue's mercs, including Fowler. Archie Tatum was shielding, though not as strongly as Ben. She took care not to accidentally hit him with the backlash as she went after the Navigator on the sealed ship. He wasn't much above a class four, or maybe a three on a good day.

She couldn't afford to wait. She found him, cracked his shield, invaded his mind, and pushed.

It took seconds.

She felt him realize what was happening and start to resist, but she had him. As he slipped into unconsciousness, she repressed a small surge of pleasure. She did it because she had to do it, not because she enjoyed it, she reminded herself. But she knew that, having been a victim once, she could very easily let herself revel in the power of knowing she'd never be a victim again.

Someone pushed back at her from the ship, a questing mind that was stronger than the Navigator's had been. One of the women from the auction, she thought. They'd hardly attempt to purchase a natural without having someone who could assess her value. This was the Empath, certainly implant-enhanced and at least a class three. The mind searched. Cara clamped down her shields. Then there was another mind in there—the Telepath, she thought. Damn, they were sisters.

On another level, she heard Ben telling Archie Tatum to send in his drill bots and then she was aware she was on the floor, resting against Ben and drawing on his strength. She jabbed at the siblings, but they had locked tightly together in a double shield.

Her head felt as though it was swelling like an overripe peach, about to burst. She screwed her eyes tight as if to stop them popping out of their sockets. Shit, not siblings, but twins, with a natural bond. She felt them blocking her as she probed for a weakness, or a tiny crack that would let her in.

"Hear that?" Ben spoke to the ship. "That's a drill bot cracking through your outer skin. And that? That's another. And another. You can take off whenever you're ready, but you'll be sucking on vacuum."

"And what about your girl, then?" The female voice sounded stressed, as well she might. Holding the shield was taking all her concentration, distracting her from what was happening in the physical world.

"Not a problem," Ben said. "The bots you couldn't hear have cracked your door seal."

The hatch blew with a pop. Syke and Fowler were first through into the cruiser.

The commotion split the twins' attention between the mental world and the physical. Cara found her crack. She reached into the Empath's mind and did the psionic equivalent of punching her lights out. That left the Telepath who was reaching for some kind of weapon. The image of a handgun clarified in Cara's mind and it was pointing at Efra.

Without hesitation, Cara dropped the Telepath where she stood. She yanked her mind out of the Telepathic link and then everything went gray.

"What's happening?" Her voice sounded shaky inside her own head.

"Our guys are in," Ben said. "No casualties, thanks to you."

A few minutes later Efra ran out of the hatch and straight into Kennedy's waiting arms, her wrists still manacled.

Cara sat on the floor, Ben supporting her. "I thought you were the one with White Knight Syndrome. How come you let Syke and Fowler take point?"

"You're always telling me not to lead with my chin. Those guys had it covered and, besides, you needed me."

She felt a faint flutter of surprise. "Bastard! I only needed you because you made me do something I never wanted to do again. Ever."

"The girl's safe." Ben kissed the top of her head. "And you're the strongest person I know. You'll be all right."

Easy for him to say. He didn't have to live with the knowledge that she'd not found it at all distasteful. And she hated herself for that.

✦ ✦ ✦

Ben dispatched Efra and Kennedy to Red One with a security detail for their protection, and then turned his attention to the crew of the *Lian-X*.

Syke did a difficult job competently. He would debrief and cross-examine the detainees, not only the ones who'd bought Efra, but all the others caught up in tonight's operation. There were now twenty-nine individuals in the cells in the militia lock-up in Blue Two. Ben didn't envy his task.

Ben and Cara went with Syke and gave their own personal statements. Cara volunteered a statement, but tried not to go into details of how she'd knocked out the three psi-techs on the crew. She didn't even want to admit it to herself. She didn't have to like what she'd done.

Syke's best interrogators were Empaths, so he tended to get the truth, or at least the truth as the detainees knew it. Luckily, they were concentrating on the traffickers. The small groups had no links with each other. They'd come from various unconnected locations across the galaxy, seeking psionically gifted individuals for a variety of reasons. One to start a breeding program, another to root out those disloyal to a petty oligarch. At least two were traders who planned to sell their purchases on for a profit.

Ben would have liked to space the traders personally, but Garrick's intention was to record and blacklist each individual, should they ever try to enter Crossways again, and then let them go.

Cara and Ben hung around Blue Two for an hour, sitting

in a waiting area, sipping from a shared bottle of water. Eventually, with a nod from Syke, they slipped away.

"I'm surprised Garrick intends to let them go," Cara said.

"They're not station citizens." Ben shrugged. "Since we don't have a prison on Crossways, all we can do is space them or let them go. Crossways has always had a reputation for working outside the law. Garrick has to change that reputation, but spacing all its former customers is a bit too radical. He needs to let the criminal element know they're not welcome here anymore."

"What about the criminals on the station? Roxburgh's not the only one."

"No, but if Garrick takes down Roxburgh, then it sends the others a clear message. Clean up or get out."

"Do you think he'll do that?"

"Yes. Eventually. When he has a good reason."

"The auction isn't good enough?"

"Technically . . . probably not."

Ben tugged at his shirt collar. His evening suit was crumpled, and Cara's gorgeous dress was fit for nothing but the recycling chute. No wonder they rarely wore anything but practical buddysuits. They'd both discarded the armored vests.

"Let's go home," Ben said. "You look exhausted."

"Forcing people into unconsciousness will do that every time."

"I'm sorry about that. I had to do something quickly before the situation escalated and it was the best thing I could think of." He took her elbow and steered her through the main entrance to where a tub cab waited in the pull-in.

"Not best for me."

"I know, but you did it and did it well."

"That's because some part of me enjoyed doing it. That's what I hate. If I ever turn into a sadist like Donida McLellan, I want you to shoot me."

"You won't."

"How do you know that?"

"I know you. I trust you."

The tub cab whirled them into the traffic lane, heading up five levels and then rimward. Ben took Cara's hand and held it, knowing anything else would be too much and anything less would be too little. He'd asked a lot of her, maybe stretched her more than he should have. Would she hold it against him? They were almost back at Blue Seven before he heard her sigh and felt her relax. That was a good sign on many levels. He raised her hand to his lips and kissed her fingertips, relieved to see her mouth turn up in a half smile.

As her lover, he wanted only what was best for her. As leader of the Free Company, he'd need her strength not her enmity.

There would be fallout from tonight. Garrick and Roxburgh were already at odds. Sooner or later, it would come to a showdown between them. When that happened, it would get messy. The Free Company would be in the thick of it. They owed their lives to Garrick and Mother Ramona. They wouldn't forget. Ben wouldn't forget.

Blue Seven was rarely still and quiet, but at this time of night activity was at a minimum.

"I hope they're all still out enjoying themselves," Cara said. "And that their parties didn't come with added people rescuing. Wouldn't it be nice for once not to be dropped into a crisis situation?"

"You'd get bored," Ben said.

"No, I wouldn't. Try me. Give me a month without a crisis or a panic of some kind. Hell, give me a week. . . ."

He swept his arm around her. "Will you settle for a night?"

She sighed. "You know I will."

Chapter Eighteen

DREAMS

GARRICK FOUGHT HIS WAY OUT OF THE BED-
clothes and sat up, sweating.

"Whassup?" Mona's voice slurred with tiredness.

He'd not intended to disturb her. "Nothing. Go to sleep.
Sorry, too much champagne. Too much cheese late at night."

He swung his legs out of the bed and sat, resting his
hands on his knees.

He knew he'd had a dream again, but it was already fading. It was the Nimbus, of course, always the Nimbus. There
were any number of other worrisome things — Roxburgh
for instance — but Garrick's dreams always returned to that
suffocating blackness, and Kitty Keely stepping into it like
it was a lover.

He needed to buffer himself against it or he'd have more
nightmares before morning. He pulled open the nightstand
drawer and took out a bulb. He snapped off the end and
jabbed the fine needle into his stomach, squeezing until all
the fluid had been absorbed.

That was better. He should be able to get some sleep
now.

"What was that?" Mona leaned around him. "You said
you'd given up using that stuff."

"I only use it when I need it. Not all the time."

"Yeah, right. You know there are side effects. Have you had your liver checked and your kidneys?"

"Of course."

"When?"

"A short while ago."

"When?"

"I can't recall exactly."

"Have you got the tremors?"

"No, I haven't got the tremors. I'm not pissing blood and my skin isn't turning yellow. I'm fine."

"Show me. Hold out your hand."

He felt the detanine beginning to take effect. He took a deep breath to steady himself and held out his right hand. It was passably shake free. Luckily, she didn't ask him to hold out both hands.

"See the doc. Get something to help you quit. I don't want to be a widow before I've had the chance to be a wife."

"I will."

But he knew he wouldn't. Mona probably knew it, too.

✦ ✦ ✦

Cara divested herself of the once beautiful dress and held it up to the light. "Do you think I could make a slinky evening top out of this if I chopped off what's left of the skirt?"

Ben showed supreme disregard for discussions about clothing. He took the tatters out of her hand and dropped them on the floor.

"I like you much better without it." He bent to kiss her shoulder. His warm breath tickled the side of her neck.

"I haven't decided if I've forgiven you yet."

"As long as you forgive yourself—"

She turned and put her finger on his lips. "Maybe we shouldn't talk about it, not right now."

"Suits me."

"Hmm I was thinking about un-suiting you." She tugged at his shirt collar.

"That suits me, too."

Her dress and his suit ended up wrapped around each other in the semidarkness of their own bedroom floor.

Afterward they curled up together, the light extinguished, both on the verge of sleep, but though Ben's breathing deepened, Cara remained wide awake.

"Do you think Garrick looked well tonight?" Cara asked.

"You're thinking about Garrick?" Ben said, half into his pillow.

"I've been away. It's the first time I've seen him in a while. Mother Ramona looked exactly the same, but Garrick — well — he was positively sparkling."

"Is that a bad thing?"

"Considering what he's been through, maybe it is. Before I left, he was looking haggard — showing his age, and more. How old is he? Fifties?"

"That would be my guess."

"Last time I saw him, I would have guessed seventy. Tonight, he looked forty. That's a big change. Is he on something?"

She felt Ben shrug. "You're the Empath. If you're worried, I'm worried."

"Maybe not worried exactly, but there's something I can't pin down. Let's keep an eye on him."

"If you say so." Ben sounded drowsy.

Cara snuggled close, trying to sleep.

"Ben?"

No answer. She closed her eyes again.

The suffocating blackness is behind her, creeping inexorably forward. She reaches for Kitty Keely's hand and they cling closely together, knowing this is the end. In the distance, the Solar Wind *winks into existence. Thank all the stars! But it's too far away, and too late. The blackness will suffocate them long before rescue. Then two figures are flying through foldspace toward the tiny, vulnerable shuttle. Yes! Yes! Come on, faster!*

Friends in front, the blackness behind. It's a race.

Kitty Keely tugs backward. "Can you hear it?" she asks. "It's singing. Come and listen."

"It's a trap. Don't listen."

The two figures arrive outside the shuttle. What next? The hatch is to the rear. The black cloud has already enveloped it.

The figures step through the forward screen as if it's not there.

"This way, come on." Benjamin is holding out a hand.

But Keely lets go. She steps into the cloud and she's gone.

Cara woke with a gasp, heart pounding.

"What?"

"Huh?"

She sat up, shivering, finding Ben also wide awake, sitting bolt upright on the edge of the bed.

"Bad dream," she said.

"You, too?"

"The Nimbus. Garrick, Kitty Keely, me, and you."

"That's where my mind took me tonight. I wonder why we both dreamed the same thing."

"The mind's a strange thing. I haven't had these dreams in all the time I've been away. Why should they start again now?"

"I hope I wasn't projecting."

She knelt and put an arm around Ben's shoulder. "Have you had these dreams all along?"

"Most nights. Sometimes more vivid than others."

"Hell, Ben, have you told anyone? You haven't, have you?"

"What's the point? They'll fade in time."

"It's been well over a year."

"Don't fuss. I can cope."

She sighed. "All right, this is me not fussing." She drew him into bed and snuggled up close. She might not fuss, but it didn't stop her worrying.

✦ ✦ ✦

Ben dressed and took a detour past the kitchen where Ada Levenson's staff kept the Free Company fed—no mean feat in itself. Ada, a fearsome woman to see wielding a meat cleaver, waved at him from the preparation counter.

"Breakfast's ready," she called. "Help yourself."

He tipped one finger to his forehead in acknowledgment, grabbed a carton of juice and a breakfast bun to go, then grabbed two more savory buns, one each for Wenna and Cara, and headed to the office.

"Report from Syke on your screen," Wenna said.

Ben's own office lay beyond Wenna's, but since his door was nearly always open, it had become merely a continuation of the shared space. He wandered through and downloaded Syke's files from his main machine to his handpad, then joined the two women in his life by Wenna's desk.

"We missed three of the naturals." Ben dropped into an empty chair planted next to Wenna's desk. He read the report from last night. "Gwala stopped four if we include Cara's water world man—"

"Lev Reznik," Cara said. "He took off by himself. Looks capable enough. I told him to come here, but if he doesn't, he's his own problem."

"Agreed," Ben said. "Port security apprehended the twins at the passenger terminal, and we rescued Efra. That's seven."

"There was an elderly man, a woman in a Japanese costume, and a white-skinned man with tattoos, possibly in his early twenties," Cara frowned. "The other two were easily forgettable: middle height; middle age; middle coloring; one male, one female; no distinguishing features. I probably couldn't pick them out of a lineup."

"Syke's militia released the old man, but not the woman in the Japanese costume. She probably lost herself in the masked partygoers." Ben looked down his list. "The tattooed man is missing and one of your middling people—the woman. They might still be on-station, but chances are they've slipped through the net and we have no way of tracking them or their purchasers."

He realized he was squeezing his right hand into a fist and forced himself to relax his fingers. Yes, sure, he'd like to plant a punch in Roxburgh's face, but the man was untouchable—for now. Old school Crossways, Garrick called him and the others like him who were reluctant to give up their criminal ways.

"We should send out a bulletin to the Monitors," Ben said.

"You're on the Monitors' most wanted list."

"That doesn't mean I can't report a crime. They know where I am—where we all are—but they're not about to come and get us. Not yet, at least."

The gate comm beeped. Wenna reached across and tapped it. "Phipps. What have you got?"

"Fellow says he's Lev Reznik, and a woman from the auction told him to come here."

Cara nodded. "I did. Can you bring him through?"

It only took a few minutes before a shadow in the

doorway announced Hilde Hildstrom and the scaly man. Hilde nudged him through the door and left them all to it.

"You look like you need more water," Cara said, springing up out of her chair and filling a large cup at the water cooler. She handed it to him.

He took a fine muslin kerchief, dunked it in the cup and tied it around his throat, then drank the rest in one gulp.

"Help yourself." She indicated the cooler, and he refilled the cup twice before slowing down from gulping to sipping.

"Well, here I am," he said. "I guess you bought me fair and square. I was angling for the two women, but they weren't interested."

"You wanted to be bought?" Ben asked.

"Maybe, if it was the right buyer."

I guess there's a story here, Cara said to Ben.

"Oh, there is," Lev said. "Sorry, you didn't mean me to hear that, I suppose. That's what I do. I can hear what you're thinking to each other. I'm not a real Telepath. I can't broadcast, but if two people are in the same room, I can hear what's going on between them, even when they don't want me to."

"You're from Aqua Neriffe?" Cara asked.

"Close—well not geographically speaking. I'm from Aqua Mirek. Aqua Neriffe was the first water world. They did a slightly better job on our throat architecture when they engineered the Mirekians. The Neriffians all talk funny. Too much sibilance on their esses."

As if to prove a point, Marta Mansoro arrived in the doorway. "I heard you got sssomeone from Aqua Neriffe," she said.

"See what I mean?" Reznik said.

"Not quite, Marta, Aqua Mirek," Wenna said.

"Oh, one of those sssmartarssses. Call me if you need sssomeone to drown him for you."

"We will, don't worry."

"Sweet girl," Reznik said to Marta's retreating back. "I think she likes me."

She flipped him the finger over her shoulder.

"I like her." He laughed.

"So what are we going to do with you, Mr. Reznik," Cara said.

"I don't know, my dear. It was your money. You tell me."

"We don't keep slaves on Crossways," Ben said. "Would you like to be repatriated to Aqua Mirek?"

"Oh, I don't think so. I had a little trouble with err . . . the government."

"Which one?"

"Both of them. I was sitting in on a trade deal to make sure there was nothing underhanded going on, but the Westphalians hadn't declared my presence to the Orcadians or to their own negotiators, and I overheard something I shouldn't have, which is how I ended up shipping out in a hurry."

Cara raised an eyebrow, which Ben interpreted as: What the hell are we going to do with this one?

He shrugged in reply.

From outside, they heard the sound of a voice raised in frustration. "I know my blasted way, Hildstrom. Let me through."

"That's Dido Kennedy," Cara said.

"Uh, what now?" Ben said.

They didn't have long to wait. Kennedy hove into view dragging Efra along with her by one hand. Neither of them had changed since the previous evening, and Kennedy's bulk wobbled along in the sparkling red dress. Efra had been crying. Kennedy's face was thunderous.

"She's all yours, Benjamin." Dido used Efra's wrist as a lever and swung her through the office door. "Turns out her parents sold her to Roxburgh's goons and don't want her back in case of repercussions. There were already a couple of suspicious characters sniffing around this morning. I sat up all night with a pulse pistol in my lap, but I can't keep her safe. Recruit her into the Free Company so that I know she's going to be all right."

"Hey, Lev." Efra's face lit up at the sight of the water man. "You signing up as well?"

"Maybe. Would you like that?"

"Of course."

"She's never had much schooling, but she's a bright little thing," Kennedy said. "Picks up ideas real fast."

Ben massaged his temples with the finger and thumb of one hand. "All right, Dido, leave her here. We'll figure out something to do with her." He looked at Lev Reznik. "With both of them."

"Jussaro?" Cara said.

"Jussaro," Ben confirmed. "Sanctuary starts here."

✦ ✦ ✦

There was no point in waiting.

"I need to see Garrick," Cara told Ben. "I have an idea." She took a deep breath. "Jussaro and I have been trying to figure out what to do about Sanctuary. Obviously bringing a bunch of deserting psi-techs to Crossways would be a bad idea for all sorts of reasons. I think—Jussaro and I think— we'd be better setting up on Olyanda."

She caught the quick turn of Ben's head. It might mean them being apart for a while. She continued before she let that thought distract her.

"Will you come and see Garrick with me? I'd like your support."

"You and Jussaro have it all planned. You don't need me."

Was that hurt in his voice? Ben had always had such a tight natural shield that she'd rarely been able to tell what he was thinking if he didn't choose to share.

"If Garrick says yes—"

"I doubt he'll say no. I presume you've worked it all out with Jussaro."

"No, not entirely. I was hoping you—"

"Cara, I—oh, just go and see Garrick."

She didn't drag it out. She put in a quick call and yes, Garrick was free in about an hour. Instead of Ben, she took Jussaro and a couple of Tengue's mercs as security.

"I'm not usually invited to meet with the exalted," Jussaro said. "I'm not expected to genuflect, am I?"

She was about to take him seriously when she saw the twinkle in his eye.

"I'm sure Garrick wouldn't mind a bit of adulation. You could try going down on one knee and kissing his ring."

"If I thought it would help, I would."

But as it turned out, ring-kissing wasn't on the agenda. Garrick welcomed them into his office rather than a formal meeting room. After the pleasantries and offer of beverages, Cara settled down to business.

"It's my understanding that since you've set up a new landing site close to the platinum processing plant, the old landing site is no longer in use. We'd like to take it over."

"'We' being Sanctuary?" Garrick asked.

"Officially, a school for the naturally psi and a training college for the newly implanted. That would include any psi-techs Crossways needed us to train. Jussaro being the main instructor, of course. It would tie in with Ben training your jumpship pilots."

Garrick shook his head. "The original landing site took a pounding from the Trust fleet. Leah Nolan's report said not much was salvageable."

"If I can take a party of Free Company down to assess it, we can see what's left. All the temporary buildings are modular, so we may be able to retrieve something. The original biodegradable buildings might only be good for another year or so, but there are also the medonite panels from the storage units, the barns, and the dining hall. We can reuse them and, possibly, the original landing vehicle."

"It took a hit in the battle."

"It did, but it might not be a total write-off. Give us a week to make an assessment. It's not as if there isn't plenty of space on Olyanda for us to build Sanctuary."

Garrick nodded. "I suppose it would be a resource for us, too. What will it cost?"

"I'll let you know after the assessment. We'll need subsidizing with supplies, but we'd need that if we stayed on Crossways. Eventually Sanctuary will supply psi-techs, pilots, and Navigators to both Crossways and the Free Company, so we're not asking for something for nothing. It's an investment."

"Yes," Garrick said. "I think we can agree to support your school on a trial basis if you find the landing site on Olyanda is usable. Let's say we give it a year and then reassess it."

Cara nodded. "A year sounds fair."

She needn't spend the whole year on Olyanda, she told herself. There would still be plenty of opportunities to be with Ben.

While Jussaro continued to work his way through the Free Company personnel, unlocking their implants so the Trust couldn't find them again, Cara spent some time in the comms chair, checking out the long-range tel-net, seeing what was happening on the inhabited worlds.

She was disturbed to find that three passenger liners,

totally unconnected with each other and on different routes, had vanished in the Folds in as many weeks. It was big news on Earth and on the inner system colonies, Mars, Trappist 1E, Chenon, and Drogan's World. Altogether, over seven thousand souls had been lost.

Two freighters had also been lost, one from Cranford and the other from Prairie, but since both were independent colonies, their loss hardly made a ripple across the net. Besides, in total, the loss of life was only fourteen; the loss of seven thousand souls overwhelmed it. It mattered to the families of the fourteen, though.

Cara logged the losses in the incident file they'd been keeping ever since the encounter with the Nimbus. They had nothing to compare the losses against, but she was sure they were escalating. She logged into the station's records and set a search for ship losses over the last twenty-five years and sent the result to her handpad.

Chapter Nineteen

GATE

A TINGLE IN BEN'S MIND ANNOUNCED CARA connecting to Valois, one of Garrick's jumpship pilots who was currently shadowing the remains of the enemy fleet left over from the Battle for Crossways.

Ben had destroyed the temporary jump gate the megacorps' fleet had used to mass close to Amarelo space before the attack on Crossways. Then in the aftermath, with the station safely in Olyanda space, he'd gone back and drawn the Amarelo jump gate through behind him. It had left the combined battle fleet high and dry, since none of the ships had their own jump drives. It would take them years to journey to the nearest usable jump gate at sublight speeds.

The megacorps had tried to build a temporary jump gate, but Ben had destroyed it. Now he had a relay of observers following the fleet in case the megacorps tried to build a new jump gate.

They were building a new jump gate right now according to Valois.

"Let's go blow up a jump gate," Ben said, easing himself into the pilot's chair on *Solar Wind*'s flight deck. He grinned at Cara, already at the comms station.

"It feels like forever since we've been on a jaunt

together," she said. "Can you call it a jaunt if you're about to go and engage an enemy fleet?"

"Whatever we call it, let's make it count."

Cara opened the comm. "Crossways Control, this is *Solar Wind* requesting exit from Port 22."

"*Solar Wind*, stand by."

"Standing by."

"Crew secure." Yan Gwenn swiveled in his seat at the systems station.

They carried a small crew: himself, Cara, Yan, Dobson in engineering, Gwala—borrowed from Tengue for his weapons skills—and Ronan Wolfe in sick bay, at Cara's insistence, because this had the potential to turn very dangerous very quickly.

No change there, then.

Jake? Ben asked Cara.

Slipped away twenty minutes ago, Cara said. *He should be in position by now.*

Good.

Ben allowed himself to blink slowly. He'd had the usual sleepless night, knowing he'd soon have to contend with the Folds. At least not sleeping meant not dreaming.

"Fifteen." He'd been keeping count despite his thoughts, or perhaps because of them. Would the void dragon manifest on this trip?

"Ten," Yan said.

Cara's voice went out shipwide over the speaker system. "Eight seconds to foldspace. Six . . . five . . . four . . ."

Ben touched the jump drive controls and reached out with his mind, linking into the ship and searching for the right path to take them from Olyanda local space to Amarelo space, two AU out from the system's star—the area of space where Crossways used to be, allowing for orbital drift—the scene of the battle almost a year ago.

"Three . . . two . . . one."

With a deep breath, Ben nudged the *Solar Wind* out of reality and into the Folds.

His stomach rises up into his throat and he swallows hard. Everything slows, or else his mind is running fast. It's pitch-dark, but he can see everything clearly outlined as a negative image. The Folds are never the same twice. He daren't think about his encounter with the Nimbus. In his mind it's an appalling manifestation of nothingness, more terrifying even than the void dragons. Because he's deliberately avoiding thinking about it, he thinks about it.

"Engineering A-okay," Dobson announces over the shipboard comm, breaking his train of thought.

"Nice transition, Ben. Medical all locked down and secure." Ronan reports. "Seen anything we should know about?"

"Nothing so far," Ben says. He knows why Cara insisted Ronan should come. His journeys through foldspace have not been entirely uneventful since he first encountered the void dragons. That trip nearly killed him. Now they're attracted to him. They know him. He only wished he knew them, or at least, knew what they were, what game they were playing, and what the rules of that game were.

"Oh, here they come . . ." Cara says.

Two otter-kind swim through the bulkhead and turn lazy circles.

Hey, baby, Cara says to one of the otter-kind as it spirals around behind her and looks over her shoulder at the comms screen before doing a lazy backflip across the flight deck.

Otter-kind, Ronan. Ben connects mentally. *Do you see them?*

He lets Ronan see through his own eyes, not something he would usually allow for anyone except Cara, but Ronan is a good friend, an exceptional doctor, and has a delicate mind-touch.

*I see them. Oh . . . * Ronan's mental voice is filled with wonder.

The otter-kind nudge Ben's shoulder one after the other before departing down into the ship.

They may be coming your way, he tells Ronan.

I'll let you know if I see anything.

Most people can't see the otter-kind and the void dragons. Not even all Navigators can see them. The ability to see them is linked to the ability to navigate foldspace in a jumpship without using the gate system that connects the vast trading networks. When recruiting jumpship pilots, Ben uses their ability to see void dragons as his first criterion. It's empirical evidence that they'll be able, with training, to fly the Folds without beacons.

He's not sure which way round it is. Does the ability to see void dragons make a good jumpship pilot or does being a good jumpship pilot imbue the ability to see void dragons? Or is it something else entirely that gives a person the ability to do both?

Cara didn't used to be able to see them, but having connected with Ben and seen them through his mind, she can now see them for herself. She's not even a Navigator, so what's that all about?

There's a disturbance in the cabin pressure and a huge dragon's head pushes through the ceiling without disrupting its solidity. It looks at him, swivels its bulging eyes to take in the whole cabin, then shrinks itself down to fit and floats gently to the deck.

Cara jumps and leans back in her chair to avoid letting it touch her.

It's here, Ronan. Ben lets Ronan in on his vision, curious to see if Ronan, like Cara, will develop the ability to see them once he's been guided in the right direction.

Yan, at the systems station, doesn't see it at all and carries on monitoring the *Solar Wind*'s path through the Folds as if the void dragon's barbed tail hasn't sliced him in half as it lashes back and forth. The creature stills and settles on its haunches. Its eyes are level with Ben's.

What do you want? Ben forms words in his mind but what he transmits to the void dragon is simply *?*

The void dragon blinks and then a picture forms in Ben's mind. It's Dido Kennedy's workshop on Crossways in the underbelly of Red One. It's quite clearly the day Ben flew Crossways through the Folds to Olyanda. But the void dragon flicks past the jump drive to the scene playing out at the side of the workshop, Gen giving birth. Cara and Max in attendance. Nature is taking its course. With a final slither Max is holding his new daughter and placing her on Gen's belly. The void dragon's vision zooms in on the pink-faced, newly born infant.

That's Olivia May Marling, Ben tells it.

The void dragon asks, *?*

Baby, Ben says. *It's how we make more of our kind.*

The void dragon shakes its head. If it understood language, that would be a definite no. Ben decides to go with it.

That's not what you wanted, is it?

The void dragon shakes its head again and its expression says it's finding the lack of communication frustrating.

You and me both, buddy.

"I can see it." Ben hasn't been aware of Ronan in his mind, but now Ronan's head and shoulders appear from the access tube. "I saw the otter-things so I wondered if . . . I can! I'm seeing it myself, not only through you."

"Welcome to the club. If only we could figure out what it wants."

"I don't think there's much doubt about that," Ronan says. "It's formed some kind of attachment. It wants to see the baby."

The void dragon offers a toothy grin and departs the flight deck the same way it arrived.

"I can't see Gen ever allowing that to happen, can you?" Ben asks, wondering what would happen if it did.

"Not in a million years."

"Seven minutes, Boss." Oblivious to the presence of the void dragon, Yan calls the time since they entered the Folds.

"Strap in if you're staying," Ben tells Ronan. The medic straps into one of the two passenger seats on the flight deck.

Ben wrenches his thoughts away from void dragons and Gen's baby and the thought of them meeting. Instead, he searches for the line to Amarelo space. That's what a Navigator does—follows the tides of the universe as they ebb and flow—knows which way is up and how to get from A to B.

He can still pick up a disturbance around Amarelo. Not surprising. The aftermath of a space battle lingers in fold-space, even more than a year on. Ben finds the line, follows it, and with a wrench they pop into realspace—not exactly where Crossways used to be, but close in space terms, somewhere ahead of the convoy of battleships.

"There they are," Ben said as Yan enhanced the image on the main screen.

At sublight speeds it would take the convoy close to twenty years to reach the next nearest jump gate. Ben felt sorry for the individual crewmembers, but having the megacorps fleet depleted was an advantage they couldn't afford to lose.

"Something on the long-range scanner," Yan said. "Looks like the fleet."

"On screen," Ben said.

"Checking the open comms lines," Cara said.

Ben knew she'd be checking both transmissions and telepathic chatter between ships. "Let me know if you find anything interesting."

At the very farthest range of their scanners a knot of vessels hung motionless in space surrounding a half-built jump gate. The gate would eventually consist of two units orbiting around each other with, when operational, a blacker-than-black two-dimensional oval void in the center. The larger of the two units, the gate impeller, was almost complete.

Arranged around the embryonic gate, in a defensive pattern, were the remains of the combined fleet, vessels of varying sizes, all armed.

"That's more like it," Ben murmured.

Their first attempt at gate building had been pathetically easy to knock out. They'd begun to build in a position some two months ahead of the fleet's then current position on the principle that the farther from the scene of the battle they were, the less likely they would be spotted.

That might have worked if Ben hadn't had a relay of pilots checking on the fleet and their potential flight path. There were only two possible jump gates within reach at sublight speed. It was obvious from the fleet's course that they were heading for the Potamis Hub. Finding the half-built gate had been easy enough. Ben had given them enough warning to evacuate the workers before blowing the gate to atoms. The construction vessel, itself a jumpship, but unarmed, had made a hasty retreat.

This time they were using a different strategy. The might of the battle fleet was standing between *Solar Wind* and the target. Exactly what Ben had expected. It would take them another twenty years to reach Potamis. They were relying on the rescue gate. No one wanted to grow old on a battleship.

"Cara?"

"The chat's all pretty banal. Some general grumbling. They're not in danger of starving, but they're starting to run low on specific supplies. One young man from the Rodontee Cruiser, *Lentik*, has a craving for peanut protein paste and he's trying to set up a deal with the quartermaster of the Arquavisa flagship to trade for a case of it, but Arquavisa is driving a hard bargain." She narrowed her eyes and cocked her head to one side. "There's a high-grade Telepath on the Alphacorp ship, Tallinn, and he's making contact calls for the crew members who have families. Some of it's hard to listen to. 'Hi, honey, I'll be home in twenty years, please tell the kids I love them, and remember to dust my fossil collection.'"

"Sticking it to the megacorps is one thing," Ben said, "but I feel bad about stranding the crews out here. A couple of years ago that could have been any of us. How many times did we put our faith in the corporations to support us, you with Alphacorp, and me with the Trust?"

"I wonder how many of them would quit their posts if they had the chance," Cara said.

"Are you thinking of offering them the chance?"

"No, of course not."

Did she say that a little fast?

"Most of them were doing their jobs," Ben said. "It wasn't personal. And now they feel abandoned. I would in their place, wouldn't you? Their bosses could send jumpships to evacuate them within a few days, but the ships and equipment are worth more to the megacorps than the well-being of their crews."

"You can still hear it in their ship-to-ship chatter," Cara said. "The crews left behind felt particularly aggrieved when Eastin-Heigle abandoned their ships in favor of evacuating their crews and none of the other megacorps followed suit."

"More than they value *some* of their crews," Cara said. "There's a lingering resentment that the more powerful psitechs were recalled and transported on the Monitor ships along with the injured. The guy on the Alphacorp ship refused to go without his crewmates and said that without at least one long-range Telepath the fleet was vulnerable."

"The Arquavisa flagship has locked on," Yan said. "We're still out of effective weapons range, but they've seen us."

"The chatter's all gone, and the alarm has spread fleetwide," Cara said. "They're ready for us."

Ben saw the evacuation shuttles springing away from the gate, playing it safe no matter how good the defenses looked. Good. They weren't underestimating him, and they

were determined to have his hide this time. Ben pushed
down a few tension-butterflies fluttering in his belly.
"Gwala, are you awake?"

"I am not only awake, I'm locked onto that big Alphacorp bastard. He's presenting us with his side, trying to
tempt us in, but he's prepping a broadside."

"When he's within range, give him something to think
about."

"Affirmative."

"Hold on, everyone."

Ben blinked *Solar Wind* into foldspace, had barely half a
second to register the change, then emerged into realspace
above the Alphacorp ship. Gwala took careful aim and sent
out two torpedoes. One plowed a channel directly between
two cruisers, the other clipped the rigging from the comms
array on the bulbous nose of the Alphacorp ship.

"Good shooting." Ben was already changing course before missiles from four different ships locked on. He blinked
Solar Wind into foldspace again for long enough to lose the
lock and then reemerged below and diagonally opposite
their previous position. Gwala released two more torpedoes and destroyed two unmanned drones without so much
as a flare. Just an imagined pop and they were gone, disintegrating in silence.

Ben barrel-rolled into foldspace to avoid a torpedo, feeling the wobble of a near miss.

This time foldspace is bright orange and the void dragon is
stretched supine across the flight deck. Ben jumps and loses
a precious second.

The void dragon says, *?*

I'll try to explain next time, Ben tells it, not knowing
whether it understands anything he says.

They emerged from the Folds on the far side of the enemy
battleships, fleeing for their lives; the gate they'd come to
destroy still intact behind them.

"Yan, evasive action," Ben said.

Six ships broke the line to pursue *Solar Wind*.

"Their admiral isn't very pleased they're giving chase,"
Cara said. "He's calling them back."

"Too late."

Yan split the screen so they had a view of the six pursuit ships and the half-built gate.

"Any time now, Jake," Ben said almost to himself. "Any time now."

The Dixie Flyer popped out of foldspace in the shadow of the gate, close enough to release a couple of preprogrammed limpets. A small fire flared and died as the oxygen inside the gate impeller burned itself out in an eyeblink and an undramatic puff of an explosion marked the end of the gate.

Three ships peeled off from the pursuit of *Solar Wind*, realizing they were following a decoy, but four of the ships that had held firm to the gate fired both DEWs and hard shell torpedoes at the Dixie.

Well done, Jake. Now beat it, Cara said. *Ben will be very unhappy if you scratch the paintwork on his Dixie Flyer. He loves that little boat.*

Yeah, right. See you on the other side, Lowenbrun responded.

The Dixie Flyer winked out of sight, and seconds later Ben followed Jake into the Folds.

Chapter Twenty

ESCAPEE

BEN DOCKED *SOLAR WIND* SAFELY IN PORT 22, having stuck to the rules and emerged from foldspace slightly more than a hundred klicks from the station.

Jake? Cara sent out a questing thought.

Home safe. The Dixie doesn't have a mark on her. Going to visit with my cousin a while.

Jake's cousin Dree was his only family. Barely more than a girl, Dree had grown up in the backroom of Sally's Bar in Montego, the biggest city—though that wasn't saying much—on the planet of Vraxos, where life was cheap and sex was cheaper. Jake had brought her to Crossways on the condition that she didn't continue her old profession. She'd surprised everyone by signing up for courses at the university as soon as it had opened again after the cleanup.

"Tired?" Cara asked Ben as they walked into Blue Seven.

"Gods, yes. My body could sleep for a week, but I haven't shed the adrenaline yet, so my brain's hunting for things to do. I'll file the ship logs and then see about taking a break. It feels as though it should be midnight, but it's still mid-afternoon. What about you?"

"Jussaro's been floating some ideas about Sanctuary. He wanted to chew a few things over."

Ben made a noncommittal sound.

Her eyes softened as she gave him a quick peck on the cheek. "You should come and talk to him."

"Later, maybe, when he's not up to his ears in modifying implants. I wouldn't want to get in the way of that."

He turned toward the office, dragging his gaze away from the sway of her hips as she walked down the length of Blue Seven toward Jussaro's room.

Ben sighed. He was going to get involved in this Sanctuary thing whether he wanted to or not. Cara was invested in the idea, and he was invested in Cara. It wasn't a bad thing, of course, but he owed his first loyalty to the people of the Free Company, the ones who'd followed him out of the security that working for the Trust provided. As it turned out, they hadn't had much choice. Job security meant nothing when your boss wanted you dead because you knew too much.

The comm on Wenna's desk beeped as he passed it.

"If that's for me, I'm not here," Ben said.

"It's a call from Crossways engineers. They're requesting assistance. They're clearing some of the subsections below Red One. There's someone injured down there. Someone's injured and there's an echo of a Telepath, but she's not responding to anything they're throwing at her."

"Okay, I'm on it," he said. "Alert Ronan, too."

"You don't need to do this personally, Boss," Wenna told him.

He shrugged. "I'll go take a look."

Ben had become intimately acquainted with the nooks and crannies of Crossways Station during the days and weeks following the battle. He'd worked with the cleanup crews as one more pair of hands, on a go-anywhere-do-anything basis. More than once he came across Garrick also trying to bury the memory of the Nimbus with sweat and dust.

He didn't recall this particular part of the station. Any station had its underbelly, and Red One had been lower than that. Dido Kennedy's workshop, close to the bottom of the central spindle, had been as low as Ben had ever wanted to go, but now he was beneath that.

Four station engineers, easily identified by their green coveralls, stood in the narrow corridor as he approached. They were obviously arguing.

"What's the problem?" he asked.

They leaped apart as if caught in some mischief. He knew all their faces. Luckily, they had name flashes on their uniforms.

"Anders, didn't we work together on the Green Four rebuild?"

"Yes, Commander Benjamin."

He didn't have a rank now, but that was beside the point. "What's going on?"

Anders jerked his chin toward an access tube, beneath which were chunks of debris. "We checked this section of the station after the battle, but we didn't clear it until about six weeks ago. We left it free of rubble. This is all fresh. There's something or someone up there, and it ain't a rat. Burgess, here, tried climbing up." He indicated a young man with a cut on his forehead and a darkening bruise. "Rats don't throw rocks."

"Okay, take a break. There will be a medic along soon. Stay within hailing distance. I'll see if I can get to your not-a-rat."

He deployed his helm and face mask. "Hey, up there. I'm on my way. I'm a friend."

He thought he heard voices, but he couldn't make out any words. He wasn't even sure they were speaking Basic. How many languages could he could say friend in?

"Umngane. Ushomi. Dost. Vriend. Sadiq. Ami. Amigo. Freund. Ven. Vän. Ystävä."

He was running out of ideas. Most colonies spoke Basic, a language that had evolved from twenty-second century English, and had been an international language of the air before mankind left Earth. Some colonies favored dialects and regional Earth languages, Arabic, Hindi, Mandarin, Afrikaans and Zulu being among the most popular, but there were regional European languages, too.

Ben cycled through his repertoire of languages again and began to climb.

The tube was way too tight and not altogether safe. Dust and debris rained down on him, but not missiles—at least not deliberate ones unless the person above him was a very bad marksman.

A block of masonry supported on a broken pipe narrowed the access. There must be hundreds of corners like this left over from the battle. Obviously, nothing vital ran through here, or someone would have noticed before now. He shoved against the masonry to see how secure it was. A small landslide of rubble dusted his helm and he paused to clear his faceplate. He had a small laser cutter, but didn't want to dislodge anything big that would hit him on the way down.

"Hey!" Ronan shouted up from the corridor.

Sorry, Ben said. *Trying to clear debris blocking the tube. I can't see what's ahead, but there's someone up here. May be more than one. I can hear voices. Damn! There's a child crying.*

How many people had taken refuge here? One slip with the laser cutter and there would be one fewer to worry about.

How many? Ronan called up to him, mind-to-mind, echoing his own question.

I can't tell yet.

Ben rapped on a piece of pipe, one of several that crisscrossed the tube. It had somehow threaded itself through the ladder which had detached from the tube side. Somewhere above was a huge piece of medonite lodged in the cradle of cables and wires.

The pipe clanged. Someone was rapping in reply.

"Hello!"

Several voices answered, all yelling at once. He clanged the pipe again. "One at a time. How many of you?"

"Four." A woman's voice, speaking Basic, but heavily accented.

"Injuries?"

"Broken arm. Head."

"Same person?"

"No."

"We're coming to get you. We have a medic. Hang on."

"Where you think we gonna go?"

Ready, Ronan?

Yeah. We could use Archie Tatum's bots right now.

Will I do?

Ben looked down to see Serafin West at the bottom of the shaft, reclining in a float chair.

What are you doing here? Ben asked.

Relax, Serafin said. *I picked up news of this on the*

Free Company's backchat. I'm not getting out of this float chair, but I've brought a satchel full of bots and I'm only using my mind to control them. I've got my new lung. This is only an infection. I'm on meds. How long have these guys been trapped?

Not that long. Ronan, is Serafin about to kill himself?
Ben was torn between his need for a flotilla of bots to chew through the obstruction, and his concern for Serafin, still on sick leave after being badly injured in a scrap with Trust assassins. He had finally decided to retire with his longtime lady friend and grow cabbages on Jamundi, but a recurring lung infection had kept him on Crossways under Ronan's care.

I'll keep an eye on him, Ronan said. *Come on down. Let the bots do the work.*

Ben inched down the tube, a five-meter drop, using handholds consisting of twisted bits of ladder and some power conduit. His gloves and his buddysuit would protect him from any live current, barring a slap across his exposed face with a loose cable.

He dropped the last two meters and brushed dust and debris from his suit.

"Shit, Benjamin, you look half dead," Serafin said. "When did you last get some sleep?"

Ben shrugged. "Why do you always say that?"

"Because it's always true. Your face is gray. In fact, I've never seen a brown face quite so gray before, not while its owner was still alive, anyway."

"It's dust." Ben pulled off his gloves and wiped his face, smearing grit into one eye. "See," he said, blinking rapidly.

Serafin harrumphed. "Shall I send in the boys?"

Ben nodded. "What have you got?"

"Cutters, drill bots, some general-purpose spider bots."

"Go to it, then."

As Serafin opened the satchel and released a number of little spiderlike machines, Ronan bent over the old man and clipped on blood pressure and pulse monitors. "You can stay as long as you're not putting yourself in danger."

"I know, I know." Serafin patted Ronan's dark curls absentmindedly. "I wrote the manual on procedure while you two were still in short pants."

The spider bots scuttled up the tube and Serafin closed his eyes. "It's messy in there," he said. "How many trapped?"

"Four," Ben said. "Two of them injured."

"Why would someone go to ground in a foxhole like that?" Serafin kept his eyes closed, seeing through the eyes of his bots. "Stand away from the bottom of the tube."

A trickle of dust turned into a cascade of rubble, followed by sawed-up sections of twisted metal.

"Take a rest, Serafin," Ronan said.

"I think the boys are almost through."

"That wasn't a suggestion."

"Just a few more seconds." Serafin's eyes glazed over as he concentrated on running the team of bots.

"Have it your own way, Old Man." Ronan pressed a blast pack to the side of Serafin's neck. "This will help, but right after this, you go straight to bed."

Serafin's only reply was, "More rubble." Ceramic shards crashed down, and as the echoes died away, Ben heard someone screaming from above. He leaped for the tube, pulling himself up with what was left of the ladder's securing bolts. He dislodged more conduit and shoved his head and shoulders through a hole barely wide enough.

In a node hub, a woman crouched with a pale-faced boy who clutched his arm, obviously in pain. An elderly man lay insensible in what little space they had left. A skinny girl, no more than fifteen, held a wad of torn clothing to the old man's temple. Her face was tear-streaked, but she wasn't crying now. Blood had dried on his bald head, washed into his ear, and soaked his collar and tunic. The child looked at Ben, eyes wide.

"It's all right. I'm here to help. Let me see."

He reached for the cloth, but she pushed between him and the old man and said something in a rapid dialect that had some words of Basic, but inflections his ear couldn't catch.

"Can you translate?" Ben asked the woman.

"Her gran'pap," she said slowly, and then pointed to herself and to the old man. "Pap."

"The girl's your daughter?"

The woman shook her head and pointed to the boy. "Mine."

Not from around here. Ben told Ronan. *Some kind of

family group. Almost certainly in trouble with someone for something. They look terrified, and it's not simply because they've been trapped in here with poor air.

"It's all right." Ben raised both hands in a gesture of I-mean-no-harm and went through all his translations of friend again. The girl let him past this time. He checked the unconscious man's pulse, weak and thready, and relayed the information.

"I'm coming up," Ronan shouted.

The confines of the tube necessitated some close maneuvers, but eventually Ben helped the woman and the boy down to the corridor below where Serafin kept them company, and Ronan climbed up.

The girl wouldn't leave her grandfather.

"He's a doctor." Ben gestured to Ronan. "He'll look after your grandfather—gran'pap." *If anyone can,* he thought.

She looked at him wild-eyed and shook her head.

Oh, heck, the child had some telepathic or empathic talent. He cursed himself for being careless and put reassuring thoughts uppermost in his mind, but all she did was scowl at him.

Ronan raised one eyebrow. "A new recruit?" he asked.

Ben stared at the child. "We can't take in every waif and stray."

"No? You make a habit of it. Cara turned out all right, and Max."

Ben sighed. "Yes, they did, but there was Kitty Keely, too."

Ronan peeled the rag from the old man's head and ran a portable scanner over the wound. He pressed his lips together, while his face took on a serious expression that told Ben the man's chances of survival were slim. Ronan slapped a blast pack to the patient's neck. "That should hold him until we can get him out of here." He rocked back on his heels. "Kitty wasn't your fault. You can only help those who want to be helped."

"That thing, whatever it was out there in the depths of foldspace, was moving so slowly. I should have been able to—"

"Cara said Keely stepped into it."

Ben nodded. "One minute I was reaching out a hand and thought we were all going to make it; the next minute there was nothing to reach out to, just an oily black cloud, darker than foldspace itself, if that's possible."

"Improbable, but not impossible." Ronan scanned the old man again. "Vitals are erratic." He administered another shot. "Anything's possible in foldspace."

The sound of climbing interrupted their conversation. Ronan was right; Kitty Keely hadn't been Ben's responsibility and her loss had not been his fault. They'd saved Norton Garrick, which had to be a bonus. Garrick might not be the only person who could run this station, but right now he was the best they had.

"Where's the patient?" Max Constant's head appeared above the top of the tube and he shoved a bag marked Dockside Medical over the lip.

Ben raised an eyebrow at the tall accountant. "Are you doing paramedic duties now?"

"Whatever needs doing. Gen said I was making the place look untidy."

"Is that my spinal immobilizer?" Ronan said. "Stop wasting time and get it unpacked."

"You heard the man." Ben grabbed the bag.

The spinal immobilizer inflated around the old man, becoming a protective cocoon that enabled them to lower him gently down the tube. Ben followed with the girl, but by the time he released her to her family, Ronan was shaking his head.

As soon as the child interpreted Ronan's gesture, she began to wail and shriek, alternately beating her breast and tearing at her hair in the biggest public display of grief Ben had ever seen.

The aunt and her son crouched down, leaning against the corridor wall, and watched impassively.

Ben looked to her for help. "Can't you comfort her?"

The aunt shook her head. "It would not be proper."

"Proper?"

"Zeroun was an elder and her gran'pap. Nairi must make . . ." she searched for the word in Basic. "Must make moan for his passing to make sure his spirit does not return."

"She must have loved him very much."

"No, she hated him."

"Huh?"

"Zeroun brought her here to sell her to a casino man, Roxburgh. I am translating for them. Zeroun does not speak much Basic. Nairi, she has . . ." The aunt whirled her finger in tight circles by her temple. "The knowing of what others are feeling."

"Empathy."

"Yes, Empathy. Casino man cannot employ dealers with implants, but no one can prevent him from employing naturals. He trains them from a young age. When we took Nairi to the casino, there was a woman there in a . . ." She waved her hands in front of her to show she meant some kind of costume or dress, and then pulled the corner of her eyes to change her eye shape.

"Kimono," Ben said. "Cara said there was a woman in a kimono."

"Yes, kimono. Woman told Zeroun that Roxburgh planned to train little one as a whore, as well as a croupier, to earn back her price. Zeroun did not believe her. Roxburgh's man said Nairi would be important for her mind. Would not be sold like the others. Would not be used for pleasure. That is a big taboo in our culture."

"How old is she? Fifteen? That's a big taboo in most cultures."

"Woman made a scene. Gave us chance to get away. We ran. Zeroun followed, and then . . . one of Roxburgh's thugs." She mimed being hit on the head.

"I can see that would spoil your day."

"Spoiled his day, bigtime. Four of us. But Zeroun hurt. My boy, too. Nairi did the right thing. Only protecting herself."

"Will you take Nairi home?"

She shook her head. "Nairi cannot go home. Empathy also is big taboo. And Roxburgh has an agent who sends him news of . . ." She whirled the finger again. "Talents."

"So Roxburgh has taken others from your world?"

"And will do again. His auctions are big business. Not always held here. Held all over. Place announced at last minute. Buyers come from far and near."

She glanced at the chrono showing on Ben's handpad. "What time did he die?"

Ben glanced at his handpad. "Four oh eight."

The woman clapped her hands and said something in a

language Ben didn't follow. The result was instant. The child stopped weeping and wailing and looked up, her eyes still a little wild and her hair mussed. She nodded.

"It's done," Nairi said in heavily accented Basic. "The bastard won't be coming back to haunt me."

Chapter Twenty-One

MONSTER

"THE GIRL'S A NATURAL EMPATH, THE ONE Roxburgh was going to keep for himself after the auction, but she escaped," Ben said as he dropped his buddy-suit on the chair and slid into bed beside Cara. "Apparently, Roxburgh's been holding auctions all over the galaxy, always somewhere different. Garrick's going to have to deal with him, and I think the showdown is coming soon."

"What about the child?"

"I think she might be one for your Sanctuary."

Cara felt the heat radiating from his body. "It's not mine."

"No?"

"It's Jussaro's."

"You've no involvement?"

"I didn't say that."

Ben sat up. "I'm aware I dragged you into all this . . . Crossways . . . the Free Company."

"You didn't drag me anywhere I didn't want to go. But I think we could do more."

"More?"

"Light." She sat up and turned to face him. "We have an opportunity. While the platinum lasts on Olyanda, the Free

Company is rich. I know we take on jobs when they come our way, but we don't need the income to balance the books."

"There's a team out right now settling a new independent colony on Yara on behalf of Cotille Colony."

"And I'm sure they'll do a great job because they're good at what they do."

"So what's the problem?"

"It's not a problem. It's an opportunity. We have a core of free psi-techs here, but throughout the galaxy there are thousands of psi-techs tied to the megacorps. Sure, some of them are happy in what they do, but others need to find a way out. We could be their way out."

"You want to develop Sanctuary into what it once was?"

"Sanctuary is an idea; it's not a physical place. To house everything together would make it too vulnerable. It needs to be a network of cells. That's what it always was. Zandra Hartwell gave Jussaro the key to the network, and she's part of it herself."

"That paints a big target on Jussaro's back. The megacorps might send another fleet after Crossways. I don't want another attack on my conscience."

"The only people to blame for the combined fleet attacking Crossways are the ones who ordered it, and you know who was probably behind the whole thing."

"Crowder."

"Your good old friend."

"I should have killed him when I had the chance."

"You thought you had."

"That was the second time. The first time I let him live."

"It's not in you to kill in cold blood."

"I think it's a talent I may be fostering, at least where Crowder's concerned."

Cara pulled Ben to her and ran her hand across his shoulders, feeling his muscles tighten. "Sit still."

She knelt over him and began kneading his neck and shoulder muscles using slow, even strokes with the palms of her hands. She straddled his prone body and gently but firmly worked her way down his back. There was the old burn scar, hardly noticeable now after treatment with stem cell spray. His skin felt like silk beneath her hands. She massaged and then slowly rubbed the heels of her hands up either side of his spine and out to the tips of his shoulders in broad, soothing strokes.

"All right, mister, turn over."

But he was already asleep. Biting her lip, she snuggled down beside him.

◆ ◆ ◆

Max Constant hadn't had an implant when he'd met Gen Marling, but he'd always been able to tell what she was thinking. Well, he knew what she was thinking now, implant or not. The mug crashed against the wall, its contents decorating the bland, beige medonite surface with an interesting splatter pattern as he ducked toward the door.

Hush, sweetheart. Daddy didn't mean it. Gen's thought echoed in his head even though it wasn't meant for him.

But he had meant it. He'd meant every damn word.

Gen hugged the monster to her breast. Liv's angry screams turned to snuffles. Max recognized the look on Gen's face. Love.

Well, yes, he loved the child, too, didn't he? He was her father, after all. Having grown up in a series of foster homes for difficult kids, Max was determined his daughter would grow up in a happy and harmonious family.

But she was making it difficult.

How could something so sweet turn so sour in such a short time? The kid was barely fifteen months old and already she ruled everything. At first it had been an endless round of food, nappies, cuddles, sleep. Max had been okay with that. If he'd harbored a few reservations about Gen's obsessive relationship with the baby, he'd shrugged them off. It was natural for a new father to feel suddenly excluded from the mother-child bond. The answer was to do some father-child bonding, to take an active interest. Max could spoon mush into her hungry mouth, and he could change nappies and do the walking-round-jiggling-baby-to-sleep thing while Gen snatched a few hours of real rest.

So he'd tried that, and for a while it had worked.

When had it changed?

Gen had taken Liv down to the surface of Olyanda while the station was in danger of breaking apart. Though Max had visited, they'd managed very well without him. Too well. Max had noticed a difference when they arrived home.

Then one day the little monster had pushed him away *with her mind*.

He'd never felt such an icy chill run down his spine. It felt like the ultimate betrayal. His own flesh and blood, the child he'd anticipated for so long, had rejected him. Thoroughly.

She wanted Mom and only Mom would do.

Not only that, but she'd weaseled her way inside Gen's head, and now Gen had rejected him, too, preferring to lavish all her attention on the monster.

It was perfectly natural, he told himself again. That's the way it was with hormones. It's how the human race survived. The mothering instinct was as natural as . . . as . . . as his daughter was unnatural.

Better make himself useful, since it was obvious his own family had no need of him whatsoever. He headed for the office.

Despite what many people thought, number crunching wasn't boring. Machines took care of the basics. It was Max's job to keep intelligent control, to look for the right opportunities to maximize profit and make short-term investments so their cash was actively working for them. Since their share of the platinum profits had begun to trickle, and then roll in, keeping a tight rein on it all was even more important.

Max needed someone reliable he could train up and leave in charge of the office on the occasions when he needed to be elsewhere. He'd finally settled on Billy Naseby, a psi-Finder paralyzed from the waist down in the Battle for Crossways. His mechanical aids were good, but Ronan, their chief medic, had advised a desk job. Billy had a sharp mind and a quick wit. Max could use someone like that.

Ronan was Max's third appointment of the day, but this time it wasn't a business meeting. He rolled up at Ronan and Jon Moon's apartment, a few units away from where Ben and Cara lived.

It was noticeable that despite all the apartments starting off the same, they quickly took on the character of their occupants. His and Gen's was messy and homely, full of baby toys lying around on a series of colorful rugs. Cara and Ben's was comfortable, but it was easy to see they were both used to moving around. Their personal touches, images in foldaway frames, were easily portable, quick to grab and pack.

Ronan and Jon's apartment was minimalist, almost clinical, all clean lines, sharp corners, and shiny surfaces. Even so, Ronan had no problem making beer-rings as he slapped a couple of cold ones on the low table where they gathered condensation and began to drip. Max wondered whether Ronan was the one who liked everything in its place, or Jon. Since Jon had taken himself off to a grapple game at the newly recommissioned stadium, it was hard to tell.

"Cheers, Doc." Max picked up a beer, popped the top with his thumb and took a swig from the neck of the bottle. The brew was flavorful, but not very alcoholic. Max concentrated on it, not speaking until he'd drunk most of the contents.

"You wanted to talk to me," Ronan said.

"About Gen and Liv."

"Things not going well?"

It may have been Max's expression, but Ronan levered himself off the sofa and, without asking, took a bottle and two glasses from the cupboard. He splashed whisky into the bottom of both glasses.

"Is it normal, Doc?"

Max gulped the amber liquid and almost choked on it. Ronan patted him on the back and refilled his glass.

"Slower this time, or I'll be sending you home to your wife bladdered. Is what normal?"

"Olivia. Gen's not expecting me back." Max slumped, elbows on his knees. "She's made it quite clear she doesn't want me hanging around her and the monster."

"Max—"

"Don't call my daughter a monster? Is that what you're going to say?"

"She's hardly a monster."

"What would you call her, Doc? She's a little tyrant— and already developing telepathy."

Ronan sighed. "To my knowledge there has never been a baby born in foldspace before."

"With a void dragon looking on." Max hiccupped and stared at the liquid in his glass. "I know. I know."

"Exactly."

"So what does that mean?"

Ronan shrugged.

"Damn it! You don't know, do you? You don't know whether she's normal or not."

"It means we do our best to adapt and learn." Ronan pointed at the glass. "Sip it."

Max did, then looked suspiciously at the glass. "Is this the best you can do?"

"In this mood, you wouldn't appreciate the good stuff. Besides, Jon heard you were coming and hid the best bottle before he went out."

"See, Doc, you and Jon . . . well . . . you're not likely to be having a family any time soon, are you? You know what I'm talking about medically, but you're not a parent, so — "

"No, I'm not a parent. Though Jon and I have talked about it and, well, maybe, one day . . . when the space station isn't disintegrating around our ears and we can offer a kid a stable life, we might find a nice surrogate mom, and have a three-parent child. I'd like kids. We'd both like kids. Thing is, Max, I know being a parent isn't easy, and new fathers sometimes find the adjustment difficult. They suddenly have to share their loved one with another person, one whose demands come before their own — "

"It's not that. I was ready for that. I wanted this baby as much as Gen did. But I didn't expect . . . the mental thing. I expected Gen to be totally absorbed." He took a deep breath. "I didn't expect the kid to reject me."

Ronan frowned. "Reject you how?"

"With her mind, Doc. She pushes me away."

"Have you had your implant checked? You're a strong Finder, but I didn't think you registered on the empathy scale. Even if you did, you shouldn't be picking up emotions from a toddler."

"I'm not picking up emotions. It's not like that. She's sending them. Loud and clear. You can't hear anything?"

Ronan shook his head. "I'm as good an Empath as you're going to find on this station, except perhaps for Jussaro. I should be picking up emotions from her if anyone should."

"And?"

"Well, as her doctor, I've picked up nothing except — "

"Except?"

Ronan shook his head. "Actually, nothing. I've picked up nothing at all."

"There! That's what I mean. Is that normal? You can pick up emotions even from deadheads. Is it likely you'd pick up nothing at all from an unguarded baby? Wouldn't you get—say—contentment or hunger or who-are-you-you're-not-my-mom kind of feelings?"

"Well, sometimes babies give off those feelings."

"Sometimes?"

"Okay, often."

"But never Liv?"

Ronan pressed his lips together.

"See, Doc, that's what I mean. She's blocking you."

"She's too young, Max. How can she—"

"Foldspace. Void dragon. Mental powers. How normal does that sound to you?"

Ronan took a sip from his own glass and grimaced. "You're right, this stuff is foul." He went into the adjoining bedroom and retrieved a small bottle, emptied both glasses, and refilled them. "Try this."

Max sipped. The golden liquid trickled down his throat, this time without choking him. "Better."

"Yeah." Ronan sipped from his own glass. "Maybe ... maybe we could get Jussaro to take a look at Liv."

"It's a step in the right direction."

◆ ◆ ◆

Garrick was at his desk. This wasn't unusual. Garrick was married to his desk lately. Mona kept after him to delegate and he would—when he felt there was someone capable to delegate to. He'd had high hopes for Benjamin. He would have drafted him in a heartbeat, but Benjamin would never leave the Free Company. Besides, the Free Company was an excellent resource in itself. Benjamin always went above and beyond.

Garrick's administrative staff had expanded beyond the capacity of his offices in the Mansion House basement and now occupied the upper floors of the block on the corner of the square, opposite Hub Park. Estelle Cray, once his secretary, had become his senior administrator. Captain Syke's militia occupied the lower two floors. Syke had so far resisted relegation to the role of desk jockey in favor of taking an active role in policing the station.

The circulating air felt cool on Garrick's face and forearms. He'd rolled up his shirtsleeves sometime earlier. Now he tugged them down again and reached for his jacket, which he'd thrown over one of the two visitor chairs. As he shrugged into it, his comm began to bleep.

It was a message from Akiko Yamada.

Garrick blinked rapidly, smoothed down his jacket as if she could see it, slid into his chair and hit receive.

Yamada's head and shoulders appeared on his screen.

"Mr. Garrick, greetings." She flattened her palms together and inclined her head politely. "It is Alphacorp's desire to lay old business to rest and discuss the possibility of new business. To that end, I would like to arrange a meeting on neutral territory to discuss the possibility of Crossways providing Alphacorp with jump drives suitable for retrofitting into ships of our courier and small freighter classes. Part of any such agreement might include the retrieval of our thirteen ships and their crew currently stranded in Amarelo space—all in exchange for suitable remuneration and a non-aggression pact between Alphacorp and Crossways. I hope we can work together. I await your reply."

Garrick had to hand it to the woman; she had nerve. Fifteen months ago, her ships had been trying to pound Crossways into surrender. He knew it was as much about the platinum on Olyanda as it was about old grievances against Crossways. Now she was looking for a deal. She'd struck a good tone, though. She'd found the right balance between ingratiating and overconfident.

He watched the message again. The time code showed it had been prerecorded and sent in a data packet via the jump gate system. It had taken thirteen days to reach him, which meant she'd sent it soon after Benjamin destroyed the most recent attempt at rebuilding a jump gate in Amarelo space. Coincidence? He thought not.

He tried to look beneath the offer. What did she want? Was it what it looked like on the surface? She must have her research and development division working around the clock to develop their own compact jump drives. It was only a matter of time before they did. Garrick was under no illusions. Kennedy had been the first past the post, but it wasn't a one-horse race. Crossways had a head start on the megacorps for now, but for how long?

Should he sell Kennedy's jump drive to Alphacorp? Once they had a working prototype, they could reverse-engineer it and produce their own. On the one hand, he didn't want Crossways to lose the advantage; on the other hand, if it was only a matter of time before it happened anyway, Crossways, and Kennedy, herself, should get something out of it.

He resisted the urge to reply immediately. This wasn't a decision he could make alone. He might be the titular head of Crossways, but he needed wise counsel on this: Mona, Ben, and Cara, for starters, plus Oleg Staple and Leah Nolan who were responsible, between them, for Olyanda's safety and the platinum production. If those five were his inner cabinet, he also needed the best expert he could find on economic networks and someone who could take apart Alphacorp's last published accounts and maybe also crack their systems to get a true picture of their current state.

And, if they were going to seriously talk about a legitimate business deal, Garrick needed to clean his own house and get it in order. The likes of Roxburgh would have to go.

Then there was only one more problem. She'd asked for a meeting somewhere neutral. There was no way Garrick was going anywhere that involved flying through the Folds. She would have to come here.

Would she be willing to do that?

And if he was willing to sell the jump drive plans, what could he get out of her in return? If she agreed to a nonaggression pact, could he rely on it to hold?

Chapter Twenty-Two

SMACKDOWN

THE WOMAN IN THE JAPANESE KIMONO, MISSing since the night of the auction, was missing no longer. Her frosted body, still in the kimono, bumped gently against the outside of the clear observation dome, tied on a short tether. Her mode of death obvious by the spike thrust through her left eye, deep into her brain, pinning to her face a flimsy with a familiar casino logo on it. The message was explicit: don't mess with Roxburgh.

"It's time," Garrick said, a soft catch in his throat as he and Ben stood looking up at the woman. A squad of militia had cleared the viewing deck of gawkers, and Syke had sent a crew to retrieve the body.

"Roxburgh," Ben said.

"Before someone gets hurt."

"Someone's already been hurt." Ben looked up. A space-suited crew was approaching the corpse in slow-mo.

Garrick nodded. "Before someone else gets hurt, a lot of someones."

"If you're going to go after Roxburgh, it has to be permanent. You can't leave him free to take another swing at you."

"I'm aware of that."

"You need to take out his captains as well, or one will fill the vacuum."

"Yes."

"It'll take some planning."

"That's why I called you," Garrick said. "It would be simplest if he were to die resisting arrest, I can't deny that, but if we can take him and his henchmen alive, they'll get due process."

"And then you'll execute him."

"Legally."

Capital punishment, banned for centuries on Earth, was sometimes the expedient way of dealing with major criminals out in the far reaches of space where the Monitors were stretched thin and there was no access to prison planets. At least with Empaths around to confirm guilt, there was little chance of sentencing an innocent.

"And what happens if you can't take him?" Ben gestured upward to where the team had now untethered Kimono Woman and manipulated her into a body bag. "You realize he's intending to provoke you. He'll be expecting you and he'll be ready to retaliate."

"I realize. There are risks." He raised one eyebrow. "I find the older I get, the fewer risks I want to take, but this time I don't have a choice. Let's do what we can to minimize them."

Four hours later, Ben emerged from the Mansion House with plans buzzing around in his brain. He found Cara in the comms chair back at Blue Seven, tucked away in the cubicle that offered isolation, though more often than not, Cara left the door open to Wenna's office, not minding the background noise.

"You're going after Roxburgh," she said as he leaned against the doorframe. It wasn't even a question.

"Garrick is."

"And you're going with him."

"We have to hit all his key operatives at once."

"Right now, when he's ready for you?"

"No, we're going to let him stew for a few days at peak readiness until his people are jittery. In the meantime, Garrick's going to look ineffectual to throw him off balance. Can you monitor the station chat?"

"Of course."

"And do we have a Finder who's keyed into Roxburgh? We need to know where he is, now and for the next few days."

"Better give Max a few credit chips and see how long it takes him to lose them at the gaming tables. Roxburgh tends to keep a close eye on his business. Max can tag him mentally."

"Good idea."

Ben began to handpick a team from the Free Company and brief them.

In the meantime, Garrick issued several public notices relating to a reward for information leading to the killer of the unidentified victim.

Four days later Garrick's office issued another notice to say they had a suspect in custody.

On the eighth day, early in the morning, Garrick made his move.

For the past five days, Roxburgh Heights had experienced several inconvenient power outages, most for a matter of minutes, but one lasted a couple of hours. Between outages, the power supply had flickered ominously.

Roxburgh had made no representations to Garrick's office personally. Instead he'd sent Ilsa Marquat, his highly efficient personal assistant, a woman who looked as though she could crack walnuts between the cheeks of her arse.

Cara had picked up some gossip she'd passed on to Ben. Roxburgh had not been happy with the answer that the power supply problem was his own fault for not allowing access for replacement cables. Miss Marquat was stuck between Garrick's office and Roxburgh's wrath, and had grumbled within the hearing of one of the croupiers. The news had spread.

To appease Roxburgh, Garrick had sent two engineers who claimed to have fixed the problem, while rigging the emergency power to fail after two minutes.

Roxburgh Heights wasn't Garrick's only target. Roxburgh had operations all over the station: his own private port, Port 46, where he kept a small fleet of vessels he preferred to call free traders; a warehouse kept under permanent lockdown in Brown Eight; five brothels scattered around the hub on different levels, and two smaller casinos, one in Green Four and another on the Saturn Ring. The Green Four casino doubled as a strip joint and venue for barely legal cage fights.

Ben, Cara, and a team of twenty, all buddysuited and armed to the teeth, were ready to take Roxburgh Heights where, according to Max, Roxburgh himself was holed up. He'd been there since Kimono Woman had been discovered. Even on a station the size of Crossways, there was nowhere sensible to run to. Not that Roxburgh had any intention of running. His intention had been to provoke Garrick into a confrontation and to force him to back down, giving Roxburgh the kind of free hand he'd always enjoyed. His casino was more than a place of business—it was a fortress.

Syke had smaller teams of uniformed militia heading for each brothel with a close-down order, and he led a larger team to the casino in Green Four. Tengue's target was Port 46 while Gwala's team hit the warehouse. Mother Ramona had taken a shuttle to the Saturn Ring in the early hours of the morning. She knew the manager of Roxburgh's casino there and believed there would be no trouble once Roxburgh himself was safely confined.

Garrick turned up at Blue Seven as Ben and Cara were getting ready to depart. "I'm coming with you."

Ben thought about trying to dissuade him but dismissed the idea. The determination on Garrick's face was plain. Ben had not been around when Garrick usurped Chaliss' place as head of Crossways in what had been—in every sense of the word—a hostile takeover, but it had obviously been a successful action. He should be able to take care of himself.

"You'll need a communicator," Ben said. "Everyone else on this trip is a psi-tech of one sort or another."

"And that means you'll all be stuck with communicators as well. Sorry."

"Don't be. I can appreciate you need to be there. Buddy-suit fully armored? Weapons?"

"Yes, and yes," Garrick said. "And I know how to use them."

"I'm sure you do. But do me a favor and hang back, okay? You're not a gang boss on the make now. The head of Crossways would be difficult to replace."

"Are you going to stand there all day lecturing me?"

Ben smiled. "No, that's all I'm saying."

Cara handed Garrick an earpiece and activated the channel in her helm. "Testing."

Garrick nodded. "Let's go get the bastard."

✦ ✦ ✦

Stay with Garrick, Ben told Cara. *I don't want any accidents because he's not part of the psi-tech gestalt.*

I will.

She hadn't intended to hang back, but appreciated that someone had to, and she could hold open the gestalt as well from the rear as from the front.

"Do we know whether Roxburgh is at home to callers?" Garrick asked as they piled into the tub cabs specially fitted with priority transmitters that automatically pushed everything else out of their way, like the ambulance cabs and Syke's militia transports.

"Max is our best Finder. If he says Roxburgh is in the casino, then he is."

Garrick scanned all the figures in buddysuits, helms, and faceplates. "Where's Max?"

"Having an early morning coffee inside Hot'n'Sweet, across the square from the casino. He doesn't need to be in the melee to pinpoint Roxburgh for us and, frankly, he's not had the extensive training these guys have had. We've stationed six more people in there, and in the pie shop next door. They're watching the front door while we go in at the back. Obviously, we don't want bystanders involved, but if there's a general exodus from the casino, we need to detain everyone in case some of Roxburgh's lynchpin operatives make a break that way."

"It should be quiet this early in the morning."

"We hope so."

The tubs split up. Cara, Garrick, and six psi-techs headed up to the service elevator three levels above the main floor of the casino.

They waited for the call from the Psi-Mech dealing with the power supply.

"Get ready," Cara told Garrick. "Power's out in three, two, one. Go."

The power throughout Roxburgh's establishment was down, though the corridor lighting was still on.

Cara hadn't expected to be back so soon, but at least she had a good memory of the area where the service elevator shaft ended up. There were stairs as well which, of course, they took, knowing the camera eyes were off briefly. They had thirty seconds to get to the bottom of the stairwell, using night-vision goggles. They ran in behind six buddysuited figures led by Alexei Kronenburg, Telepath and combat veteran. They pelted down the steps, acutely aware of the time. Kronenburg's wingman shattered the camera eye at the bottom of the stairwell with a spider bot. When the emergency power kicked in, that eye would be out, as would the eye where the other group, led by Ben, had entered.

Right on cue the emergency power came on. Two minutes. Cara counted down. She could hear Garrick breathing softly beside her, but no one else made a sound.

Exactly two minutes later the emergency power flickered and died. They moved out smartly, heading for the main floor of the casino. Ben's team, she knew, would be looking for Roxburgh himself. Max said he was in his suite, so that was the first place they'd hit. No doubt there would be personal guards there, but they didn't know how many or what capability they had. Surprise was their best weapon.

Breaking out on to the casino floor and spreading out, Kronenburg activated his microphone. "Stay where you are and no one gets hurt."

A couple of people, outlined as shadows in the night-vision goggles, were close enough to make a break for the door. There was a staccato burst of fire, well above their heads, which stopped them in their tracks.

"I hope the rest of you have more sense," Kronenburg said. "Everyone on the floor, face down. NOW!"

His words had the desired effect, but there was movement behind one of the banks of chance machines. Someone made a run for it. Four figures appeared in the main entrance. Shots cracked out and the figures collapsed to the floor.

"Stunners." Cara subvocalized to Garrick, repeating what everyone knew through the gestalt.

Another figure appeared from behind the bank of machines, running low in the opposite direction. He carried a weapon and was bringing it to bear as he ran. A single shot rang out.

Garrick.

"Not a stunner," he said.

Cara knew via the gestalt that Ben's team had made its move at the same time as Kronenburg had burst into the casino. There was the sound of shooting, some of it from the Free Company, some toward.

Mentally connected to the gestalt, Cara felt the punch as Ben's suit deflected a shot which grazed his ribs, but she knew the shot hadn't penetrated. Jon Moon fell, tripped in the dark. The night-vision goggles weren't perfect. She could feel him scrambling to his feet again and Ben pushing him down as one of Roxburgh's goons took a shot. It whistled above both their heads.

She had the impression of light as they burst into Roxburgh's apartment, which must have been on a different emergency power supply. The brightness was temporarily blinding. Ben switched off his lenses. In the middle of the floor Roxburgh stood, unruffled. Sitting on a chair in front of him was Mother Ramona, hands bound behind the chair, her figure swathed in a thick vest with a single wire poking out above her heart.

Roxburgh smiled, but it didn't reach his eyes. He held a tiny controller in front of him, his thumb pressed down on it. Ben recognized it immediately. It was a fail-deadly. If Roxburgh's thumb pressure was released, the bomb would activate.

"Gentlemen, I'm so glad you could call," Roxburgh said. "I ask you not to make any sudden moves. This good lady's life depends upon it, and your own also."

"No!" Cara gasped and drew Garrick to one side. "I thought Mother Ramona was going to the Saturn Ring."

"She left early this morning."

"Roxburgh's got her. Come on."

They backed out of the casino. One of the other buddy-suited figures followed them out. *Can I help?*

Archie. Is there anything in your bag of tricks that can diffuse a body bomb?

I can try. He reached into his bag and took out a spider bot no bigger than his thumbnail.

On our way, Ben.

Thank goodness Roxburgh didn't have an implant. But Mother Ramona did—at least she had a receiving implant.

She needed a Telepath to link her into any communication, but her personal Telepath, Ully, was also missing—and it was quite likely they'd been traveling together. Cara liked Ully, a powerful mind in a frail body. She hoped the old lady wasn't hurt, or worse.

They bounded up a flight of stairs, Cara explaining the situation to Garrick as they ran. At the head of the corridor leading to Roxburgh's quarters there was a body slumped as if pointing the way. Cara signaled for quiet. They stole across the remaining distance and slipped silently inside the anteroom where four more bodies lay sprawled in death. Archie let the spider bot go and sank down next to one of the bodies, eyes closed, subsumed into the bot's progress. Defusing a bomb was going to be tricky.

Cara reached for Mother Ramona. *Are you okay?*

If you call being tied to a chair with a bomb strapped round my torso okay, then I'm fine. Not injured, anyway.

Ully?

I don't know. If the bastard's hurt her . . .

Don't twitch when a spider bot climbs up your leg and under your vest.

As if. You haven't got a Black Widow or something venomous for my friend here?

One thing at a time. Garrick's with me.

Tell him not to do anything heroic.

I'll make sure he doesn't.

Ben had followed the conversation. As ordered, he'd put the gun in his hands down on the ground, but Cara knew it wasn't his only weapon. He carried at least one more gun, probably a stunner, and a pair of knives, each in a quick release harness, one on his left breast and another on his left sleeve. The rest of the team had followed suit with their own weapons. Jon Moon, who'd been behind the rest, had managed to roll to one side while still in the anteroom and was out of sight of Roxburgh, fully armed. He crouched on the opposite side of the doorway to Cara, Garrick, and Archie. They exchanged nods.

Archie looked up.

What's the matter? Cara asked. *Can't you defuse it?*

It's linked to another device.

Oh, shit! Ben's thought echoed her own so closely that Cara didn't know which one came first.

What kind of device and where?

Big, and I don't know. I guess Roxburgh knows he won't stand a chance once he presses the trigger on Mother Ramona, so if this doesn't work, he either plans to go out in style, or he hopes to get away in the aftermath. I suspect the bomb's somewhere vital and likely to rip the guts out of Crossways and blow a hole into space.

So we need to defuse the second device first, Ben said.

That's about it.

We need every Finder, now. And every Psi-Mech and ordnance expert we can muster.

They didn't need to be right here, of course. With a station the size of Crossways, they'd never get here in time to be useful, so what they needed was an accurate vision of what to search for.

"Let's talk about this, Roxburgh." Ben began stalling for time.

Cara quickly updated everyone and collated news from the other teams. The smaller casinos, the brothels, and the private dock were under control. The warehouse in Brown Eight had a small defense squad, and they'd settled in for a siege. Gwala was trying to reason with them rather than blow the doors and go in hard. The warehouse itself was in the oldest section of the station, in what had once been the primary ring before the additional outer rings had dwarfed it.

"You don't suppose he'd build a bomb in his own warehouse, do you?" she whispered to Garrick, pulling him down to sit next to her.

"The bastard's mad enough, especially if he had an escape vessel moored on the opposite side of the station."

What do you need? Max appeared in the doorway and hunkered down on the other side of Archie.

To find this. Archie shared what his spider bot had found in the innards of Mother Ramona's vest.

Max mouthed, "Oh shit," without making a sound.

By this time a squad of Finders had joined the gestalt. Max shared the image Archie had put into his head. It wasn't a picture—they didn't have a visual—but it was an idea expanded from the body bomb. Cara felt herself sucked along with the hive-mind, and though she wasn't a Finder, she experienced what they experienced through the link. She kept Ben out of it. She could sense he was bringing all his negotiation skills to the fore as he tried to talk Roxburgh down.

She caught part of a phrase, "Didn't think he'd have the balls to do it ..." and a harsh laugh. It showed Roxburgh had seriously underestimated Garrick. She wondered when he realized Garrick was about to make a move. Probably Mother Ramona heading out for the Saturn Ring had alerted him. The bastard probably had someone from Crossways Control in his pocket. If they all lived through this, they could find out who later.

Max stiffened beside Cara and his palm landed on her thigh—arm rigid.

Got something?

Brown Eight. There's something against the outer skin of the ring.

Brown Eight, she relayed to everyone. Roxburgh had planted the device in his own warehouse.

Gwala and Hilde and their team were currently laying siege. Gwala had a receiving implant, but Hilde was easier to communicate with, being a full Telepath, if not long-range.

Hilde, did you get that? Cara asked.

Yes, got it. No blasting the doors open. Going to have to do it the hard way and talk the bastards out. I guess they don't know they're sitting on a bomb. That gives us bargaining power.

While Ben tried to delay Roxburgh, Hilde and Gwala tried to talk sense into the small crew holed up in the warehouse. Cara could only wait. *Get out of here, Max,* she said. *We're armored. If that bomb goes off and you're in casual clothes, Gen will never forgive us if we get you killed.*

Right now she might thank you for it. He levered himself up. *Okay, okay, I'm going.*

You've done your bit. Cara might have time to quiz him about the odd remark later, but it was likely he and Gen had simply had a tiff, something which would soon blow over.

The minutes stretched while everyone did their jobs to the best of their ability. How long could Ben string out the confrontation with Roxburgh? He had to make it appear as if the negotiation had plenty of scope. Roxburgh mustn't feel as though he was out of choices.

How are you doing? Cara asked Hilde.

Explaining some of the facts of life and death to the guys in the warehouse. Trying to tell them that taking a bomb in the guts is above their pay grade.

And?

I think we're getting through. At least, they've gone looking for the device to see if what we're telling them is true.

Cara began counting. She felt as if she should have reached a thousand already, but it was only a hundred and fifty-four.

Warehouse door's opening. They're coming out, Hilde said. *Manny's gone bomb hunting . . . Easy when you know where to look.*

Have you got someone to—

Defuse it? Yeah, Walker's here. He's the best we've got. Stand by. You'll know if he gets it wrong.

One minute stretched to two—two of the longest minutes in Cara's life. Ben was still trying to reason with Roxburgh who insisted that Garrick present himself personally, on the count of three. She felt Garrick stiffen against her.

"No heroics. Ben's got this."

"One."

Garrick pulled free of her warning hand and stood up.

"Two."

Cara leaped to her feet beside him. She grabbed his hand. He dragged her into the doorway, which had not been her intent.

"Ah, Garrick," Roxburgh said. "Late to the party, but now you're here, we can get started."

"Mona."

Done. Bomb defused and safe, Hilde said.

"Garrick, damn it. Get down," Mother Ramona shrieked.

My turn, Archie said.

Ben stepped sideways in front of Garrick as Cara pushed him down from behind.

"Two for the price of one," Roxburgh said. He jerked Mother Ramona to her feet, pushed her toward Garrick, and took his finger off the switch.

There was a click. Mother Ramona fell to her knees.

Garrick drew his pistol and fired between Ben's ankles. A bolt of energy hit Roxburgh under the chin and blew off the top of his head at the same time as Ben's thrown knife hit his throat.

Mother Ramona slapped the top of her explosive vest and came up with a tiny spider bot cradled in the palm of her hand.

Chapter Twenty-Three

AFTERMATH

WITH ROXBURGH DEAD AND HIS CAPTAINS held securely, his organization collapsed in on itself. Garrick took a message from Cooper who ran Roxburgh's casino on the Saturn Ring. He wandered into the bedroom, where Mona was fresh out of the shower and drying her hair.

"Cooper is more than happy to keep his position as manager and pay his profits, as taxes, to Crossways."

"Smug isn't a good look on you, Garrick." Mona hadn't quite forgiven him for almost getting her killed.

"I rock the smug look, especially tonight." He grinned at her as he stripped off his shirt and dropped it on the floor. "With Roxburgh on the slab, and his six heavies in the slammer, I have a right to be smug. So do you."

"I'm still shaking inside, and I can't stop thinking about Ully. I'll never sleep."

"Benjamin's Finders are looking for Ully. They'll let us know as soon as—"

"I know, but . . ."

He thought about offering her a shot of detanine, but it would only start another row between them. He glanced at the nightstand where a pack of four bulbs sat calling to him silently. He hadn't taken a shot yet. If Mona would come to him, he wouldn't. Not tonight. He wasn't in the drug's grasp. He could leave it alone whenever he wanted to. It just so happened he hadn't wanted to until now.

Sex and smugness would surely give him a good night's sleep tonight—the sleep of the victorious.

Mona tutted at him and bent to retrieve his shirt. As she came upright, he stepped up and took it from her, grasping her slim waist and pulling her in close. Her hair smelled of freesia blossom and was still a little damp from the shower.

"You're surely not going to hold a grudge?"

She softened against him as he hardened against her.

"Maybe not." She reached up and pulled his mouth down to hers.

Later they lay in a tangle of sheets in the darkness.

Sex had certainly worked for her. She was relaxed against him, not exactly snoring, but breathing a deep, regular purr that made Garrick smile against the top of her head. He'd hoped that the sex would do it for him, too, but here he lay, wide awake, planning to deal fairly with Roxburgh's employees, and unfairly with the six thugs in Syke's lockup.

Garrick didn't want this to be a takeover of one crimelord by another. There had been plenty of that in Crossways' past, but it wasn't the way of the future, not if the station was going to become legitimate. All the profit had to go to Crossways, to effect repairs and to improve infrastructure and services.

He'd deliver the whorehouses to the workers, on condition they ran as a co-op, and paid Crossways market-value rent for the premises, plus a fair tax based on earnings. Any girls working under coercion could leave with no recriminations. Next, he'd close down the smaller casino. Its position in Green Four made it valuable as real estate and he disliked its reputation for sleaze and a quasi-legal fighting cage.

The big casino at Roxburgh Heights might take a little more sorting out. Denied the top three levels of management, who were all in lockup, the staff could choose to stay or leave. He'd have to put a couple of Empaths and his own security in there, at least during the transition. An immediate pay raise should help to offset whatever they'd previously skimmed from the games. If the house belonged to Crossways, it had to be clean.

All that didn't take long to work out. Garrick lay there again, desperately tired, yet unable to close his eyes.

That's when the Nimbus came to him.

He hadn't even realized he'd fallen asleep. Maybe he hadn't. Was it real?

He jerked awake. "Lights." He said it so loudly that they came on full. Mona mumbled and turned over, freeing his arm from beneath her shoulders.

His voice shook and his breath came in uneven gasps. Sweat prickled his scalp. His mouth tasted like a garbage can. He swung himself upright to sit on the edge of the bed, his arms and legs trembling all over, his eyes blurry.

He blinked against the light and scanned the room.

No Nimbus.

"Lights down."

He could think of only one thing.

Detanine.

Eyes closed, his hand brushed the top of his nightstand. Nothing there. Where was it? Panic welled up. He needed it. Now.

He forced his eyes open. Sure enough, the nightstand was empty of detanine.

Where the fu—

There. A single bulb lay on the floor. Relief flooded over him. He reached down for it, overbalanced, and fell to his hands and knees, grabbing his prize as he did so. He rolled over into a sitting position, naked on the floor, leaning against the wall and clutched the single bulb. He popped the top and jabbed the needle into the skin of his stomach, squeezing so quickly that the force stung. He welcomed the pain. As warmth began to spread through his body, he spotted the remaining three bulbs under the bed. He must have knocked them off during sex. He began to chuckle and then to laugh.

"Whasso funny?" Mona's voice slurred with sleep.

"Nothing at all."

He crawled to the bed, pulled himself to his knees, and then managed to get his feet beneath him, almost falling into the covers.

Mona snuggled toward him. "Hey, big boy, wanna go again?" She pushed her hand between them, but the detanine had him in its grip now and he didn't rise to the occasion. "I guess not. Shit, Garrick, when are you going to get help? That stuff will kill you."

"I can handle it."

"No, you can't. You might have been able to if you'd quit sooner, but you didn't."

"Don't say I told you so."

"Okay, I won't."

But she didn't need to.

✦ ✦ ✦

Braced by detanine, Garrick paced into Roxburgh's casino, currently closed to the public, and addressed the staff. They'd had time to think and wonder where their next paycheck was coming from. He had his own security team around him, so anyone with a grudge would think twice before doing anything stupid.

"It's like this," Garrick told the assembled workers. "If you're not in jail yet, you're not likely to be, but I'm watching you all. Whatever you did in this establishment for Roxburgh—bar staff, croupiers, cashiers, cooks, waiters, cleaners, escorts—you can continue to do, but from now on you'll be working for Crossways."

"Does that mean we'll be working for you?" someone yelled.

"In effect, yes, but not me personally. Crossways gets the profits, but in return we'll service the building and equipment. We'll even fix your power supply . . ."

A few people sniggered, having figured out the joke, but the vast majority simply stared, some shifting from foot to foot uncomfortably.

"And we'll put in new management. Whatever you did previously, you'll be running clean games in the future. If you don't like the idea, you can get out now. Anyone caught cheating customers or lining their own pockets will be off Crossways immediately, and you'll be very lucky if there's a ship waiting for you on the other side of the airlock. Do I make myself clear? I said: do I make myself clear?"

There was a small chorus of yesses.

"And in case you think you can buck the system, I will warn you that there will be Empaths on staff."

He stared down their low rumblings of discontent. "Not on the tables, of course, but on staff and among the patrons. Consider this a warning. You're all on probation. One last thing—does anyone know the location of Ilsa Marquat?"

He hadn't expected anyone to come forward, and no one did. Miss Marquat's absence was a puzzle, as was Ully's. It was entirely likely that Marquat, seeing which way the wind was blowing, had gone to ground, or even left the station before the brown stuff hit the whirly. But it was also possible that Roxburgh saw her as a liability who knew too much.

Ully's continued absence was worrying. Mona adored the little old lady, even though she rarely said as much. Ully had been with her for close to twenty years. Neither the Free Company Telepaths nor their best Finders had been able to come up with anything. They were still trying, but Garrick's unvoiced fear was that she was floating out in the black somewhere, frozen and alone.

He took a cab to Blue Seven from the casino, still surrounded by his guards, all anonymous in their buddysuits and wearing helmets so he didn't have to. He'd hate to have to go everywhere fully armored. In fact, how nice would it be to stretch out, semi-naked, on a sun-drenched beach with Mona by his side and simply shrug off the cares of management? One day, when he'd purged Crossways of its undesirables and set it on the road to legitimacy, he might announce an election, leave it up to someone else, and retire. Thanks to the platinum, his own personal fortune was sufficient for ten lifetimes, and, presuming enemies didn't catch up with him, even with rejuv treatments he wasn't going to make it much beyond another hundred years. Of course, since he was never going to venture into the Folds again, his paradise beach had better be available somewhere on Olyanda.

Blue Seven was bustling as usual. He left his guards at the entrance and passed through the barbican alone. The receptionist had already called ahead, so Ben met him on the other side.

"Have you eaten?" Ben asked.

Garrick's belly growled at the thought. "Not since breakfast."

They walked down to the dining area. It was set where the roadway opened out, making it feel light and airy, a neat trick on a space station. The kitchen itself was covered, but the tables were all sociably in a plaza. It was all very egalitarian. Ben mucked in with everyone else. There was no priority seating or special table for the boss.

"What'll you have?" Ben passed Garrick a tray. "I can recommend the beef."

"Beef? Real beef?"

"Jake Lowenbrun's been making the most of that little freighter, and Ada Levenson's been giving him a shopping list every time he goes somewhere."

"Speaking of the freighter . . ." Garrick said as he piled beef and potatoes on his plate and followed Benjamin to a table, "our diplomatic mission returns soon, I believe."

Garrick had been happy to lend his yacht, the *Glory Road*, to Ben's grandmother for her mission to recruit independent colonies to the Crossways Protectorate, but it would need its regular berth in Port 22 when it returned.

"I've been thinking, Benjamin, since Roxburgh no longer needs it, how about the Free Company takes over Port 46 and gets the hell out of Port 22? Forty-six is more convenient for Blue Seven anyway."

Ben's face lit up. "Are you kidding? That would be excellent. We'll pay the going rate for it, of course."

"I don't see why you should. Roxburgh never did."

"I'm not Roxburgh."

Garrick smiled. "Okay, I take your point. Rent to Crossways gratefully accepted. There are a few ships in it, and a few more out on runs, probably due back with illegal cargoes. You'll need to deal with those potentially hostile arrivals. Take over the ships for your trouble. Keep the crews out of my hair, and we'll call it straight for services rendered. Unless you were planning to give me a bill for the Roxburgh takedown."

"You know I wasn't. This station's better off without the likes of him."

"Indeed it is, and it acts as a warning to the other crimelords. Clean up your act or leave." Garrick speared a cube of potato, cooked to perfection, almost more of a luxury than the beef on a station where many foods arrived dehydrated. "Mmm, I should make a point of calling at lunchtime more often."

"It's always lunchtime here, Garrick, and you're always welcome." Ben waved his hand at the openness of the warehouse above their head. "It's the best kitchen in town."

"I've had an inquiry." Garrick changed the subject abruptly. "Miss Yamada of Alphacorp wants to let bygones be bygones. She wants to buy retrofit jump drives, and as part of the deal she wants her fleet retrieved from Amarelo space."

"Do you believe she's on the level?"

"I believe she wants jump drives. Though when she can commission new jumpships from scratch, I wonder why she wants retrofit ones. Of course, once she gets her hands on one drive, she can have her research and development labs reverse engineer it pretty quickly."

"Well, there's never been a huge market for jumpships. New ones are, on average, fifty percent more expensive to build, and the capacity to build them is limited. There are only a couple of shipyards that specialize, and they're usually working two to four years behind their order books. Retrofitting existing ships is going to be faster and cheaper—depending on how much she's willing to pay for either the drives or the plans to build them. Have you given her an answer?"

"Not yet." Garrick's plate was now empty and his stomach pleasantly full. "There's a lot to consider, including, of course, that someone may come up with a retrofit solution of their own."

"It's only a matter of time, I guess. Have you discussed it with Dido Kennedy?"

He shook his head. "Crossways paid her for the invention, but since most of that went to the citizens of Red One, she should make something else out of it if we sell it. I want to bring together an advisory body—a council, if you like. Crossways shouldn't depend on one person."

"Even if that person is you?"

Garrick laughed. "Not even then. Crossways isn't a monarchy. Crowns are heavy and I have no children to inherit. Will you join me? Cara, too, of course."

"I can't speak for her, though I see no reason why she wouldn't."

"And yourself?"

"Yes, count me in." Ben offered his hand and Garrick

took it. "So, speaking as a member of your council, what are you going to do about Roxburgh's captains? You said they'd have a hearing. Are you going to make a show trial of it?"

"It's tempting, but nothing so high profile. We'll simply put them on trial for aiding and abetting Roxburgh in his illegal activities. We'll have a panel of three judges, and two independent Empaths. I'm expecting all the accused to be as guilty as hell. Most of them have killed, or ordered someone killed, either on their own behalf or Roxburgh's. I doubt any of Roxburgh's former employees will come forward with specifics—they care too much for their own skin. As for the soon-to-be-found-guilty, since we don't have any way of imprisoning them long-term, and since I'm reluctant to simply float them out of an airlock without specific murder charges, I'm proposing we dump them on one of the Monitor's prison planets. I suppose it's illegal, but once they're dumped no one will be any the wiser."

Ben nodded. "There are no guards on a prison planet, just a planetary net to stop unauthorized ships. The real punishment is trying to survive, and there's always someone bigger and meaner."

"Can you get through the planetary net? Surely it's set up to stop prison breaks."

"I have a contact in the Monitors. I may be able to work around the problem."

"Sounds perfect."

Garrick and Ben shook hands on it. It wasn't until Garrick was on his way back to the Mansion House that he thought about detanine and began to sweat.

❖ ❖ ❖

Ben wasted no time in taking over Port 46.

After more than a year of sharing Port 22 with Garrick and Mother Ramona, it was going to be strange for Tengue's security team who would henceforth be working independently of Port 22's militia.

"We can handle it, no problem," Tengue said as they discussed the details of taking over the port. Roxburgh's men were gone, of course, but there were three vessels currently mothballed in there, two of them runabouts and the other, the *Gambit*, a larger vessel which was furnished for any number of illegal activities. They were still discovering

hidden compartments and compiling a list of her armaments. Ships like this didn't come with a user manual. She'd
originally been a small cargo vessel, but her modifications
were extensive. Where *Solar Wind* was lean and mean,
Gambit looked unassuming. On closer inspection, however,
she had a wealth of modifications.

Yan Gwenn was all over her, delighted with what he
found. Within half a day he'd called in Dido Kennedy and
they were making arrangements to retrofit a jump drive.
Ben tried not to smile as he watched them working together. Their relationship had deepened in the last year.
Despite their difference in age—Kennedy was at least ten
years older than Yan and twice his width—they were a comfortable couple. Kennedy no longer slept on the couch in
her chaotic workshop and, except when he needed to be on
hand for work, Yan was frequently absent from the single
unit allocated to him in Blue Seven. Ben had enquired dis-
creetly and discovered they had a small apartment in Red
Two, directly above Kennedy's workshop in Red One. Yan
had no doubt installed an access tube between the two. The
last time Ben had visited the workshop, Kennedy had allowed a pack of her semi-feral kids to move into her old
sleeping space. They were better guards than a flock of
geese.

Both Yan and Dido oohed and aahed over *Gambit*. No
doubt Ben would get to check her out in time, but his immediate problem was the lack of information about Roxburgh's missing ships. Would they return or not? It all
depended on whether they'd heard the news that Roxburgh
was dead and his operation shut down. There were no records. Maybe there had been, but in securing Port 46 during
the smackdown, the crew who had been here—four guards,
three maintenance workers, and a duty controller—had
managed to erase the records. The duty controller was currently awaiting trial along with Roxburgh's six heavies,
though Garrick couldn't find anything more than obstruction and destroying evidence to charge her with.

Franny Fowler had been first into the port office in the
aftermath of the takeover, and she'd spent the last two days
drilling down through what records remained.

"I've found something." Her voice came over the speaker.

Ben climbed the stair to the port office. "Show me."

"I cross-referenced the records from Crossways Control with what was left on the system here. There may be others, but I pinpointed these two. The *Hastings*, a medium-sized freighter, left port fifteen days ago. She filed a flight plan for the Dromgoole Hub, but wasn't required to specify a final destination."

Since the Dromgoole Hub was a twelve-gate nexus, *Hastings* could be anywhere by now. If the pilot had been warned, it was likely she wasn't coming back.

The second ship, the *Cotton*, had departed barely an hour before the smackdown. Ully and Ilsa Marquat were still missing. Could *Cotton* hold the answer?

✦ ✦ ✦

Cara gazed around Port 46. If it hadn't been for the internal decor missing the flashes of color provided by Garrick and Mother Ramona's logos, it would have been easy to think she was standing in Port 22. There was *Solar Wind*, and the Dixie Flyer; both had been turned and were ready for immediate takeoff.

Her eyes strayed to the two smaller ships overshadowed by *Gambit*. They were typical runabouts, one slightly larger than the other. She checked them both. One was a six-seater with a small cargo area. The other would seat ten. It had a slightly larger cargo area and also had a couple of crew berths, a small galley, and an even smaller washroom. Perfect.

"So let me get this straight," she confronted Ben. "We're paying rent for the port, but whatever is in it is ours to keep."

"That's right."

"And you're fitting a jump drive into *Gambit*."

"Dido and Yan are doing it right now."

"What about the two little runabouts?"

"I haven't thought that far yet. They're not big enough for jump drives."

"That one is." Cara pointed to the ten-seater. "The *Flint*. She's bigger than the Dixie and you managed to get a jump drive in that."

"The Dixie was in better condition."

"So you don't want the *Flint*?"

"I didn't say that. A ship's a ship." He grinned at her. "What are you hinting at?"

"Sanctuary could use a ship like that."

"You know the Free Company will provide whatever transport you need."

"I know, but if we're resettling psi-techs where the megacorps can't find them, it doesn't make sense to have any number of pilots in on the secret. We need something more secure."

"You'd need to find your own pilot."

"We can do that."

Chapter Twenty-Four

ULLY

BEN SOUGHT MAX OUT IN HIS OFFICE WHERE Billy Naseby, Max's new assistant, had his own desk which he could adjust for either his float chair or his standing harness. He was working now, so absorbed in whatever he was looking at on screen that he never even noticed Ben in the doorway.

Ben jerked his head and Max followed him. "Do you fancy a little trip outside?"

"Why, Commander Benjamin—a date at last. I didn't think you cared."

"I meant outside. The real outside. I need a Finder who can track through foldspace if necessary."

"What are you looking for?"

"Not what, who. Roxburgh sent a little ship out shortly before we took him down, and Ully and Ilsa Marquat are still missing."

"I've never met Marquat."

"But you know Ully."

"Not well, but yes, I know her. I'd probably need something that belongs to her—a valued personal possession, maybe."

"Whatever you need."

Max nodded. "Now?"

"Now. I can wait ten minutes while you tell Gen."

"No, that's okay."

"You'll need your buddysuit anyway."

"Yes, of course." Max looked down at his soft green tunic and black trousers and shrugged. "I guess I'm a bit under-dressed."

Was it Ben's imagination that saw reluctance as he turned toward his apartment?

"I'll meet you in Port 46." Ben went to gather his crew.

Thirty minutes later they were all aboard *Solar Wind*. Their quarry, the *Cotton*, was small, but she belonged to Rox-burgh, so she'd be armed. Ben was prepared. He had Dobson in engineering, Tengue and a contingent of his mercs strapped down in the cabins, with Ronan and two med-techs in sick bay. Every position on the flight deck was filled: Cara on comms; Yan Gwenn on systems; Gwala and Naomi Patel on tactical, and Max in one of the two bucket seats.

Just as they were clearing for departure, Crossways Control asked them to wait. Ten minutes later, Mother Ramona arrived on the dockside, dressed in a practical buddysuit and flanked by two of her security guards.

"I'm coming, too," she said, taking the spare bucket seat. "If you find Ully, I want to be there."

The *Cotton* wasn't fitted with a jump drive, so she had to enter and exit the Folds via the jump gate system and there had to be records. Ben had Cara download the information.

"Found it," Cara said. "The *Cotton* filed a flight plan to the Dromgoole Hub."

"Damn!" Mother Ramona said. "Twelve potential gates out of there. Too many choices."

"Max?" Ben said.

Max shook his head. "Not much. An echo around the jump gate."

That was hopeful. If the pilot of the *Cotton* had been intending to dump bodies, he could have done it anywhere this side of the jump gate, in which case they could float forever unless someone stumbled upon them accidentally, or unless a Finder was on the case. It was good news that Max couldn't locate Ully immediately.

Rather than using the jump drive, Ben filed a flight plan for the Dromgoole Hub and prepared to follow the *Cotton*'s trail.

Prepare for foldspace, Cara told the crew. *Any time—*

Now.

Entering foldspace from a jump gate should be no different from entering via a jump drive, but somehow it is. It's as if there are echoes of every other ship that's ever passed through, and a well-worn track that stretches to a vanishing point ahead. Close to the gates foldspace is redolent with comings and goings. The tracks in front of them converge, and they jump out of foldspace at Dromgoole Hub without incident.

Cara gave a false ident for the *Solar Wind*, one of the ones supplied by Mother Ramona for such an eventuality. They docked against one of the outer rings of the hub. Cara logged into the station network.

"Don't waste your time," Mother Ramona said. "I bet none of you came prepared with a false identity, did you?" She looked around at their blank faces. "Then I'll get this." She flashed a warrant card from her breast pocket that identified her as Investigating Officer Rae Fields.

"If you get caught impersonating a Monitor, you'll spend five years on a prison planet," Ben said, frowning.

"Then you'll have to come and get me, Benjamin. Or better still, I won't get caught."

Officer Fields exited the ship and Ben pulled up the ramp behind her.

"How long should we give her?" Max asked.

"As long as she needs," Ben said. "Cara's keeping contact."

Cara nodded.

It took about three hours for Mother Ramona to return to the dock, this time on a neat little transporter driven by a young man in the uniform of hub security. Ben watched Mother Ramona shake his hand before walking sedately up the ramp, glancing once at the camera eye and winking.

"Did you find it?" Cara asked as Mother Ramona climbed up the tube to the flight deck.

"Nothing. No arrival or subsequent departure. I'm as sure as I can be that the *Cotton* never reached here." She turned to Ben. "Is it possible she changed direction while in the Folds?"

"It's not impossible, but it would need a pilot who was a high-grade Navigator."

"Ack!" Max butted in. "Is now the time to say I've had no sense that Ully passed through here at all? I sensed her presence in the Folds, but I lost it once we passed through the gate. I thought she'd probably been and gone, but it could be that she was never here."

Ben felt a buildup of tension in his belly that heralded not so much a flutter of butterflies but a whole flotilla. Into the Folds and straight out again; that was the way he liked to do things these days. Crashing around in there searching for Ully could bring them to the attention of all manner of nastiness, chief among them being the Nimbus itself.

They are in the Folds once more and all's quiet. Ben tells Max to concentrate on Ully. The faster they can get out of here the better.

"Five minutes." Yan calls the time and Ben knows that even five minutes is too long in this limbo.

"Max?" he asks.

Max has his eyes closed now. He points.

Using him as a compass, Ben turns the ship. He has no idea of distance and would be surprised if Max did, but speed isn't relevant in this place.

"Are you sure you know what you're doing, Benjamin?" Mother Ramona asks, but her voice sounds as though she's under water even though the flight deck looks normal.

Cara has set the audio comm so they can hear every part of the ship.

"What's that, man? Get it off me!" Comes from one of the cabins.

"Wake up, you're dreaming," says another voice, female this time.

Cara switches the video to the cabin where four of Tengue's mercs are strapped into transit seats. There's a faint ripple on the screen that Ben recognizes.

"Relax. You're not seeing things," Ben says over the comm. "It's one of the otter-kind. It won't hurt you."

But where the otter-kind are ...

A big snout pushes its way through the aft bulkhead. Ben swivels to face it. The prehensile claws on its beard take on a life of their own. The creature noses Max and the claws comb through his hair, but he has his eyes closed and obviously feels nothing.

? the void dragon asks.

Searching, Ben says, trying to make the thought imitate the word. He pictures Ully in his mind as he last saw her: slight build, lined face framed by an explosion of fine white hair. Then he adds Ilsa Marquat to the image.

The void dragon looks at Max and projects a picture of Red One.

Kennedy has jury-rigged a jump drive to Crossways and they're trying to maneuver the station through the Folds. Gen goes into labor and drops out of the gestalt. The void dragon is curious enough to turn its attention to the little miracle as Gen gives birth.

Yes, he's the father, Ben tells it, trying to project the relationship.

? the void dragon asks again.

"Cara, can you connect me to Max, so I can show the void dragon what he's doing?"

Cara smoothly forms a triad channeling Max through Ben to the void dragon.

There's a feeling of understanding. Its head disappears, but the ship moves as if the void dragon is guiding it.

The head reappears and Ben gets a sense of *!* before it pops out of existence.

"External views all round," Ben says.

Yan flicks the external sensors on to panels on the forward screen. There's something out there in the darkness.

"Is that the *Cotton*?" Mother Ramona asks.

Yan magnifies the image. A small ship is mired in something dark.

Ben's heart begins to pound. Nimbus!

Between the *Solar Wind* and the *Cotton* something smaller floats alone. He hears a sob from Mother Ramona. The cloud of white hair haloing out from the slender corpse is all that's needed to identify her.

"*Solar Wind* to *Cotton*," Cara says. "*Solar Wind* to *Cotton*. Are you receiving me? What is your status?"

There's a fountain of static and a female voice answers. "Oh, God, *Solar Wind*. Our drive has died and there's this thing."

"Identify yourself," Cara says.

"Ilsa Marquat, and my pilot is James Beech."

"Your purpose."

"What?"

"What's the purpose of your journey?"

"Courier for Lord Roxburgh."

"Not murder?"

"What?"

Mother Ramona lurches across the flight deck and screams over Cara's shoulder, "That's my friend out there, you bitch!"

"It's getting closer. Help us." Marquat begins to gabble. "You don't understand. We were taking her to safety, but she died. Such an old woman. Must have been a heart attack. We said the words and buried her in space. Oh, God! It's getting bigger."

"Stand by, *Cotton*." Cara turns to Ben. "What next?"

Ben is ready to turn and run. One close encounter with the Nimbus is enough for any man.

"Benjamin, you can't leave Ully behind." Mother Ramona's face is streaked with tears. "Get her back."

A weight settles on Ben's shoulders. That's the Nimbus out there, and he has a full crew to keep safe, but leaving Ully's body is not an option.

"Tengue, I need two people suited up and at the upper hatch on tethers in five minutes. Not the man who saw the visions."

He considers telling Tengue that they don't actually need to suit up as long as they believe they can breathe. Foldspace isn't like the deep dark of realspace. Since nothing is real within foldspace, even you, then you can survive if you believe you can. Ben is living proof. So is Cara. So is Garrick.

It's not the time to start a philosophical debate.

He nudges *Solar Wind* toward Ully's floating form, sees that the airlock is cycling.

"Target acquired," Tengue says. Airlock secured.

Ronan and his med-techs are waiting for them in the suit locker, a space wide enough for a gurney. Ben can see it all on the screen.

"Ronan?"

"Dead," Ronan says.

There's a heavy thump in Ben's belly. Until that moment

there was always a chance that Ully had believed and that foldspace had been kind to her.

"If they're claiming it was a heart attack," Ronan said. "I never saw one that left contusions on someone's throat."

"Bastards!" Mother Ramona clutched the rail at the top of the access tube. "Murderers. Make them pay, Benjamin."

She slides down the tube and moments later appears in the suit room, bent over the gurney with its sad burden.

"Are you coming to get us, *Solar Wind*?" Marquat's voice comes out as a squeak.

"Stand by," Cara says. She turns to Ben.

On the forward screen, the view shows the Nimbus has already shrouded half the *Cotton*. When it had been Garrick in danger, he hadn't hesitated. Maybe he could do the same again, by floating across foldspace and pulling Marquat and her pilot out of the doomed ship.

"Which one of you did it?" Ben asks.

"Did what?"

"Strangled Ully. It's your last chance for a clean confession. When that cloud of black reaches you, you're gone."

"No! Get us out."

"Which one of you did it?"

"He did. He killed her. You've got to help me!"

"She's lying." A male voice this time. "Roxburgh told us to get rid of her and bury the body where no one would find it. She did it. The old woman hardly put up a fight."

Ben has heard enough. He edged *Solar Wind* away from the *Cotton*.

No one speaks as the gap between the two ships widens.

"Wait. Hel—"

Cara flicks the switch, and Ilsa Marquat's last words are lost.

"If anyone has anything to say, say it now," Ben says.

He's met with silence.

"Let's go home."

He powers up the jump drive and looks for the line for home.

◆　◆　◆

"You're sure this is a good idea?" Cara asked.

"Have you a better one besides spacing them all?"

Garrick had held his trial, with witnesses from the

casinos and the whorehouses giving testimony, some reluctantly, presided over by a panel of judges and a pair of independent Empaths.

The former controller of Port 46 turned out to be up to
her neck in people trafficking. Four of the heavies had multiple counts of murder against them, and the other two
were guilty of intimidation, inflicting bodily harm, and kidnapping, including the snatching of Mother Ramona and
Ully.

Garrick would have been happy to space all of them, but
he'd promised they'd get a fair trial and a fair punishment.
Mother Ramona had argued that the ones who snatched
Ully were also guilty of murder. She'd wanted to see them
floated out of an airlock, but the judges, well versed in in-
tergalactic law, said if they were trying this case anywhere
other than Crossways, they'd hand the prisoners over to the
Monitors for deportation to a prison planet for life.

Ben had said he knew a man who might be able to help,
which was why Cara found herself with a dilemma.

"You want to talk to the Monitors?"

"Unofficially, and only to Jess. He might not be inclined
to help, but it's worth a try."

"Should you remind him where you are?"

"The Monitors have known where I am since the battle."

Cara frowned. "They might hesitate to try to come after
you officially, but there have been two attempts on your life.
It might have been them."

"Extra-judicial killings? I don't think so. I'll take my
chances."

"We'll take our chances. Don't forget I'm on their list
also, as is everyone in the Free Company."

"If you think we shouldn't . . ."

She sighed. Ben knew more about the Monitors than she
did. "I think we should, but with due caution."

Not knowing where in the Galaxy Jess Jessop was wasn't
a problem. Cara had met the man and could find him mind-
to-mind if she had to. She closed her eyes tightly and concentrated. Jess wasn't his real name, of course, but he'd
suffered from the usual Monitor nicknaming as Ben had
and it had stuck. Ben Benjamin instead of Reska, Jess Jessop instead of . . .

"What's Jessop's given name?" she asked Ben.

"Rich, I think. Yes, I'm pretty sure it's Richard, but no one ever calls him that."

"Just checking." She continued drawing a complete picture of the man in her mind. When she was fully familiar with it, she sent a thought questing out across the galaxy.

Who wants to know? Jessop didn't immediately recognize Cara's mental handshake. That was good. She brought Ben into the conversation and took herself out of it, listening but not interrupting.

Jess, it's Ben.

What the hell, man?

Can you talk?

Wait a minute. There was a short silence. *I was on the bridge. I think my crew might have noticed something.*

Your crew? You made Prime.

There was a vacancy. You might have had something to do with that. I inherited the Carylan and Alexandrov's crew.

He's not someone I'd like to follow into a job.

Cara felt Jessop's full agreement. *There were a few discipline problems, but I sorted them out.*

I'm sure you did.

This isn't a social call, is it? What do you want, Ben? I should be setting a Finder on you right now.

Don't bother. I'm on Crossways. Any time you want to come and visit, let me know.

The communication wobbled. If Jessop didn't get him, Cara thought she might kill Ben herself . . . slowly.

Do you mean that?

I do, though not if you arrive with a warrant. Garrick's cleaning up Crossways. I know it's unlikely, but things are changing around here. There's been a purge, and we have seven perps who would be ideal candidates to spend the rest of their lives on a prison planet. We need you to make the arrangements.

You can't send people to prison planets without a trial.

They've been tried by fully accredited judges, with qualified prosecutors and defenders. Garrick even had two Empaths to see there was no miscarriage of justice. They're guilty. I can send you the charge sheets and the trial proceedings. In the old days Garrick would have floated them out of an airlock, but as I say, things are changing. If they'd been tried anywhere in the galaxy, they'd all get life on a prison planet.

I still can't take the law into my own hands.

There was a pause. Cara felt Jessop pull back, thoughts spinning.

Do you trust me, Ben?

There was a time, out on the Rim, when we were both straight out of the academy, that we had each other's backs.

Will you let me take your request to Rodriguez?

Cara almost dropped the connection. Sebastian Rodriguez was the head of the Monitors. The buck stopped with him.

He's a fair man, Ben. If the records are all squeaky clean, there's no real reason why he shouldn't sign off on the order. I can do prison transportation. I'd need the charge sheets and the court records, of course.

And you'd want to come and pick up the prisoners on Crossways.

I'd be obliged to if we're keeping this legal.

I'm going to have to vouch for you to Garrick.

And I'm going to have to vouch for you to Rodriguez.

Fair enough.

Chapter Twenty-Five

COLONIES

BEN WAS BOTH LOOKING FORWARD TO JESS Jessop's visit and dreading it. His time in the Monitors had been fraught with trouble. His first posting had been to a system with five well-established colony worlds. Lots of work there for an eager new copper. He'd had a good boss, and Jess and he had been both working partners and friends.

But once he'd been posted out to the rim under Alexandrov, the job turned to shit. Alexandrov was on the take, and the Monitors ended up policing the dispute that turned into the Burnish War. Helping Burnish refugees to freedom and then confronting Alexandrov had effectively ended his Monitor career.

He might have left the job, but the job hadn't ever left him. How many times had he been told he had White Knight Syndrome? If he could make a situation better, he felt obliged to or—at least—to try.

If he'd still been in the Monitors and someone—maybe even an old friend—had given him carte blanche to land a fully armed ship on a station full of people wanted by the law, he might be very tempted to do as much good as he could by taking out as many criminals as he could find.

He hoped Jessop didn't have White Knight Syndrome. In

fact, he was counting on it. Jess was older and wiser now.
While Ben had been running colony missions for Crowder
and losing time in cryo sleep, Jess had been living steadily
toward middle age.

Ben and Cara waited in the port controller's office with
Franny Fowler, who had taken over the general running of
Port 46, both security and shipping.

"I could dock him in one of the external cradles," Fowler
said. "He could only bring a small shuttlecraft on to the
station, then, and—poof!—the threat is eliminated."

"I thought about that, but if Garrick is legitimizing the
station, we have to trust the Monitors sooner or later."

He turned to Cara for confirmation, but her face was a
mask. *Don't ask me. I agree with Franny.*

Fowler had turned to her holographic screen. "They're
on final approach now," she said, adjusting her earpiece.
"Okay, Crossways Control, I see them." She brought the
Monitor ship in slowly, a great lumbering beast of a thing
three times the size of *Solar Wind*.

"Come on. We'll be the welcoming committee," Ben said.

He'd asked Cara to stay outside the port gate, safely hidden with Tengue and his crew, but she'd insisted on coming
with him. The Monitor pilot turned the ship in its own
length, as skillful a maneuver as Ben had seen in a long
time, and sat the *Carylan* on the slipway, ready to depart
before she'd even settled in.

Cara made a rumble deep in her throat as they approached. "Is that deliberate? They could open their hatch,
snatch us both, and be out of here before Tengue had time
to blink."

"Got to show a little faith," Ben said.

"Are you even armed?"

"Not even a derri. And I asked you not to carry."

"I'm not—well—not quite. I stashed it in the office with
Franny."

"Oh, great. She's—"

"Mouthy but not insane. That's why she's got this job."

"Yeah, right."

Carylan's hatch hissed and cracked open a couple of
centimeters before the top half hinged up and the bottom
lowered to form a ramp.

It was only when Jessop stepped on to the ramp alone

and dressed in a uniform rather than a buddysuit, that Ben realized he'd been holding his breath. His first impression was of a middle-aged man with faded, thinning hair. Then Jess smiled and it was as if no time had passed since their last encounter.

They met at the bottom of the ramp with a huggy, back-slappy greeting and then stepped apart so Jess and Cara could shake hands.

"I wondered if there might be a bigger welcoming committee," Jess said.

"My security guards are close by, but out of sight, just in case."

"Mine are lined up by the hatch. Shall we say that we don't need their services today?"

"A wise move."

"Stand down." Jess waved toward the hatch, no doubt with telepathic orders to secure the ship and wait for further instructions. Jess was a psi-tech whose telepathy had always been stronger than Ben's.

"I can't stand down my security," Ben said. "They're for your protection—and ours, too, come to that." He indicated Cara by his side.

"Too many potshots at Ben, Prime Jessop," Cara said.

"Please, call me Jess."

She nodded. "And there would be a few people who might consider it open season on any Monitor rash enough to step onto Crossways. It's not that long ago that a couple of your heavy battlewagons stood by while the megacorps tried to pound us all to space dust."

"I know, and I'm sorry for it." He shrugged. "Crossways has a certain reputation for lawlessness."

"I hope that's soon something you can say in the past tense," Ben said. "Garrick is sincere in his intention to make Crossways legitimate. I'm not saying there isn't still a criminal element, but the worst of them—"

"Roxburgh."

"That's right, Roxburgh. Now that he's gone, a few other organizations are reassessing their position."

They reached the port's blast doors. Ben slid his hand-pad past the plate to identify himself and keyed in a security code. "Of course, the majority of the station's inhabitants have committed no crime worse than being born here."

The door slid open. Jess started visibly at the sight of Tengue's best troops, all kitted out for a rumpus.

"Jess, this is Morton Tengue, our security chief."

Jessop recovered himself almost immediately and shook hands. "Geez, Ben, did you lay on the heavies for my benefit?"

"Just another day on Crossways. Until I saw it was you on the ramp, that ship could have been filled with shock troops."

"I'd hate to have to be so paranoid."

"I do. Welcome to my life."

✦ ✦ ✦

Cara liked Jess Jessop, his easy manner, and the way Ben relaxed into their old friendship. Much as he meant what he said, Jessop would still report everything he found of interest on Crossways, and that meant showing him only what they wanted him to see. They couldn't avoid the tub cabs, of course, but they weren't going to take him as far as the hub, so they scrambled out of the tub cab on the sixth level and walked him through the piazza, around walls built from piles of rubble, past the stalls and Cara's favorite barista.

"You want coffee?" Cara asked. "Joe makes the good stuff, though Ben doesn't drink it, of course."

"He always drank tea," Jess said, "or beer."

"Not so much beer, now," Ben said. "I need to keep my head clear."

Cara waved at Joe and held two fingers up for coffees.

Jess laughed. "Did you ever tell Cara about that time on Kalvin Station?"

"Oh, don't remind me. I had a hangover for a week."

"We were young and foolish." Jessop eyed him sideways. "Done a few years of cryo, I guess. You don't look anywhere near as old as you should."

"Yes. Sorry about that. My brother makes the same complaint."

"Your family well?"

"Yes, all of them. I have nephews now, and Nan is still active."

Cara smiled to herself. Nan was more than active. She was away being Crossways' ambassador to the independent planets. Jess didn't need to know that.

Joe handed over the coffees, complete with lids, and Cara passed her handpad over the reader to pay for them.

"It's up here." Ben led the way through an open blast door and up a bland staircase, leaving Cara and Jess to walk together.

"So are you on the level, Jess?" It was the kind of direct question that could sometimes shock enough of a wobble out of someone for Cara to pick up intentions.

He grinned at her. "You're an Empath. I read your file."

"Sorry, I had to ask."

"And what do you think?"

"I think you are, but I don't know about your bosses."

"I'll not lie to you; there are problems within the Monitors."

"Alexandrov?"

"He was a real liability, but he's gone now. Rodriguez is doing a great job of getting rid of the deadwood. He's only been in the top job for three years, but already there's a big improvement. If Crossways wanted to sign up to the Monitor charter and turn legal, he'd support you in any way he could."

"That's good to know."

"That's not me guessing. Rodriguez actually told me to pass the message on. Nothing in writing, though. Not yet."

"I'll tell Garrick."

"Of course, there might be issues."

"You mean like the charges against all of us?"

Jess shrugged.

"You know they were all trumped up?" Ben called over his shoulder.

Jess raised his voice to carry forward. "I figured kidnapping thirty thousand settlers might be beyond even you, Benjamin. Besides, it's not your style."

"It's certainly not. Those settlers are safe, now, and the Trust is never going to find out where."

They reached Blue Seven and brought Jessop into the heart of the Free Company.

"You've a sweet setup here." Jess looked around. "Well protected."

"Crossways has been good to us." Ben didn't mention how profitable their small percentage of Olyanda's platinum profits had been.

Cara led the way to their apartment and opened the double doors onto the garden. "How do you want to handle the prisoner transfer?"

They made arrangements to have the prisoners taken securely to Port 46 in an hour, and so Jess' visit was shorter than Cara suspected either of the two men wanted to make it. She watched them catching up, Ben as casual as she'd ever seen him. When it was time to go, Ben and Jess parted with regret at the short visit but pleasure at the renewed acquaintance.

As Cara and Ben watched the *Carylan*, loaded with the new prisoners, glide down the slipway from the safety of the port office, Cara heard Ben sigh.

"Did that achieve what you wanted it to achieve?" Cara asked.

"Well, I don't think it did any damage. If Crossways is going to straighten itself out, it needs to have a working relationship with the Monitors. We'll get there—in small steps."

✦ ✦ ✦

Ben snapped awake instantly as Cara poked him. He swung his legs out of bed. All too often a nudge in the middle of the night heralded trouble.

"Relax, it's not an emergency this time. Your Nan and Ricky are on their way home. Listen." She brought him into the conversation. Nan was talking through Chander Dalal, a long-range Telepath from the Free Company who had been with her since she set out on her diplomatic mission more than a year ago.

We're coming home, Nan said.

When? Ben asked.

Just wrapping up negotiations here on Cranford. It's our fifty-sixth colony. We need to take a break. We'll come to Crossways first, and then I promised Ricky a trip to Jamundi to see his dad and Kai. He won't say it, but he's missing them.

The megacorporations were vastly powerful when pitted against one colony, or even two, but against fifty-six they started to look like less of a force.

For want of a better name the alliance had become the Crossways Protectorate. As long as they didn't realize

Crossways' power to protect had been diminished by the battle, everything would work out. One thing Crossways could do, however, was to provide platinum at a price much lower than the megacorps. By cutting out the middleman, Crossways made a better profit and the colonies bought at a lower price. It enabled them to run their own fleets more economically.

The *Glory Road* slipped gently into Port 22 and dropped into the place *Solar Wind* had recently vacated. She dwarfed all the other runabouts, even Mother Ramona's best smuggling vessel, *Needle*. A yacht in name only, *Glory Road* was as big as most cruisers, sleek and luxurious. Garrick had loaned her to Nan for the duration of the diplomatic mission on the understanding that the best way to attract help was not to look as if you desperately needed it.

"Nan! Ricky!" Ben was waiting at the bottom of the ramp as the passengers disembarked.

Ricky launched himself from the ramp toward Ben and then pulled up at the last minute, awkward, as if wondering whether a hug or a handshake was most appropriate. Ben solved the problem by drawing him in for a hug, resisting the obvious comment about the boy's growth spurt. At thirteen, Ricky had become a gangling youth, no longer a child. Rion was going to get a surprise when he saw his son again. He looked more like his older brother Kai now.

"Reska!" Nan was the only one who ever used Ben's given name.

"Nan!"

Ben let Ricky go and embraced his grandmother. She never looked any older. Tall for her age and with skin like leather from her years working outside on the Benjamin family farm, Louisa Benjamin hugged her grandson fiercely. Ben laughed. Fierce was Nan's fundamental nature.

"Should we have rolled out the red carpet, Madam Ambassador?"

Nan laughed. "I'd be surprised if you have any red carpet. This place looks like a wreck."

"Compared to the way it was when you left, it probably does. Compared to what it looked like after the megacorps had finished pounding on it, I can assure you it's a palace."

She sniffed. "I'll take your word for it. Where's Cara?"

"Blue Seven, making sure your accommodation is comfortable. How was Garrick's yacht?"

"Luxurious. Better by far than a lot of the garbage cans I've traveled in. Captain Dorinska knows her job and Chander has taught Ricky the art of Asian cooking while we've been planet-hopping." She reached up and touched the side of Ben's face, her pink fingers contrasting with his darker cheek. "How are you?"

"I'm fine, Nan. We're all fine."

"I wanted to come back—after the battle."

"There was nothing you could have done. I was glad you were out of it." Ben glanced at Ricky.

"Yes, you're probably right. Though the boy has shown signs of extreme common sense this year. I'm proud of him. We might make a negotiator of him when he's old enough to get his implant if he can resist the lure of becoming a pilot."

"We've had a number of naturals turn up who don't need and don't want implants. Perhaps Ricky might like to talk to them."

"Hey, I'm here," Ricky said. "If we're talking about implants, I think I'm ready now."

"Don't be too eager," Ben said. "Keep your options open. You may be a natural."

"So if I'm a natural, think how much stronger I'd be with an implant. You'll not dissuade me, Uncle Ben. I've made up my mind."

"Does he remind you of anyone?" Nan asked.

Ben grinned. "I guess he does. All right, Ricky, if your father gives his permission, you can sit your aptitude tests with Jussaro as a preliminary, and I'll make you an appointment to see Vina Daniels."

"I thought Civility Jamieson was your top implant surgeon."

"He is, but Vina is his best student and much friendlier than Jamieson."

"A student?"

"She's a qualified doctor, but still working with Jamieson. That makes her the second-best implant expert on Crossways."

"Second best?"

"Trust me, that puts her way above any of the Trust's experts."

"If you say so."

"But it doesn't mean you'll get your implant straight-away. You're still young for the process."

Nan sighed theatrically. "Don't think I haven't told him."

Ben shepherded them out of the dock onto the con-course where a tub cab, decorated with bright swirls of color, stood waiting for them.

"Ah," Nan shaded her eyes as she climbed in. "I haven't missed these at all."

Ben punched in the destination and the tub cab bounced them round toward Blue Seven, a second cab following dis-creetly.

"Is that Gwala behind us?" Nan asked.

Ben sighed. "There's usually security around somewhere close. Tengue is very good at his job. Even though I think it's overkill, I don't interfere. They can't cover every even-tuality." He hadn't worried her with details of Swanson and the attempt on his life. No one had been able to find any connection between Swanson and any of the megacorps, so investigations were at a dead end. He switched to mind-to-mind communication to cut out Ricky. *Crowder's still out there, and for all we know he may have already sent a hit man, or more than one.*

Have you taken out a contract on him?

*I haven't. Grandfather . . . *

Yes, he's keeping a close eye on Crowder, but I doubt even your grandfather can get an assassin inside the high-security accommodation in the Trust Tower. You should have killed Crowder when you had the chance.

I thought you were a negotiator.

With a sideways glance at Ricky she said, *Sometimes it's better to bury the bodies than leave a live enemy behind you, especially someone like Crowder.*

"Are you talking about me?" Ricky asked.

"No, honey," Nan said. "We're talking about war and some of the more distasteful aspects."

"Are we at war with the megacorps? If so, I should get an implant right now. I can help."

Ben shook his head. "It's never what you think it's going to be. I was caught up in two local wars when I was in the

Monitors. You need to be in a war to appreciate it, preferably on the losing side. You won't love it so much after that."

Ricky's eyes widened. "Will you tell me about it?"

"Someday. It wasn't fun. Though that's how I met Mother Ramona. I had some Burnish refugees to smuggle out of the danger zone. A promise I'd made to someone who died."

"So what ha—"

"We're here," Ben said. "Let's get you settled."

✦ ✦ ✦

"Nan!" Cara hugged Nan, then Ricky. The boy was taller than she was and, though lanky, was heading for the same height as his father and his Uncle Ben. "Good to see you. I've put you in the same guest accommodation you had before, right above me and Ben. All you need to do is bang on the floor and we'll come running."

"I'm sure we'll manage without disturbing you," Nan said. "Lord, but it's good to see you again. Keeping in touch mentally isn't the same as seeing everyone in person. But we can't stay long. I think Ricky's been missing his dad and Kai."

Ricky shot her a look as if to say he was perfectly okay, but Cara caught a wave of emotion from him. "I'm sure you have, too," she said.

"Truth to tell, I have," Nan said. "I'm ready for a break, and Jamundi sounds very tempting. I never thought I'd say this, but I miss the farm."

"Come down to our apartment when you're ready. I begged some good beans from Ada—dark roast—or I can make tea."

"Ah, excellent. I remember your coffee."

It took less than half an hour for Nan and Ricky to arrive at Ben and Cara's door. While Ben made tea for himself, Ricky, Nan, and Cara settled with satisfied grins and a large mug of hot, strong coffee each.

"So, before I go and report to Garrick, I guess you want to know how it went," Nan said.

"I've been keeping score," Ben said. "But it's not just about the numbers."

"You're right. It's not. In general, the independents are very unhappy about the price they are paying the megacorps for platinum; it raises the price of imported goods artificially. Some of the colonies have their own fleets to maintain. The megacorps are charging a premium for platinum rods and extra tariffs at the jump gates."

Ben nodded. "To be expected, I guess."

"Some of the colonies are self-sufficient. Those were the ones who were most eager to join the protectorate. The opportunity to buy platinum from Crossways at a fair price was one of the things that made a difference. I hope Olyanda is as rich in platinum as everyone thinks."

"It is. Even richer than expected."

"Good, because I've promised plenty."

"Fifty-six colonies. That's good going."

"Fifty-seven. Velleda wasn't going to join, but the elders changed their mind after we'd left."

"What about the colonies that aren't self-sufficient?"

"They fall into two categories. Some rely on imports for nonessential goods that they can't produce themselves. A colony isn't going to fail because they can't get hold of chocolate, coffee, and sugar, so I'm not worried about them. I am worried about the ones that can't grow enough staples to feed their colonists. They are potentially unviable without the goodwill of their neighbors to sell them protein powders and grain. Five or six of the colonies are not in a good position. Three of them are mining operations, with not much of a toehold on the planet they're inhabiting. They produce high-quality exports, but their land is largely infertile. Two others produce very little except dissatisfied settlers. I'd like to persuade them to resettle and combine with another colony. They're not so populous that we couldn't move them."

"What about Guggenheim, Nan?" Ricky asked.

"Ah, yes, Guggenheim. It's a dead-end sort of place, but their youngsters are tough as nails and often eager to sign up for military service so they can get off-planet."

"It's not foot soldiers we need, it's pilots and ships," Ben said. "Crossways Protectorate would be hard-pressed to respond if there was a major incident. We need to be ready. What defensive capabilities do the colonies themselves have?"

"It varies. Some of them have navies of their own and are willing to send ships to a combined fleet. Others have nothing. The major problem is that if we want their ships elsewhere, they are reliant on the jump gate system which means the megacorps can use the jump gates as a choke point."

"So they need to know how to build Dido Kennedy's jump drives and they need plenty of platinum rods."

"That's what I've promised them."

"Then we'd better talk to Garrick about making good on your promise."

"There's one more thing," Nan said. "I'm not even sure it's significant, but in talking to the colonies I have noticed a worrying trend. There have been enough mentions of ships going missing in the Folds to begin to ring alarm bells. Each colony on its own may only have one or two incidents to report, but added together, there's something wrong somewhere. It may not be the Folds, of course. It may be human predators. Ships belonging to the independents are a soft target, or at least they were. Hopefully, the Crossways Protectorate will change that."

Chapter Twenty-Six

AMARELO

"MR. CROWDER, THERE'S A REPORT ON YOUR desk that I think you will want to see first thing." Stefan French met him at the office door with a coffee.

"Thanks, Stefan. Report?"

"From Lawrence Archer on Chenon, sir."

Archer was his hands-on man in Colony Ops, a competent administrator, but he didn't have much vision. Crowder had enjoyed the complexities of organization when he'd been in charge. Now he'd worked his way up the Trust ladder, he had to do it all via underlings.

He lowered himself into his float chair and plugged in the datacrystal. The holo-screen shimmered in front of him. He almost lost his breakfast. The video looked like a slaughterhouse. It was a few moments before his ears caught up with the voice track.

"... images from New Canada received late last night. The colony log shows that a ship claiming to be a humanitarian transport requested permission to land. The colonists billeted refugees with volunteers in the town. The carnage began shortly after midnight. The civilian population was completely unprepared. Resistance formed around the town hall. The adults sent children into the bunker beneath the building for safety. They survived, but their accounts are confused and confusing. The perpetrators didn't appear to want anything except mindless killing."

Crowder put it on pause and rubbed his hand across his eyes, then hit play again.

"By the time the Monitor relief ships arrived, the perpetrators had departed."

Stefan cleared his throat. "There's been a similar attack on an Alphacorp colony. We don't have any details yet."

"Do you know where?"

"Perseus Arm, not even in the same sector as New Canada. Speculation suggests that Crossways is behind both raids in retribution for the attack on the station last year."

Crowder shook his head. "Where did you hear that?"

"Several media channels are speculating."

Crowder would always be happy to let the media do his dirty work for him, but he knew this wasn't Ben Benjamin's style. Besides, the man had been the one to set up the colony on New Canada on behalf of the Trust. He had friends there. If he was going to attack anywhere, it wouldn't be New Canada.

✦   ✦   ✦

Can you come to the office?

Cara connected with Ben while he was in the training gym where he'd stopped off to see Ada Levenson's session. Despite her reluctance to get involved, Ada put down her opponent in less than thirty seconds and then gave a demonstration of throwing techniques with kitchen cleavers. Not a woman to get on the wrong side of.

Something wrong? Ben asked.

I've been monitoring the S-logs and psi-net chatter . . .

And?

Two colonies have gone dark. One belongs to the Trust and one to Alphacorp. There's speculation that it might be us. Retaliation.

They don't even know what happened, yet they're blaming us?

They do know what happened — at least they believe they do. They were both small colonies, both recorded taking in a boatload of refugees, then nothing. The Trust planet was New Canada.

There was a silence while Ben digested the information.

He'd spent almost a year on New Canada working with the colonists on a virgin planet. He'd made friends.

What happened? They didn't find platinum, did they?

No. Nothing like that. The Monitors sent ships in. There were only a few survivors.

"Dead? How?" Ben had reached the office where Cara was waiting.

"Slaughtered," Cara said. "Messily. A variety of ways: handguns, knives, sidearms, small automatic weapons fire. It looked like a gang of maniacs had gone through the place with a kill order."

"They were good people on New Canada: farmers, teachers, scientists, artisans, laborers, administrators, technicians. When we left, they'd hired a crew in from the Trust on long-term contracts: Telepaths, Psi-Mechs, and a couple of Finders."

"The psi-techs were killed, too."

"And the Trust thinks it was us?"

"There's no obvious motive. Nothing stolen."

"The survivors?"

"In their statements they said the refugees, who'd been billeted around the town and the surrounding small settlements, turned on them in the middle of the night. Like unstoppable soldiers, they said, even the ones who looked frail and elderly."

"Could it be their attackers simply had the element of surprise? Sounds like a pirate tactic to me. Let me know if you hear anything else. We should warn the Protectorate planets."

◆ ◆ ◆

Cara went with Ben and Nan to the Mansion House.

Norton Garrick was in a charming mood today.

"Miss Benjamin, nice to have you with us again. We've been following your many successes with interest." Garrick shook Nan's hand.

Cara noticed how Nan shook hands then fixed her face into a neutral half smile. Was she picking up something odd from Garrick? With her Empathy dialed up to ten, Cara thought she detected what had impacted Nan's calm. Garrick was hiding it well, but beneath his geniality there was something going on. Agitation? Stress, perhaps?

Garrick led the way to one of the Mansion House's smaller reception rooms. This was the place of complex deals and mutual, if unwritten, understandings.

Mother Ramona, already seated at the dark polished wood table, gestured to the chairs and they all sat—herself, Ben, Nan, and Garrick. There were two seats to spare.

"I hope you don't mind. I invited Oleg Staple and Leah Nolan to join us," Garrick said.

The door opened again and a stocky man entered, his hair shaved down to almost nothing, which emphasized the roundness of his head. Staple was a handspan shorter than Ben, but he had a powerful frame and shook hands with a viselike grip. He commanded the fleet that protected the planet and now, by default, the Crossways fleet, too. He'd taken the two fleets after the battle and made one good one from the pieces of both.

Nolan was a few paces behind. She was a woman of middle years, middle height, and middle coloring. It was the first time Cara had met her face-to-face, but she knew from handling comms to and from the planet that Nolan was a nononsense administrator, given to quick decisions that were logical and thoughtful. She was in charge of the mining activities on Olyanda; effectively, she looked after everything on the ground.

The visitors' arrival made no difference to Garrick's mental state. Whatever he was feeling had nothing to do with today's meeting.

Nan presented the results of her mission on a datacrystal which detailed each colony, its strengths and weaknesses, its exports and imports, its population, its status with regard to self-sufficiency, and the number of ships it could field for its own defense, as well as the number it could contribute to the Protectorate should the need arise.

Nolan took it all in without making notes. Staple said little but jotted down numbers as the meeting progressed. Mother Ramona, all business today in a sober suit, wrote notes on a desk pad.

"I must admit," Garrick said. "Your success has been beyond my wildest hopes." He smiled at Nan somewhat ruefully. "Fifty-seven colonies joining the Protectorate is almost embarrassing—"

"Especially since you can't protect them."

Cara tried not to smile at Nan's directness, but probably failed. She pressed her lips together. Was Nan poking at Garrick deliberately to see if she could stir up something?

"But they can protect each other," Nan said. "Isn't that right, Commander Staple?"

"The figures certainly add up." Staple regarded his notes. "With the addition of a few heavy-hitting battleships, we can make a fleet like that work. They'll need retrofitted jump drives, of course . . ." He stared at his figures. "And we'd need to instigate training and set up a chain of command." He tapped his stylus on his pad twice. "But I think we can make it work."

"We might be able to do something about the heavy-hitting battleships," Ben said. "When we stranded the enemy fleet in Amarelo space, Eastin-Heigle abandoned their ships so that they could repatriate their crews. It may be a specialist job to break in safely, but theoretically those ships are subject to the laws of salvage. If we can get them, they're ours. We'd have to check what's out there, but I guess there might be at least five usable ships."

"You're suggesting we steal Eastin-Heigle's battleships?" Garrick asked.

"Not steal," Ben said. "Salvage. Legally."

"If these ships are accessible, why didn't the other megacorps salvage them?"

"The ships are useless unless someone can retrofit a jump drive or is willing to take them home the long way through realspace," Ben said. "We can fit jump drives."

"And how are we going to find crews?" Garrick turned to Cara.

"When Sanctuary is in business, they'll find us . . . eventually."

"Is that wise?" Garrick asked. "How can we tell they'll be loyal?"

"It's almost impossible to lie mind-to-mind," Cara said. "Especially to a good Empath. It's not foolproof, obviously. Someone can be absolutely sincere one day, then change their mind the next, but we'd spread the new recruits among seasoned loyal crews. It's worth a try."

"So . . ." Garrick rubbed his hands together. "All we need to do to make this work is to steal—sorry—salvage five enemy battleships, refit them with jump drives, find pilots, and teach the colonies how to retrofit jump drives to their exist-ing fleet."

"That's about it," Ben said.

The platinum profits would finance a new retrofitted fleet made up of colony volunteers and salvaged battleships, while Cara and Jussaro tried to set up Sanctuary on Oly-anda.

Nan waited until they were well away from the Mansion House. "How long has Garrick been like that?" she asked.

"You noticed it, too?" Cara said.

"He's a troubled man, desperately trying to do what he feels he has to do before he breaks apart. He thinks he's living on borrowed time."

Cara stole a glance at Ben. It wasn't news to him.

"Let me tell you about the Nimbus, Nan . . ." he said.

◆ ◆ ◆

Solar Wind emerged from foldspace ten thousand klicks from Crossways' previous position in Amarelo space, allow-ing for orbital drift around the star. Ben thanked provi-dence for an uninterrupted flight through the Folds.

Cara had taken Archie Tatum and a team of Psi-Mech engineers to Olyanda to assess the old landing site, so Lynda Munene had taken her place. A competent class two Telepath, she could handle comms well enough for the cur-rent job, but Ben missed Cara.

He'd sent Nan and Ricky home to Jamundi with Jake, promising to visit as soon as he could.

After a year, the debris field from the battle was widely dispersed, already orbiting Amarelo on a predictable path.

"Engineering A-okay," Dobson checked in.

"Medical, A-okay," Ronan said over the comm. "Not that you're likely to find anyone still alive unless there's an oc-casional cryo pod that everyone missed after the cleanup."

"Oh, damn!" Yan said. "There's something out there with an active gravity generator."

A significant amount of wreckage drifted as a large mass.

"Scanners," Ben said.

"Scanning now. There it is." Yan flicked the image, much magnified, to the forward screen.

"It's the farm," Ben said, "Or what's left of it."

Crossways' farm, a segment of a repurposed O'Neill

cylinder, had been one of the first casualties of the battle. How many had died sucking on vacuum when the farm had been ripped apart from the station?

The remains of the farm had attracted a significant amount of debris over the past year. From this distance, some of the pieces were big enough to be whole ships, abandoned deliberately, or gutted and dead.

"Let's see what the megacorps left behind," Ben said. "I know we're here for ships, but we'll not leave pods behind whether their occupants are alive or dead."

"Scanning for escape pods now," Yan said. "You never know ..."

Ben nosed *Solar Wind* into the outer layer of debris. Though dense in space terms, they could still navigate safely without colliding.

"Pod," Yan said, and relayed the coordinates. "No life signs."

"Ours or theirs?" Ben asked.

"Theirs."

"Let's be sure. Dobson, deploy the grapple."

"I'm on it, Boss."

Ben maneuvered the *Solar Wind* until they were alongside the escape pod. Dobson brought it on board with no trouble at all.

"Body," Ronan relayed from the hold. "One of theirs. Lieutenant Charles Strachan. Alphacorp. Looks like he died of his wounds before the cryo kicked in."

"We'll take him back for funeral rites and notify Alphacorp," Ben said. "They did the same for ours in the aftermath."

They nudged farther toward the center of the gravity well.

"Ship ahead," Yan said. "Cruiser size. No ID yet. It's not broadcasting any kind of beacon, but it looks—uh-oh."

"What's wrong?" Ben asked.

Yan magnified the image on screen. The ship looked whole until they passed beneath it. The far side had burst open like an overripe plum.

"There might be salvageable parts," Yan said. "Dido said not to miss anything potentially valuable."

"She should have come herself, then."

"You know what she's like in space."

"She lives on a space station."

"Yes, but she can convince herself that it's big and solid. Not at all like knowing there's only a thin skin between you and a vacuum."

"Mark the wreck as worth investigating later and we'll send in a scavenger crew, but right now we only have time for whole ships."

Ben was already moving toward a second set of coordinates.

Ronan emerged onto the bridge.

"Deja vu."

Ben shrugged. He'd come here in the aftermath of the battle, not once but three times, searching for survivors. It had been a tricky operation, since the enemy fleet was re-grouping and the Monitor battlewagons were still looming.

"Grim days," Ronan said. "Even when we found them, we couldn't always keep them alive."

"You took some of them personally," Ben said.

"Well, I like to keep my reputation intact."

"You like to win."

"We're not dissimilar in that respect."

Ben felt a smile tugging at the corner of his mouth. There was a reason he and Ronan got on so well.

"We won more than we lost," Ben said.

"The last time we were here, there were too many bodies," Ronan said. "I sincerely hope there are no more bodies today. Let Lieutenant Charles Strachan be the only one, please."

They nosed through more debris. "Ahead, Boss," Yan said. "It's an Eastin-Heigle cruiser. It looks to be intact. No life signs."

"Let's take a look."

Just because Eastin-Heigle had abandoned their ships in favor of taking the crews home, didn't mean to say they'd left them unprotected. It was very likely they were booby-trapped unless you had a set of Eastin-Heigle recognition codes. This was going to be tricky.

Ben left Yan to maneuver *Solar Wind* into place off the cruiser's port side while he suited up along with three psi-techs, Issy Monaghan, Corin Butterfield, and Lynda

Munene, who was a Psi-Mech as well as a Telepath. Issy had been working with Dido Kennedy and Yan Gwenn retrofitting some of Crossways ships and was there primarily to assess whatever ships they found for refit.

They checked each other's suit seals and made their way down to the cargo airlock, which was big enough to take all four of them. They tied onto a line for the journey across to the waiting cruiser. Lynda opened up a communications network.

The airlock cycled and the outer hatch slid open.

Ben and Corin, at either end of the line, fired their suit thrusters and eased all of them to within fifty meters of the ship, then floated silently to the emergency hatch on the port side.

Corin examined the hatch. *Come on, baby, talk to me.*

He put his face close to the mechanism, leaning his suit helmet against the side of the ship. They had no way of knowing whether the ship had been locked down tight with all life-support systems mothballed, or whether it was operating on a sleep cycle which would restore power on detecting a human presence.

Or it could be booby-trapped to hell and back, Ronan said, following everything from the safety of *Solar Wind*.

Could be, Corin said. *I need to connect and—* He grasped the hatch opening. *Here we are.*

The emergency hatch was wide enough for two suited bodies at a time.

Ben itched to join Corin, but protocol said he should let the engineers take the risks. It didn't feel right to send in Corin and Issy first, but that was their job. Ben let them do it.

Clear, Issy said. *There's stale air in here, but no life support. The power's on standby, though, so we should be able to cobble something together. Come on in.*

Ben went in with Lynda. The ship was dim and tomblike with no gravity and a fine rime of ice on anything metallic.

Engineering's through there, Corin said, pulling himself hand over hand along the corridor grab-rail. *I sent a couple of spider bots ahead. It's dark and creepy, but there are no obvious booby traps. It wouldn't make sense if there were. They pulled their crew out, but they know the ship's here. They've left it in working condition, possibly hoping to* *be able to salvage it themselves at some future date. It's one hell of an expensive piece of hardware.* *

They followed him.

**Lights,* * Issy said, and they were rewarded with a gentle glow.

**Looks like I can give us quarter-grav,* * Corin said. **And reinstate life support so that—oh, shit!* *

**What?* * Ben said.

**We've tripped something. Self-destruct sequence initiated.* *

**How long?* *

**Five minutes. Less now.* *

**Can you figure out how to stop it?* *

**Sure, but not in five minutes.* *

**Everybody out. Now!* * Ben pushed Issy toward the corridor they'd entered by. Lynda was close behind. Ben turned. Corin had lingered by the engineering console. **Corin, out, now.* *

**I'm just—* *

**Now!* *

**Yessir.* * Corin pulled something out of the console and pushed off toward the exit.

**Yan, we need a quick exit. Do a close pass and have the jump drive online.* *

**Coming now.* *

The emergency hatch cycled too slowly. **Blow it,* * Ben told Corin who sent a couple of bots into the lock. A small, quiet puff of the internal lock and then a louder clang as the outside hatch popped and flew off, driven by a rush of stale air.

Ben clipped a line on Issy and sent her up the hatch, then Lynda, Corin, and finally himself.

**Three minutes.* * Corin had been counting.

Solar Wind loomed in front of them. They all jetted for the open cargo hatch, tumbling inside as gravity took hold. Ben unclipped his line and ran for the flight deck as fast as he could while fully suited. He popped the seals and stripped off the gloves as he ran, dropped them on the floor, and jumped onto the first step of the access tube. *Solar Wind* was way too close. She'd be wiped out if the cruiser blew. He emerged onto the flight deck and flung himself into the pilot's chair as Yan rolled out of it. His hands found the controls. Yan released his helmet seal for him and still had it in his hands as he slid into the systems station. "Jump drive ready, Boss."

"Go!"

And just like that they are in foldspace with thirty-four seconds to spare. Ben takes a deep breath. He hasn't even had time for the usual doubts.

Well done, everyone. Lynda is still holding the comms link open and Ben feels everyone's state of alarm. *Debriefing after we exit from foldspace.*

He blinks rapidly. The void dragon is on the flight deck. He'd not noticed it arrive.

? The void dragon says.

You know, I wish I could tell you. He tries to imagine an explosion.

Does the void dragon understand? Ben feels a sudden *Ah-ha!*

The void dragon explodes.

Ben begins to duck but there's no real explosion, only the appearance of one. Scales are embedded into the bulkhead. Ben's heart is pounding, but before he can react, the void dragon returns and the scales realign themselves.

EXPLOSION, the void dragon says it quite clearly in Ben's head.

A word. It says a word.

An actual word.

Maybe it's worth the explosion.

Predictably, the void dragon disappeared as they popped out of the Folds into Crossways space.

"Did you see anything, Yan?"

"Such as?"

"A void dragon."

"No. I don't know whether to be grateful for that or not."

"On balance, I think you should. Can you fly the bus? I need to debrief."

Ben peeled off his suit. It would need a thorough check, especially the glove seals where he'd ripped them apart. He made his way to the mess where Ronan, Lynda, and Issy were already waiting. Corin slipped in behind him and sat at the table with a cat-that-got-the-cream grin.

"You look very pleased for someone who nearly blew us up," Lynda said.

"Hey, it wasn't me. Blame Eastin-Heigle. I got it."

"Got what?" Ben asked.

"The systems download. With this, we should be able to tell how they safeguard their ship so we can disarm it."

"You mean you've figured out how to untrap the booby?" Issy asked.

"Well, not quite, but the way to do it should be in here." He waved the crystal. "Any other Eastin-Heigle ships out there should follow the same protocols."

Ben held his hand out. "Well done, Corin. One of Mother Ramona's specialists should be able to crack this."

Chapter Twenty-Seven

OLYANDA

CARA STOOD ON THE EDGE OF THE LANDING pad in the rain, enjoying the weather on Olyanda after the weather-free atmosphere on Crossways. She left her hood down and let the rain slick off her short hair and trickle down her face. She was happy to make her home wherever Ben and the Free Company were, but there was no denying she preferred her feet on solid ground.

If only she could persuade Ben down to the planet, but Garrick called on him more and more frequently these days. It was almost as if ... She didn't want to think about it, but it was almost as if Garrick was grooming him to take over one day. How old was Garrick? He couldn't be more than twenty years older than Ben. There was plenty of life left in him.

Yet ...

They'd all noticed a difference in Garrick since the attack on Crossways, and Cara didn't think the space battle was to blame. She was pretty sure the close call with the Nimbus was what was weighing on his mind.

Cara had been monitoring the S-Logs for chatter about foldspace. There was nothing about the Nimbus, and no one else had seen the void dragons, or more likely they weren't saying anything if they had in case they were sent for a neural examination. But, worryingly, two more passenger vessels had disappeared in the Folds within the last couple of weeks. Vessels occasionally disappeared in foldspace, but not so many in such a short period of time. They had nothing in common except they'd used the jump gates. Not even the same jump gates—she'd checked.

Stand by, Jake said. *Anticipating touchdown in ten minutes.*

Waiting for you on the field. It's raining.

Ah, my bad luck. Jake had a pilot's disdain for weather systems. They were nothing but a nuisance as far as he was concerned.

No crosswind, though.

Olyanda could be subject to sudden fierce storms, which caused everyone to take shelter, and closed down the spaceports and all traffic.

That's one blessing.

Jake brought in the *Bellatkin* in slightly under ten minutes, set her down on the landing pad, opened the hold hatch, and released the unloading ramp.

Lots of goodies, courtesy of Crossways.

Including my exoskeletons?

Them, too.

You're a star.

Yeah, right. I suppose you want some help with the unloading.

If you're offering.

Jake climbed down from the pilot's hatch and stared at the remains of the little town they used to call Landing. "It's not exactly prime real estate, is it?"

"It used to look better than this. It took a battering both before the Crossways battle and after. Apart from the occasional solar flares that send us all running for sun block and the violent storms that send us running for shelter, Olyanda's a decent planet—at least around the equatorial belt."

"Yeah, I saw the polar ice on the way in."

"It's retreating, but the ice goes in cycles. As far as we can tell, it's never completely covered the whole planet, but sometimes the temperate equatorial band narrows considerably. It might be a couple of thousand years before the next ice age or a couple of hundred, but it won't happen overnight. In the meantime . . . look." She gestured beyond the compound to where a fat silver river rolled gently across a wide valley floor. On the far side of the valley giant hoodoo-like pinnacles rose and beyond them mountains, grayed out by the rain.

"The mountains sparkle in the sun," Cara said. "Mica, in case you're wondering."

"I figured you might have mentioned it if they'd been made out of diamond."

The remains of a road, laid down for the original settlers, ran parallel to the river. In the far distance, a collection of buildings squatted close to trees that Cara had ceased to think of as strange, but when she'd first set foot on Olyanda they'd looked like giant heads of purple-green broccoli. The name had stuck, as had the name for the town.

"Those are the infamous broccoli trees, huh?" Jake asked.

She grinned. "The settlers decided to call their first town Timbertown, but it was always Broccoliburg to us. The refugees Garrick sent down from Crossways after the battle have taken over the buildings there, and the crops that the settlers broke ground to plant are doing well."

"So how much of what's here is salvageable?"

She sighed. "The landing vehicle is completely gone. Gutted. Nothing left to strip out, so we can't retrieve any tech. A couple of ground cars can be repaired with parts from the chewed-up ones. There were five flyers still operable after the bombing, but Leah Nolan's guys took them in the early days. I've asked for them all, but I'll be happy if I get two."

"Accommodation?"

"Tengue's guys salvaged some of it already. They camped out here for a short while after the settlers left—"

"They were originally Ari van Blaiden's squad, right? I heard the stories."

Cara sincerely hoped he hadn't, at least not all of the stories.

"Tengue's mercs had been hired by van Blaiden, but they were a professional crew and van Blaiden being very dead at the end of the confrontation, they considered that contract ended and were happy to sign on as security for the Free Company."

Tengue rarely talked ethics. However, Hilde had once told her that he'd had serious second thoughts about van Blaiden, but having signed a contract felt honor bound to stick to it.

"Come on, I'll show you around before we unload your cargo."

Something blue-green whizzed past their legs at knee height. Jake jumped, startled.

"What the heck was that?"

"Trikalla. Native wildlife."

"It looked like a jellyfish."

"Yes, almost, except it floats on air, on a cushion of air to be precise. And it squirts out jets of air to steer, kind of like farting, except we're still not sure whether it has a rear end or whether both ends are the same. Don't worry, they're not dangerous—not to flesh-and-blood creatures anyway. They live by ingesting metal. Copper's their favorite, but they're willing to try anything new."

"Okay. Anything else I should know about?"

"Not unless you take a trip into the mountains where you should watch out for lyx packs, six-legged things about the size of a wolf. Be careful in swamplands, too. Reptans are the most dangerous creature on Olyanda. They look a bit like a cross between a beaver and a flying squirrel. Do not engage. They leap for your face and latch on, and their underside is covered in venomous barbs. Neurotoxin. You'd last about half an hour and it would be the longest half hour of your soon-to-be-over life."

"Jeez! Can't this place come up with fluffy bunnies?"

"I once asked Ben exactly the same question. He said that if it did, they'd eat all the crops."

"Yeah, he might have a point."

Cara led Jake into the middle of the compound where what had been a geodesic meeting hall now stood like a skeleton, spurs reaching into the sky, defying gravity. Some of the clear panels lay splintered and crushed, but alongside the dome was a sealed tunnel-shaped structure made from whole panels.

"At the moment that's our only weatherproof structure. We eat and sleep there."

"What's that about people in glass houses shouldn't throw stones?" Jake asked.

"Or maybe that should be: people in glass houses shouldn't."

Jake laughed. "Yeah, not much privacy, huh."

"Not much. We'll get the privacy thing sorted out now we have the exoskeletons. We need some help with the heavy lifting to move the medonite panels from the old risers. There isn't one still complete, but there are plenty of panels that are reusable. There are enough to make shelters for us and the animals."

"Animals?"

"The settlers left behind all their livestock when we had to get them off planet in a hurry. Garrick's refugees started to round up horses and cattle, but there are still more out there. We've liberated half a dozen riding horses already."

Jake shuddered visibly. "I'll stick to a more predictable mode of transport if I can."

She grinned at him. Typical flyboy. He'd fly a bucket of bolts through the Folds without blinking, but he was nervous of anything planet based.

"Come and eat with us, and then we'll get your cargo unloaded."

At the far end of the glasshouse, they'd set up a camp kitchen, presided over by Blake Morgan, one of Ada Levenson's food wizards. He took care of all the domestic arrangements, which let everyone else get on with their jobs.

"Hello, Jake." Jussaro waved from the table where he was tucking into a bowl of Blake's fragrant risotto. "Get yourself a bowl of this and come and join us. Tastes great, but don't ask what's in it."

"Hey, I heard that," Blake called from the other side of the kitchen. "I'll give you the recipe if you like."

Jussaro chuckled. Archie Tatum glanced up from his own bowl, smirked, and continued eating.

"Do not piss off the chef, my friend," Lev Reznik pointed at Jussaro with his fork. "I once worked in a restaurant, I know—"

Cara turned away to get a bowl. The friendly banter was good. She hadn't known what to do with Reznik. He'd had several sessions with Jussaro and was currently trying to decide whether he wanted to be fitted with an implant, at the same time as Jussaro was trying to decide whether he could cope with one. There was every indication that with an implant he could be an excellent long-range Telepath. Cara had been pleased he'd volunteered for the Sanctuary working party.

Ben had given her ten Free Company psi-techs, mostly Psi-Mechs under Archie Tatum, but she'd also brought Efra, Dido Kennedy's protégé from Red One. Dido was worried that someone would try and snatch her again. If she joined the Free Company, they could protect her.

They also had Nairi, the child Ben had rescued from the tube. Her family had gone home on the understanding that Nairi would stay with the Free Company until she was old enough to decide her own future. Jussaro had paired her up with Efra and the two girls were becoming firm friends. With Efra's help, Nairi's Basic was improving. If one decided to have an implant fitted, the other probably would, but they didn't have to make that decision yet.

One by one, another eight psi-techs filed in for food. Morale was good. They had a simple job to do: clear the site and recycle what they could. Cara realized she was happy here. Life in the open air with no distractions was remarkably restorative.

◆ ◆ ◆

Ben arrived back on Crossways. The apartment felt empty without Cara. She was too far away on Olyanda for him to contact her mentally. His Telepathy was strictly short-range. He had to wait for her to contact him. She usually came through late in her day, but not always at a regular time. It was as if he took second place to her establishing Sanctuary.

He knew Sanctuary was important, but he had too much to do to give it much thought. Cara and Jussaro were perfectly capable of handling everything. She spent much of her time with Jussaro these days. He could be jealous, but—well—it was Jussaro. Cara treated him like a favorite uncle.

Her absence shifted the comms work onto the shoulders of the Free Company's class twos. Some of them had to work in tandem to match what Cara could achieve on her own, but Ben was the first to admit that tying Cara to monitoring long-distance comms was a waste of her talents.

They needed to recruit a few more class one Telepaths

for the Free Company, but that wasn't as easy as it sounded. They were rare, and the Free Company was a tight unit, formed in adversity. Even if they could find people with the appropriate skills, integrating newcomers wouldn't be easy.

He called into the office first to find Wenna in her usual place. Sometimes he wondered if she was hardwired to her desk.

"Heard from Cara?" Wenna asked.

He shook his head. "You?"

"Not since a request for a couple of exoskeletons a couple of days ago to help them shift wreckage. I guess Sanctuary's going to take a lot of resources."

"Yes. What do you think about it all?"

Wenna rocked back in her chair. "If you'd asked me three years ago, I'd have shrugged it off. I was nice and comfortable, working for the Trust. It felt like security. I would have followed the company line and said anyone who went rogue was ungrateful when the megacorps gave them so much. Sure, I'd been on some shitty missions . . ." She waved her prosthetic arm. "But even though I knew things could get rough, I still trusted we'd be looked after. I trusted that Crowder would look after us." Her mouth turned down. "But that was before the Olyanda mission. We've all gone rogue together and with good reason. We were lucky not to be fighting the system on our own."

"That's what Cara did," Ben said, "and Jussaro."

"And I respect them for it. I'm not sure I would have the guts to do what they did. So the short answer to your question is yes. I think creating Sanctuary here on Crossways, or down on the surface of Olyanda, is the right thing to do. If Jussaro and Cara are willing to do it, I think we should give them all the backing we can." Her eyes narrowed. "You miss Cara, don't you?"

"Is it that obvious?"

"Only to me. And maybe to Ronan."

"It's pretty much an open secret, then. Though Cara may not have noticed."

"That's between you and her. You should talk about it."

And how would that work out? His mind flitted across possibilities. They were drifting apart. Did he have the courage to relax and trust that she'd come back?

"I said you should talk about it," Wenna said.

He nodded.

"Soon," she said.

"Soon." Ben turned to leave. "I'll be with Garrick and Mother Ramona if you need me."

Wenna was right. Probably.

Chapter Twenty-Eight

THIEF

THEY'D BEEN ON OLYANDA FOR SIX DAYS. Once they had the exoskeletons that Jake had delivered, the job of clearing went much faster. Cara worked in one, strapped into it like the soft heart of a powerful robot. She'd not used one since the early days of settling Olyanda with the Ecolibrians and it had taken her a couple of days to remind her muscles how to move in one of the lumbering machines, but now she used the machine like an extension of herself, to clear rubble and haul usable panels and equipment. They'd borrowed an earth shovel from Leah Nolan and sorted the debris into recyclable and non. They used the non as a foundation for a rampart around the compound. They'd eventually top it with a perimeter fence, but that was a task for later. They'd also set aside material to be recycled by the settlers in Broccoliburg who were expanding outward.

"Hey, Carlinni." Jussaro nudged her foot as she lay, fully clothed, on her bed.

"Can't a girl get some sleep?"

"I brought you coffee."

"Oh, sure, that will help me sleep." She sat up and pulled a blanket around her shoulders.

Jussaro handed her a mug and sat on the empty bed next

to hers. The air mattress dipped under his weight. The other beds were still unoccupied since there was a giant mojo tournament taking place at the other end of the shelter. Voices rose and fell with every shake of the twelve-sided dice.

"Our week is up tomorrow. The next year depends on the assessment. Your assessment, I guess, as the project leader."

"I'm only taking point on the site reconstruction. Sanctuary is yours."

"All right, first things first. Are you going to report that the site can be salvaged?"

"I think we've proved that."

"Then what?"

"As I said. Sanctuary is yours."

"I want to share Zandra Hartwell's knowledge with you, the contacts and the unlock codes . . ."

She opened her mouth to protest, but he silenced her with a wave. "You don't have to do the actual unlocking, but you may need to pass on the knowledge one day. And I want to bring in Vina Daniels. We're going to need an implant specialist and she's the right one for the job. I'll give her the unlock codes, too, and also—unless you can see any reason why not—I'll give them to Civility Jamieson. What do you think?"

Cara tried to gather her thoughts. "I think Vina is the perfect choice if she'll take the job."

"And Jamieson?"

"He's an arse, but he's brilliant at what he does. He can help people with those codes, and that's what he's good at. He doesn't actually give a shit about the individuals, but he likes to win. Those codes are made of win as long as they stay secret."

"And you?"

"Let me think about it. There's Ben to consider."

"He's not a great believer in Sanctuary."

"He is, but it's not his primary concern right now. He's trying to keep the Free Company together and support Garrick while keeping an eye out for what the megacorps are going to do next."

"And he wants to do all that with you at his side."

"He does. And I want to be at his side, or I want him at

mine." She sighed. "Garrick pledged to support us for a year, and Ben agreed. I'll give it a year and then I might want to reassess."

She sipped her coffee.

"I'll leave you to think about it. Get some sleep."

"Sleep? You brought me coffee," she said to his retreating back.

❖ ❖ ❖

"I heard your trip didn't exactly go according to plan." Mother Ramona crossed her elegant legs and sipped from a glass of iced tea.

Ben had opted for hot tea, and a mug sat steaming and ignored on the small table beside his understuffed arm chair.

They were in Mother Ramona's retreat, a corner of the Mansion House that she'd managed to make look like the den she used to favor when she lived alone. It was messy and organic, with a sagging couch covered in throws, overcrowded shelves stuffed with memorabilia and a few real paper books—antiques by the look of the bindings—and file boxes. Datacrystals lay scattered in front of the holographic screen on her desk. It blinked occasionally as it cycled through a holding program.

"Not exactly. We weren't planning to get blown up, or lose a potentially sound ship, but one of my crew retrieved the ship's system files. I'm looking for someone who can crack them. I figured you might have someone on staff."

"You need a good thief."

"Isn't that a contradiction in terms?"

"Okay, you need a thief who's good at the job."

"I'd have to be sure of loyalties. I still have a bad taste in my mouth about the Alphabet Gang."

"Yes, they were a disappointment. Garrick has made it clear they're no longer welcome on Crossways."

Mother Ramona uncrossed her legs and sat forward. "I have someone in mind—a pair of someones actually: J.P. Lister and his wife Pamela, known as Pami. They're a bit of an odd couple, but they're not likely to turn assassin. When you see them, you'll understand why. I'm not sure J.P. actually has a first name. No one ever calls him anything but J.P."

"You trust them?"

"They're in it for the money. Offer them enough, and they'll take the deal. I trust them enough not to sell out to anyone who offers them more. A deal is a deal as far as they're concerned."

"That's refreshingly—honest."

She laughed. "Honor among thieves."

"Okay, set up a meeting."

"I already have. I anticipated your needs. They'll be at the Koshee Corner House for the next hour."

"How will I know them?"

"Ask for table 24. J.P. is the brains, but he wouldn't be able to function without Pami. Don't assume she's purely decorative. She is that, but she's a lot more as well."

He levered himself out of the chair. "Thanks for the tea."

"You haven't touched it."

He leaned forward and picked up the mug, still a little too hot. He sipped twice and put it down again. "There."

Mother Ramona chortled and waved him away with one hand. "Keep us informed."

The Koshee Corner House was one of the station's premier meeting places. Plenty of deals took place here, so each table was equipped with privacy baffles. It had come through the battle without a scratch thanks to its position close to the hub on the second level.

"Table 24," Ben told the receptionist. "I'm expected."

He followed her into the restaurant, ordered tea, and turned to meet the Listers. Mother Ramona had only half-prepared him for the odd couple before him. J.P. was in a float chair, a stick-thin man, sharp-featured, possibly in his late thirties, and with a bush of ginger hair that waved as if in a breeze, despite the air being still. Pami was probably the most beautiful woman Ben had ever seen. Every feature was perfect, including her dark eyes, unblemished mid-brown skin, straight nose, and kissable lips.

Stop! What was he thinking?

He lips twitched up at the corners. She knew what effect she had on him. It was probably the same effect she had on every straight male within a radius of a hundred meters. She half raised one eyebrow.

"Commander Benjamin. We were expecting you. Say hello, J.P."

"Hello, Commander." J.P. elevated his chair, so he was on Ben's eyeline. "Pleased to meet you. Mother Ramona told us you might have a job for us. Do sit down."

Ben sat and J.P. lowered the chair so that he was at the same height as Ben.

"A job, yes, I need a security system cracked."

He held out a datacrystal, a copy of the original. Pami leaned forward across the table showing cleavage that ate a corner of Ben's rational mind. He didn't know where to look. Well, yes, he knew, but the jiggling beauties were trying to claim his attention. The eyes, Ben. Look at the eyes.

Pami took the datacrystal, examined it, and handed it to J.P.

"Eastin-Heigle." J.P. saved the day by drawing Ben's attention to himself as he wrapped his fingers around the crystal and closed his eyes. He had a light voice that had a tendency to squeak like a teenager. "Interesting, Commander Benjamin. What would you have us do?"

"Crack the security and tell us how to access the ships safely."

"You need someone to break in," Pami said. "Don't let my husband's physical appearance fool you. Losing the use of his legs didn't damage his ability to work."

"And by work you mean—"

"Steal. Yes. I'd like to think that, given time, there isn't a security system in the galaxy that J.P. can't crack. There isn't a single item we can't retrieve."

"Safely?"

"Of course." She almost purred. "But it's inanimate objects only. We don't deal in kidnap."

"Fair enough."

Eyes, Ben, look her in the eyes! Her face was distracting enough in itself.

"How long?"

"How long have we got?" J.P. asked. "Is it a rush job?"

"It's not life or death, but we'd like to address it as soon as possible."

J.P. cleared his throat. "We haven't talked a fee."

"I don't suppose telling you the station will be very grateful would carry any weight?"

J.P. cocked his head to one side, raised one eyebrow, and gave Ben one of those looks.

Ben sighed. "I didn't think so. What's the bottom line?"

Pami smiled. "Five thou retainer while J.P. looks at the systems, then twenty-five thou per vessel recovered. The first twenty-five thou to be deposited in escrow before we depart Crossways."

"You're coming on the actual job?"

"I said not to let J.P.'s mobility fool you. We need to be there. Deal?"

"Deal."

◆ ◆ ◆

Cara waited for Ben on the landing field, her bag packed. She'd had a sleepless night and then in the early morning had come to a decision. It was her turn to wake Jussaro for a change. She had a slight headache from the infodump, and now all that knowledge was rolling round in her brain. She'd need a while to sort it all out. The megacorps would kill for the unlock codes and information about Sanctuary that she now carried.

Thanks, Jussaro. Once more I'm a target, or I would be if anyone knew about this.

You're welcome, Carlinni. He picked up her thought and tossed it back at her.

Jussaro and Archie Tatum were continuing the cleanup in her absence.

She was jittery with the thought of seeing Ben again. She missed him. It had only been a week, but there had been the months before that when she'd been hunting for Zandra Hartwell. Her time at home had been too short and interrupted by her work and Ben's.

Home. She examined the concept. Yes, impersonal as it was, she considered their small shared apartment in Blue Seven to be home.

She didn't try to contact Ben while he was dropping into the atmosphere from Crossways. He was an experienced pilot, but drilling down through the atmosphere was still dangerous, so she didn't distract him.

She heard the ship before she saw it and knew immediately it was Ben's small Dixie Flyer, not the *Solar Wind*. Strictly speaking, it was the Trust's Dixie Flyer. No psi-tech ever owned the expensive equipment they operated. Not that the Trust was ever going to get the Dixie back—though it was probably one more thing on the charge sheet that sat in every Monitor station on this side of the galaxy.

Solar Wind purred, the Dixie screamed as she dropped down. Then the tone lowered as she made her final approach and settled neatly onto the landing field on her antigravs.

Cara waved, picked up her bag, and began to walk.

Ben opened the side hatch and stepped down the ramp, austere in his black buddysuit. Her own buddysuit moved with her like a second skin as she picked up speed. Three paces away she dropped the bag and reached for him.

"Missed you."

"Missed you, too."

His hug was warm, but his kiss was only a peck on the cheek. Then he held her at arm's length.

"It's happened, hasn't it? Jussaro's given you the codes."

She nodded. "How did you know? Am I suddenly walking around with a sign on my forehead that says: *Open here for secret information*?"

"Not quite, but I know you. You look as if you're carrying an extra burden."

"Well, in a way, I suppose I am."

He pulled her to him again and she didn't resist.

"You could have said no," he whispered.

She shook her head against his chest. "I couldn't."

He kissed the top of her head and let her go. She slung her bag aboard the Dixie and climbed in, settling into the passenger couch with a sigh. "I could do with a nice long space voyage so I can rest up. I'd forgotten what hard work an exoskeleton is. It's been like the early days with the Ecolibrians, but at least we've gone a whole week without a storm, and the guys at Broccoliburg traded us some fresh meat for sugar, so there have been a few high spots. Are we going straight to the wrecks?"

"No." Ben shook his head. "I've hired a couple of Mother Ramona's retrieval specialists—"

"You mean thieves."

"Precisely. J.P. Lister and his wife, Pami. Let's call them an unusual couple and leave it at that. J.P. cracked the safety codes from Eastin-Heigle's system download in less than twenty-four hours. I'm taking them out with a retrieval team to see if we can liberate a battleship."

"Oh." Cara bit back her disappointment.

"Wenna's looking forward to having you back in the comms chair."

"It's about time we recruited another class one."

He compressed his lips and gave Cara a long look. "Sorry about that. You understand why I have to go with the retrieval team."

He did look sorry. "I guess so."

It should make it easier to tell him she'd promised a year to Jussaro and to Sanctuary, but somehow it didn't.

The trip to Crossways was a short, six-hour hop, not even needing a jump through the Folds. Though they were next to each other on couches in the small cabin space aboard the *Dixie*, conversation was desultory . . . almost forced.

They landed in Port 46, a few hundred meters from the *Solar Wind*.

Ben pecked her on the cheek again. "I have to go."

"Right now?"

"Sorry. We delayed the launch by half a day so I could come and pick you up, but we're scheduled to depart at eighteen hundred hours."

Lynda Munene gave Cara a wave as she made her way across the hangar.

"Who are they?" Cara jerked her chin toward a couple heading for *Solar Wind*: a man in a pair of close-fitting kinetic legs, rolling across the floor at walking speed next to a tall, elegant woman.

"That's Mr. and Mrs. Lister, J.P. and Pami."

"Really?"

"He's the brains, she's the b—"

"Beauty? Were you going to say beauty?"

"No. Is she? I hadn't noticed."

"You hadn't?"

"I was going to say brawn."

"I think you were right the first time."

As Pami Lister turned to glance in their direction, Cara pulled Ben to her and kissed him full on the lips. She felt his surprise and then his gratifying response.

"Take that for now, Mr. I-Hadn't-Noticed." She grinned and slapped him lightly on the arm. "Look after yourself."

"You know I always do."

"No, you don't. You always take care of other people

first. Why do you think I've insisted Ronan join the mission?"

"Point taken. I will be careful, I promise."

She let him go and caught a tub cab to Blue Seven where she dumped her underwear in the laundry and repacked the bag. Self-cleaning underwear would only last for so long.

She felt a little empty.

Cara, are you back on Crossways?

Just arrived, Jake. Where are you?

Would you believe it, at my cousin's graduation ceremony.

I would believe it. Tell Dree congratulations from me.

She'll be looking for a job now.

Are you hinting?

Just saying.

*You know the Free Company doesn't take on . . . * She'd been going to say deadheads, but she pulled herself up in time. *normals.*

I know. She'd be willing to have a receiving implant if that would help. She's real smart.

Dree had been disappointed to learn she wasn't psi-tech material.

No matter how smart, a receiving implant would still put her at the bottom of the pecking order in the Free Company. She's worth more than that.

I get it, but—

I tell you what, Jake. If she doesn't get her dream job offered, we'll talk again. All right?

Yeah, thanks.

Sanctuary would need a good administrator, and being a deadhead might be an advantage.

Chapter Twenty-Nine

SALVAGE

BEN NOSED *SOLAR WIND* INTO THE KNOT OF debris that had almost proved fatal on their last trip. This time they had the Listers on board.

"Potential Eastin-Heigle ship dead ahead," Yan called.

"On screen." Ben watched as the bulk of a battleship hove into view. "Is that the *Howling Wolf*?"

"I believe it is." Yan's voice held a note of awe. "I can't believe they didn't scuttle her before they left."

"She's a thing of beauty. Maybe her captain didn't have the heart, or maybe she's booby-trapped up the wazoo and waiting for us to trigger one huge explosion."

"So we get to see if the Listers are as good as their talk."

"We do, indeed." Ben spoke over the comm. "Suit up, everyone. We're going after the *Howling Wolf*."

J.P. had an adapted space suit that worked in tandem with his kinetic legs. As a Psi-Mech, he controlled the mechanical leg sheaths with his mind, so he had full mobility. Pami had taken Ben aside in a waft of expensive perfume and explained that he didn't always choose to use the kinetic legs because they took up a proportion of his thoughts and sometimes he needed his full attention on something else. Ben hoped he had a hundred percent of his attention on cracking the Eastin-Heigle security program.

There was a reason Ben had wanted Cara occupied elsewhere while he took a crew to diffuse a bloody big bomb.

"Stand off a hundred klicks once the away team has latched onto *Howling Wolf*, Yan."

"What if you need fast extraction like last time?"

"We have more intel than last time."

"You trust the Listers?"

"They're still alive."

"It's your fu— err, choice."

Ben laughed and left the pilot's chair to Yan.

"Look after my ship."

"Since I can't fly her through the Folds without a jump gate, you'd better come back, or Crossways will have to send out some rookie jump pilot to rescue us. I can't tell you how embarrassing that would be."

Despite his otherwise excellent piloting abilities, Yan couldn't see the void dragon. He'd never grasped the technique of entering and exiting foldspace without a gate.

Ben climbed down the access tube to the suit room where Lynda Munene was already waiting. Issy Monaghan and Corin Butterfield were on standby. There was no use risking more personnel than absolutely necessary. For the same reason, Ronan wasn't going across with the first party.

Pami was helping J.P. into his suit, her own fastened as far as her waist with the top half dangling down behind her.

"Okay, sweetie?" she asked.

"Fine." J.P. did a series of squats in the suit, testing his connection with the legs.

Pami shrugged into her suit.

"Let me help you with that." Ben had stepped forward before he'd even put his brain into gear. Pami's buddysuit hardly disguised her hourglass figure. Ben put his thoughts on lockdown as he checked her fastenings and clipped the helmet to her collar. He tapped the helmet to remind her to reset her comm. "Everything all right in there?"

"A-okay, Commander Benjamin."

Ben busied himself getting into his own suit and let Lynda check it for him. *Are we set?* he asked.

Set, the Listers said in unison.

Set, Lynda said.

Ronan entered, already fully suited. *Set,* he added.

We are. You're not, Ben said.

Would you like to explain that to Cara, or shall I?

Ben thought about it. *You're sure?*

Sure.

Okay. Set, Ben said.

They cycled through *Solar Wind*'s airlock and, tied on a line, jetted across to *Howling Wolf.*

Main airlock, J.P. said. *That's the only place I can disable the intruder protocol.*

They moved as a unit to the main lock. J.P. and Pami unclipped themselves from the main line, but stayed clipped together.

We have a window of eighteen minutes after the hatch opens, J.P. said. *It will take six of those to cycle through the airlock, so stay cool. Mark the hatch opening in three ... two ... one. ... Now.*

Ben activated his timer and followed the Listers into the airlock. At least this one was big enough to take all five of them at once.

Howling Wolf, Ronan said. *She has a bit of a reputation.*

She has, indeed. Ben looked around the airlock, bland and workmanlike. *I was on her once before, when I was in the Monitors. It was during the Burnish War. She'd been sent to put down the rebels with extreme prejudice, but her captain, Jeb Nash, gave me a window to take out a party of refugees—families of the rebels, mostly women and children. He agreed he wouldn't notice them slipping away.*

Sounds like a compassionate man, Ronan said.

Not compassionate enough to spare the rebel base, but, yes, it was a small mercy, and I made the most of it.

We're in. J.P. cut across Ben's reminiscence.

The airlock finished cycling, and the inner door cracked and shooshed open. Emergency lighting shone around them, but the long corridor in front of them was dark.

There's atmo, Lynda said, *but it's only residual. Life support is off; ship's systems are locked down. It's colder than Hell.*

Find me a systems station, J.P. said. *I expected one right here.*

Ben's chrono, showing on the heads-up display in his helmet told him they had ten and a half minutes left. Without gravity, they pulled themselves along the corridor, pushing

off and floating where there was enough of a sightline to tell
them where they were heading.

I thought he'd studied the download, Lynda said.

Everyone's a critic, Pami said. *That was for a cruiser,
dumbass.*

Right. Cruiser. Battleship. Try this way. Ben turned left
at a junction and slapped the wall. The ship's plan sprang
into life.

Three doors down, Ben said. *Let's move it.*

They found a secondary station, turned on the emergency lighting, and stood aside while J.P. and Pami went to
work.

J.P. stared at the control panel for longer than Ben expected, then with gloved fingers, tapped a couple of controls. A second panel lit up, much more complex than the
first, and J.P. examined it.

Can he do this or not? Lynda asked.

No distractions, Pami snapped.

Ben glanced sideways at J.P.'s faceplate. Was that sweat
beading on his forehead?

Six minutes to go.

Time stretched unbearably slowly. Finally, J.P. moved. He
pressed both hands onto the console and leaned forward.

Four minutes to go.

He's in, Pami said.

"Self-destruct in three minutes," the ship announced
calmly.

Can we do anything? Ben asked.

Stay out of his hair, Pami said, but her own mental
voice sounded strained.

J.P. clutched the console with his hands.

Legs, he said.

Pami grasped him around the waist and anchored him.

He'd abandoned control of his legs in order to give the
ship's systems all his attention.

"Self-destruct in two minutes," the ship said.

There was no point in running for the door. The airlock
was on a six-minute cycle and *Solar Wind* was standing well
away. At least she'd be out of the immediate blast radius.

And Cara was safe.

Ronan inched toward him until their suits were touching.

They'd been side by side in life-or-death situations before. There was nothing to say.

"Self-destruct in sixty seconds," the ship said in a slightly grating voice.

"Self-destruct in fifty seconds."

"Self-destruct in forty seconds."

"Self-destruct in thirty seconds. Twenty-nine. Twenty-eight. Twenty-seven."

Ben tried to shut the countdown out of his mind. The Free Company would be all right. Garrick could solve any problems Crossways hit him with. He was sorry he'd not had the opportunity to see Rion again, but his brother would be fine. He was resilient, and he had Nan, and Ricky, and Kai.

"Nineteen. Eighteen."

He didn't want to die.

"Seventeen."

Not here, not now.

"Sixteen."

Still too much left to do.

"Fifteen."

And there was Cara. She would be all right. She was capable . . .

"Fourteen."

But, oh, he didn't want to leave her . . .

"Ship's systems restored."

He sucked in a deep breath . . .

"Self-destruct terminated."

And relaxed.

"This is *Howling Wolf*, Captain Jeb Nash in command. How may I help you?" The generated voice almost sounded real.

Quarter gravity bound Ben's feet to the floor. He wanted to kneel and kiss it. *Everyone okay?*

J.P. sank to the floor, his legs sticking out at odd angles. *I am now,* he said.

Pami knelt by him and tapped the faceplate of her helmet against her husband's.

I think I've tested my buddysuit's plumbing to destruction, Lynda said. *But, yes, okay, now.*

Okay, Ronan said, his mental voice steady.

Have you got nerves of steel? Ben asked.

Ronan shook his head. *No imagination. It helps tremendously.*

But Ben had seen the beads of sweat on his face. He touched his friend's arm, briefly. *Let's go see if we have a functioning battleship.*

Link me with Solar Wind, Lynda, please. Yan. You can come alongside now. Send Issy and Corin over. She's ours.

Okay, Boss. Stand by.

Issy, Corin, and Lynda settled themselves into engineering and checked out the ship's systems. There was some superficial damage. She'd taken a couple of hits in the battle and showed signs of one section having been depressurized and restored again, but they pronounced all sections safe and life support online again. The air was breathable, and the heating systems would achieve a safe temperature for humans in less than thirty minutes.

Having done their job, the Listers expressed a desire to find a cabin and rest. J.P. looked exhausted. Pami heaved him to his feet, and he took over control of his legs again.

"That was a close one, Commander Benjamin. I don't mind admitting it." J.P. said. "I think I earned my cut."

"Yes, you did. Are you still willing to try for any other ships we find?"

"If they're Eastin-Heigle, they'll be easy after this one."

Ben and Ronan set off to explore the ship. They found crew quarters and sick bay on this level.

"Just a quick look," Ronan said. "I heard the sick bays on these ships were state-of-the-art." He stared at the gleaming surfaces. It didn't look as though it had been abandoned in a hurry. Everything was in its place.

Through sick bay was a mortuary alcove. An array of lights showed that three of the cold chambers were occupied.

"I guess when they transported the living, they didn't have room to take the dead," Ben said as Ronan pulled out each of the drawers in turn.

"Odd that they didn't simply hold a funeral and cremate them. Uh-oh. Did the ship say that Nash was captain?"

"Yes. He must be coming up for retirement sometime soon."

"Looks like he's been retired permanently," Ronan said.

"Asphyxiation. He must have been in one of the depressurized compartments. Same with the other two bodies."

"Ah, sorry to hear that. Nash was a good man and a fine captain. We'll deal with the bodies later."

"Oh, shit!"

"What?"

"There's someone in the emergency cryo chamber. Not dead. They left someone behind!"

"Badly injured?"

"Not injured at all as far as I can tell."

"Any notes?"

"Aww, hell. He's in cryo storage pending neural reconditioning. No more details, though there may be a personnel file on him somewhere. His name's Oliver Lopez. He's a pilot."

"Is he safe where he is?"

"He's not going anywhere anytime soon."

"Then he's a problem for another day."

They checked the ship plan on the sick bay wall and made their way up to the bridge. After *Solar Wind*, it felt enormous. There was a captain's chair as well as a pilot's station and a nav chair. There were additional stations for a comms tech, a systems tech, and two gunnery operatives, a weapons systems tech, and a defense station. Next to them was a dedicated damage station.

"All the bells and whistles you could hope for," Ben said.

"Or not hope for if you happened to be on the other side."

"Indeed."

Ben sat in the captain's chair and flicked on the holo screen. "Pretty big chair to fill," he said. "Nash was vastly experienced."

"Do you fancy yourself in that seat?" Ronan asked.

"No. Not my style. Garrick will find someone. Maybe Oleg Staple can use her as a flagship—presuming the engineers say she's suitable for a jump drive."

Hey, Boss. Lynda cut in from engineering.

Lynda, how goes it?

Corin and Issy are here. On first examination, it looks like we can fit one of Kennedy's Mark II jump drives. There's some repair work to do to the damaged sections, and refitting the jump engines will take about eleven days.

What's her capability now?

Sublight engines are online. We can get her out of the debris field and give the engineers room to work on her.

Stand by.

Yan, did you get that? Rendezvous one hundred klicks outside of the debris field.

I'll follow you.

Ben abandoned the captain's chair and took the pilot's console. *Sublights online. Let's go.*

For such a big vessel, *Howling Wolf* was remarkably responsive. Ben nudged her through the densest part of the debris field without mishap and covered the hundred klicks in barely ten minutes, half of that being deceleration.

How does she handle, Boss? Yan sounded eager.

Sweet as a nut. She's all yours for the refit.

I'm looking forward to that.

Ben rounded up Lynda, Issy, and the Listers while Ronan prepped Oliver Lopez' cryo pod for transfer across to *Solar Wind*. They left Corin in charge of engineering, and Yan Gwenn took over as captain and pilot. They'd send a team to install a Mark II drive and make repairs.

I want this on my résumé even if it is only temporary, Yan said from *Howling Wolf* as Ben settled in to take *Solar Wind* through the Folds to Crossways.

✦ ✦ ✦

Crowder took the invisible glass elevator right to the top of the building for a full board meeting. Tori LeBon had given him a heads-up late the previous evening. They'd lost three colonies, now, though they'd managed to keep two of the losses completely secret in case it affected their stock figures. Ditto the ship losses.

Five years ago their ship losses in foldspace had been in line with everyone else's, one or two a year. Accidents happened. They were sad, but statistically there were more deaths from accidental drownings on planet Earth than from flying the Folds.

That was five years ago.

They'd tried to keep a lid on the news. Three years ago, however, they'd lost ninety-six flights, most of them freight but some passenger flights. Not all of them under the direct control of the Trust, of course; some were colony-to-colony routes, which enabled them to fudge the figures.

Then two years ago they'd lost a hundred and forty-five ships and last year two hundred and six. This year, so far, was looking no better.

Crowder leaned against the invisible glass-steel wall, trusting his bulk to what looked like nothing. He'd never liked heights. Taking this elevator as opposed to the conventional ones was his way of testing himself.

If the new settlers knew the rate of loss, they wouldn't be so eager to sign up for off-world travel—hence one of the reasons for keeping quiet. They hadn't told the crews either, but rumors were rife and even the frequent changing of routes and the splitting up and relocation of crews didn't help. Everyone knew someone who was no longer responding to messages.

Were other corporations losing ships and colonies and, like the Trust, squashing the news in case the value of stocks fell?

The elevator slowed and the door opened onto the plush carpet and refined opulence of the executive suite where a pretty young thing in a traditional Zulu beadwork collar against a dark-brown, flesh-colored singlet and a multihued wraparound skirt offered him a beverage of his choice.

"Iced coffee." He needed the caffeine, but it was too hot for regular coffee.

Yolanda Chang, in charge of the research and development division, entered the suite from the far door. Had she been talking to Tori LeBon in advance of the meeting?

Isaac Whittle, the vice-chair, was thirty seconds behind Chang. Damn, that was ominous. Thirty seconds behind Whittle, the door opened again to reveal Le Bon. She'd had a complete makeover since the last time he'd seen her, possibly a rejuvenation treatment or three. She was taller by ten centimeters and thinner by twenty. Maybe Crowder should have taken advantage of his doctor's offer. He pulled in his gut and then released it with a grunt. Dammit! If his brain wasn't enough, he might as well retire now.

The elevator announced its presence again with a chirpy beep. Adam Hyde and Beth Vanders arrived together, like they always did. Crowder had made it his business to check that out. Neither his wife nor her husbands knew about their shared past. Vanders and Hyde had had a child together, and though they were not lovers now, they'd always retained an affection for each other.

Sophie Wiseman and Andile Zikhali were the last two to arrive, in the same elevator, but a professional distance apart. Wiseman was a wild card, easily swayed by rhetoric and ruled by her heart. Zikhali was ruled by his head, cool and logical and always looking at the bottom line.

"We're not late, are we?" Wiseman asked as she looked around and counted heads.

"Not at all, but now we're all here, I suggest we get started." LeBon led the way into the boardroom with its round table, but no gallant knights. "You all know why we're here. As of today, five hundred and eighteen Trust ships have been lost in the Folds in the last five years as compared to thirteen ships in the preceding decade.

"Our ships are now impossible to insure at any price. We bear the financial losses in their entirety."

Isaac Whittle cleared his throat and looked at her pointedly.

"Of course," she said, "our primary concern is the loss of life."

"Do we have a figure on that?" Vanders asked.

"I have it here." Whittle's handpad projected an interactive holographic screen. He stared into it. "In round figures, it's almost fifty thousand. If you want the exact numbers, it's forty-nine thousand, eight hundred and ninety-two, including five thousand and thirty-eight psi-techs. Our psi-techs, hence the recruitment drive in the last couple of years."

"They weren't all ship crews," Zikhali said.

"No. Two thousand five hundred from the crews, mainly Navigators, Telepaths and Psi-Mechs. The rest were Special Ops, Colony Ops, and—in one spectacular loss—a thousand troops on their way to deploy on the rim to try and de-escalate the Burnish War."

"Madam Chair." Crowder inserted himself into the discussion. "One doesn't have to be a mathematician to run the numbers. The ships that have been lost in foldspace were all transiting via the gates. Only one ship out of five hundred and eighteen was a jumpship. While I appreciate the percentage of jumpships in use is tiny, I would like to bet it's more than point two percent. Until now, jumpships have been an expensive alternative to jump gates, but maybe that's about to change. How many more ships can we afford to lose? Jumpships would give us a very nice edge."

And they would also be very useful against Crossways.

Benjamin had run rings around the megacorporations after the Crossways debacle. He'd stranded them in fold-space, dammit. Something he couldn't have done if they'd been fitted with jump drives.

Adam Hyde, always keen to increase his own standing to the detriment of someone else, looked directly at Yolanda Chang. "Perhaps Miss Chang can tell us how long R and D are likely to be before they can provide us with the plans for a retrofit jump drive such as we believe Crossways has access to."

"My best people are working on it." Chang didn't look happy. The pressure was on.

"Wasn't your department trying to get hold of one of those retrofit ships?" Crowder asked, knowing full well that was the case. Hyde was a particularly ineffective Special Ops director. Crowder wouldn't mind the job himself in the next shuffle.

"We've had our ships looking for one for the last year, but they didn't look any different, post refit, so capturing one and hauling it off to reverse-engineer the drive has proven difficult."

Crowder suppressed a smile. Ships without the drive were easy to capture, but of no use. They'd accidentally taken three of those and had to officially lose them in the Folds to cover up their mistake—easy enough to do right now. The ships that did have the drives tended to use them to evade capture.

"I have it on good authority, Mr. Crowder, that Alphacorp has approached Crossways to buy their retrofit drive." Dammit! Vanders always backed Hyde.

"That may be so, Mrs. Vanders, but I also have information on good authority, and my good authority tells me that Crossways has not yet agreed to sell, though negotiations are ongoing."

"If they do, it will put them two jumps ahead of the Trust. I understand that after the Olyanda affair, it's likely to be a cold day in Hell before Crossways trades with us."

"The very fact that Alphacorp is desperate for the retrofit jump drive shows that in all possibility their ship losses are as bad as ours, if not worse."

"If I could make a suggestion," Andile Zikhali said. "We should make representation to all the other megacorporations and even to the smaller corporations and the independents to find out, in confidence, how widespread this problem is."

Chapter Thirty

LOPEZ

"DON'T STAND OVER ME. THIS IS TRICKY."

Ben stepped aside as Ronan plumbed in lines to the frozen psi-tech's groin and underarms. He was usually on the receiving end of the cryo process, so seeing it from this end was something of a novelty.

"How long, Doc?"

"Can't rush the revival process. Six hours, maybe. He should be close by then."

"I'll come back in five."

"You do that." Ronan dismissed him from the infirmary with a wave.

Cara was working a full shift on comms. The apartment felt empty. No doubt there were a hundred and one things in his office that needed attending to, but right now he didn't feel like settling down to mundane matters. Wenna could and would deal with most of the questions that fell across his desk.

He wandered down the length of Blue Seven to the refectory. Food was a good idea.

The Listers were sitting with full plates before them. J.P. was in his chair and Pami was fussing over him. She looked up and saw him approaching. Her face lit up, and Ben felt his insides lurch. What man wouldn't when a woman who looked like that delivered the ultimate smile?

"Commander Benjamin, we were discussing the next outing," Pami said as she collected a mug of tea and slid into the seat opposite. "And thank you for prompt payment for *Howling Wolf*."

"You're welcome. You did a good job. Not too tired, I hope."

"I could sleep for a week," J.P. said. "I always can after a job. Pami has different needs."

The way he said *needs*, and the way Pami looked at him, made Ben hot in regions he shouldn't be thinking about. He took a long pull of his tea and scalded his tongue. Blast!

"There's a pile of work waiting for me," he said. "Tomorrow we deliver a Mark II engine, engineers, and supplies to *Howling Wolf*. The day after we'll go hunting for another Eastin-Heigle prize. Can you be ready?"

"I'm always ready," Pami said.

He felt his face grow hot like a schoolboy. Good job a blush hardly showed on his brown skin.

What troubled him as he walked to the office was that he found himself thinking how easy it would be to accept her unspoken invitation. And if he did, he'd regret it for the rest of his life. He'd better steer clear of Pami Lister in future.

"Hey, Boss." Wenna looked up from her screen. "Max was looking for you, and Garrick asked if you could call and see him."

He caught a tub cab to the Mansion House. Garrick was in his office on the ground floor, the public level of the Mansion House below the colonnaded main entrance.

"Are you on your own today?" Ben asked, looking around for Mother Ramona.

"Yes, Mona's taking care of a diplomat with a sudden need to be elsewhere."

"Business as usual, then."

"More or less. Well done on *Howling Wolf*."

"She's exactly what Oleg Staple asked for. I've sent you a full report."

"Thanks. That's not why—" He brushed a hand through his hair. "Do you dream?"

"Most people do."

"I mean, about . . ."

"The Nimbus."

"Yes."

"I do."

Garrick closed his eyes and swallowed hard. "I thought it was just me."

"You should have said something sooner."

"I couldn't . . . I didn't . . ." He took a deep breath. "I've been taking care of it." He pulled a bulb out of his pocket. "With this."

Ben frowned. The little bulb was anonymous.

"Detanine," Garrick said. "It helped me to sleep at first—five or six hours of dreamless sleep. Now I get barely two."

"Have you spoken to anyone?"

"Besides you? No. Mona knows. I see her looking at me, but . . ."

"You need to talk to someone—a specialist."

"There isn't anyone who specializes in what we saw. What was it, Ben? Did we look on the face of a god?"

"Don't ask me what it was, but it wasn't a god no matter how powerful." He took a deep breath. "When you learn to fly the Folds, your teachers tell you that sometimes you hallucinate in foldspace."

"That was no illusion."

"Of course not. They're real. I don't know why some people see them and others don't."

"But I don't even have an implant."

"It doesn't matter. Ricky doesn't, but he can see void dragons. He'll be a jumpship pilot one day if that's what he decides to do. You went down a different route. Did you refuse an implant?"

"Ha! They didn't offer an implant program in juvie detention."

Ben laughed. "Believe me, the training program I went through was like juvie detention with added exams!"

"So—the Nimbus . . ."

"A lot of ships are vanishing in the Folds lately. Maybe we lose them to the Nimbus."

"You think?"

"I don't know, but I'm not ruling it out. If I were still in the Trust, I'd be pushing for a change in training, but I'm not and I can't. There is one thing I know, though. What's in the Folds can't come through."

"You're sure?"

"The laws of physics are different there."

"So unless I go back into foldspace . . ."

"It can't get you. Not in daytime. Not in your dreams."

"You're sure about that?"

"It's the fear that will eat you if you let it."

"Right, I'll work on that."

"Good. If it helps, I'm still working on it, too."

Ben stayed with Garrick for longer than he anticipated, so with silent apologies to Max, he headed straight to the infirmary in Blue Seven. Oliver Lopez should be thawed by now.

"How's he doing, Doc?"

"He should be coming around soon. If he was scheduled for Neural Readjustment, maybe he's had some sort of psychotic break, or an episode, or he's done something antisocial."

"I can hear y . . ." The body on the bed spoke. He cleared his throat and tried again. "I can hear you talking about me. None of those things." He began to cough. Ronan flipped the top half of the bed up until Lopez was in a sitting position, and then raised his feet a little for comfort.

"Just stay where you are for a moment, Mr. Lopez." He squirted a puff of something in the man's face. "Breathe. It will help to clear your lungs."

Lopez breathed. "I can hear them creaking like old leather."

"It's only temporary. Cryo has all sorts of unlovely side effects." He grabbed a bowl as Lopez threw up. "Like that."

"Man, I feel like shit."

"Here, drink this. It's Chembal, the single worst tasting thing in the universe."

Lopez took a sip and grimaced.

"It's to get your electrolyte balance back to normal. Did you know they could make it taste like anything? It could be hot chocolate or a rich red wine, but instead they choose to make it taste like earwax, or maybe sprout juice mixed with chlorine. That's to take your mind off how your body feels."

"Yeah, it's working." Lopez held out the cup. "Can my electrolytes stay out of balance for a while longer?"

Ronan took it. "Unless you fall over and froth at the mouth, though for all we know, that's why you were in cryo in the first place."

"No." He shook his head. "I was in cryo because I said I could see something in foldspace. When they told me it was an illusion, I told them, hell, no, it wasn't. I touched that thing. It had scales. It spoke to me."

"It wasn't an illusion," Ben said. He activated the holo image on his handpad, a drawing of the void dragon.

"Shit! That's it!" Lopez pressed himself into the bed.

"What did it say?" Ben asked.

"It said *explosion*."

"Explosion. You're sure?"

"You don't forget something like that."

"Did it say anything else?"

"It said a name."

"What name?"

"No one I've ever heard of: Olivia May Marling."

Ben felt as though his stomach flipped right over and then settled with a kind of sick inevitability, somewhere close to his boots.

✦ ✦ ✦

"It said what?" Max's lips felt rubbery and numb. He took a deep breath. "No, don't say it again, I heard you the first time. I needed time for my brain to catch up. A void dragon said my daughter's name to a random Alphacorp pilot before she was even born?"

His legs couldn't hold him up anymore. Luckily, Ben's couch caught him. He stared at Ben and Ronan, two people he would trust with his life, who were now babbling impossibilities.

Ronan knew about his difficulties with Gen and baby Liv. Ben was perceptive enough to have picked up some of it, though he hadn't asked, and Max hadn't offered details.

But now this . . . this was in the nature of a threat. All of Max's paternal instincts stood to attention inside his head—and his gut, too, if he was honest.

"We're not even sure if the void dragons experience time in the linear way that we see it," Ben said. "Communicating with them has been pretty damn near impossible, but we have no reason to believe they're antagonistic. One watched your daughter being born, and all it seemed to exhibit was curiosity."

"That's my daughter we're talking about!" Max wanted to jump up and shout, but his legs felt like jelly.

"And that's why we wanted to let you know what Lopez said." Ronan actually patted Max on the shoulder, then retreated quickly when he saw Max's expression. "It probably doesn't mean anything."

"Young children are generally not allowed into fold-space. Maybe there's a reason for that," Max said, trying to keep his voice from shaking.

"Pregnant women generally don't travel the Folds after the first trimester," Ronan said, "but Gen was piloting *Solar Wind* with an eight-month bump."

"Is that supposed to be a comfort? How many babies have been born in foldspace?"

"To be honest, I don't know—"

"That was a rhetorical question, Ronan. The real question is what do I do? What do we do?"

"Nothing, for now," Ben said. "I doubt you were planning to take Liv into the Folds anyway."

"You're looking uncomfortable, Ben. What else is there I should know?"

"I didn't think much of it at the time, but when we jumped into Amarelo space to look for salvage, we encountered a void dragon. It didn't identify Liv in as many words, but it had an image of a newborn in its mind—a picture of Dido Kennedy's workshop and Gen on the couch giving birth. I told it that the baby was Olivia May Marling."

Max's rubbery legs prevented him from leaping forward and throwing an unwise punch at Ben. Unwise because he was an accountant and Ben was the stuff that hard-hitting heroes are made of. Max regretted that he hadn't kept up with the fitness regime. He was going soft sitting on his arse in an office on Crossways.

Ben tapped himself on the chin with his own fist. "I don't need you to sock me on the jaw to feel bad about it."

Max grinned ruefully. "Was I that obvious?"

"Don't worry. No one's getting at Liv except through the entire ranks of the Free Company."

Max felt a little better at that, and then his heart hit his boots. What the hell was he going to tell Gen?

✦ ✦ ✦

Cara thought it was about time she showed sisterly solidar-
ity and went to visit Gen while Max was hard at work cooking the books or whatever he did in the accounting office.
She took two carry-out cartons of Blue Mountain coffee.

Gen and Max had snagged a new apartment at the far
end of the block, a ground-floor one with a door into the
communal garden. It had two bedrooms, one of the first
family-friendly living units. It would be nice to see more.

"I brought coffee," Cara said, holding out a cup of Blue
Mountain.

"Oh, you shouldn't have—"

"It wasn't a problem."

"No, I mean, literally. I'm still breastfeeding Liv . . . only
at night to settle her down for bed . . . and . . . the caffeine . . .
you know."

Cara didn't know, but she hoped she might find out one
day if things ever settled down.

"It's a lovely thought, but you'll have to drink both of
them."

"I can do that, but now I feel mean."

"No need. I have some decaff. It tastes almost like the
real thing." She laughed. "At least that's what I keep telling
myself."

Gen waved Cara to a seat. Liv, who had been pushing a
model tub cab around the central rug stood up and came to
Cara's knee.

"Cara," she said quite clearly.

"Hello, Liv. What are you playing with?"

"Tub cab," Liv said. "Ride 'round the station."

"Yes, that's right."

"Sometimes they bump." She bent down and picked up
a second tub cab, even more garish than the first. "Like
this." She crashed them together, laughing as she did it.

"Now you." She pushed a tub cab into Cara's hand and
dropped in a small articulated person. Then she crashed her
own cab into it so the person bounced out. "He fell."

"Yes, he did," Cara said. "But people don't usually
bounce out of tub cabs."

Liv wrapped her arms around her chest in an imitation
of a baby harness.

"Well, yes, they might if they don't wear straps."

Liv put the person in her own tub cab and crashed it once more into Cara's, flinging the cab and its passenger onto the rug.

"How are you getting on?" Cara asked Gen as Liv bent to retrieve the figure and the cab. "We've hardly seen each other with you going down to Olyanda and then me going to find Zandra Hartwell. Since Wenna's organized a pair of class twos to do a shift on comms, I've got a couple of hours. I thought we could catch up."

"And you thought you'd come and check to see how I took the news that a void dragon is interested in my little girl."

"I'd have come anyway, but . . . how are you taking it?"

"Probably better than Max."

"Void dragon, Mummy. My friend."

Cara looked at Gen and raised one eyebrow.

"I made her one out of cloth. It took a bit of doing to get the right proportions, but she loves it. Show Cara your dragon, sweetie."

Liv dutifully dropped the tub cab and ran into the bedroom, returning with an exquisitely made soft toy with perfect proportions and finely stitched detail.

"Gen, I didn't know you were so clever with your hands. That's beautiful."

"Issa void dragon," Liv told Cara. "It came for my birthday. When I got borned."

"It did," Gen said. "Cara was there."

Does the dragon talk in your head, too? Liv asked Cara, mind-to-mind.

Gen! Cara gasped.

"Ah, yes. I was going to tell you." Gen's gaze caught Cara's briefly and then slid off. "She's a natural. Probably should have mentioned it sooner, but . . . you know . . . Max already thinks she's a freak. I didn't want anyone measuring her for a Free Company buddysuit. She gets to make her own decisions when she's old enough. I'd take her to Sanctuary before I'd let her be pushed into doing something she didn't want to do."

Cara blinked at Gen's strength of feeling. "I guess that's what being a mother is all about."

Liv's question kept hammering on the inside of Cara's

skull. Does the dragon talk in your head, too? It was one question beyond the child being naturally telepathic. She tried not to let the disquiet show on her face.

Gen chuckled. Maybe she hadn't caught Liv's question. This time she did look Cara in the eye. "It rearranges your hormones completely. You'll see when it's your turn. I used to think people were speaking figuratively when they said they'd kill for their children, but now I know it's literal."

All through the rest of the visit Cara kept returning to the twin ideas that Liv was already a telepath, and she had the void dragon in her head.

Ben?

Cara, where are you?

Just back from visiting Gen. Where are you?

On my way from Garrick's. You went to see Gen at last. That's good.

Yeah. I feel guilty, but I've been avoiding her. I mean—she's so mumsy and I have no experience of babies. When I offered to babysit and she refused me, I'm ashamed to say I was relieved.

Gen had no experience either until she developed a sudden yen to be a mother. You think we should talk about having babies?

The question drove Cara's thoughts about Liv and the void dragon right out of her head.

Babies!

Now that would be a commitment. She'd never allowed herself to think about having a family, but she'd never been against the concept. And if she was going to have children with anyone, Ben Benjamin was definitely the one. He'd make a great dad.

Eventually, she said. *When it's safe. I'd like that. What about you?*

Yes, probably. Like you say ... when it's safe. Phew, now we've got that out of the way ...

Is it?

Didn't we decide that eventually, when it was safe, we'd think about babies?

I think we did.

How do you feel about that?

Good, I think, she said. *How about you?*

Yes. Good.

Ben Benjamin, are you, y'know, smiling?

I might be.

Gen's got her hands full. Did you know Liv's a natural telepath?

Seriously?

Oh, yes, most definitely. And she thinks she can talk to a void dragon, too. No wonder Max was rattled by what Oliver Lopez said. She told him about Liv's natural telepathy and the void dragon. *Should we worry?*

The answer was a long time coming.

I don't think so, as long as we don't let the kid anywhere near the Folds.

It was impossible to lie mind-to-mind, but for a moment Cara felt a thought stirring in Ben's mind that he squashed quickly. He had an idea that he didn't want to share with her. She'd have to wait for the right time to ask what it was.

Chapter Thirty-One

BUTTERSTONE

BEN FELT GOOD. NOTHING HAD EXPLODED; no one had gone missing, and Jussaro was still down on Olyanda, keeping himself so busy that he wasn't demanding Cara's attention. She'd assured him that once they'd established Sanctuary, Jussaro wouldn't need her there permanently.

They'd taken time for not only a long night which, to be fair, included some periods of sleep, but a lazy morning and a meal together that was either late breakfast or early lunch.

Cara had relayed more details of Liv's emerging talents. A child with an invisible friend wasn't exactly an unheard-of phenomenon, but a void dragon ... That was new. Combined with the idiosyncrasies of Liv's birth, it presented a conundrum. Cara said Gen had made Liv a toy void dragon. Which came first, the toy or the invisible friend in the child's head?

Did Liv think the void dragon was speaking to her from the Folds? Was that even likely? Telepathic communication between realspace and foldspace simply wasn't possible, or, at least, to Ben's knowledge it had never happened.

Maybe Jussaro would know more.

Cara had volunteered to take an extra turn in the comms

chair in the afternoon to make up for leaving so much of
the routine work to a bunch of class twos, while she searched
for Hartwell. When Ben reached the office, Wenna was
wearing a frown. Under normal circumstances, it took a lot
for Wenna's emotions to show on her face.

Ah, well, the peaceful day had probably been too good
to last.

"Is something wrong?"

"I had a request from the president's office on Butterstone last Tuesday. They have fifteen youngsters identified
as potential psi-techs. We booked them in with Civility Jamieson to have implants fitted here, and then promised
them some basic training."

"Sounds reasonable."

"I tried to contact them via their regular comms network
to sort out details, but no one is answering. They have two
long-range Telepaths that they hired in from Ramsay-
Shorre, already trained, so someone should be on duty, but
I can't raise them."

"Who did you use?" Ben was aware that their own long-
range telepathic strength was limited since they'd lost Cas
to the battle and Saedi Sugrue to Jamundi. It was one of the
reasons he wished Cara wouldn't tie herself up quite so
much with Sanctuary.

"Lynda Munene and Chander Dalal in tandem."

Either one of them should be able to contact Butterstone. Two should be overkill for a job like that.

"Ask Cara to try," he said. "Keep me up to speed with
your results."

It didn't take long for Cara to come into his office. "Butterstone," she said. "Nothing."

"Oh, shit. After New Canada, and those colonies that
you said had gone dark . . ."

"I tried to follow the reports on New Canada, but there
wasn't much information. I suspect a news blackout, though
I don't know why."

"Did you say that refugees were involved?"

"That was in one of the first reports from New Canada,
but then it was redacted."

"I'm going to Butterstone," Ben said.

"I'm coming with you."

Of course, it wasn't as simple as taking *Solar Wind* and

jumping off to Butterstone. They needed to prepare for
whatever they might be likely to find. A colony going dark
could be caused by anything from natural disasters, or
plague, to a sudden attack by well-armed pirates chasing
whatever the planet had most of. Ben had been on the receiving end of that kind of attack on Hera-3. But it was rare
for something to happen so quickly that there was no time
to get out a message or a cry for help.

"What do you think it might be?" Garrick asked when
Ben commed him.

"I have no idea, but since this is a Crossways Protectorate planet, response should be official. Do I have your blessing to make it so?"

"Yes, of course. Do you need any extra assistance?"

"We've loaded disaster relief equipment, and I'm taking
twenty psi-techs on *Solar Wind*. Jake's standing by here
with the *Bellatkin*. If we need anything extra—trained
troops, medics, supplies—we'll shout. You send them with
Jake."

"Yes, of course. I hope it's simply a communications
glitch."

"So do I."

But it wouldn't be. There were too many psi-techs on
Butterstone. With Cara's telepathic reach, she should have
been able to contact someone, even if something had happened to their long-range Telepaths.

Yan Gwenn was still refitting the *Howling Wolf*, which
was taking longer than expected. Naomi Patel had taken his
place on *Solar Wind*'s flight deck. She had flown a hornet
during the Crossways battle, and had proved herself quite
capable of handling a jumpship. One third of their team
consisted of Psi-Mechs, their versatile bots being invaluable
in an earthquake, flood, or landslide situation. Including
Ronan, they had four doctors, ten med-techs, and six of Tengue's mercs headed by Gwala and Hildstrom.

It was a good team for a tight situation. Ben was hoping
this wasn't going to be a tight situation, but he wasn't taking
chances. First rule of thumb: if there's no response from air
traffic control, scan as your descent through the atmosphere
allows, then do an exploratory fly past. See what's on the
ground, see if anyone throws rocks, or worse.

"Nothing," Cara said as she tried to contact someone,

anyone, on Butterstone. "No telepathic chatter, no mechanical comms."

"Naomi what can you get on the scanner?" Ben asked.

"From this distance, not much. The settlement is small and the farming areas look quiet."

The farming areas, worked by robust agri bots, had a relatively small labor force. Butterstone was a promising colony, but still young. Most of the population was concentrated in a very limited area, little more than an outpost that hadn't yet grown to its full potential. The real estate in the temperate zones suited humans and their animals well. Wheat and corn grew abundantly, and Butterstone looked as if it might become the breadbasket of the Onix System, supplying food crops to Ironhold, which, as its name suggested, was rich in minerals, but poor in land and slightly too far away from the system's star to have a good growing climate. Even the equatorial region was barely a cool ten degrees at the height of summer. Ironhold specialized in heavy industry and the kind of high-tech infrastructure that supported it. With their plentiful supply of raw materials, they produced high-value, low-weight goods for export and had three thriving shipyards in orbit.

"Cara, anything from Ironhold?"

"They lost contact with Butterstone about the same time as we did."

"Have they had any problems?"

"No, but they say they turned away a ship of refugees on account of the fact that they're in the middle of their storm season. They suggested Butterstone, and Butterstone agreed to take them in."

"Refugees." Ben felt a cold knot in his belly. Coincidence? Probably not. "Just how many refugees on that ship?" Ben asked.

"Forty. Not enough to cause major trouble."

"From where?"

"Apparently somewhere called Barra."

Ben had never heard of a planet, or place on a planet called Barra.

"Boss, look at this."

Naomi magnified the aerial scan of Rhyber, Butterstone's only town. It was still a long way off, but there were shadowy marks on the streets. Ben felt goose bumps on his arms and the back of his neck prickled.

"Can you magnify it?"

"Trying now . . . There."

"Those are bodies," Cara said.

Ben took *Solar Wind* in a low, slow pass over Rhyber. No one shot. No one threw rocks. The only people visible were lying in the street, splayed in death, not comfortably sleeping.

"Check out the landing field," he said.

"No movement," Naomi said.

"What about the refugee ship?"

"No sign of it."

Ben brought the *Solar Wind* in to land close to what passed for a spaceport. Butterstone's main export was compressed flour blocks. A freighter sat empty waiting to be loaded, but there was no activity. The doors to the terminal building were wedged open by a woman who looked as though she'd collapsed.

Ben scowled. *Ronan, get your team ready.*

After a routine examination of the atmosphere for anything toxic, Ben cracked *Solar Wind*'s hatch and the mercs deployed with their usual efficiency, Gwala leading and Hilde at his back.

Ben followed their comms chatter.

"Spaceport clear," Gwala said. "Fifteen bodies. We haven't moved any of them, but there are no outward signs of violence. No blood, but their color isn't normal. The doc will confirm it, but I'd say they've been poisoned. There's no airborne toxin, however, at least not now."

Ronan and his crew moved out of the ship and into the spaceport. Ben left Naomi in command of the flight deck and he and Cara followed cautiously. They were all fully buddysuited and helmed with breathing tubes at the ready in case of toxins.

An eerie scene greeted them in the spaceport. Apart from the woman who'd fallen between the doors and had died there, everyone else was behind the counters or in the office. It wasn't a huge spaceport. It was possible that whatever had struck had done so at night as there were only a few members of staff present. One of them had died on the washroom floor, curled around her belly. Two had made it as far as the sick room and on to the narrow beds there. Five had died in the office and a sixth close by. They looked as if they'd been affected within a few minutes of each other. Number seven had fallen in the corridor, eight and nine on the stairs, and numbers ten to thirteen in the air traffic tower.

It was almost more than Ben wanted to take in. They looked like ordinary people who'd upped and died for no apparent reason. He'd been half-prepared for violence, man-made or natural, but to see the people of Butterstone casually dropped to the floor, unmarked in death, gave him the creeps more than dealing with the aftermath of a massacre. The dead didn't scare him, but the manner of their passing disturbed him more than he wanted to let on.

Cara looked pale, too. Anyone who'd lived through the Battle for Crossways had seen their fair share of death, but the bodies had shown their reasons for dying: crushed skulls, bleeding wounds, burns, puncture injuries, and the blue-lipped victims of asphyxiation, but on Butterstone there was nothing to bandage.

The moment Butterstone had lost contact it was already too late.

"Almost certainly poison of some kind," Ronan said. "But I'll need to do a full analysis to be sure. No one touch anything with bare skin. On no account breathe unfiltered air or ingest anything we haven't brought with us ourselves."

"Can we do anything?" Cara asked.

"Look for signs of life in the town. See if anyone has escaped this."

"No one has come running from that direction," Ben said. "I'd say that was a bad sign. Let's move out into the town."

With Gwala's mercs taking point and the psi-techs ranged behind them, they headed for the town center. Built on a circular plan, four wide avenues converged on a central area that had been laid out as a social space with shops, a couple of taverns, a hotel for incomers, and beds of flowers that sparkled like jewels in the afternoon sun.

Behind the plaza were neat houses, little boxes typical of colonies everywhere, but a little farther out, people had started to build bigger, less utilitarian houses in the yellow stone that had given the planet its name.

There were a few bodies in the street, but most of them were in the houses.

Cara opened up a channel to Ronan. *More bodies, Ronan. No one left alive, at least no one we've found yet.*

I need to carry out a few more tests, but my best guess is a poisoned water supply. Possibly a super-concentrated arsenic derivative. I'd say everyone I've seen so far died about twenty-four hours ago, give or take. The poison is easily detectable in water, but only if you're looking for it.

Cara opened up the communication so everyone could hear Ronan's warning. *Don't mess with the water.*

"Hey, over here," Hilde called. "Manny's found something."

Ben turned.

Gwala had a bundle in his arms and he was carrying it as if it would break.

"I found a baby," Gwala said. "In its cot with its dead mother right there next to it."

"Manny are you crying?" Hilde said.

"I got some dust in my eye."

"Sure you did." She bent over to look.

"Poor little thing is all floppy and weak," Gwala said. "Dehydration, I guess. Luckily, it didn't get fed with contaminated water."

"Ronan has baby formula in the emergency supplies," Ben said.

"Maybe it was breast-fed," Hilde said. "That's why it survived. There, little thing, we'll take you to Uncle Ronan for a checkup and a nice drink of formula."

She held her arms out for the baby, but Gwala wouldn't let go. He walked off in the direction of the landing field.

"It almost feels like a triumph, doesn't it?" Cara said.

Ben shuddered. "One survivor out of a colony of five or six thousand people isn't much of a triumph. Let's see if we can find the water treatment plant and trace this to its source. Cara, Hilde, you're with me. You, too, Dingle." He picked one of the Psi-Mechs, a thickset woman with a satchel of bots slung over her shoulder. "The rest of you continue the house-to-house search. Maybe there are more babies, or folks who didn't drink the water."

"There's not much town, but where do we find a water pumping station?" Dingle asked.

Ben pointed at the edge of the built-up area, to a concrete bunker with air vent pipes. "That looks like an underground reservoir to me."

In the middle of the long side was a concrete doorway and a medonite door, hanging off its hinges.

"This looks like the place." Ben drew his sidearm and stepped inside, blinking as his helm adjusted to night vision in the darkened corridor. There were steps going down and the distinct swish-swish of running water. Hilde covered the rear. Behind Ben, Cara drew her own weapon and clicked off the safety.

Ro Dingle, behind Cara flipped open her satchel. "Should I send a bot down, Boss?" she asked in a soft voice.

"Yes, do that." No sense in taking stupid risks even though it did look as if this whole place was a ghost town.

Ro sent down a couple of small spider bots, one on the stair and one clinging to the side wall close to the ceiling. Her eyes had that faraway look of one who's seeing something else entirely. "Two bodies, Boss," she said. "It doesn't look pretty down there. Some kind of fight. No sign of life now."

Ben didn't holster his sidearm, but he ran down the stairs without checking around corners. He heard footsteps behind him, keeping up.

In the deep chamber below, the sound of fast-flowing water blotted out everything else. He felt Cara make a four-way connection between them all. Water flowed in, gushing through a narrow channel into a well. Presumably the town's water pipes flowed out, hidden below the churning surface of the water. On the concrete apron at the foot of the stair lay two bodies, one sprawled in death, the other curled into a fetal position. There was blood—more than one person could afford to lose.

Ben checked the sprawled corpse. It was a woman, maybe fifty years old, dressed in clothing that had once been a smart business suit, not at all the kind of thing that Butterstone's colonists wore. The front of her suit was soaked in blood from a gut wound.

This one's still alive, Cara called and brought Ronan in on the communication. *Ronan, it looks like a knife wound to the chest. There's a lot of blood. The knife's still in.*

Don't touch it, I'm on my way.

Ben came to stand over Cara. The man was barely conscious. Dressed in basic coveralls, very much like colony clothing, he looked like the tech who should have been looking after this place.

He's a deadhead, Cara said. *I already checked. His coverall says his name's Denton.*

Denton's fingers spasmed. Cara took his hand. "It's okay. The doctor's on his way. We've got you now."

His lips moved. Ben thought he said, "Water," but his voice was so soft and low that it was lost in the noise echoing in the chamber.

Denton's eyes flickered toward the prone body and his lips twitched. Ben bent his head to catch the words. "She put something in the water. I . . . I had to . . ."

"It's okay. We know." No use telling the man he was too late.

Ronan and his crew arrived. Ben surrendered Denton to their care and took another look at the woman. She looked like anything but a mass murderer.

Ronan can you spare someone to take this body into custody? I want to know who she was and where she came from. I'll bet she's not one of the colonists. Maybe she's one of the refugees. If she is, she's the only obvious one we've found so far.

Though it looked as though they'd found the source of the poison, there was still going to be a long cleanup operation. Ben straightened up and gave Cara's hand a quick squeeze. *You doing okay?*

About as okay as possible in the circumstances.

They headed into the center of town together.

◆ ◆ ◆

Cara was bone-weary. She'd been doing the heavy lifting on comms, and when not required for that had taken her turn identifying and bagging bodies. The cleanup operation on Butterstone took the best part of a week. They brought in extra hands to cover it and set up a couple of mortuary tents in the central plaza and a small temporary hospital on the edge of town.

There were survivors, but not many. Three babies, presumably breast-fed, had been saved by their mother's choice of nutrition. A drunk found in the backroom of a tavern, sleeping off a massive binge was all right except for a hangover to end all hangovers. Predictably, he knew nothing about the tragedy and couldn't take it in when told.

In the small hospital, there was a woman in a coma and a man who'd had stomach surgery who was receiving all his fluids via intravenous drip. Luckily, the machine looking after him hadn't run its complete cycle, so his recovery was progressing normally, or as normally as it could when he'd lost his entire family.

They'd found eleven agri-engineers out in the far fields working on the machinery, apparently in the middle of a two-day shift. They all thought the comms array had gone down again, a not uncommon occurrence and normally nothing to worry about.

The poisoner struck in the early evening when people were dining late, or drawing water for a last cup of tea before bed, or taking a shower or cleaning their teeth. The poison hadn't acted instantly, so it was likely the first few people to feel ill had taken meds with a glass of water and then taken to their beds to sleep it off—except, of course, death had caught up with them while they slept.

Ronan had worked out that the time of death for most people had come between midnight and three in the morning. A few had been later and had obviously witnessed the disaster, but not knowing the cause, had ingested water that was still contaminated.

Ben had called for a specialist team to clean up the water supply, but the poison had already flushed through the system and gone on to present problems to the waste disposal engineers and to the ecosystem surrounding the sewage and drainage.

The survivors, without exception, didn't want to stay on Butterstone, but there was fertile land and infrastructure, so maybe there was a potential home for new colonists.

Roger Denton had the constitution of an elephant. After six hours in surgery and a couple of days of continuous observation, he'd recovered enough to speak. His story wasn't wildly different from the few words he'd gasped out when they'd found him. He'd seen someone breaking into the water pumping station, but only found the refugee woman after she'd dropped something into the well. She'd gone for him with surprising strength and agility for someone who looked like a middle-aged businesswoman, but he'd grappled with her and cut her badly with her own knife before she'd stuck him between the ribs with it. She'd bled out, but the knife itself had plugged Denton's wound and saved his life.

He didn't have family, but he'd lost most of his friends. A couple of the farm mechanics came to visit him daily. Cara understood they spent their afternoons talking in low voices and crying together.

Chapter Thirty-Two

DNA

ON CROSSWAYS, CARA SPENT A GRUELING DAY alongside every long-range Telepath they could muster, contacting the colonies of the Protectorate and warning them not to allow ships claiming to be refugees to land under any circumstances. Worryingly, two more colonies from the Crossways Protectorate had gone dark. Garrick had sent out ships to check on them, but it was too early to expect to hear anything.

By the time she'd had a quick snack and crawled into bed beside the heavily sleeping Ben, Cara was exhausted to the point of unconsciousness. The bed swallowed her and that was the last she knew.

There was no time between sleeping and waking. First, she was asleep, then she was awake, but she couldn't tell how much time elapsed between one state and the next.

She opened her eyes and knew only blackness. Was she blind? She raised one hand to touch her eyes. Soft eyelashes brushed against her fingers. Yes, her eyes were open. Her heart pounded. The darkness was all around her, suffocating her, drawing out of her all that made her real. Unmaking her, but filling her with unbounded yet terrifying joy.

"Cara?"

The voice made her flinch. It took her a moment to identify it and to tie it to the warm body lying beside her.

"Ben?"

"Who else might it be?"

"Sorry . . . I was dreaming and then I wasn't, but the dream is . . . Can we have some light?"

At the word, light, a dim glow illuminated the area around the bed. She put her hand to her chest and could feel her heart pounding.

"Oh, I thought . . . Never mind." She bit back what she'd been going to say because it sounded mad.

"You thought what?"

"That the darkness was somehow solid and that I was inside it. I must have been dreaming."

"If you were dreaming, so was I."

"You mean?"

"I was in the shuttlecraft and the Nimbus was creeping toward me. Kitty Keely was there, then she let go and the Nimbus smothered her. Then there was only darkness. Being inside it. Trapped. Helpless. Yet at the same time exhilarating. Like the biggest drug buzz ever."

"I'm sorry. I must be projecting. That was my dream, except I wasn't seeing it from my own point of view, I was seeing it from Garrick's."

"Did I give the dream to you, or did you give it to me?"

"Neither. I think we both got it from the same source. Do you ever get these dreams when you're not on Crossways?"

"I have lots of dreams." Ben's words almost choked him. "Most of them not good."

"But this one, in particular, where you're Garrick?"

He nodded.

"Have you ever had it while you were off-station, or while Garrick was?"

"I don't know. I don't think so."

"I don't think you're projecting it. I think Garrick is."

"Garrick hasn't got an implant."

"Maybe he doesn't need one. The three of us were within a whisker of the Nimbus together. We may be attuned to each other. We need to see Garrick."

"To what end? To politely ask him not to send his dreams

to us because we already have enough of our own? Ask him to wear a tinfoil hat?"

"A tinfoil hat. Yes, perfect!"

"What?"

"Ask him to wear a damper. He's a deadhead. He's probably never even considered it might be necessary. Maybe he's getting dreams from us. This might work both ways."

"It's worth a try."

"We need to see Garrick."

"First thing in the morning."

✦ ✦ ✦

Seeing Garrick dropped to the bottom of Ben's priority list when the reports came in that the two colonies that had lost contact were both dead, in the worst possible way.

"Your Telepaths need to spread this news." Ben handed Cara a dataslide and she docked it with her handpad.

"It looks like another long day," she said.

The reports were fairly succinct and didn't dwell on the carnage, but Ben's imagination supplied what the reports missed out. The colonies were both small, concentrated into single settlements, and there were few survivors. One was agricultural, the other an isolated mining operation, importing subsistence goods and exporting gold, diamonds, and a modest amount of platinum.

The mining operation had not had the resources to support three hundred refugees but had agreed to let the vessel land on hearing they had technical problems and only needed to stay for as long as it took them to effect repairs.

Both attacks took place at approximately the same time.

"Two refugee ships, both telling the same story," Ben said. "Bigger than the ship that landed on Butterstone, so there are at least three ships. Who the hell is responsible for this?"

"The megacorps, trying to lay it at our door," Cara said without hesitation. "They don't care about a few small colonies, but they do care about discrediting us and splitting the Crossways Protectorate apart. What good is a protectorate if it doesn't protect?"

"You might have a point." Ben shrugged. "But I'm not sure."

"Crowder was willing to wipe out the colony on Olyanda to get at the platinum."

Ben nodded. "He was, but . . ."

"You're not going to defend Crowder, surely?"

"Oh, he's as guilty as sin over the whole Olyanda thing, and trying to get the megacorps to pound Crossways to dust. There was profit in that, profit for the Trust and promotion for Crowder, but chewing up colonies for nothing more than publicity—I don't think that's his style."

"He was willing to wipe out ten thousand on Olyanda and a million people here on Crossways. You think he wouldn't hesitate to kill a few thousand on an isolated colony?"

"I think his reasoning is twisted, but I think he'd draw the line at that. There's no immediate profit in it. Besides New Canada was one of his colonies. I set it up, but it was his project."

"So not the Trust. Alphacorp, maybe? Or maybe several megacorps acting together. After all, they lost significant face, not to mention crews and ships when they took a poke at Crossways and failed."

"Could be. I wish I knew."

✦ ✦ ✦

Ronan had taken DNA samples from the refugee woman on Butterstone, and they'd run them through every available database without finding her. Cara had checked the personnel files of the megacorps involved in the Crossways attack, but there was nothing.

"There must be a database somewhere that this woman is on," Cara said, as her last possibility came up blank. They were working in the captain's cabin on *Solar Wind*.

"Did the crack for the Trust's colony database work?" Ben asked. They'd had J.P. Lister use his extensive talents on finding a backdoor into the system. Although he claimed the job was beneath him, he'd not only cracked the Trust's settler database, but those of all the megacorps.

"It worked, but we drew a blank on all of them." Cara chewed her lower lip. "The only one I haven't checked is the

Monitor database and while I guess J.P. might be able to crack it, I doubt he could do so without someone noticing."

"Well, I have an idea," Ben said. "Could you link me with Jess Jessop?"

Cara found Jessop easily and linked Ben with him.

I'm happy to tip you off about something, Ben said, *if you're happy to keep it under your hat for now.*

Tell me and I'll decide.

You've had a couple of colonies go dark, settlers killed. Am I right? I'm being blamed for one of them, but you know that's not my style.

Go on, Jess said.

We've lost three. The entire population of Butterstone killed by poison in the water supply. The other two were more ... messy.

I'm sorry to hear that. We've had three now, including New Canada.

I set up New Canada. Survivors?

Eighteen children, plus a few from outside the main settlement. I figured it wasn't your handiwork. I wasn't so sure about Crossways.

Not ours. Not any of it.

The inner systems press is blaming Crossways.

Yeah. Why am I not surprised? We wouldn't destroy our own colonies, Jess, you know that. Besides, I had friends on New Canada.

Have you any idea where the attacks are coming from?

None. We've got one of the perps, or at least her body. Butterstone took in a shipload of refugees shortly before it happened, and I'll lay odds she was on it. The refugees have gone, of course. Took off before we arrived, but we have her. We've checked her DNA through every database we can access, legally and not, but we can't find her. Can you check her through yours?

I can, but I'm guessing you're looking in the wrong place, Jessop said. *How far back have you checked? You know we recovered some refugee bodies from the first colony that was lost.*

Cara said it looked like some kind of news blackout.

There was a reason for that. The refugees, well, they might have been refugees, but they weren't from where they claimed. We DNA-checked them and found matches.

Go on, Jess, you're killing me. Don't stretch it out.
They were from ships lost in the Folds almost a hundred years ago.
Oh, shit!
I couldn't have put it better myself.
Cara silently agreed.

✦ ✦ ✦

"What does it mean?" Cara's face had gone white.
Ben felt light-headed.
"I don't know. Refugees lost in the Folds, coming back. The dead returning."
The image of his parents as he had last seen them swam into his head, or maybe it was a memory of the portrait that had hung on the wall at home: a tall, light-brown man with a reassuring smile, and a petite, dark-brown woman who, even though it was a still photograph, looked graceful. If he thought hard, he could almost recall their voices.
Almost.
He'd been so young when they'd been lost in the Folds.
He couldn't even remember the moment when he'd learned that they weren't coming home. He remembered the emptiness of a sleepless night and crawling into Rion's bed in the early hours of the morning to find his big brother's pillow was wet with tears.
Ben's mind leaped around in jerky circles.
Were all those people lost in foldspace not lost at all? Were they waiting for rescue, locked in some kind of endless time loop? Hell, did time even pass for them?
"We rescued the ark." He reached for Cara's hand. "If we'd been brave enough, bold enough, could we have rescued other ships lost in foldspace?"
"If you're asking whether you could have rescued your parents, the answer is no. How old were you when they went missing? Six? Seven? How many years elapsed before you earned your pilot's ticket? Even if you'd absconded with the first jumpship they let you fly, how would you ever have found them? You could have spent your whole life looking."
"I guess, but maybe other ships, ones lost recently . . . I could ask the void dragons."
"There's a small matter of not being able to communicate with them."

"I bet I know who could communicate with them. She told you so herself."

"You don't mean . . ."

"Olivia May Marling."

"You wouldn't—"

Wouldn't he? It depended what was at stake. Maybe he could persuade Gen and Max to come on a trip into the Folds. What if it were the only option? Gods, he hoped it wasn't, but the void dragon's persistence came back to him. It wanted Olivia. He had a sick feeling in the pit of his stomach. He thought he knew the reason why.

◆ ◆ ◆

"Ben, you're going to want to take this comm direct," Cara said over breakfast in their apartment. "It's Saedi Sugrue, calling from Jamundi."

"It's not Nan, is it, or Rion?"

"No, it's not about your family. Here . . ."

She pulled him gently into the conversation.

Saedi, what's wrong?

There's a refugee ship requesting permission to land.

While Cara was holding the communication open for Ben, she contacted Phoebe Tilston, Mother Ramona's latest in a string of Telepaths trying out as a replacement for Ully. Cara thought that this time she'd found the right one. Phoebe linked Mother Ramona into the call and brought her up to speed.

Is Garrick with you? Cara asked Mother Ramona.

He's—not well.

Shit, Garrick surely couldn't be off his head on detanine. Not now, not when they all needed to pull together. Cara eased into the conversation between Ben and Saedi, keeping Mother Ramona in the loop.

Hell, Saedi, Ben said. *You haven't given permission for them to land, have you?*

Of course not, but they're saying their ship's losing integrity and they're coming in with or without permission. I guess they've been turned away from other colonies, and they're not taking no for an answer this time.

Okay, tell them you're prepping the landing ground and delay them. We're on our way. It's about time we got the jump on these maniacs, whoever they are.

There was a pause while Saedi relayed the information.

Is Jack there? Ben asked.

Cara liked Jack Mario. He was Saedi's partner and the Jamundi colony's chief administrator. Victor Lorient was supposed to be the colony director, but since the death of his son, Danny, and the scramble to save the Olyanda settlers from both the Trust and Alphacorp, he'd been a changed man. Diminished. Rena, his mild-mannered wife, had blossomed and now headed the colony in all but name.

Jack's here and Rena. I called Gupta and Doctor Hoffner, too. They're on their way.

Good, Ben said. *We need a plan. You'll have to mobilize every spare hand you've got. Call in all the psi-techs and build a secure compound. On no account let any of the refugees out into the town. Keep them on their own ship for as long as you can, then fence them in.*

Got it.

Ben was already dressed in his buddysuit; Cara was still half-dressed. While she relayed messages for Ben, she pulled on her buddysuit trousers and top and sealed the two halves together.

Ben called Tengue to gather his mercs together.

What do you need? Mother Ramona asked.

We need you to alert Syke to keep everything locked down on Crossways while we're away. We're taking Tengue and most of his mercenaries and forty of the Free Company. If we need backup, we'll send for it. Wenna's in charge while we're away.

Understood.

Cara could sense Mother Ramona snapping out orders via Phoebe's telepathic link.

Jake, are you still asleep? Cara called.

I was, and I was having this dream ab—

Get to the Bellatkin. We have a serious emergency. Need to get Tengue's mercs to Jamundi.

When?

Yesterday.

I'll be at Port 46 in ten minutes. Jake asked no more questions.

Ben rattled off a list of psi-techs and then cursed because Archie Tatum was still on Olyanda with Jussaro.

Will I do? Serafin butted in.

You're on sick leave and almost retired, Ben said.

I'm still the best you've got, and besides, Jamundi's where I'm going to retire and Suzi's already there.

If you can get to Solar Wind *before we take off, you're in,* Ben said, *but we can't wait for you.*

I'm on my way.

By the time Ben had called the psi-techs to action, Cara had her buddysuit on straight and they ran for the dock.

Chapter Thirty-Three

JAMUNDI

SERAFIN MADE IT ONTO *SOLAR WIND* BARELY a minute before Ben locked down the doors. With Cara by his side, Ronan in charge of the med bay, and Serafin leading the Psi-Mechs, Ben felt like they'd got the band back together. Suzi, Saedi, and Gupta were waiting for them on Jamundi.

"Room for one more on the flight deck?" Max poked his head up above the rim of the access tube.

"I don't recall asking you to come?" Ben said. "I thought you preferred accountancy to hard action?"

Max shrugged. "You might need a Finder."

Ben bit back the comment that he hoped Max had squared it with Gen before volunteering for what could be a dangerous mission. If those two were still having problems, it wasn't for him to interfere.

He released the docking clamps and nudged *Solar Wind* out into space, clearing the immediate area of the station before picking up speed.

Cara held open a link. Ben said, *Jake? How are you doing?*

Loading the last of Tengue's mercs now, and their equipment. These guys carry around a whole arsenal.

Let's hope we don't need it.

We'll be away from here in ten. See you on Jamundi.

Respecting the station's hundred-klick safety zone was for the times when it wasn't an emergency. At fifty klicks Ben engaged the jump drive.

Though ever-present in his dream, Ben hasn't let himself think too much about the Folds during waking hours, but here he is again in that liminal space between realities. He tries not to think of the void dragon in case the thought attracts it, but not thinking of something is always the way to have it uppermost in your mind. Sure enough, a void dragon comes. Its scaled head fills the flight deck, but then it shrinks in size until it's barely the size of a well-grown crocodile though way more beautiful than a croc. It flexes its wings, which shimmer with rainbow colors despite being black as the void itself.

EXPLOSION! The void dragon says straight into Ben's head—though he may also have heard the word with his ears. That's new.

"No explosion today," he tells it.

BENNN. It knows his name. That's new, too.

"Are you talking to the thing that knows my daughter's name?" Max asks from one of the two bucket seats reserved for non-flight crew.

"You can't see it?"

"Do I want to?"

"Did you see it when Gen gave birth?"

"I saw something. A ripple in the air. Something not quite there and yet . . . I tried to forget it again as quickly as I could."

"It's the same something."

MAAXX, the void dragon says, and turns toward him.

"What? Oh! Wait a minute. Go away!"

Ben sighs. Max can hear the void dragon and the dragon has another word.

OLIVIA MAY MARLING, the dragon says suddenly. OLIVIA MAY MARLING. There's a strong sense of *need*.

"You are not getting anywhere near my daughter," Max says. "Hear me. I mean it."

MEAN IT. The dragon repeats. MY DAUGHTER.

And then Ben finds the line and they pop out of fold-space above Jamundi.

"Can that thing follow us through?" Max asked.

"I don't think so," Ben said.

"Don't think? Aren't you sure?"

"I used to be sure that it was all in my imagination," Ben said. "All I'm sure of now is that I've never seen or heard of a void dragon in realspace, and one has never tried to cross over with me."

"How come we can cross into its dimension, but it can't cross into ours?"

"You've got me there."

"Why is it so fixated on my daughter?"

Ben shrugged. "I wish I knew." He had an idea about it, but he wasn't telling Max yet. If there ever came a time for that, he knew they'd be on opposite sides of an argument.

The planet now filled the forward screen. Bathed in light from its yellow sun, Jamundi was blue-green. With intermittent light cloud cover and polar ice, it looked a lot like Earth but with two moons.

"What a beauty!" Max gazed at the screen. "Prettier than Olyanda."

"And not as likely to be affected by solar storms, either," Ben said. "It's altogether better real estate. The settlers got a bargain—eventually—though they paid for it in other ways, I'll admit."

"Like nearly getting wiped off the face of the planet," Max said.

"Something like that. Yet here they are on their own planet."

"With psi-techs," Max said. "That's not exactly what they wanted."

Ben shrugged.

Victor Lorient was psi-phobic, but his wife Rena had declared the Free Company welcome and had even accepted psi-tech help to get the new colony established.

When Crowder had gone after his family, Ben had moved them to Jamundi. Rion, his brother, and Rion's elder son Kai were settling into their own farm. Young Ricky wasn't cut out for farming, though, any more than Ben had been, even though he'd been raised to it. And Nan? Nan would stay near her family, no doubt, but she wasn't the kind of woman to retire and grow old gracefully.

Cara interrupted his thoughts. "Saedi says the refugee ship is touching down now."

"Let's go in as quietly as we can."

Ben activated the heat shield as they breached the outer atmosphere then deployed *Solar Wind*'s retractable wings for atmospheric flight. He brought her in two hundred klicks south of Jamundi's main settlement and skimmed the ground, raising dust but staying hidden as much as possible. He dropped the ship into a quarry, temporarily silent. The forty psi-techs, all armed and protected by buddysuits, formed up and trotted toward the town where Jack Mario was waiting for them in the newly constructed town hall.

The small enclave built around the landing site on Jamundi had grown into a proper town since their last visit. The Psi-Mechs had cleared hectares of forest for crops and building land while the settlers' own carpenters had built houses out of wood with stone foundations. Suzi Ruka's agriculture team had already harvested three crops of fast-growing grain and several varieties of vegetables, so the settlers weren't reliant on imported staples.

"Jack, good to see you again." Ben shook hands with the administrator on the town hall's doorstep under the portico. "You've managed to keep them in their ship, I take it."

"So far." Jack ran his hand through thinning hair and shrugged his broad shoulders. "They're not happy about it. Gupta's policing it, but I'm sure he'll be grateful for the backup."

Shorter than Ben by half a head, Jack was thickset and muscular. Saedi, frizzy fair hair forming a halo around her pink face, was the same height as Jack. She nodded a greeting, but Ben recognized the faraway look. She was obviously in the middle of a communication. He didn't interrupt her.

"Jake Lowenbrun is about ten minutes behind us with fifty of Tengue's mercs on board."

Jack shuddered. "Aren't those the guys who were trying to kill us on Olyanda?"

"Only because they'd been hired by the wrong side. They work for us now."

"You trust them?"

"I do. We pay their wages."

"And what if someone paid more?"

"I'd still trust them—at least to warn me they'd had a better offer." He grinned.

"Good enough for me," Jack said.

"Have you built a secure compound?"

"In such a short time? We've done our best. With your guys as guards, it should work. What if the refugees are genuine, Ben? What if they need humanitarian aid and all we've given them is a wire fence and a couple of big tents?"

"No one is going to deny them help, but that will be only under secure conditions. Ronan has a portable DNA testing lab. We'll match them against our database and see if their story checks out."

Ben heard the *Bellatkin* screaming in to land next to *Solar Wind* in the shallow quarry. She wasn't exactly subtle, but Jake did the best with what he had. Tengue's mercs arrived at the double in full battle gear, taking no chances. Jack directed them to the compound, where they set up an outer perimeter with a charged security screen, and then formed up to create a human corridor from the refugee ship to the compound.

"All right," Ben said to Saedi. "You can invite them to disembark and make their way to the reception area where we have shelter and medical staff."

"Done," Saedi said.

The ship itself was a passenger transport, capable of carrying four hundred people in reasonable comfort. The refugees hadn't been crowded together in the hold of a scow; they'd had contour couches, water, and food.

"There's a registration plate on the ship," Ben said. "Can you run it through the database?"

Cara brought up the holo display on her handpad and punched in the registration numbers. "Whoa!" she said. "It's listed as the *Barbary*, an Eastin-Heigle passenger ship reported lost in the Folds last year with only thirty-four souls aboard. How many refugees is she carrying?"

"Three hundred and eleven, including crew, according to their report." Ben's eyes narrowed as the main hatch cracked open and a passenger ramp extended.

"Some need medical help," Saedi said. "They sound pretty desperate."

"So are they genuine or simply good actors?" Cara asked.

"That's what I was wondering," Ben said. "After so many attacks it's surprising that they're still using the same excuse to land. It's not very imaginative. If I were planning to infiltrate and destroy several colonies, I would vary my story for getting my ship to the surface. Though to be honest, why land at all? An attack from the air would be much more devastating."

Ben had firsthand experience of that, and he never wanted to see a colony go through it again.

A single person appeared at the top of the ramp. He was in his fifties and wore a crumpled, teal-green flight suit that matched his claim to be James Bridgwater, captain of the *Barbary*. Tengue's men surrounded the bottom of the ramp, but James Bridgwater didn't look dangerous. He even stumbled as he walked down the ramp.

"He looks exhausted," Cara said. "Not much of a threat."

"I wonder if the colonists on Butterstone thought that when their refugees arrived." Ben stepped forward with Cara at his side. Ronan was a couple of paces behind. "Captain Bridgwater," Ben said. "Welcome."

"I'm sorry. You have the advantage. Not sure who you are or even where we are. Are you in charge here?"

"Ben Benjamin. I'm in charge of your reception. We have medics standing by. Unless your passengers would prefer to stay on the ship."

"I'm sure they'd prefer to stay anywhere but the ship."

"We need to verify who you are and where you're from."

"Of course, Mr. Benjamin, of course. Happy to tell you everything you want to know. May we disembark, now?" He wobbled and would have fallen but for Ronan.

"You don't look in such good shape yourself, Captain. Come with me." Ronan flashed a private comment to Ben and Cara. *Whoever he is, he believes he's telling the truth.*

"I agree with Ronan," Cara said. "There was no hint of anything untoward in Captain Bridgwater's mind. We'll know more when the med team has done a DNA match."

One by one, the crew and passengers of the *Barbary* descended the ramp. They were all ages from teen to elderly and showed a varying amount of physical distress. Ben and Cara watched them walk, shuffle, limp and—just two of them—run the short distance between the ship and the compound.

The people of Jamundi had provided blankets and spare clothes. Rena Lorient delivered them, all piled on a mule cart led by a couple of men who immediately started unloading and passing the bounty to a chain of Gupta's security team.

"Are you sure these people are dangerous?" Rena Lorient paused by the fence next to Ben and Cara. "They look like they need our help."

"I'm not sure," Ben replied, "but I'm not sure they aren't dangerous either. We know of six colonies that have been destroyed so far. Do you want Jamundi to be the seventh?"

She shuddered. "Of course not. Your instincts have served us well, Commander Benjamin. I'll back your decision, whatever it is."

"We'll give them medical help, food, and shelter. I guarantee they'll not be harmed unless they start something, but I'm not letting them out of here until we're sure."

"They don't look fit enough to start anything but a prayer meeting," Rena said.

"That's the truth," Ben muttered as Rena walked away.

"We came here full of suspicions," Cara said, "but if the other refugees were as convincing as this, I can understand how they were accepted. I've had my Empathy dialed up for anything untoward, and so far they're all genuine. It was a different bunch who attacked Butterstone—smaller group, smaller ship. We don't know about the other colonies. Maybe these folks are exactly what they appear to be."

"I hope you're right," Ben said, "But there are too many coincidences. And the *Barbary* was reported lost in the Folds."

"I know. I know." She paced back and forth. "What are we missing?"

Ben wished he had an answer for her.

Ronan and Mel Hoffner, along with four med-techs, established a medical tent inside the compound perimeter, separated from the refugees' accommodation by a single fence. There were no signs of violent injury, though some of the refugees had had relatively minor accidents, and some were suffering from stress and long-term medical conditions exacerbated by their recent circumstances. Tengue and Gupta between them arranged a permanent watch on the compound.

With everything secure, Ben and Cara retired for the night to the Benjamin family farmhouse, a short way out of town.

◆ ◆ ◆

"Rion's been busy," Cara said as they pulled up in the borrowed groundcar.

"Maybe not Rion. That's a new house, not a new barn." He pointed to a traditional wooden building across the yard from the original house, a basic modular dwelling with pods added for private rooms for Nan, Ricky, Kai, and, more recently, Thea.

The family all assembled in the yard. Ricky threw himself at Ben and immediately started gabbling all the news he could think of.

"Hold on, young man," Ben set him on one side and embraced Rion. They must have looked more like brothers once, but Ben had lost several years in cryo, so he was still thirty-four, while Rion had lived all of those years and was now closer to fifty, his hair sprinkled with gray and his skin weathered to dark brown leather with liver spots showing on his temples.

Nan, who'd also lost years in cryo during her time as a negotiator for the Five Power Alliance on Earth, and later as a freelancer, didn't look a day over seventy despite her outdoor skin and gray hair swept up into an untidy knot. Cara knew she was at least eighty in biological time, but she'd been born well over a century earlier. One day she'd like to have a long sit-down with Nan and learn some real history.

"Ah, here they come," Nan said as Kai and Thea crossed over from the new house to greet them. Thea hung back a little and Kai cradled her shoulders to draw her into the family circle. Cara saw immediately why Kai had built the new house. Thea looked about seven months pregnant.

"Congratulations," Cara gave the freckled redhead a hug. "You look as though life is treating you well."

"It is." Thea's pink cheeks deepened several shades. She was one of those pale-skinned women who blossomed in pregnancy.

"Come in. Come in." Rion waved them toward the farm-house door.

"Ah, young people these days," Nan said as she put a tray of tea on the large kitchen table and indicated they should all sit and drink. "Always putting the cart before the horse. These two should be standing up together and declaring their marriage, don't you think so, Ben?"

"You mean like you did, Nan?" Kai grinned at his grand-mother. He was a handsome young man, lighter skinned than his father and with Ben's height and supple grace.

"There were reasons your grandfather and I didn't marry," Nan said stiffly, and then her face cracked a smile. "I simply can't remember what they were after all this time. He's still around, you know." She winked at Ben. "And I don't think he's currently married. Maybe we'll do it one day—we still had a spark the last time we met, though I haven't seen him in person for a long time."

"You never talk about him, Nan," Ricky said. "Like he's some well-guarded secret."

"Well, I suppose he is, or was at any rate. He's about to retire from politics now, so I don't suppose it will matter then."

"He's a politician?"

"Oh, yes. Malusi Duma is the outgoing president of Pan-Africa."

"*The* Malusi Duma?" Ricky's jaw dropped.

"I've mentioned him before. I knew you were only half-listening."

"I was listening. I heard the name, only I didn't know much about Earth history until you made me take a class in it while we were traveling."

It wasn't news to either Ben or Rion, but Thea's eyes grew as round as saucers. "Even I've heard of Malusi Duma," she said. "Didn't he push through the Pan-African charter?"

"One of his finer moments," Nan said with a wink. "At least, one of his finer public moments."

"Nan, you don't mean . . . ? Euwww!" Ricky screwed his face up.

"I don't know what you're thinking, young man, but I was thinking about him brokering the trade agreement with Europe. Most of that had to be done behind closed doors."

Cara laughed at Ricky's discomfort and then felt mean.

"So what about this ship?" Nan asked. "Where's it supposed to have come from? What's the story?"

"We don't know yet," Ben said. "We'll know more tomorrow when we can interview some of them. They don't behave like homicidal maniacs, but I guess Butterstone's refugees appeared legitimate, too. Otherwise, why would they have been billeted in people's homes?"

"Are the refugees dangerous?" Ricky asked.

"Well, there are three hundred of them, but they're safely contained in a compound," Ben said. "Only a few at a time are allowed into either the medical facility or the interview room. Most of them don't look fit enough to do serious damage, given that they aren't armed. The engineering team is checking over their ship for signs that it's been involved in any kind of violence, traces of blood on garments or on shoes, or maybe even in the passenger seats. Ronan's medics are also running DNA samples. We should have the results soon."

"Do you need some help with the interviews?" Nan asked.

Cara had been hoping she'd volunteer. She was one of the best Empaths this side of the Rim. If anyone could ferret the truth out of the refugees, Nan could.

Chapter Thirty-Four

REVENANT

"MIGHT AS WELL START AT THE TOP AND work down," Ben said.

Cara settled into her chair. Their interview room was little more than a hastily-assembled, tunnel-shaped riser made of medonite panels clipped together. It didn't have any windows, but light filtered through the translucent walls. The Psi-Mechs had assembled it in half a day, and divided it into two rooms. Though it was basic, it wasn't unpleasant. Nan and Vijay Gupta had taken over the second interview room.

The door opened. One of Tengue's mercs ushered in Captain James Bridgwater.

"Captain Bridgwater, please sit down," Ben said. "I hope you're feeling better. Doctor Wolfe tells me your blood pressure is stable now, but you've been under some stress."

"It's funny how you don't notice it until it's not there, isn't it?"

"Stress?"

Bridgwater nodded. "I feel as though someone's pulled the plug out, Commander Benjamin. By the way, I must apologize for calling you mister yesterday. I didn't mean to be rude."

"You weren't rude. Commander is a courtesy title. We don't have ranks in the Free Company."

"But you captain your own ship?"

"As do you, Captain Bridgwater. You do understand I have to ask a few questions, don't you?"

"I do. Go ahead."

"Your ship, the *Barbary*, was reported lost in the Folds with thirty-four souls on board, including yourself. All crew. You were on the way to pick up passengers on Kemp's World, thereafter headed for Chenon."

Bridgwater blinked twice. "Ah, yes. That was it. Kemp's World to Chenon. A regular run via the Dromgoole Hub. I remember now."

"You're a little vague."

"Am I? Well, a lot's happened since then."

"How long ago was it?"

"Oh, at least two weeks. I'd need to access my ship's log to tell you exactly."

Ben glanced at Cara and she frowned. She leaned forward and held Bridgwater's gaze. "Would it surprise you to know it was last year, Captain?"

"Last year? No. I don't think that could be right." He closed his eyes as if in thought. "Three weeks. At the most."

He thinks he's telling the truth, Cara said on a tight link to Ben.

"How did you get your ship out of the Folds? You don't have a jump drive."

"Jump drive? No, nothing like that. I guess we must have got lucky."

"You're a Navigator as well as a pilot?"

"I wish I was. I have a great Navigator, though. She's a whiz. She found a line to a jump gate. Pretty scary at the time, but no damage done."

"If you have a great Navigator, how did you get lost in the Folds in the first place?"

He frowned. "I'm sure it will come to me. The gate ... which gate? Ah, yes, Dromgoole E. That's it. It will all be in the ship's log."

"Unfortunately, all of your ship's log has been erased, including your crew manifest."

He shook his head. "Those things are impossible to erase."

"Agreed. They are, which is why yours being erased is highly unusual."

"No." He shook his head. "I'm sure it's okay. I made an entry in it as we landed here."

"What happened between entering the Folds through Dromgoole E and arriving here? Where did all your passengers come from?"

"Couldn't leave them behind. Humanitarian aid, you understand. Never fail to answer a distress call."

"This distress call, tell us about it."

"Distress call."

"From a ship? From a planet?"

"Yes, distress call." Bridgwater's eyes began to droop and his head bent forward.

"Is he going to sleep?" Ben asked.

"He's exhausted," Cara said. "It's more like his brain is shutting his body down. Better get a medic."

She called for Ronan, but Mel Hoffner arrived instead. She ran a scanner over Bridgwater and looked at them sharply. "What have you been doing to him, Boss? He's in shock."

"Just questions, polite ones," Ben said. "No raised voices, nothing awkward. He's got a distorted idea of time. Thinks his ship has only been out of contact for two or three weeks, and can't remember how they escaped from the Folds, or, apparently, where they picked up the refugees."

"I'm going to have to put him on a monitor."

She called for a med-tech with a float chair and wrestled an unresisting Captain Bridgwater into it, clipping a safety strap across his middle.

"Keep us informed, Mel."

"Don't worry, I will." She pushed Bridgwater's chair out of the interview room and let the door close behind her.

"Well, that was unexpected," Ben said. "I wasn't too harsh on him, was I?"

Cara shook her head. "You were gentler than I would have been. If he has no memory of events, what has happened to him?"

"Let's see what the next one says."

Their next interviewee was the *Barbary*'s second in command, David Cho. He appeared more alert than his captain had been. He was firm on the Dromgoole Hub and entering the Folds via the Dromgoole E gate, but then began to exhibit the same vagueness. No, he wasn't sure how they exited the Folds and, although he knew they'd answered a distress call, he couldn't recall the circumstances. Ben stopped pushing him before he started to shut down like Bridgwater had done.

"Perhaps we'll have better luck with the passengers," Cara said. She flashed a message to Mel. *How about you pick us out a passenger who's in robust health,* she suggested.

I've got one here you should find interesting. She's in excellent health for someone who's a hundred and ten years old according to the birth date she gave us, but doesn't look a day over forty. I should have her DNA results in about fifteen minutes.

Does she have a name?

Ms. Catherine Ashbeck of the Boston Ashbecks. When I reminded her Boston, Massachusetts, didn't exist anymore, she said if we thought a little thing like a meteorite strike was going to take down her family, we should think again. They are apparently now based in Boston, Lincolnshire, even though they've retained their American accent. To hear her tell it, they own most of Lincolnshire and were single-handedly responsible for saving the town. When the sea rose, it was their money that paid for the evacuation and the new town site fifty miles inland.

"This should be interesting," Ben said to Cara.

The door opened to admit a woman who carried herself like she was certainly a member of the richest family in Boston.

"Ms. Ashbeck, please sit down." Ben made the introductions and polite enquiries as to Ms. Ashbeck's health and well-being before getting down to the serious questions. "Can you tell us how you came to be on board the *Barbary*?"

"Certainly. My companion and I were aboard the *Pride of Kashmir*, cruising to Appledore where my family has business interests."

"Your companion?"

"A secretary. He's of no consequence."

"Is he still with you?"

She frowned as if she couldn't quite remember. "We must have separated." Her voice faltered for the first time.

"So what happened?"

"There was an emergency."

"What kind of emergency?"

"You think they tell the passengers? A red-flashing-light-sirens-in-the-night kind of emergency. The kind they drill you for. I grabbed a breather mask and strapped into my cabin couch." She frowned again. "I must have passed out. When I came to, I was on the *Barbary* in one of those dreadful recliners, sandwiched between an elderly gentleman and someone who looked like a vagabond." She brushed her own clothes as if to say, I have standards.

I have the DNA results, Mel interrupted without coming into the room. *She's exactly who she says she is. Reported dead sixty years ago with the loss of the* Pride of Kashmir *in the Folds.*

"How long have you been on board the *Barbary*, Ms. Ashbeck?"

A frown flickered across the woman's face like a brief shadow passing across the sun. "Since the day before yesterday."

She believes that's true, Cara said. *There's not a flicker of doubt, and she's not deliberately lying.*

"Thank you, Ms. Ashbeck." Ben tried to give nothing away in his tone of voice. "We might need to talk to you again, later, but that's all for now."

"What happens next, Commander Benjamin? Are you sending me back to that squalid tent? Don't you at least have better accommodation? How long do we have to wait before we're repatriated? We are going to be repatriated, aren't we?"

"All in good time, Ms. Ashbeck. I can't answer all your questions yet."

"If you get word to my family, they'll send the yacht for me."

"I'll see what we can do."

Ben screwed his eyes up tight and opened them wide again as Catherine Ashbeck exited the room, back straight, not looking over her shoulder. "What the hell is going on here? Bridgwater thought it had been three weeks, Ashbeck thinks it's closer to three days. It has to be something to do with the Folds. Time doesn't pass in there in the same way as it does out here, but it still doesn't make sense."

"You said it yourself once when you were talking about the void dragons," Cara said.

"What?"

"Their time isn't always linear. Things that are sequential to us maybe aren't, not in the Folds, anyway."

There was a knock at the door. Without waiting for a response, Tengue opened it a crack and stuck his head inside. "Is your next interviewee lined up?"

"Not yet," Ben said.

"Well, I think you're going to want to see this one right away."

"We are?"

Tengue grimaced and pushed the door all the way open.

Standing in the opening, looking as if she hadn't died a year ago, was Kitty Keely.

The sight of her bumped Ben's mind back to the moment of her loss. He remembered it so clearly.

They are searching in the Folds for Garrick and Keely, adrift in their tiny two-man shuttle. Ben settles *Solar Wind* in the black depths of foldspace, cuts the drive, and listens. He closes his eyes. Foldspace isn't black; neither is it empty. It glistens like moonlight on oily water. He can sense the lines that have the potential to lead to anywhere, but those aren't what he's looking for.

Tracks disturb the ripples, faint whispers in the fabric of spacetime, maybe where some ship has once passed, maybe a void dragon or the otter-kind.

There's something out there, like a crosscurrent. What has been smooth becomes choppy.

"There's something on instruments," Cara says.

Ben closes his eyes for a few seconds longer, trying to feel the shape of it in the iridescent black. He blinks them open again.

"What is it?" Gwala asks, his hands twitching toward the weapons control panel.

"It's like nothing I've ever seen," Wenna answers from the systems station.

The void dragon swirls into the flight deck and asks, *?* Ben gets the impression of *OTHER* without any actual words. The void dragon is worried.

"What is that?" Cara asks.

"A ship." Ben recognizes it. "Garrick and Kitty."

As Ben fires up the maneuvering thrusters, the otter-kind tumble into the flight deck, become agitated, and shoot out again. The void dragon swirls around twice and then disappears.

"Whatever's out there, the big fellow doesn't like it," Ben says.

"I'll try the audio," Cara says.

"*Solar Wind* to shuttle. Come in, please. *Solar Wind* to—"

"Cara? Ben?" Kitty answers. "Oh, gods, come and get us. This thing—"

"We can see something on the scanners. What is it?"

"Stay back, Ben," Garrick says. "If it touches you, you'll be stuck here like us."

"I don't intend to let it touch us," Ben says, "but we've got to get you out."

"Oh, yes, please," Kitty says. "It's swallowing the shuttle."

"Explain."

Garrick says. "At first it was the tail of the craft that was mired, but it's drawing us in. Half the shuttle is—I don't know—dissolved into this darkness."

"Can you still move around freely?"

"Yes, within this half of the cabin. Neither of us has tried to touch the shadow-thing. It gives off a fearful sense of—I don't know—otherness."

"Okay, we're coming to get you."

Ben nudges *Solar Wind* ever closer to the shadow. Dread builds inside him until his bones rattle with it.

"I'm not liking this," Gwala says.

"I thought it was just me." Wenna tries to keep her voice light, but it cracks.

"Cara?" Ben asks.

"All of that and more."

As *Solar Wind* nudges closer, the shadow billows like a cloud.

"That's as close as we can get," Wenna says. "The shuttle's embedded too deeply."

"We can see you," Garrick says. "You're still too far away."

"Do you trust me?" Ben asks.

"Yes."

"Then all you have to do is step through the front screen of the shuttle and cross foldspace like you were taking a stroll in the park. You can step straight through *Solar Wind*'s skin."

"Oh, yes, that's likely!"

"Everyone doubts."

"Shall we suit up?" Cara asks.

"No. They'll never trust us if we don't trust ourselves. As soon as we break the integrity of their shuttle, they'll choke on vacuum because that's what they believe will happen."

"So we simply step out of the airlock?"

"More or less, yes, but we don't need the airlock. We can go out through *Solar Wind*'s skin, pass through it like the void dragons do."

"And what happens if you don't come back?" Wenna says.

"Believe that we will."

Cara grabs Ben's hand. "Let's do it."

They push off together, then rise to the ceiling and through it into the wonder of foldspace. Momentum carries them forward. The skin of the shuttle gives way beneath them and they land gently in the small space.

Garrick grins, incredulous, but hopeful. Kitty collapses into the pilot's couch. "You can't . . . You didn't."

"Can and did," Ben says. "It's the only way out. Or are you going to sit here and wait for that to catch up with you?"

The aft section of the shuttle, including the hatch, is wreathed in what looks like dense black smoke, but it remains coherent, as if it's contained. It exudes a terrible nothingness.

"I'm with you," Garrick says.

"I . . . can't," Kitty says. "Couldn't you have brought pressure suits?"

"There wasn't time." Ben eyes the tangible darkness. It's almost touching the back of the couch Kitty has sunk into. "It's up to you, Kitty. It's save-yourself time."

"Save myself for what? You're going to have to get rid of me, aren't you? What will it be? An airlock accident?" She looks at Garrick. "A hundred-year sleep to wake, when and where? My mother abandoned. Alphacorp—"

"You have to help yourself," Ben says. "Come on. There's still time."

"Why would you care after what I've done?"

"Why not?" She's a spy, not a mass murderer.

The darkness roils toward them.

Ben links hands with Cara again. Cara grabs Garrick, and Ben holds out his free hand for Kitty.

She hesitates.

"Come on, Kitty."

He reaches out for her, but the darkness beats him to it. A tendril swirls around her waist, draws her into its embrace.

Her eyes widen. "Go!" she mouths. Without a sound, she steps into it and disappears.

"Quickly," Ben says as the darkness boils toward them. They push off, through the shuttle skin and dive for *Solar Wind*, landing in a heap on the flight deck floor.

"What the hell was that thing?" Garrick asks.

"Nothing I've ever seen before," Ben says. "The void dragon calls it *other*. Let's hope we never see anything like it again."

Without waiting to be told, Wenna fires the thrusters and *Solar Wind* slides away as the shadow swallows the nose of the shuttle and balloons outward toward them.

"Kitty . . ." Cara says.

Ben takes a deep breath. "She made her choice. Sometimes all you can do is hold out a hand. It's up to them whether they take it. Let's go home."

Ben blinked at the woman in the doorway.

Yes, it was definitely Kitty. Definitely not dead.

Chapter Thirty-Five

ATTACK

CARA STARED AT KITTY KEELY.

Not dead, then, she thought. She was swallowed by the Nimbus, but here she is.

The Nimbus was the stuff of nightmares. An alien thing, unable or unwilling to communicate, ineffable.

"Kitty," Ben said. His voice nearly broke.

Even though Ben had said all the right things about holding out hands and Kitty not taking them, he always blamed himself when someone got hurt. It was his big flaw. Ronan called it White Knight Syndrome. If anyone needed rescuing, Ben would volunteer. But he couldn't be responsible for the safety of everyone in the galaxy, nor for everyone on Crossways, not even for everyone in the Free Company.

That didn't stop him trying.

Cara had her Empathy cranked up to ten to see what emotions she could get from the person standing in front of them. She looked like Kitty Keely, sounded like Kitty Keely. Was there even a small chance she was not? Was this some elaborate hoax?

Even as she was thinking that, she dismissed it. No one could have guessed Kitty would come face-to-face with the very people she'd betrayed. No, betrayed wasn't the right word. Keely had been a spy, an infiltrator right from the start. She'd fed information to Alphacorp, doing the job she'd been sent to do. Alphacorp had a hold over her, her ailing mother, so wherever Kitty's sympathies lay—and Cara had reason to believe she was not unsympathetic to Crossways—she was never going to turn away from Alphacorp permanently.

"Sit down, please." Ben indicated the chair and Kitty sat.

Cara felt no emotion emanating from her at all, neither fear nor surprise. She looked the same as she'd looked on the day she died, dressed in a borrowed flight suit with the Crossways logo on the breast pocket.

"Are you well?" Ben asked.

"I believe so, though your doctor would be able to tell you the state of my health better than I can. Doctor Hoffner, I believe."

"You remember her."

"I didn't know her well, but we had passing acquaintance."

Mel, have you processed Kitty Keely's DNA results yet? Cara asked.

She checks out, except her file says deceased, which she obviously is not.

That's okay. We'll sort out that one.

"Could you tell us how you got here?" Ben asked. He didn't add, especially since we saw you die.

Kitty's expression went blank for a moment. "When you left me on the shuttle, I called for help and luckily the *Barbary* was close enough to pick me up."

Cara felt Ben cringe when Kitty accused him of leaving her behind, but he didn't deny it. "Do you remember exactly what happened?"

"There's not much to remember. I kept wondering if you'd come back after you took Garrick, and then I thought maybe you'd left me deliberately. You obviously didn't want an Alphacorp spy on Crossways. There's no jail there, so I expected you'd float me out of an airlock sooner or later. Perhaps leaving me in the Folds was simply a way of getting rid of me. What did you tell people?"

"The truth: that you were swallowed up by an alien cloud."

She raised her eyebrows. Cara detected nothing but

genuine surprise. "And they believed you?" she asked.
"That sounds pretty lame."

Ben cleared his throat. "So, the *Barbary* picked you up—
in foldspace—and then what?"

"Then we came straight here. I'm glad I didn't have to
spend more than a couple of days with all those refugee
folks. Some of them were in a pretty bad state, and I'm not
a trained medic. I volunteered to help the flight crew. Their
Navigator was strictly a gate-to-gate man and had lost the
beacon. I helped him find it. I flew them out of the Folds."

"You're Captain Bridgwater's whiz of a Navigator?"

"Is that what he said? He told me I could have a job any
time I liked. Unless you particularly want to float me out of
an airlock, I might take him up on that. See if the Rodontee
Corporation will buy my contract."

"I never wanted to float you out of an airlock, Kitty, believe me. The worst we'd have done to you would have been
to return you to Alphacorp."

"And here's me thinking you wanted to dump me in the
middle of foldspace."

"What do you remember of the Nimbus?"

"The what?"

"The black cloud in the shuttle."

"There were a few wisps of smoke from a burned-out
panel, that's all."

She's telling the truth as she believes it happened, Cara
said. *Though there's something else underlying what she's
saying. I didn't get that from the other interviewees. There's
more to Kitty than is immediately obvious. Perhaps I'm only
picking this up because I knew Kitty before.*

We're going to have to go deeper, Ben said to Cara.
Perhaps Ronan's regression therapy.

Good idea.

◆ ◆ ◆

Ben was puzzled. There had been no sign of aggression.
None of the interviews had turned up anything unusual in
what the refugees believed, but their stories still didn't tie
in with the truth as Ben understood it. The passengers all
had different recollections of their various ships getting into
trouble and the *Barbary* picking them up, but some of them
had been lost in the Folds as recently as a couple of months

ago, while others had been lost a century earlier—yet here they all were, alive and looking as they had the day they were lost.

"Ideas?" he asked.

They were all sitting around the big table in *Solar Wind*'s mess, the biggest communal space on the ship. A beverage machine burbled quietly to itself on the counter. Ben helped himself to a hot tea before they started, and offered drinks to the visitors.

Cara, clutching coffee, was by his right hand, as usual—he liked that, though he'd never clip her wings by telling her how much—Ronan sat opposite, with Nan and Tengue. To Ben's left were Vijay Gupta and Max. At the head and foot of the table, respectively, were Rena Lorient and Jack Mario. Ben had always valued Jack. He'd been an ally even when they'd appeared to be on opposing sides in the early days of the Olyanda settlement. Ah, those were the days, when they'd thought their only problem was the enmity between settler and psi-tech. Rena was an unknown quantity. She'd appeared compliant when they'd been on Olyanda, but as her husband had diminished, she'd grown to take over the colony in his place.

"Can we repatriate them?" Rena asked.

"They're dangerous," Ben said. "I don't know how and I don't know when, but no matter how pathetic they look, they present a danger. Don't trust them for a moment."

"We haven't told them yet what year it is," Ronan said. "Imagine the shock of finding out you've been legally dead for a century. They all think they've had a bit of an adventure that's lasted a week or two at the most."

"What's our best guess as to what has actually happened to them?" Jack asked.

"I know this sounds like science fiction," Ben said, "but alien abduction would be my theory." He held up his hand to quell the murmurs around the table. "Yes, I know that during all our time exploring the galaxy we've never actually come across a sentient civilization, even if we've found life-forms on other planets, but these aliens are not from our dimension."

"Do you think it's your void dragons?" Gupta asked.

"I'm not an authority on these things, but the void dragons are benign, so far—more curious than anything," Ben

said. "They don't communicate like we do. They're telepathic. We can occasionally pick up feelings from them, but
we don't have any commonality that enables us to work on
building a shared vocabulary."

"If it was the void dragons," Cara said, "surely they
would have attacked us."

And that's when the alarms began to sound.

◆ ◆ ◆

Tengue leaped to his feet, one hand on his communicator.
"Question answered. They've massed by the fence and
they're trying to claw their way through it."

Ben had moved *Solar Wind* out of the quarry to a landing pad on the far side of town, but it would still take them
almost five minutes to run to the compound from here. Ben
and Tengue were first down the ramp, Cara and Ronan
close behind. There was one groundcar parked close by. It
was a four seater, but with Ben and Tengue in the front,
Cara, Ronan, and Gupta jumped in and squashed into the
back.

Arriving at the compound Cara could see the refugees
clawing at the fence in a frenzy, each one trying to climb the
mesh or push it over. The fence was beginning to wobble. If
they breached it, then the mercs' charged security screen
was the town's last defense against what was nothing short
of a ravening horde.

Space zombies, Cara thought and then immediately dismissed the idea. Whatever they were, they weren't mindless
creatures. Or, at least, they hadn't been until now.

The mercs were standing their ground supplemented by
the psi-techs, outnumbered three to one, but with vastly su-
perior technology on their side.

"They're in some kind of hive-mind state," Cara told
Ben, "but not on a wavelength I can break into."

"Can you sense if anything's controlling them?"

"No. That's not to say there isn't, but I can't sense it.
They're locked together in some kind of mental bubble."

"Set your weapons to stun," Tengue yelled. Cara opened
up a channel for Ben. *You heard him,* Ben said. *Weapons
to stun. Let's not kill anyone's grandma if we can help it.*

What if Grandma's trying to kill us? Serafin asked.

Don't die. That's an order. And Serafin, get out of there now. Stand aside.

Or what? You'll retire me?

Cara heard Ben curse under his breath.

We can't let them get through that fence, or they'll kill themselves on the security screen, Ben said. *Okay, Serafin, make yourself useful. Get your Psi-Mechs to rig up a water cannon. Quickly.*

The town had fire hoses; all they had to do was point them in the right direction.

Cara watched as the fire hoses drenched the refugees, but the dousing didn't deter their frenzy. Even the elderly ones, who had been so frail when they arrived, were climbing over each other in an effort to get out of the compound.

"We don't know if they're irredeemable," Ben said. "Deadly force has to be our last option."

The fence wobbled dangerously and began to sag. The refugees put more effort in, this time working together.

"Tengue's perimeter shield is strong enough to kill an ox," Ben said. "We can't let them through the first fence."

Serafin, increase pressure on the hoses.

In answer, the water scythed from the hoses, bowling over the refugees on the edge of the crowd and slamming the ones in the middle backward into their fellows. One or two lay where they'd fallen, but the others simply climbed onto their feet and kept coming.

"Shit! Tengue, use your stunners. Knock them out. Let's get them restrained however we can before they break the fence."

The mercs began to fire stun bolts into the crowd. Whenever one person fell, the people behind them merely stepped over, or on top of their fallen companions and kept pushing at the fence. With a shriek of tearing mesh, it gave way and the rearmost trampled over the foremost to get out of the compound, barely meters in front of the force wall. Tengue's mercs tried to cut them down with stunners before they got that far, but for every one that fell, one made it through and suddenly the air was full of cries and the stench of singed flesh. Tengue's men didn't give way. They stood their ground and continued to fire. Every person who fell to a stun bolt was one less collapsed in the perimeter shield.

It might have been minutes. It might have been an hour. Finally, there was no one moving.

Cara wrenched her gaze away from the heaped bodies and looked at Ben. His face, gray with shock, said it all.

"Medics and first responders!" he yelled, and backed it up with a thought.

It was like a battlefield. No, it was worse than a battlefield, because these people hadn't been soldiers, or at least not soldiers as Cara knew the term. She couldn't believe how frenzied the attack had been; even the old ones were super-strong. Now, in the aftermath, a deadly silence had descended.

Serafin retracted his lobstered helmet and stood hand in hand with Suzi Ruka. "I think that's me done with carnage," he said. "I'm ready to retire and grow cabbages. I'm going home with Suzi now. Would you have someone pack up my stuff and send it on next time there's a ship passing?"

"Sure, old man," Ben said. "But if you get bored, you know where to come."

"He won't get bored," Suzi said. "I have plans."

They turned and walked away.

There was only the soft whir of machinery as the Psi-Mechs began to replace the fence. Those outside it were either dead or unconscious. It was difficult to tell which. The med-techs were already moving among them with psi-techs and mercs working together as stretcher bearers, carrying them inside the compound, dividing them into two groups, the dead and the living. Cara was horribly aware that the dead outnumbered the living by more than three to one.

"What can I do?" she asked Ronan.

"Go to the triage station. Restrain the uninjured and put them under guard. I can't guarantee they won't start to go mad again once they wake up, but hopefully the stunners will have disrupted whatever brain pattern drove them into that frenzy."

"Do you think they were being controlled?"

"By what? By whom? We found nothing when we examined them. Obviously, we need to look deeper."

She shrugged. "Right now, Ben's alien abduction theory is the only one that fits."

Ronan didn't offer her an opinion. He handed her a sedative spray and a tranquilizer gun, fully loaded. "When they start to come around, give them a whiff of sedative if they're anxious. If they're a danger to themselves or anyone else, put them under with one dart."

"I know the routine. One dart to sleep, two gives them a chance, three darts kill."

"Usually." He nodded. "Ben gave Crowder three darts and he lived. I don't know how. Keep the safety on."

"Of course." She coded the safety to her thumbprint.

Ben was already moving among the fallen across the compound. He felt her light telepathic touch and looked up. *Some of them look as though they're sleeping, but I know they're not. How could I let this happen on my watch?*

It's not your fault. Most of them did it to themselves, though they weren't in their rational minds.

They certainly weren't. Let's see what we can do for them, and then we need to find out what's going on.

As Cara waited in triage, it became evident that more and more bodies were piling up and fewer and fewer survivors were in the group for treatment.

"So many dead," Cara said softly as Mel Hoffner called it for Captain James Bridgwater. The man had hardly a mark on him. No burns, no obvious trauma. "What do you think killed him?"

"We're going to have to do autopsies."

"For all that lot?" Cara jerked her head to the area where the bodies were piling up.

"Don't they deserve it? Don't their relatives, or maybe their descendants, deserve to know how they died?"

"I don't know. Will it help anything? They already know they've been lost in the Folds. Do they need this extra pain?"

Mel brushed a stray lock of hair out of the way. Her pretty blue eyes glistened with unshed tears. "If it were my relative, I'd want to know."

"Would you? Have you ever lost anyone in the Folds?"

Mel shook her head.

"Did you know Ben's parents were lost in the Folds when he was about six and Rion was nine?"

"I didn't know they were so close in age."

"Rion's never done cryo. Never even been off Chenon until Ben hauled him off for his own safety. I suspect losing their mom and dad in the Folds had something to do with that."

"It didn't stop the boss."

"I think it affected him the opposite way. Chalk and cheese, the pair of them. But I see it in Ben's eyes when he looks at these people. Might his parents still be out there? If they are, can he reach them? Can he bring them home?"

"He rescued the settlers from the ark. You all did."

"That was different. They hadn't been lost in foldspace, they'd been dumped in it, in cryo. They'd had no contact with whatever entities are out there. No trauma."

"You think these people have been in contact with the void dragons?"

"No, I don't. The void dragons could have attacked the *Solar Wind* at any time. Ben's made himself vulnerable to them on several occasions, but he's still here."

"So what else is there?"

"There's the Nimbus."

"I've got a live one," a tall med-tech called as he wheeled a gurney into triage. "Female. According to the DNA database, she's Kitty Keely."

"Kitty may be the key to it all," Cara said. "We saw the Nimbus take her, yet here she is. Whatever you need to do, keep her alive."

Chapter Thirty-Six

AUTOPSIES

"THREE HUNDRED AND ELEVEN SOULS," BEN said, "and only fifty-three survivors. How did we manage to kill two hundred and fifty-eight civilians? All right..." He raised one hand. "I know what the autopsies are saying. Heart failure. The poor devils simply used themselves up with that superhuman frenzy. And those who didn't were fried on the security barrier or trampled by their friends."

"You're blaming yourself again," Cara said as Ben paced up and down their cabin on *Solar Wind*.

"No, I'm not—well—yes, maybe a little, but I know it wasn't me. I wish I could have done something to prevent it. If we get another shipload of refugees requesting to land, next time we sedate them right from the beginning, separate them, in case this was some kind of mass hysteria."

"Are you wondering what you'll do if your parents turn up?"

"No." He sighed. "Uh ... yes. It's in the back of my mind, I confess, but thousands of travelers have been lost in the Folds. There's no reason to suppose ... At least that's what I've been telling myself."

"You're right. There is no reason to suppose anything, but it has to be something you've thought about. How must

Nan be feeling? She lost a son. You were lucky you had each other."

"Yes, we were."

"Be kind to her before we leave for Crossways."

"Am I ever not kind to her?" Did his face show a degree of shock?

"Sometimes you take her for granted."

"Do I?"

"In the way you take us all for granted. You know that we know what we're doing, so you let us get on with it."

"As a leadership style, it works pretty well."

"Do you think you could stop being my boss for a few moments?"

"Why?"

She stood up and blocked his way as he turned. "Because I think we both need to remind ourselves that we're still alive." She pulled his face down to hers and kissed him.

"Ah." He felt himself relax into her arms.

✦   ✦   ✦

Kitty was out cold for three days and then groggy from the low-level sedatives, but she spoke rationally when Ben visited. The frenzied fury had dissipated and though she recalled that there had been some trouble, she didn't remember what had caused it.

There were fifty-three survivors, including Kitty, none of whom could be trusted no matter how docile they appeared now.

Ben and Cara met with Rena Lorient and Jack Mario in the new town hall. It was ten days since the frenzy as they were all beginning to call it. Time for decisions.

"We can't leave them here."

"You can't leave them here."

Ben and Rena spoke in unison after the initial pleasantries.

"Well, at least we're agreed on that," Ben said.

The town hall was the settlement's main administrative building, featuring double-height rooms and lofty windows that let in the slanting late-afternoon sun. The furniture was plain, but functional. A large table, used for council meetings, and somewhat unforgiving chairs. It was the sort of place that said *we care about the people more than our-*

selves. Someone had painted a portrait of Victor Lorient, and hung it on the wall behind the head of the table. It was a little amateurish, but gave a certain impression of the man's vitality, or at least what it had been. Ben had always found Victor Lorient difficult to deal with, but he hated the idea of seeing him diminished. He was almost pleased that during their whole visit he'd made no effort to get involved with the refugee problem. Mel Hoffner confirmed he'd had a slight stroke, which had left him weakened. No wonder Rena and Jack were doing all the work.

"I'm sorry for the refugees," Rena said. "They were ordinary people with a life ahead of them and whatever happened to them—whenever it happened—ended that. I sympathize, but we're not equipped to either look after them or restrain them here."

"We wouldn't dream of leaving you with the problem," Ben said. "We still don't know whether they'll continue to be dangerous; whether the frenzy will happen again. We need to find out as much as we can, but this isn't just our problem. The megacorps are losing colonies, too."

Rena shivered, as well she might.

"I know how you feel about the Trust," Ben said. "Knowing Crowder is out there makes me feel like there's a target painted between my shoulder blades, but rest assured, there's no way he will ever find Jamundi. Its sun is not even on any star charts; our hackers made sure of that. And in case one missing star was ever picked up by an eagle-eyed astronomer, they erased another hundred as well."

"I leave the altruism up to you, Commander Benjamin, but thank you for your reassurances. We had a council meeting and the area of the compound is going to be kept as a peace garden as a memorial to those poor people. Thank you for the list of names."

"We have their DNA records and their ashes will be repatriated. We'll find a way to do it."

"How will you examine the survivors?"

"Ronan Wolf is highly skilled in psychological regression. We know the Nimbus swallowed Kitty Keely, so we'll start with her. David Cho, second in command of the *Barbary* also survived. We'll take them both to Crossways and observe them carefully."

"And the rest of them?"

"Another round of interviews, but then we'll put them into cryo and ship them off to the Monitors with as much information as we have."

"Can you deal with the Monitors without getting captured yourselves?"

"I have a contact who will cut me some slack if I'm being useful."

"Good luck, Commander Benjamin."

The interviews took three days, by which time Jake had collected cryo pods from Crossways and returned with all the equipment Ronan and the med-techs needed to freeze the survivors.

Ben asked Cara to contact Jess Jessop, whose first comment after a string of expletives was to say: *You want what?*

I want you to collect fifty-one cryo pods from Mirrimar-6. I think you'll find them very interesting.

How am I supposed to account for them?

A tip-off. Ben laughed.

Some tip-off. I'll tell you what; make it Mirrimar-10, which we're due to check into in four days' time. That will make more sense to my bosses.

Mirrimar-10, it is. I'll rent a warehouse under an alias and send you the details.

So are you going to give me a clue?

We had a warning about a shipload of refugees landing on one of our protectorate planets. We arrived before anything kicked off and corralled them. They appeared perfectly normal at first—that is if you consider that some of them went missing sixty years ago and others barely a year. We kept them in a compound rather than making the mistake of giving them access to the colony. It's as well we did.

He gave Jess a rundown of what happened.

And now you're dumping the problem on us.

Not so much a problem, more an opportunity to do some research. Besides, I figure you can deal with them better than we can—more humanely at least. They have the potential to be dangerous, but I doubt it's their fault.

Ben sent Jake and a small crew of Tengue's mercs to deposit the cryo pods in storage on Mirrimar-10, a small hub near Cygnus Alpha.

Naomi Patel took temporary command of the *Barbary*. She'd have to travel to Crossways via the nearest jump gates, so it would take her close to eighteen days allowing for sublight travel time.

Ben took Kitty Keely and David Cho in *Solar Wind*. Ronan had charge of them in sick bay, each one mildly sedated and secured to a contour couch. To be safe, Ben stationed four guards outside the door.

He watched the *Barbary* claw its way into the air and up into the stratosphere and then turned to say good-bye to his family.

"It was good to see you, brother." Rion clapped him on the back of the shoulder in that awkward way brothers have. Kai shook hands like the man he'd become, and Thea, almost too round in the belly to reach, stood on her tiptoes and kissed him on the cheek.

"If it's a boy, we're going to call him Robert like your dad," she said. "And if it's a girl, she'll be Anju like your mother."

"That's good to know. I hope Nan didn't twist your arm in the matter of names."

"No, it was my idea."

"You're a star, Thea," Ben murmured. "Look after the boys—and I include Rion in that."

"I will, Uncle Ben."

Then it was Nan's turn.

"Are you sure you won't come with us, Nan?"

"I'm going to stick around here for a while, at least until Thea pops out the next generation of Benjamins. Call me if you need a negotiator."

"You'll be the first person I'll call."

"Can I come with you, Uncle Ben?" Ricky asked. "I won't get in the way, promise."

"I know you won't, Ricky, but your Nan has an advanced course in mathematics for you to study. If you want your pilot's ticket someday, better do the groundwork."

"She says I have to do history as well."

"Psi-techs have to have a good background in all the major subjects," Ben said. "Jussaro gave you the green light for an implant as soon as you turn fifteen."

"I have to wait that long?"

"Two years is not a long time. Pass all your courses with good grades and we'll ask for another assessment when you're fourteen."

"Oh, wow!"

"If your dad agrees." Ben grinned at Ricky's expression. "Better do all your chores on the farm, so he knows how responsible you can be."

"I can do that."

"Good man."

Ben swore he could still see Ricky's smile from orbit as *Solar Wind* climbed into the black.

"Are you going to bring Ricky into the Free Company?" Cara asked as Ben prepped for jumping into the Folds.

"I doubt I'll have much choice. He can't stay on Jamundi if he gets an implant, and Rion won't want him rattling around the galaxy on his own. Do you mind?"

"No. He's a good kid. Pretty grown up for his age."

"Except when he's not."

"He's a Benjamin. He'll get there in the end."

"Ready for foldspace jump," Ben said.

"All clear, Boss," Dobson said from the systems station.

Cara relayed it throughout the ship, receiving affirmative responses from the forty or so psi-techs.

"Folds coming up in three, two . . ."

With the feeling that something had imploded, *Solar Wind* popped out of existence in realspace.

They emerge into the oily black of foldspace.

Are you all right? Cara asks.

So far, so good, Ben says. *No void dragons yet.*

Ben, there's a void dragon half as big again as my sick bay cramming itself in here, Ronan calls. *It's fascinated by Keely and Cho.*

Cara flicks the image of sick bay on to the peripheral screen. There's a shimmer on the screen that could be a void dragon looming over Kitty.

"Are you recording?" Ben asks Cara.

"Yes."

See if you can get any information from it, Ronan, Ben says.

How can I do that when we have no common language?

How are Keely and Cho reacting to the dragon?

Ronan checks readouts on his screen. *Keely's agitated, but her vitals are within normal range. Cho's terrified. Heart rate through the roof.*

They can both see it?

Without a doubt.

When I interviewed Cho, he didn't react to the void dragon image.

Well, he can certainly see it now.

I can hold us in foldspace for a while longer. See if you can get either Keely or Cho to say something.

I'll try my best.

Ben can't simply put *Solar Wind* on automatics unless it's a dire emergency, but he keeps flicking his attention to the screen to see what's happening in sick bay. The shimmer that might be the void dragon, hitherto still, suddenly whirls around and pops out of existence.

That's weird, Ronan says. *The void dragon looked terrified and—*

Vanished. I saw.

Oh, gods! Get us out of here, now! The tone of Ronan's voice changes completely in an instant. Ben can't see anything on the screen.

What's happening?

It started as a dark smudge in the air on the far side of sick bay. Now it's as big as a fist. I think it's your Nimbus.

Shit!

Ben touches the controls and reaches for the line with his mind.

Exiting foldspace on my mark. Three. Two. One.

They pop out of the Folds into realspace.

Ronan's face was ashen as he described the Nimbus. Everyone else had disembarked from *Solar Wind*. Med-techs had taken Kitty and Cho away in float chairs. Ben and Cara met Ronan in the now-deserted sick bay.

"It was there, but not there," Ronan said. "I'm beginning to wonder if I imagined it . . . except I'm still shaking."

Nothing had shown up on the video feed, though that wasn't necessarily proof of anything. The void dragons never showed up on actual recordings, not even as a disturbance in the air.

"Tell us what you saw," Ben said.

"I'm not sure when it manifested. I saw a wisp of something, but it might have been there for some time. Both Keely and Cho were becoming more agitated and I was concentrating on them."

"Was it the Nimbus that was causing their agitation?"

"Presuming whatever I saw was the Nimbus."

"Let's say it was."

"Cause and effect? Again, I don't know. They may have been able to sense it coming, or they may have simply reacted when it was too small for me to notice it. I did . . . feel something, though. A chill and a wave of animosity. I thought that was probably Keely and Cho, pissed off at me for having them in restraints, but it might not have been. Then the Nimbus started to coalesce and, small as it was, it was utterly terrifying."

"Your med-techs?"

"In the outer room, strapped in for the jump."

"So no one else saw anything?"

"Just Keely and Cho, woozy under sedation, so they won't be much use. I sensed it wanted something. I don't know if that was me or Keely or Cho, or all three of us." He frowned. "Although . . . maybe I do . . . know, I mean. Keely and Cho were its focus. I'm not sure where that left me. I think I was a tasty bonus."

Ben looked at Cara. "Does this implicate the Nimbus in what's been happening to the colonies?"

"You mean it's sending humans that have been lost in the Folds back out into realspace to attack other humans? Why would it? What does it have to gain? Things that happen in realspace don't affect foldspace and the other way around."

"Unless they do and we simply don't know about it."

Chapter Thirty-Seven

QUESTIONS

THEY WERE STILL THINKING ABOUT WHAT had happened on Jamundi when news came in of another attack on a colony—this time one belonging to Arquavisa. The details were sparse, but from what Cara could gather from the amalgamation of half a dozen separate news broadcasts, a ship had attacked a well-established colony, dropping wide-dispersal canisters of Agent Topax from the air on all three major centers and every hectare of cultivated land. A corrosive herbicide and defoliant, Topax was designed for use on uninhabited planets as a prelude to terraforming. It was deadly to all carbon-based life and remained active for three years from the time of deployment. It was also now banned by interstellar treaty.

Digging a little deeper, Cara discovered that the ship was one of Arquavisa's own, though Arquavisa was strongly denying it. Why would a megacorporation attack one of its own colonies with its own ship? Answer—it wouldn't.

Cara accessed the files that J.P. Lister had cracked and began digging through the records of lost ships dating back to the first use of Topax and the last—a period of only thirty-two years. That narrowed it down.

Nothing.

She extended the search to five years either side. The

earlier years when Topax would have been in development, and the later years when, though banned, there might still be stocks in existence.

There. An Arquavisa transport had been lost in the Folds seventeen years ago. Her cargo manifest included Topax. Had it come back with deadly intent?

If so, how?

Cara's grasp of foldspace physics had never been much more than she needed in order to do her job. In other words, as long as she could hurl messages across the vastness of the galaxy, the deep questions on the nature of the Folds weren't relevant.

She had a working knowledge of celestial mechanics, orbital mechanics, and time dilation, but when Ben asked her to help him check for recent research into foldspace dynamics, she figured she needed backup.

"Can you put me in touch with your best astrophysicist?" Cara asked Garrick.

She'd made the trip to the Mansion House while Ben, whose knowledge of foldspace physics was much better than hers, pored over available research.

Garrick looked . . . stretched thin. She didn't know how else to describe it. It was as if his skin didn't quite fit him. She wouldn't have been surprised if, when he blinked, his eyelids were translucent. She found herself watching.

He did.

They weren't.

But all the same, something was wrong. A little knot of worry lodged somewhere behind her sternum. Garrick was a friend, but more importantly he was the driving force behind Crossways' lurch toward legitimacy. If something happened to him, the strongest crimelords would come circling like sharks.

Garrick cleared his throat and frowned at her, not quite focused. He fiddled with a stylus on his desk. He picked it up, turned it around in his fingers, put it down again. He didn't look her in the eyes when he said, "You're particularly interested in academic research now because?"

Garrick, of all people had a right to know. "Because we have evidence that the refugees who attacked the colonies came out of foldspace. Some of them had been in there for a very long time, but were no older than when they went in.

Others had been in there for less than a year." She let him digest the information. "Kitty Keely was one of them. She thinks it all happened a few days ago. Has no idea a year has passed."

Garrick leaped to his feet and then sat down so hard in his float chair that it hit the floor and bounced back. He said nothing, but his face went through several changes. Shock and awe pretty well covered most of it. He put one hand up to his mouth and pinched his lips in an effort not to speak until he was ready.

"You're still having nightmares, aren't you?" Cara asked.

"How did you . . . No. Well, yes. Sometimes."

"You mean every time you close your eyes?"

"Not always the same. Not always the same . . . intensity."

Garrick's knuckles were white as he grasped the arm of his chair.

"Did you ever take the implant aptitude tests when you were a teen?" she asked.

"Ben asked me that, once. Like I told him, they don't test you in juvie detention or on the streets."

"So you've never been tested at all?"

"Why would I?"

"Because you're transmitting those dreams to me and Ben. I don't know if they're going any farther, or whether we're getting them because we were with you and saw the Nimbus for ourselves."

He gave her a disbelieving look.

"You dream of being inside it, right?"

"How did—? Yes." He inhaled and blew out a long breath. "Will it ever end?"

She shook her head. "I don't know. Your dreams are nature's way of telling you that you have something to deal with. If you're projecting, you may need a damper."

"Will that stop the dreams?"

"Sadly, no, but it may stop you projecting them. What does your physician say?"

Garrick shrugged. "Says she knows nothing about fold-space."

"And that's the big problem," Cara said. "Nobody knows. Hence, I need to talk to the station's best theoretical physicist. Maybe part of the solution is learning more."

It turned out the person Cara needed was Doctor

Christa Beckham. Tempted away from Earth to teach at Crossways' embryonic university, she'd been injured and spent seven months recovering from leg and spinal surgery—time she'd used to work on a paper about foldspace illusions. Since getting out of rehab, she'd started to teach again, but continued working on the paper.

Cara slipped into the back of her class and caught the last ten minutes of a lecture that made her glad her student days were behind her. She approached Doctor Beckham after the lecture theater emptied.

"Doctor Beckham."

"You're new. I don't do catch-up sessions, so if you missed anything, you'll have to ask one of the other students. Try Altberg. She has a brain and she almost knows how to use it. Avoid Pashley. He thinks he knows what he's talking about, but he hasn't a clue."

"I'm not a student."

"No? Well, good day to you, then."

"I am interested in your work on foldspace illusions. They're not illusions, you know."

"And you know this because?"

"I've seen them."

"People see illusions. The clue is in the name."

"Do people hear illusions, too?"

"Hmm, interesting. Tell me what you know."

"I'd have to take you to see Ben Benjamin. I'm from the Free Company and we need to talk to you about the latest research into foldspace dynamics."

"Benjamin. Isn't he the one who—"

"Flew this space station through the Folds, yes."

"I was in surgery at the time. Missed the whole damn thing. Pity, it would have been a perfect opportunity."

"Opportunity?"

"I've devised an apparatus that I believe will show minute temperature and pressure variations if these foldspace illusions are real, but I haven't had the opportunity to test it yet."

Cara smiled. "I think we might be able to help each other out. Will you come to Free Company headquarters at Blue Seven and hear what we have to say?"

"When?"

"As soon as you can."

"I'll get my coat."

Cara was able to study Christa Beckham on the way to Blue Seven. She was hardly middle-aged, but she moved as though she was practicing to be an old lady someday soon. She walked with a cane, slowly, and with a pronounced limp. She kept her eyes cast down to the ground, taking care where she put the tip of the cane and her own feet. She climbed into the tub cab awkwardly and sat down with a thump, strapping in and leaning slightly forward, resting both hands on the curved handle of the cane. Her shoulder-length hair, black with a sprinkling of silver, flopped forward around her face.

"How do you like teaching at the university?" Cara felt the need to start a conversation.

"They're morons, but maybe not quite as moronic as the kids at Oxford."

"You taught at Oxford? Earth Oxford?"

"I don't know of any other. The kids there were all acutely aware that their parents were somebodies: rich, or politically notable, or maybe media stars, or famous for being famous. With the very occasional exception, they weren't there to learn, or, at least, not there to learn physics. Oxford is famous for its politicians; those guys aren't interested in what makes their world tick. They honestly believe it ticks around them anyway." She shrugged. "The kids here don't have much except ambition and raw talent. I can make something out of that. And, of course, I have time and funding for my research. That was part of the deal when they hired me."

"You were one of the ones Garrick hired before—"

"Just before Crossways got pounded on. A block of masonry fell on me."

"I'm sorry."

She shrugged again. "They put most of me back together, and it didn't cost me a cent. You have time to think while you're lying in a hospital bed. That's what I'm good at, thinking."

The tub cab drew up outside Blue Seven. One of the gate guards stepped forward to help Doctor Beckham out of the cab.

"Don't I know you?" She craned her neck to look up.

"I volunteer at the hospital, ma'am. I believe I pushed your float chair around once or twice."

"Graham, Lew Graham, I remember. You're sweet on that nurse. What was her name? Liza, that's it."

"Liza Roberts. We tied the knot a couple of months ago. Baby's due any time now."

"Well, congratulations, Mr. Graham. Girl or a boy?"

"Girl."

"When she's old enough, send her to my physics class."

"I'll be sure and do that."

Cara smiled at Graham as they passed into the barbican. She felt vaguely guilty for not knowing he'd married and was expecting a child. She sighed. Ben probably knew. It was good that the mercs were settling in and putting down roots, though.

Ben, we're here. Where are you?

Office. I'll see you in the meeting room in five minutes with Ronan.

Cara had time to visit the food counter to get coffee and sandwiches for herself and Doctor Beckham. She settled their visitor in the meeting room before Ronan arrived.

"Ah, good, I won't be eating alone." Ronan had a large insulated mug and a substantial piece of chocolate cake. "Would you like me to rustle up more cake?"

Cara looked at the sandwich and wondered why she hadn't ordered cake as well, but Doctor Beckham was already shaking her head.

Are you bringing cake? she asked Ben.

I wasn't, but I could.

She smiled at him mentally, a warm huggy feeling.

I'll bring extra.

He arrived with a tray with not only cake, but also some of Ada Levenson's pastries.

"Do you treat all your visitors so well?" Doctor Beckham asked.

"Only those we want to butter up for favors," Ben said. "We need information on any new developments and research on foldspace—anything that might have been flagged recently, particularly if it's unusual or unexpected."

"I need some context," Doctor Beckham said. "Tit for tat."

Ben nodded. "Last year I ended up flying *Solar Wind* out of the docking bay and straight into foldspace with four limpet mines attached to her belly, ticking down to boom." He shrugged. "Long story. Please take my word for it."

Cara knew the story, but it still made her flesh creep. She'd so nearly lost Ben. It took days for him to find his way back and he brought a fantastic story with him. It had sounded far-fetched at the time, but she'd seen things since that verified every word of it.

Ben kept the frills to a minimum. "Pilot-Navigators are taught that what they see in foldspace isn't real. I always tried to believe that, though there are times when your brain and your gut instinct have to tough it out on opposite sides. On this occasion, I was alone on the flight deck and there was this creature—a dragon."

"Dragon?"

"A void dragon. Huge. Like a cross between a winged lizard and a sea horse with eyes as black as the depths of foldspace." He closed his eyes for a moment. "Scales and leather. It was the kind of black that's iridescent, like oil on water."

"You thought it was real?"

"It was real. It is real. I've seen it since. We all have. It doesn't show up on security video except sometimes as a heat haze if you know where to look, but this is a drawing."

Ben activated his handpad and a hologram of the void dragon popped into being. Doctor Beckham swayed in her chair. "Not everyone can see them, or it. We don't know whether there's one or many, but those who can, those who are already Navigators, that is, are likely to have the talent to be able to fly a jumpship through the Folds."

"What about those who aren't Navigators or who don't have implants?"

"Some of us can see it, especially when we know what to look for," Cara said.

"In my case I had to see it through Ben's eyes before I could see it for myself," Ronan said.

"My nephew can see it," Ben said. "He doesn't have an implant yet, though he's showing potential."

"So you're sure it's real?"

"Sure. Remember I'm in a ship with four limpet bombs attached, alone, in foldspace with a void dragon. Right?"

She nodded.

"We're taught that void dragons aren't real, but what if nothing is real inside foldspace—including you, the ship, the very air you breathe. What if it's only real as long as you keep believing it's real? The ship lost gravity, I kicked off and headed for the ceiling, but for a moment I guess I forgot reality. I shot through the skin of the ship into foldspace itself. I won't bore you with the panic, but I suddenly realized I was still breathing. I grabbed the void dragon and hung on. It took me around the exterior of the ship, and I yanked off the limpets and hurled them away. Eventually, I found my way back into the ship, but I forgot to believe in air at some point. That was nearly a fatal mistake. I was in pretty bad condition by the time I made it home."

"You can put down most of that to hallucinations."

Ben nodded. "Agreed, but when I arrived back, there were no limpets on *Solar Wind*, and my implant was gone. I guess I'd forgotten to believe in it. I know. I know." Ben raised his hand. "It can't happen, but it did. You can ask the surgeon who replaced it."

"But why should it look like a dragon if it's an alien entity—and I believe that's what you're trying to tell me— right? Why should it look like a creature from our own mythology?"

"It's telepathic to a degree," Ben said. "But we don't have common ground on which to base vocabulary or concepts. I believe it encountered a human at some time and took the most awesome image in his or her mind."

"I'm not sure the latest scientific papers are going to be any good to you," Doctor Beckham said. "You've gone further than any other researchers I know of, though . . . there was something at a conference recently about the effects of belief in foldspace. Tell me, Commander Benjamin, are you the only person who has ever breached the skin of a ship and lived to tell the tale?"

"He's not," Cara said. "We both did when we rescued Garrick from the Nimbus."

"Nimbus? What's that?"

"We don't know for sure, but it's terrifying," Ben said. "A dark mass, sentient, smothering. Different from the void dragons—but we escaped and thought that was an end to it. However, colonies have been attacked in the last few months, and the attackers are all people who have been lost in the Folds, some a century ago, some last year. One, in particular, we can vouch for personally. Cara, Garrick, and I saw the Nimbus swallow her, yet she turned up in a ship which tried to attack a colony. None of the returnees think any time has passed."

"And when we brought two of them back to Crossways," Ronan said, "while we were in the Folds, the Nimbus, or something very like it, began to develop on the *Solar Wind*, in the sick bay, where they were."

"So what does it all mean?" Cara asked. "What's the true nature of foldspace?"

"How the hell should I know?" Doctor Beckham said. "What you've told me pulls the rug out from under my research, but I'll do you a deal. Take me into foldspace with my equipment, and I'll try and answer some of your questions."

Cara wondered if Ben would go for that. It might mean extending the time he spent in foldspace, which was surely the last thing he wanted. She glanced at him, but his face was set in a resolute expression.

"Done," he said.

Chapter Thirty-Eight

PUZZLES

"**L**ET'S TALK TO DAVID CHO FIRST," RONAN said. "I've been watching them both, monitoring their interactions. Kitty's still adamant she knows nothing, but Cho has moments of remorse. I think we might be able to get through to him, appeal to his humanity."

"Do you want me there?" Ben asked.

"I'd like you both to observe. Cara might pick up something that I miss."

So Ben and Cara ended up behind a one-way panel of glass-steel, opaque from the other side but so clear that, from their side, it might not have been there.

Ronan ran through the usual set of questions about who Cho was, how he'd become a psi-tech, where he'd trained to fly. Cho had no problems answering until Ronan began to dig deeper into his last mission. Cho denied any knowledge of the Nimbus, but when Ronan described it and how it grew inexorably, swallowing everything in its path, he broke down and began to weep.

"I think he's ready to talk," Ronan said. "We should get answers tomorrow."

But in the morning David Cho was dead. Not a mark on him.

"I'll do an autopsy, of course," Ronan said. "But it looks as if he simply gave up and died."

"How's Kitty?"

"She's fine, for now, but I'll keep her under full surveillance."

An hour later Ronan was standing in Ben's office, livid scratches on his face and a developing bruise on his forehead.

"Don't tell me . . ." Ben said.

Ronan sighed. "Yes, partway through the exam, it was as if someone flipped a switch. Kitty went for one of my medtechs, as vicious an attack as I've seen. I swear if we hadn't pulled her away, she'd have chewed the poor girl's throat out. Afterward, she didn't know she'd done it."

"Any permanent damage?"

Ronan shook his head. "We stopped her in time. But Kitty's going to have to be restrained or in lock-down."

"Whatever you think is best. We will need to talk to her, but perhaps you should try deep regression first. See if you can find the Kitty we used to know. She may have been a spy, but she wasn't a monster."

Ben had arranged to take a new batch of potential pilots out for an assessment run. To be honest, he was pleased to be able to leave the problem of Kitty Keely for a while and get on with the business of flying, even if it was with a bunch of pilot-Navigators he hadn't personally recruited.

He thought three of the five might do very well. One was borderline but willing to learn. The other, sadly, had faked the initial test. There was no way in hell he'd ever seen a void dragon. Someone had probably primed him with the right answers in advance of the interview.

After the training flight, Ben dropped into Garrick's office to give him the assessments and advised him to send the dud back to where he came from. He was undoubtedly a competent pilot, but he didn't have the instinct to fly a jumpship safely.

"I had Syke in to see me this morning," Garrick said. "He's heard you've got Kitty Keely in your infirmary. You know he used to be sweet on her?"

"Did he? I know he kept in touch after Orton died. I didn't realize it had developed any further."

"You know Syke. It might have taken him a few more years to get around to telling her."

"Not exactly impulsive, is he?"

"You've noticed."

"He still calls me Commander Benjamin."

"That sounds like Syke." Garrick smiled. "Anyhow, I think he'll come to see you about her, so be prepared."

"I'm not sure she's ready for visitors. She tried to tear out a med-tech's throat this morning."

Garrick winced. "Well, whatever you and Ronan think best. I thought I'd give you a heads-up."

"Much appreciated."

By the time Ben arrived at Blue Seven, Syke was waiting for him.

"Kitty," Syke said. "Alive."

"Yes," Ben confirmed. "But the Kitty you knew might not exist anymore."

He wondered if allowing Syke to see Kitty would be good for either of them. Would it advance their understanding of what had happened to her in the last year, or would it simply be a kind thing to do?

"I want to see her." Syke's voice trembled. His hands, balled into fists, betrayed his tension.

"It's not every day someone is resurrected," Ben said. "Ronan's still running tests."

"I want to see her." Syke's voice had gone very quiet, but his hands hadn't relaxed.

"As long as you know what she's done," Ben said. "She's dangerous."

Syke shook his head as if he couldn't envisage Kitty being dangerous.

"She tried to rip out a med-tech's throat this morning. We need to discover what happened to her. It's been a year, but Kitty thinks she's only been gone for a few days. Maybe it was, for her. Time in the Folds is strange. Or maybe she's been brainwashed—manipulated. It only took one woman on Butterstone to poison the colony's water supply. Imagine what someone determined and resourceful could do on a space station."

"I understand."

"I can show you the live feed to her room. She's restrained, of course, and watched constantly."

"I'd like to see for myself."

Ben brought up the holo screen. In a room bare of obvious equipment, Kitty lay strapped to a contour couch. A female med-tech sat in a corner and the two of them were chatting casually. Kitty had a reading tablet close to hand and earbuds for music.

"That conversation is being recorded, of course," Ben said. "There was another survivor, David Cho, second in command of the *Barbary*. He died this morning for no apparent reason."

"She looks the same." Syke's voice cracked and he cleared his throat before continuing. "Her hair hasn't even grown."

"Good point," Ben said. "That never even struck me. So she's either been in suspended animation for a year, or her elapsed time is only a few days, or whoever had her for the last year has hairdressing facilities. Thanks, Syke. Maybe you could sit with her for a while, see how she reacts. It would all have to be monitored, of course."

"I get that. Fine. Yes, sign me up."

✦ ✦ ✦

It was time to talk to Kitty.

Cara wasn't looking forward to this. The whole situation was getting more complex all the time. Earlier that morning Cara had taken a communication for Ben from Jessop. The transport that the Monitors had sent to collect the cryo capsules from Mirrimar-10 had successfully loaded them, entered the Folds via Mirrimar-10's main gate . . . and vanished. Cara wondered whether the Nimbus was reclaiming its own. Perhaps that's what it had been trying to do when it materialized in *Solar Wind*'s sick bay on the journey from Jamundi. Ronan thought Kitty and David Cho had been its main focus.

Could Kitty tell them more?

Ronan brought her into the interview room, secured in a float chair. Ben and Cara were already waiting. They'd agreed in advance that Ben would do all the talking while Cara and Ronan listened with all their senses to see if they could get a sense of anything underlying Kitty's answers.

"I'm sorry about the restraints, Kitty," Ben said as Ronan locked the chair to the floor and took a seat to one side and slightly behind her. "You understand why they're there."

She scowled. "I'm a dangerous criminal. I tried to kill Etta Langham."

"That's true, but it's in the past now. We don't think you wanted to do that. You were acting on orders from Alphacorp. You let yourself be caught before you could do any damage."

"Yes. Orders." Her face cleared. "I guess Alphacorp can't do much to me now—unless you're going to send me back."

"Would you like that?"

She stared at her knees and shook her head, then looked up. "Alphacorp has my mother. Unless I do as they say, they'll slap her with a big medical bill, a financial hole she'll never climb out of."

"Alphacorp thinks you're dead."

"Oh. Do you think Mom will get the death-in-service bonus?" She brightened considerably. "I guess that works out all right, then."

She sounded calculating rather than emotional, as if her mother was some distant problem that had suddenly been solved.

"We're not here to talk about Alphacorp," Ben said. "We need to know what happened to you after you disappeared into the Nimbus."

"The what?"

"You were on a shuttle with Norton Garrick, in foldspace. We found you, but the Nimbus, a black cloud that we think might be sentient, swallowed you up before we could get you off the shuttle."

"That's not—"

"How you remember it, no. But that's what happened."

"You left me, and the *Barbary* found me."

"How long do you think it's been?"

"I don't know four days? Seven maybe?"

"It's been a year."

"What? How can it be a year? I would know."

"Would you? Maybe you were in cryo or some kind of suspended animation."

She shook her head and repeated more firmly, "I would know."

"Did you talk to your fellow passengers on the *Barbary*?"

"Not much. They were all a bit odd."

"Some of them thought they'd only been on there a few days, but their records show they were lost in the Folds sixty years ago."

"How can that be?"

"You tell me. People lost in the Folds decades ago suddenly come back to realspace and start attacking colonies."

"Attacking colonies?"

"You thought Jamundi was the only one?"

"I . . . we . . ." She shook her head. "It's all a bit of a fog after we landed. Attack, you say? What happened?"

She's genuinely confused, Cara said to Ben.

"I can show you. We have video. What I can't tell you is why it happened or what the outcome was meant to be."

Ben flicked the image onto the wall from his handpad. Security cameras had captured the incident from several angles. Kitty watched in silence as she and her fellow passengers stormed the fence. She didn't even flinch when Tengue's mercs began to drop individuals with tranquilizer darts and stun bolts, and she showed no emotion at all when a mass of civilians drove forward through the mayhem to smash themselves against the security screen.

"Well?" Ben asked when the last image faded.

"Well what? What was that?"

"That was you and your fellow refugees almost chewing your way through three layers of security to attack the colony."

"No way." She shook her head. "You faked it."

"Why would we do that?"

"I don't know, but there's no way I could forget something like that."

Ben looked at Cara.

She absolutely believes what she's saying, Cara said.

I concur. Ronan nodded.

"Thank you, Kitty. We'll leave it there for now." Ben nodded to Ronan.

"Wait, you can't finish like that. You've accused me of something I didn't do. Don't I get the right of reply?"

For the first time Cara felt a flash of emotion, though it was mostly righteous indignation.

"Go ahead," Ben said.

"One minute we were all sitting around, bored out of our skulls because there's only so much you can do in a large tent, and the next thing we knew your savages were among us with stunners. You're trying to cover up your inhumane treatment of us."

"Why would we do that?"

"I don't know. You made a mistake. Whatever. Thought we were something we weren't."

Ben fiddled with the control on his handpad. The images sprang up on the screen only this time slower and in close up. He focused on one face in the crowd.

"Take a good look, Kitty."

"It looks like me, but it can't be. I'd remember."

She was still muttering, "It can't be," when Ronan called a med-tech to take her to her room.

"Opinions? Ideas?" Ben leaned back in his chair and looked at Ronan and Cara.

"She believes what she's saying, but she has fuzzy areas that she's trying to work around."

"Medically, she's the woman who left here a year ago," Ronan said. "There's no trace of cryo chemical or anything else unusual in her blood. Mentally, she's a little confused. I thought it was deliberate at first, but now I'm convinced she doesn't recall the Nimbus, or what happened during the missing year, or even trying to storm the fence on Jamundi or attacking Aster this morning."

"What about David Cho?" Ben asked.

"There's no reason he died. Historically, there have always been sudden unexplained deaths. Statistically, it was mostly young Asian men. The superstitious used to call it various things. In China, they called it being crushed by a ghost. Sometimes it's undetected arrhythmia, but I checked David Cho personally when we brought him in. I would have picked up anything abnormal in his heart, however mild. Ever since this sudden unexplained death syndrome was noted, there have been five percent of cases that remain consistently baffling. This is one of those."

"Kitty shouldn't be vulnerable to that, should she?" Cara asked.

"She shouldn't be, but neither should David Cho. Kitty's problem is in her head."

Cara nodded. "Kitty believes everything she says, but that doesn't mean the memories are real. Neural readjustment screws with your head. Has she been programmed by an expert?" Donida McLellan was never far from Cara's thoughts. It didn't even matter that the woman was dead.

"Syke's a solid part of her past here," Ronan said, "It might help to have him babysit her for a while. It might also help to sit her down with Garrick."

Cara frowned. "What might that do to Garrick? He's still a bit fragile. A lot fragile, in fact."

Ronan frowned. "Yes, you're probably right."

Chapter Thirty-Nine

KITTY

AS SOON AS GARRICK HEARD KITTY KEELY was back from the dead, he knew two things. The first was that he had to confront her, the second that it would be the most difficult thing he'd ever done in his life.

So he put it off for a few days. Tried to pretend everything was normal, but it didn't stop his gut from churning. This was real. Kitty had been with him when he'd met the Nimbus, heard its voice. She would remember. There was something important that had been missing inside him since that day, something he needed to do. Or maybe something he needed to understand.

At last he decided. He didn't waste any more time thinking about it because he knew he'd chicken out if he did. He didn't even talk to Mona about his decision. He simply called his two bodyguards and let them get him a tub cab to Blue Seven. He left them in the reception office with Tengue's duty sergeant and two other gate guards, and passed through the barbican alone.

Blue Seven was busy with people coming and going. The offices close to the entrance were manned, their occupants visible through the glass panels. In the distance, straight down the concourse, was the central dining area and kitchen. To his left the infirmary nestled between the offices and the main accommodation block, and to his right were a gymnasium, a cluster of workshops, and an equipment maintenance department.

Gen Marling was walking her toddler along, bent over, holding the child's hands in her own. Every few steps she lifted and swung the child, getting an excited giggle in return. Gen raised her head, smiled at him, and picked up the child who pointed at him excitedly. Garrick had never felt less like smiling, but he conjured one up from somewhere, hoping it looked genuine enough not to set the child crying.

He met Ronan Wolfe on the threshold of the infirmary.

"Hope you're not in a rush to go somewhere, Doctor Wolfe. If possible, I'd like to see Kitty Keely."

Wolfe looked surprised, but he invited Garrick to follow him into the infirmary.

"Her memory has gaps. Please don't be surprised if she's a bit vague. She's been sedated because she's dangerous, but we can't keep her that way. Neither can we keep her in restraints, so she's behind a clear glass-steel screen. Sound goes through in both directions, so you can talk to her as if there's nothing between you." Ronan gave him a long, level look. "Are you sure about this?"

"I hope so."

"We'll need to record everything. We're looking for any clue about what happened to her."

"I understand."

"Do you want someone in there with you? You may find the experience stressful."

Ha! If only Doctor Wolfe knew. Garrick swallowed hard to try to clear the lump in his throat. He tried to keep his voice even and neutral. "Not especially. I'm sure you'll be watching."

Damn, Wolfe was an Empath; he was bound to have picked up Garrick's agitation.

"Yes. I'll be watching. Don't worry. If you need anything, you only have to yell. Are you sure—"

Garrick swallowed again. "Quite sure."

Kitty was sitting at a table with an interlocking puzzle in front of her. She didn't look up when Garrick entered. "More questions?"

"An apology."

At the sound of Garrick's voice, her head jerked up and

she sprang from the chair, knocking it backward and scattering puzzle pieces across the table and on to the floor.

"You." She ran forward and beat both fists on the clear screen—once, twice—as if she wanted to strike at Garrick.

Garrick stepped back. He saw the screen shake slightly under the pounding, but when she dropped her arms to her sides, it resumed its original shape, neither dented nor scratched.

"You remember me, then."

"Of course, I remember you. We were out there together, decoys. I was supposed to be taking you to surrender the station, but that wasn't the real plan, was it? I never stood a chance of getting back home, did I?"

"It was about fifty-fifty. If Benjamin hadn't been able to fly Crossways through the Folds, you'd have been home free, and I'd have been in a jail cell—or possibly dead." And that might have been better than being free and having the memories eating at his soul every single day since. "It was all about getting a ceasefire for long enough to give Benjamin a chance to get Crossways to safety. Getting lost in the Folds wasn't part of the plan."

"But they came for you—Benjamin and Carlinni. They came for you and left me behind."

"That's not how it happened."

"That's what they say." She heaped the emphasis on *they* and jerked her head at the recording eye on the wall. "They're trying to twist my memories. Next you'll be telling me it all happened over a year ago."

He shook his head. "It's not my job to convince you of anything. Yes, it was over a year ago. You only have to look at the white in my hair to see that, but I want to talk about the black cloud. They're calling it the Nimbus, as if by naming it they can make it more understandable." He let out a laugh that was anything but mirthful. "I've been having nightmares ever since. That's a lot of nightmares. Sometimes I wonder how much longer I can hold it all together."

He scrubbed his eyes with the heels of his hands. "Do you remember when the whole thing began? You were trying to find the line to a jump gate. Any jump gate, you said. Then my breath started to cloud. I asked you to check life support, but you said everything was normal. Then you started to shiver. A terrible cold seeped from the rear of the shuttle. There was a darkness at head height, like a small black puff of cloud no bigger than an eyeball. It began to grow."

"I don't know what you're talking about."

"You do. You have to. It was you that heard it first."

"Heard what?"

"You said it was singing to you."

There was a moment of stunned silence, and then Kitty burst out laughing.

Garrick had been prepared for hysterics, or terror, or anger, but laughter diminished everything he'd gone through. He'd thought Kitty of all people would understand, would get where he was coming from. He'd shared the Nimbus' song with Kitty, felt its call. How could she laugh?

Something inside him swelled and broke into a thousand pieces. He ran out of the room, across reception, past a surprised med-tech. He bumped into Ronan as he reached the door to the concourse, but barely felt the jolt. He stumbled. The floor rushed up to meet him. For a moment, he saw the seam in the flooring. Something in his brain knew he was about to meet it percussively, but he couldn't get his hands between him and the ground.

✦ ✦ ✦

Max was sitting at his desk, running some figures for the cost of outfitting the *Howling Wolf* when he heard the commotion outside. He abandoned his desk and went to the door, only to see a knot of people gathered around someone who'd fallen close to the infirmary entrance.

Gen was there, kneeling to help. Letting curiosity get the better of him, he wandered over.

Garrick was on the floor, fallen but neither conscious nor unconscious. He was having some kind of fit, and Gen was holding him almost steady while Ronan tried to position a hypospray for best effect. A burly med-tech added his weight. Ronan activated the spray, and Garrick went limp.

"Are you okay?" Max offered a hand to Gen, but she didn't need it.

"I'm fine. Don't interrupt your day for us. Come on, Liv."

She turned, but Liv was nowhere in sight.

Gen gasped and reached for Max's hand.

How long had it been since Gen had reached for him voluntarily?

"It's all right." Max felt his Finder's connection to his daughter. "She's not gone far. This way."

He didn't let Gen's hand drop from his own as he led the way into the infirmary, following a series of open doors until they came face-to-face with Kitty Keely. She was kneeling in front of a clear panel with her right hand pressed to it. Liv stood on this side of the screen with her right hand pressed against the glass to Kitty's.

"Liv." Gen snapped out her daughter's name, but the child didn't move. "Liv!"

She pushed forward, but Max held on to her hand. "Wait. There's something going on. Don't wrench her out of it. You may do more harm than good."

"To hell with that!" Gen shook him off, but this time she approached more carefully. "Liv, sweetie, we mustn't disturb the nice lady."

Olivia dropped her hand from the glass. "She's not a nice lady. She wants to kill everyone. Dead."

"Did she tell you that?" Max asked. "Did she say she wanted to kill everyone on Crossways?"

"No, silly. Not here. Everyone. All the people. Everywhere." She turned to Gen. "She says she wants to go home."

"Home?"

"To the funny black thing."

Max looked at Gen. "We need to tell Ronan and Ben. They'll want to talk to Liv."

"Not now," Gen said. "Ronan's taking care of Garrick, and in case you hadn't noticed, our daughter is a bit too young for all this."

Max tried to interpret Gen's glowering look. Now what had he done?

Chapter Forty

RESEARCH

CARA HAD TO SIDLE THROUGH *SOLAR WIND*'S flight deck now that Christa Beckham's equipment filled up half the available space. Ben had had a couple of men help to haul it up the access tube, set it up, and strap it down in front of the pair of bucket seats that were for passengers.

Maybe she should introduce Doctor Beckham to Dido Kennedy. If Dido had been able to make the jump engines small enough to retrofit, she could probably reduce Beckham's equipment to the size of a suitcase.

"I need to check it now and then check it again while we're in realspace," Beckham said. "Then see what we get in the Folds." She bent to the equipment, made a slight adjustment, and looked up. "Do you think I'll be able to see them?"

Ben shrugged. "Did you test for an implant when you were in your teens?"

"Of course, but no aptitude, I'm afraid."

"It still doesn't mean anything. You might, or you might have to let your machines do your seeing for you."

"I would so much like—"

"You might not," Cara said. "There are some who can't cope with what they see in the Folds."

"I know, I know, but still . . ."

"Coming aboard." Ronan's voice sounded below. Within seconds, he emerged from the access tube followed by Jake. Ben was using this trip as an opportunity to drop Jake off to bring the *Howling Wolf* back through the Folds to Crossways now Yan and his crew had retrofitted the jump drive.

With Ed Dobson and a small crew installed in engineering, they were ready for departure.

Doctor Beckham glanced sideways at Ronan as he slid into the second bucket seat alongside her, carefully avoiding contact with the equipment. "Am I likely to need medical intervention, Doctor Wolfe?"

"I certainly hope not." Ronan smiled. "But I confess I'm curious, and in case everyone else is busy, I will be able to alert you to the presence of void dragons should you not be able to see them for yourself."

"Tactfully put, Doctor."

"And if you need me to do anything, please let me know."

"It's hardly likely, but thanks for the offer. Don't touch anything and we shall get on very well."

She pursed her mouth, but a small smile reached her eyes.

"Oh, I'm happy to simply watch and learn," Ronan said.

Cara took the comms as usual while Jake slid into the systems station.

"It seems like a small crew for so complex a ship," Dr. Beckham said.

"That's the beauty of *Solar Wind*," Ben said. "She's streamlined in all her operations. If necessary, she can be flown single-handed, though I wouldn't recommend it for extended flights."

"Is the ship armed?"

"She is, but we're not anticipating running into the kind of trouble that needs torpedoes."

One hundred klicks out from Crossways, Ben brought the jump drive online. "I doubt whether we'll be visited by void dragons on this section of the journey, Doctor Beckham. It's a very quick jump to Amarelo space to rendezvous with the *Howling Wolf*. Even so, please strap in. The effects of foldspace can be somewhat strange."

"Are you trying to make me nervous?"

"Not at all. Just cautious, which is entirely the right way to approach foldspace."

"I did go through the Folds to reach Crossways in the first place, you know."

"On a regular passenger vessel?"

"Yes."

"It's likely they put a mild sedative into the cabin air. It's standard on commercial passenger ships and it saves people from freaking out should there be any so-called illusions."

Doctor Beckham's mouth formed an "oh" shape.

"Should I switch on the equipment now?"

"No harm in letting it run," Ben said as he connected with the jump drive, feeling *Solar Wind* from the inside. "Foldspace coming up in three . . . two . . . one."

The flight deck lighting fails, but Cara looks over in the gloom and Ben doesn't appear to need it. After a few seconds it flickers on again, but softer and more golden than before. She forms a mental gestalt with all the psi-techs on board, which is everyone except Doctor Beckham. Mustn't forget Doctor Beckham. She's all right with Ronan to steady her. At least, she's not screaming, which is a good sign.

An eerie rainbow of light begins somewhere above Ben and grows until all the colors merge and the flight deck is engulfed in pure white light.

"Pretty col—" Doctor Beckham begins, but then has to screw up her eyes against the brightness. With one hand shading her eyes, she presses a couple of switches on the equipment. "Is there anything?"

"No." Cara, Ben, and Ronan answer at the same time. No void dragons. Not even a visit from the otter-kind.

They pop out of the Folds, blinking at the sudden change of light.

"Was that it?" Doctor Beckham asked.

"That was it," Ben said, smiling a relieved kind of smile.

"It was so—"

"Quick?" Cara suggested.

"We'll stay longer on the return journey," Ben said. "As long as it's safe."

"Is safety an issue?" Doctor Beckham said.

"It depends on what we see, or what we're seen by."

Cara hailed Yan Gwenn.

Howling Wolf sent out a launch to exchange Jake for Yan, who emerged on to the flight deck smiling. "Jake's going to enjoy bringing that ship home," he said. "It's been a privilege to be her captain, even though it was only temporary."

Ben welcomed him with a wave. "Welcome to the real world, Acting Captain Gwenn. Now get your backside into the systems chair and let's be away and leave Jake to play with his new toy for a while."

"Yessir!" Yan gave a very smart mock salute.

Ben introduced Doctor Beckham and explained the purpose of her research trip. "Keep the time, Yan. We'll stay as long as it's safe."

"Mr. Dobson." Ben used the mechanical comms as a courtesy to Doctor Beckham.

"Yes, Boss."

"I want your engineers positioned as we agreed in case we get any unwelcome Nimbus-shaped visitors."

"On it, Boss."

"And while we're in the Folds, I want everyone in gestalt. If there's any danger, I want to know the instant it's spotted."

Cara opened up links with Dobson and the five engineers as they positioned themselves at strategic points.

"Right. Doctor Beckham, please make the most of this. I don't want to have to do it twice," Ben said.

This was the first time Ben had deliberately extended the time *Solar Wind* remained in foldspace since rescuing Garrick and losing Kitty Keely. Kara knew he had to be all kinds of nervous, but as usual he didn't show it. He brought the jump engine on line.

"Preparing for foldspace in three, two, one."

Instead of the bright white light this time everything is misty for a while. The mist gradually clears from the deck plates upward until there's only a layer of fluffy cloud lining the ceiling of the flight deck. It dissipates.

"Everything all right, Doctor?" Ben asks. "Recording?"

"Yes, audio and video and more besides. I have the baseline from the first journey to compare it to."

"One minute," Yan calls.

"That's funny," Doctor Beckham says. "My clock says two and a half minutes."

"Time is strange in the Folds," Yan says. "One minute, thirty."

In the gestalt Cara feels Ben looking for the line to Crossways Station and Olyanda. He finds it, but lets *Solar Wind* coast.

"Are we moving?" Doctor Beckham asks.

"Yes . . . and no," Ben says. "It's relative. Movement, time, space, spacetime. You're the theoretical physicist, Doctor."

"Two minutes," Yan calls.

"Yes, but this is a practical application of—"

"They're here," Ronan says for Doctor Beckham's benefit. "Otter-kind. Small and sleek, moving like otters in water."

Beckham checks her machines, but it's obvious she can't see them.

"Where are they?"

"Rolling around each other close to the ceiling. They look as though they're playing. They buzzed Yan's head."

"They did?" Yan looks up, but he can't see them either.

"Ah, here's the big one," Ronan says as the big void dragon noses through the bulkhead, the clawed strands on its prehensile beard waving as if there's a breeze.

"Three minutes," Yan calls.

The void dragon shrinks down to a size to fit the flight deck and looms over the doctor's equipment.

"It's right here," Ronan whispers.

"Damn! I hoped I'd be able to see it."

The void dragon turns to Ben and asks *?*

"Scientific study." Ben says the words as well as puts them into the forefront of his mind.

Cara's not sure whether the void dragon has any frame of reference for either Doctor Beckham's equipment or its purpose.

OLIVIA MAY MARLING, the void dragon says.

An image develops in the gestalt mind. Red One. Dido Kennedy's chaotic workshop. A hastily rigged controller to the jump drive Kennedy has built into the station. Ben's flying the whole thing through the Folds, out of danger from the combined fleets of four megacorps and into the middle of the battle taking place over Olyanda. The Trust fleet versus Oleg Staple's defense force.

Only now it's from the void dragon's viewpoint. Cara sees Ben sink to his knees, desperately holding on to the path to fly the station through and out the other side. Then Cara sees herself hugging Ben from behind. She remembers that moment. She was pouring in all the energy she could spare into him.

Gen has just given birth. She huddles next to Max who is holding his daughter, as yet unnamed. Max doesn't flinch from the void dragon. Cara's not sure if he can see it. The dragon homes in on the baby, the unformed human mind open to so many possibilities, and plants—what?

A seed of understanding.

The void dragon tells the baby in thoughts if not actual words, *Cherished/beloved.*

And the tiny newborn understands.

"Four minutes," Yan calls.

OLIVIA MAY MARLING, the void dragon says. And they all get a strong impression of place which translates as, BRING HER HERE.

Suddenly the temperature on the flight deck drops. Oh, that can't be good. The otter-kind swirl around each other and dive through the bulkhead, leaving no trace. The void dragon stiffens and jerks to one side.

Hanging about two meters in the air in the center of the flight deck is a small dark ball of swirling cloud. A line of ice shoots down Cara's spine and she wants to throw up. No—she wants to run away screaming and then she wants to throw up. She fights the urge to bolt down the access tube.

She struggles to hold the gestalt together.

She can feel Ben fighting down panic, but he keeps his voice even. "Keep your equipment running, Doctor," he says, bringing the jump engines on line.

"What's that?" Doctor Beckham asks. "Good God! What the hell is it?"

"It's the Nimbus. Small, but growing," Ben says. "You can see it?"

"I can see it," Yan says, who has never seen a void dragon in his life.

"Oh, yes." Doctor Beckham breathes. "Though I wish I couldn't. Is this what you meant? About the scary things?"

"This is orders of magnitude worse than the void dragons," Ronan says, still managing to sound calm. "Ben, are we getting out of here anytime soon?"

Ben's holding the line. Cara doubts he's as calm as he sounds. "You are recording everything, aren't you, Doctor Beckham?"

"Yes. Can we go now?"

"Cara?"

"The rest of the ship is clear."

"Five minutes," Yan calls.

"What is it?" Ben asks the void dragon. *?*

EXPLOSION, the void dragon says, and dives through the floor plates.

It's the only word it has for something that's not good.

They exit foldspace. The Nimbus vanishes.

Cara held her head in her hands.

"Are you all right?" Ben asked.

"No, I'm not all right. I'm about to start giving Garrick nightmares. Couldn't you get out any faster than that?"

"I wanted to give Doctor Beckham's equipment as long as I could."

"I'd have settled for less," Doctor Beckham said, "though the rational scientist part of me says I should have stayed longer, recorded more."

"How soon before you find out what you've got?" Ben asked.

"I'll start the analysis as soon as I get the equipment back to the lab, after I've changed my underpants."

✦ ✦ ✦

"It's real." Christa Beckham's voice rattled out over the comms feed to the apartment's wall plate. Her face was pale, her hair mussed, and her eyes red-rimmed as if she'd been up working through the night. "Okay, I know you knew it was real, but my readings prove it. This is going to change the face of foldspace physics and the way they train Navigators. . . . I'm going to write a paper on it and maybe attend the conference in the—"

Cara slid a mug of tea into Ben's hands and a savory breakfast roll. She settled on a stool on the opposite side of the table with her own plate and mug, out of the range of the cam. She still had that hair-mussed-just-out-of bed look, even though she was up and dressed in a casual softsuit. Blue. Ben liked Cara in that particular shade of blue.

He huffed out a breath and dragged his thoughts away from Cara and the way the softsuit draped over her trim figure.

"Whoa, Doctor Beckham. Take a breath," Ben said. "Start again."

"Okay, okay. The readings prove, without a doubt, that there's something in foldspace."

Ben took a deep breath. In his head, he did a huge air punch. Yes! He'd been sure all along they existed, yet doubtful that Doctor Beckham's equipment could measure what he'd experienced.

She was already continuing. "You're quite right; the cameras don't record an image, though there's some distortion around where the image should be. If I combine it with the temperature readings and thermal imaging, plus the tiny ripple in spacetime it creates—"

"It creates a ripple in spacetime?"

"That's what I said. So if I combine all those together and push them through an imaging system, we get this." She flashed an image on to the screen which looked like a void dragon drawn as a negative image. Some of the detail was absent, but it was quite clearly dragon-shaped.

"How do you like that?" Beckham asked.

Cara leaned across the table and squeezed his buddy-suited forearm. He covered her fingers with his own.

Ben grinned. "I like it very well. And the little critters?"

"Not quite otters, though I can see why that's where your mind takes you."

"Jake calls them snakes."

"That, too." She flicked a second enhanced image on the screen which showed two amorphous blobs changing shape as they moved like a murmuration of starlings: now long and lean, now wide and globular.

"I'm not actually sure these are single creatures. I think they could be a cooperative flock of something much smaller. Look . . ." As the otter-kind passed out of the flight deck, they appeared to shatter into thousands of tiny pieces the instant before they disappeared.

"But the void dragon doesn't do that?"

"No, but it doesn't conserve its own mass when it reduces in size to fit into the available space in the flight deck."

"And what about ... the other thing, the developing Nimbus."

"We only recorded a few seconds of it. It's a pity we couldn't get more data to see how it grew ..."

"Trust me, it isn't. Did it register?"

"In a way."

"In what kind of way?"

"There was a complete absence of reading, not even any kind of cosmic background. It was the very definition of nothing."

Chapter Forty-One

OLIVIA

CARA SAW THE SCIENTIST'S IMAGE FADE FROM the screen. "Well, they can't deny the existence of fold-space creatures now," she said. "Christa Beckham's a respected scientist. If she publishes a paper on this, it has to change the way everyone trains their Navigators. It's going to have huge repercussions. That's what you wanted, isn't it? It's your moment. Everything you've said—theorized about—proven." She squeezed his arm again.

Ben nodded, but Cara could tell he was already thinking ahead, maybe about something else entirely.

"While we were in the Folds, the void dragon put something into my mind that I've been trying not to think about." He massaged his forehead with the tips of three fingers. "It asked for Olivia May Marling again, and then it showed me an image of Crossways' jump through the Folds. I saw the whole thing from its perspective. While we were struggling to bring the station home, the void dragon was fascinated by the sudden appearance of a very new and unformed human mind."

"It wasn't only you. We all saw it via the gestalt."

"You did?" Ben sounded relieved. "Then you can back me up. The void dragon gave the baby something—put something into her mind. I think Gen and Max's baby is the key to communicating with the void dragon. That's why it keeps asking for her."

"You want to take a baby into the Folds?"

"No, I don't, but I think we might have to."

"Who's we? Don't make me a part of this. I'm going to be on Gen's side when she says a very firm no to the idea."

He huffed out a breath and stared into the distance for a while.

"There's something out there. Something that's taking more and more ships in the Folds. And the people it's taken are coming back and trying to kill us. If we have a chance of finding out what and why, shouldn't we take it?"

"Not if it means exposing a baby to the void dragon."

"Maybe with the right safeguards in place . . ." Ben stood up. "I'm going to talk to Gen and Max."

"No, Ben, you can't. Ben. Ben!"

But she was talking to empty air. He'd stalked out without a backward glance.

Cara stood in stunned silence for a moment and then shoved her bare feet into her shoes, and raced after him, catching him at Gen and Max's door.

"Ben, this is unthinkable," she said. "You can't—"

"Can't what?" Max asked as he opened the door wide.

Gen stood across the room with Liv on her hip, the toy dragon clutched in the child's fingers.

"Can I come in?" Ben glanced down at Cara. She felt as if he'd suddenly slapped her across the face and forced her away.

"Can we both come in?" She pushed past Max and went to take up a position behind Gen.

"What's this all about?" Gen asked.

"The void dragon and your daughter," Ben said. "It's asking for her."

Gen clasped the little girl tight.

"When she was born, it gave her a gift. I think that gift is understanding. I think she can interpret what the void dragon is trying to communicate."

"You're nuts," Max said. "She's barely eighteen months old."

"And already speaking in sentences."

"Short, simple ones."

"Shut up!" Gen yelled. She lowered her voice once she

had their attention. "You can argue all you like over what she can and can't do, but I'm her mother and she's not going into foldspace. Not for any reason whatsoever, especially to talk to a void dragon."

"I'm with Gen," Cara said, putting one hand on her friend's shoulder. "It's too much to ask. The risks . . ."

Ben closed his eyes and took a deep breath. "I know, I know, but unless we find out what's going on, we're going to lose more and more ships and colonies. Thousands of people. The void dragon is trying to tell us something, and Liv could be the only one who can translate it."

Max and Gen stood intransigent, and Cara couldn't blame them.

"We'll take every precaution," Ben said. "We'll have a full crew, including Ronan, and a backup jumpship pilot. Gen, you could even do that yourself, so you could bring us out of the Folds at any time. You've flown *Solar Wind* often enough."

Gen growled—actually growled. Her voice came out low and raspy. "I don't know you anymore, Ben Benjamin. Get out of here. Now!"

Max inserted himself between his family and Ben, going toe to toe. "You heard Gen. I may not be much of a fighter, but so help me if you come near my daughter I'll punch your teeth down your throat. Leave now, and don't come back!"

Ben pressed his lips together, turned on his heel and left, his shield so tight that Cara didn't know what he was thinking.

Max slammed the door behind him and leaned against it.

"Are you all right?" Cara asked Gen.

"Yes. No. I don't know. I'm shaking like a leaf. How could he—"

Max moved in to put one arm round Gen and by default, Liv. "Thanks for the backup," he said to Cara. "I thought you'd support him."

She shook her head. "Not on this."

Gen gave her a wan half smile. "Yes, thank you."

"He's suggested we should have children," Cara said. "I'm not sure I could trust him after this. He's normally so . . . so Ben. Always doing what's best for people. Compassionate, even. And yet . . . I know he's desperate to find out what's going on in foldspace. Colonies are being destroyed. People are dying, and he thinks it's his job to stop it. But since the void dragons have been making an appearance regularly, and then the Nimbus, and all the dreams . . . Did you know he's been having nightmares every night for over a year? And they're not even his. They're Garrick's nightmares— somehow we share them."

"But Garrick's not psi." Gen's alarm showed on her face.

"No, but he is the one who's come closest to the Nimbus and lived."

Liv began to wriggle. When Gen put her down, the child stomped off into the middle of the floor. "Want to talk to dragon," she said. *Uncle Ben, want to talk to dragon!*

"Sweetheart, the void dragon is a toy. It's a story." Gen knelt beside the child and offered her a furry kitten made from marmalade-colored fur with tufted ears and a tiger-striped tail. She looked up at Cara. "Ever since her first words she's insisted there's someone in her head. Then it came out that it was a dragon. I made her the toy thinking she'd transfer the idea to something she could touch, but she knows. She hears the void dragon. How can that be? It's not even in the same dimension."

"No." Liv batted the kitten to the floor and clutched the void dragon toy to her chest. "I remember."

"How can you remember, sweetie, you were a new-born?"

"I was new and there was a dragon."

Tell her no, Max said.

We said we'd never lie to her.

"Tell me," Liv said.

"It was a special time." Gen adopted her Mummy-to-child-soothing-voice. "The station—all of it—flew through the Folds."

"That's where the dragon lives."

"That's right. And while the station was there—"

"With Uncle Ben."

"Yes, with Uncle Ben."

"I saw a dragon."

"I'm not sure you could have seen it. You were busy coming out of Mummy's tummy."

"It came to visit."

"It did."

"It had a beard with . . ." She flexed her fingers into

claws. "And they moved." She rubbed her toy dragon's chin, devoid of prehensile strands of beard.

"Claws in its beard?" Max asked. "Have you ever told her that? Is that even a thing?"

"I might have."

"Well, I didn't know about it."

The dragon has a wavy beard. Want to see dragon! Liv broadcast loud enough to be heard throughout Blue Seven. *Want to go with Uncle Ben to see the dragon.*

The door opened without a warning knock. Ben stood in the doorway, his face deadly serious.

"Uncle Ben!" Liv scampered toward him holding out her arms wide. He scooped her up in his left arm, drew a pistol, and shot Gen first and then Max.

Cara stood stunned for vital seconds.

"Soft stun bolts," Ben said. "They'll be all right."

"You've taken their daughter. They'll never be all right again."

"I'll bring her back safely. I swear it."

"And what if you can't?"

"I will. Come with us."

"You can't do this." She took three steps toward Ben before he squeezed the trigger again and everything went black.

✦ ✦ ✦

Ben hadn't known he was capable of kidnapping a toddler and shooting his best friends until he heard Liv's cry: *Uncle Ben, want to talk to dragon!*

But he had known Liv was the key to all this. She could talk to the void dragon. Gods, he wished things hadn't come to a head right now while the child was so small, but people were dying—thousands of them. Weighing the risk to one child against the slaughter of whole colonies, surely he was right to do this?

But Liv was an innocent. Gen and Max were his best friends. They didn't deserve this. And neither did Cara.

Cara.

He'd stunned her alongside Gen and Max, firstly because she could alert the whole station to what he was doing, but secondly, and perhaps most importantly, because it would protect her from the backlash. This was his decision, and he would bear the cost of it alone.

He flashed a command to Yan Gwenn to prepare the *Solar Wind* for a fast exit with a full engineering crew, then alerted Ronan, Naomi Patel, and Lynda Munene. Finally, he borrowed Gwala and Hilde—Gwala for his prowess at the tactical station and Hilde in the hopes that she could babysit Liv while he flew them into foldspace.

No one asked him any questions as he strode out of Blue Seven with the child in his arms, who was obviously delighted to be going for an outing. He'd told her Mummy and Daddy were sleeping—which was the truth, though they'd wake with murderous headaches and probably murderous intent.

He didn't know how he was going to fix this with Gen and Max, or even if it was a possibility. He might have split apart the Free Company for good, which would—if he let himself think about it—break his heart. And Cara. Had he lost her forever? After this, he might as well take the Dixie Flyer and go somewhere, anywhere, and start a new life. But if he could find out what was killing colonies and taking ships . . . if he could save lives and actually protect the Crossways Protectorate, shouldn't he at least try?

Liv put her arms around Ben's neck. "Don't be sad, Uncle Ben."

"It's all right, Liv. Everything will be all right."

"We're going to talk to the dragon."

"Yes, we are."

As Ben climbed into a tub cab, Gwala and Hilde emerged from the guard station and squashed in beside him.

"Where's Cara?" Hilde asked as the cab whirled them into the traffic stream.

"Not coming on this trip. I left her sleeping."

"You're taking the baby?"

"Talk to dragon," Liv said.

She stood up on Ben's thigh with her hands on his shoulder and twisted in his grip. She stared first at Gwala, then at Hilde then at Gwala again before quite calmly holding out her arms to him. Ben let her go.

Gwala bounced Liv up and down on his knee until she giggled.

Hilde smiled. "Don't you love a man who's good with babies?"

"I didn't realize it was one of Gwala's hidden talents," Ben said.

They crossed the floor of Port 46 at a dead run. Ben had a dread that Gen, Max, or Cara would come to and give the alarm before they disembarked and hit the Folds. He might return to face all of the Free Company wanting to roast him alive, but he'd get the job done first.

Gwala slid into the bucket seat with Liv as Hilde took the tactical station. Lynda was already in the comms chair and Yan at the systems station.

"What about me, Boss?" Naomi said as she came up the tube on to the deck.

"You're my spare. Take one of the bucket seats."

"Am I late for the party?" Ronan climbed up on to the flight deck, saw Liv, looked around for Gen and Max, and gave Ben a hard stare, which he ignored.

Lynda commed Crossways Control. "*Solar Wind* ready for departure."

"Flight plan, *Solar Wind*?"

"Is that you, Roebuck?" Ben said into the comm. "Emergency. We'll file a plan once we're clear of the station."

"Do I need to place a bet on this?" Roebuck said. "One hundred klicks before you hit foldspace."

"No problem, Crossways Control."

"Clear for departure," Roebuck said.

"Thank you, Crossways Control."

"Ben, is there something you need to tell us?" Ronan asked.

Ben let *Solar Wind* glide out on her antigravs and then brought the sublight engines online. She emerged into the black, gradually building speed as she pulled away from the station.

"You mean about kidnapping Liv? I'm taking her to talk to a void dragon, okay?"

Thirty klicks out, Wenna's voice came over the comm. "Ben, what the hell are you doing? Have you gone mad?"

"Very possibly." Ben looked at Ronan. "Have I?"

"Do you want my professional opinion on that?"

Ben powered up the jump drive, and *Solar Wind* hit the Folds.

✦ ✦ ✦

Cara felt as though she'd been hit with a club. She groaned and rolled over. She'd been drooling on the floor, not her own floor; this one had a soft covering, baby friendly. Gen and Max's floor.

Oh, shit!

It all came back to her, crashing over her head in a wave.

Ben—oh, Ben—what have you done? I don't know you anymore.

There was a groan to her right. She managed to hoist herself up onto all fours and open her eyes. Max had woken. He'd raised himself on one elbow, but he looked as though simply breathing was an effort. Gen was still out cold, which was perhaps as well since she'd wake up wanting to kill Ben. Right now, Cara wasn't sure she would stop her even if she could.

Ben. She had to stop *Solar Wind* from taking off with Liv on board. She tried to contact Ben, but her head was splitting apart and her implant might as well be turned off. Until the effects of the stunner wore off completely, she could barely throw a thought the length of this room.

Wenna. She might be able to reach Wenna.

Cara? What's the matter?

Wenna, Ben's gone off the deep end. He's stunned Max and Gen—and me—and he's taking Liv into the Folds to see if she can translate for the void dragon. Stop him.

Are you all right?

Will be. She wished she was wearing her buddysuit. Right about now, it would be administering a shot of analgesic. *I'll see to Gen and Max. It's about all I'm fit for. You stop* Solar Wind. *Don't let Ben do anything stupid.*

Ben doesn't do stupid, Cara.

He does now.

"Was that Wenna?" Max asked.

Cara nodded and then wished she hadn't. She crawled over to a chair and hauled herself upright on it like a baby learning to walk. Her legs would barely support her, so she sat on the chair.

"Have you any painkillers?"

"Bathroom."

"For all of us."

"Still bathroom."

Max had managed to get as far as sitting up, leaning against the wall. Gen began to stir. He inched his way over until he was beside her and started massaging her hand.

Cara risked standing. She staggered unsteadily to the bathroom and immediately vomited into the pan. She rinsed her mouth quickly, not sure whether she felt better or worse for having lost the contents of her stomach. She grabbed three analgesic blast packs from the cabinet and gave herself one. It stung the side of her neck. By the time she got back to Max, Gen's eyes were open, though she was still horizontal.

Beginning to feel insulated from the headache, Cara gave Max a shot of painkiller and then together they man-handled Gen into a sitting position.

"Here, this will help you feel better." She cradled the blast pack to the side of Gen's neck.

"I doubt it, though my head might not hurt so much. Liv?"

"Wenna's trying to get to Ben before he gets off-station."

Gen scrubbed her face with her hands. "She's gone. I've lost the link. She's in the Folds. I will kill Ben Benjamin when I catch up to him."

"Get in line," Max said.

Too late, Wenna said. *He's off and away.*

We know. Gen knows. Liv's in the Folds. Where's Jake?

Where he's been since he brought that battleship back.

Is Howling Wolf *ready to fly?*

Yes, Jake's been putting her through her paces.

Where's she berthed?

She's currently on the docking cradle above Blue Eight.

Tell Jake to prep for departure. We're on our way.

"Can you two move yet?" Cara said.

"It's my daughter out there. Of course I can move." Gen stood up and wobbled.

"Get into buddysuits, both of you," Cara said. "If we're going into foldspace, you'll need them."

By the time Gen and Max had suited up, Cara was start-ing to shuffle off the effects of the stunner. She jogged to their apartment, changed into her own buddysuit, and lib-erated Ben's dart gun from the locker as well as her own derri. Then the three of them headed for the antigrav tube up to the docking cradle where Eastin-Heigle's finest bat-tleship waited.

Captain Lowenbrun, three to come aboard.

She heard Jake chuckle as he met them in person at the hatch.

"Hey, we're ready," he said. "Where are we going?"

"Into the Folds." She quickly told him what had happened.

"No shit!" Jake's smile faded rapidly. "Come up on to the flight deck."

Cara didn't recognize any of the crew. They weren't Free Company.

"Oleg Staple's boys and girls." Jake introduced them, but Cara barely retained their names. There was a helmsman, a comms operator, a systems operator, and two tactical officers. Three other stations were empty.

"Ready to roll?" Jake asked.

"As soon as you are," Cara said.

"Max, if you're going to be doing the Finding, take the captain's chair," Jake said. "Gen—"

"I'm okay here." She slipped into one of the empty stations and Cara did the same.

Jake nodded to the crew. "Take us out."

There was no real sense of movement as the *Howling Wolf* slipped free of the docking cradle and left the station behind.

"Stand by for the Folds," Jake said from the nav station.

"Stand by for the Folds," the comms operator repeated shipwide. "Three, two, one."

The Folds sucked them up like sherbet through a straw.

"Yan Gwenn did a great conversion job," Jake says. "The *Wolf* flies like a dream. All you have to do is tell me where to point her."

Cara looks around. Max is already questing for his daughter, using all his Finding skills. Gen is sitting quietly, but she's on edge, as well she might be.

"Follow wherever Max points," Cara says. "I know that's not very scientific."

Jake keeps his eyes on Max and gives succinct commands to the helmsman.

"They're close," Max says.

"Screens," Jake says. "Proximity alarm. If they're out there, we'll find them."

"One minute thirty seconds," the woman at the systems station whom Cara remembers is Libby, calls out time. And then a short while later, "Two minutes."

Max keeps pointing.

At two minutes thirty his hand veers to the right by twenty degrees.

Jake adjusts their course.

"There!" Gen spots it first, *Solar Wind* hanging motionless in the void.

Jake adjusts course again and *Howling Wolf* gradually comes alongside. In practical terms, about half a klick away.

"Do you want the launch?" Jake asks.

Cara shakes her head. "It will take too long, and we couldn't dock against *Solar Wind* without cooperation."

"You don't think Ben will let you on board?"

"I'm damn sure he won't unless we're already too late to stop him. We'll float across."

"With or without a space suit?"

"With," Cara says. "Let's not test belief too far."

"I'll show you the suit room. Helm, keep her steady."

"Yes, Cap."

Jake guides them through *Howling Wolf*'s complex corridors to the forward suit room and helps them into the flexible silver suits, checks their helmets, and taps Cara on the faceplate to get her attention. He puts his forehead to the front of her helmet. *Don't be too hard on him. You know he's doing it because he's weighed up the options and this is the least worst of all of them.*

Cara glares at him, but through the faceplate the withering effect is probably less than she intends.

They launch themselves into foldspace through the forward airlock, all tied on to a single line and using slimline backpacks to steer.

Okay, Max? Cara is very aware Max has little experience of spacewalks.

Ask me that when we're aboard Solar Wind.*

With Gen and Cara on each end of the line and Max in the middle, they make their way across from one ship to the other. Ben has to have seen them coming. Cara wonders whether he'll wait until they get close and then pull away, but she's sure he knows who's coming after him. Cara doesn't think he'll willingly endanger any of them even if he doesn't want them on board.

But then, she'd never suspected he would kidnap Liv, either.

As they approach the matte-black surface of *Solar Wind*, Cara stops herself from reaching out to Ben mentally. Let him make the first move if he dares.

Instead, she reaches out to Ronan.

Cara!

Gen's with me, and Max. Jake is standing half a klick off the starboard beam with Howling Wolf. *What's the situation?*

*We figured there was something wrong as soon as we hit foldspace at the thirty-klick mark. No one's saying very much. Ben's—well—he's the boss and he's Ben, so . . . *

How's Liv? Gen can't wait.

She's fine. Happy. Excited. She keeps talking about the dragon as if they're old friends.

She'll be scared out of her wits when she sees it for real. She thinks it's like her stuffed toy. A dragon-shaped puppy dog.

Kids are tremendously resilient, Ronan said. *Hang on. While we've been talking, I've been making my way to the emergency hatch. Stand by. I'll let you in.*

Did Ben see you? Cara asks.

He didn't say anything, but I'm pretty sure he knows. I guess he figures it's too late now. We're in the Folds with Liv. What will happen will happen.

What will happen is that I'm going to kill him, Gen says.

After me, Max says.

You didn't know he was bringing her into the Folds? Ronan asks.

Do you mean before or after he shot us all with a soft stun?

He did what?

By the time we came around, it was too late.

Oh, shit.

The hatch springs open by a centimeter. Cara grips the handle and pulls it open the whole way. *Max first,* she says.

I'm not going to be all gentlemanly. Ladies, after me.

They cycle through the small airlock one at a time and strip off their space suits. To their credit, neither Max nor Gen rush up to the flight deck to confront Ben.

"How do you want to do this?" Ronan asks.

"There's no point in being all dramatic about it," Cara says. "He knows we're here, and he'll be conscious of not upsetting Liv any more than necessary. She hasn't seen the void dragon yet?"

"It's a no-show so far."

Cara finds herself conflicted. If Ben is right and Liv is the missing link to understanding the void dragon, there should be something to show for all this upset. But if he's wrong, then the whole thing has been for nothing. Either the void dragon will stay away, or it will materialize and the child will be scared out of her wits and, possibly, traumatized.

Or instead of the void dragon, they'll have the Nimbus to contend with, and then it's likely that no one will get out alive.

"Let's get this over with." Cara's hand brushes lightly over the dart gun at her side. She hopes she won't need it. One dart for sleep. Two darts for an even chance at recovery. Three for certain death.

Chapter Forty-Two

EXCHANGE

CARA'S HERE MUCH SOONER THAN BEN EX-
pected. The game is up.

Liv is happily playing with her toy void dragon. Sitting on Gwala's knee, she pretends to fly the dragon over his arms and around his head. Gwala cooperates with her game and makes whooshing noises that set her off giggling.

Ben is risking everything, and what for?

So far, nothing.

Ronan is first up the access tube on to the flight deck.

"Reska Benjamin—"

Ah, if Ronan is going to be formal, it's bad.

"I know, Ronan." He puts both hands up. "I've gone too far."

Cara is right behind him. She doesn't say anything, but the look she gives him is all disappointment and bitterness. It wrenches his heart. If she'd say something, anything, then he might be able to explain. Does the end ever justify the means? He's risked Liv, yes; ruined his friendship with both Gen and Max, and probably driven away the love of his life.

All for nothing.

Ben stands up, heart thudding against his rib cage. "Naomi, you'd better take over the ship while we're in the

Folds. Yan, you're in charge. I'm officially handing over *Solar Wind* and putting myself under arrest pending charges of kidnapping."

"Momma, the dragon's coming!" Liv jumps off Gwala's knee, takes little toddler steps, and flies her toy dragon right into Gen's arms making the whooshing sounds Gwala has been making. Gen drops to her knees and puts her arms around her daughter, burying her face in the child's hair.

Max strides past them, straight up to Ben. Ben sees what's coming and neither blocks nor ducks the fist aimed at his jaw. To be honest, it's not the hardest blow he's ever taken, but it hurts more in so many ways.

Ben staggers against the bulkhead while Max cradles his hand and swears. "That was worth breaking my knuckles for, Benjamin, you bastard."

"Would it help to say I'm sorry?"

"Not even a little bit," Gen says. "We're finished."

"Cara—" Ben starts to speak, but she cuts him dead.

"I don't want to hear it." Her look rips him apart from the inside.

"We know what you tried to do, Ben, and why you tried to do it, but it hasn't worked. Let's go home." Ronan is the single voice of reason, though it must be costing him to see people he trusted, friends, on opposite sides of a tear that will never mend.

Yan swivels round in his seat. "You're all making the flight deck untidy. Crew only. The rest of you find a cabin and strap in for the return journey. And that includes you, Commander Benjamin. Gwala and Hildstrom, please secure Commander Benjamin in his cabin pending a hearing. Lynda, tell *Howling Wolf* to get out of the Folds and go back to Crossways."

Ben presses his lips together and nods. It's only what he deserves.

"I told you it would come!" Liv's excited voice makes them all turn around.

The void dragon slides through the bulkhead, sees Liv, and immediately shrinks its body to the size of a large dog, though its tail snakes around the floor. The wildly waving prehensile beard, complete with claws retracts into its jaw, and it takes on the rounded shape of her toy.

Liv shrieks in delight, wriggles away from her mother's

embrace, and flings herself at its neck. It rubs its scaly jaw across the top of her head. She giggles.

OLIVIA MAY MARLING, it says.

Gen pushes herself upright and starts forward, but Cara holds her back. Max looks around as if trying to pinpoint the void dragon by everyone else's position. He steps forward slowly, kneels behind Liv, and puts one arm around her tiny waist.

MAAAXXX, the void dragon says.

It looks at Gen and nods.

"That's Mom," Liv says.

MOMMM.

Ben shakes himself free from Gwala and Hilde who have moved to either side of him. He kneels where he is, barely a couple of meters away from the child and the dragon.

"Can you understand it, Liv?"

She frowns. "Sort of."

The void dragon changes shape again. It sits on its haunches and rears up, stretching its back, elongating its front legs to arms and its back legs to . . .

Human. It suddenly appears human in shape though the skin on its back and legs still looks like dragon scales while the skin on its front looks like a buddysuit. It's possible it doesn't understand the difference between clothing and skin. There's no reason it should.

Liv reaches out her baby arms.

The void creature, hardly a dragon now, takes her into its arms as it has seen her mother do.

Ben starts forward, a little quicker off the mark than everyone else, but the void creature is faster than thought. It pops out of existence, taking Liv with it.

Ben crashes into Ronan who has started forward from the opposite side. They rebound off each other and exchange a look that says the worst thing that could happen has happened.

Gen makes a sound as unlike a scream as it can be, but it means the same thing. Her baby is gone.

Simply gone.

Max is silent, white with shock.

Cara . . . Ben didn't dare look at Cara. I-told-you-so would be the kindest thing she could say.

And Liv . . .

Is gone.

Ben doesn't even think. He launches upward, through the skin of the ship into the foldspace, searching for the void creature, but there's nothing there except an absence of light. He's carried forward away from the *Solar Wind*.

As long as he believes he can, he knows he can breathe out here—he's done it before—but he's not sure how he can maneuver without a line or a jet-pack. He angles his body as if he were in water. He's turning, or at least he thinks he is. It's difficult to tell in this void.

Isn't he supposed to be the one who knows which way is up?

He searches mentally for the right heading to take him to the ship, hoping he can follow it.

A beam of light cuts the blackness.

Another beam sweeps side to side, up and down, or maybe it's the other way around.

Ben!

Cara.

Hold on, we can see you. We're coming.

One of the light beams catches a space-suited figure. Both light sources converge on him.

Got you. Cara grabs his arm with her gloved hand and follows up with every expletive in her vocabulary, most of them vulgar. He gets the idea.

The second figure takes his other arm. *What she said.* Ronan can hold his curses as well as he can hold his liquor. *What were you hoping to achieve?*

I thought I might be able to follow if I could make it out here fast enough—

And . . .

Not a thing in sight.

Got him, Cara beams a thought to the *Solar Wind* and all her external docking lights come on at once.

Ben isn't as far away as he feared. He's managed the turn and he's been drifting toward the ship. Would he have been able to make it under his own steam? He's not even going to guess at the possibility. There's a thought in the back of his brain, and it's repeating over and over again.

She came for me. Cara came for me. Maybe she's only going to deliver him to the Free Company for a hearing, but she hasn't washed her hands of him completely.

They reach the hatch and Ronan swings him toward the grab rail by the main airlock. There's room for all three of them. The airlock outer door closes behind them. He breathes shallowly while it cycles.

Cara and Ronan remove their helmets.

Who's going to speak first?

There's a long silence.

"Thank you," he says to both of them.

Cara grunts at him and gets on with the business of peeling herself out of her suit. She and Ronan help each other with the tricky bits. Ben doesn't offer and she doesn't ask for his help.

They troop up to the flight deck, Ronan, himself, and Cara in order, not speaking.

Gen looks up, suddenly hopeful as they emerge. Ben doesn't meet her eyes.

"Nothing," Ronan says.

Max curses softly.

Ben has no words of comfort. No words of hope.

They sit staring at nothing, hoping against hope the void dragon will return with Liv safe.

How could he have misread the situation so badly? Ben had been sure the void dragon wanted to talk to Liv. If he'd thought for one moment that she'd be taken, he'd have spaced himself rather than bring the child out here.

There's a susurration, a rustling like a gentle wind through leaves. From somewhere far off he can hear two voices, one of them deep and the other girlish, though not as young as Liv.

The void creature appears again and this time it has an older child in its almost-human arms. The girl is about ten or eleven years old. She has Gen's almond eyes, but Max's smile, and already she's beautiful in that half-formed way of prepubescent girls.

Ben stares open-mouthed.

Gen makes the first move. She reaches toward the child. "Liv?"

"Hello, Ma. Goodness, you look young." She turns to Max. "Dad! I never thought . . ." She flings herself into his arms. "I've missed you."

"Haven't you missed your mother?"

"I only left her a few minutes ago. Well, an older version of her, anyway."

"And not me?"

Her face clouds.

The void creature makes a sound like clearing its throat. She nods. "I'm here as a translator."

"Where's my baby?" Gen asks. "Baby Liv."

"Both of us can't be here at the same time," Liv says. "You're looking after her. The other you, the older you, that is. The one I've just left."

"Time travel?"

Liv shakes her head. "No. Everything is happening at once in the Folds. There is no time."

"There's a future me in the Folds?"

The void creature makes a sound again.

"I'm sorry; I can't say anything more without complicating your timeline. You told me not to do that."

"I did?"

"The other you."

Ben edges forward. "Liv, what does your friend want to tell us?"

"Oh, you must be Ben Benjamin." She swivels round. "And you're Cara, and you're Doctor Ronan."

Ben wonders what happens in the future that Liv doesn't recognize them, but he bottles up the question and sticks to the pressing issue. "Does your friend have a name?"

"Yes, of course." She tries to put her mouth into a shape, and then frowns. "It's pretty unpronounceable."

"Never mind. Can you ask it a question?"

She nods. "It can hear you through my thoughts."

"Can it understand what I say?"

She blinked. "Sort of. It can understand what you mean but might not know every word."

Right keep it simple. "What's the black cloud, the thing we call the Nimbus?"

"It's bad."

Well, at least the void dragon agrees with them.

"Though it's only trying to protect itself," Liv says.

"It's hurting people," Ben says.

Liv frowns and shakes her head. "People are hurting it."

Now it's Ben's turn to frown. "How are people hurting it?"

"Not people. Their ships." She trails one hand through the air. "Platinum residue."

"Platinum?" Cara says behind him. "The platinum lost in the Folds. It's a pollutant."

"Does platinum hurt the dragon?" Ben asks.

Liv shakes her head. "Dragons are different."

Ben notices she says dragons. They've always wondered whether it's one dragon or if there are a number of them.

"What about the otter-kind—the little creatures?"

She hesitates as though waiting for an answer from the void dragon. "They're a different species," she says at length. "The platinum doesn't hurt them, either."

"Do dragons hurt people?" Gen cuts into the conversation.

"No. They're curious about us, and about space outside the Folds, but they can't cross over into realspace."

"Does the Nimbus hurt people?" Ben asks.

"It makes them into weapons to hurt each other." She claps her hands together. "It thinks that if there are no more people, there will be no more platinum."

"Does it know how many people are out there in realspace?" Cara asks.

Liv shrugs. "It learns from the people it takes and uses them as puppets." There's a pause as if she's talking to the void dragon. "It can sense the platinum and it's drawn to where the largest concentrations are. It's like a dog that bites at a flea. It's a reaction, not a plan. At least that's how it begins. But then it discovers people. Organic life." She pauses again. "It's still learning."

"I bet it is," Cara says. "Humanity—all that's good and all that's bad. What will it learn from a psychopath?"

"It's taken a few military ships, too," Ben says. "That means it has people with a skill set it can use against us."

"How long has this been going on?" Ben asks. "Damn, that's the wrong question if time doesn't exist in the Folds."

Cara leans forward. "Why now, Liv?" She turns to Ben. "People have been passing through the Folds for three hundred years. What's changed?"

"Platinum," Liv says after a pause. "There's more than there was. I'm not sure how to translate this." She looks at the void creature as if listening intently. "I think there's a tipping point." She looks at Gen. "That's what you said, Ma, or what you will say. It reaches critical mass."

"It's building up," Cara says. "Our platinum is building up, so the Nimbus is reacting to the level of pollution."

Liv nods. "At first it took ships randomly, but then it learned that some humans had more knowledge than others. Knowledge that was useful for its own purpose—stopping the platinum."

"It's taken some military vessels," Ben says. "Is that deliberate?"

"It has all of foldspace to pick from, from the very first ships to the last."

"What happens to the humans the Nimbus takes?" Ben asks.

Liv frowns. "Nothing. There's no time for anything to happen. They're here until they're not, but there's no time happening for them."

"That explains a lot," Ronan says, "but not how it gets inside people's heads, turns them into something they're not."

There's a pause while Liv talks to the void dragon. "We can't tell you because we don't know. The void dragons are frightened of the Nimbus. They leave it alone and it leaves them alone."

"If it's drawn by the concentration of platinum," Ben says, "maybe that's why most of the ships that have been lost have been between gates. Very few jumpships have gone missing."

"So it's using humans against humans," Ronan says. "If humans are a virus, it's fighting the virus with more of the same—sending altered bugs to kill off the bugs that are hurting it. Biocontrol. It's a logical move. It has no concept of the value of life. Humans are simply a virus it needs to destroy, any way it can."

Liv is staring from one adult to the other, trying to follow the conversation.

"Hold on, we're going too fast," Ben says. He speaks directly to Liv again. "Ask the dragon. Is there one Nimbus or lots."

"Lots," she says, "but they're all part of the one." She frowns. "Is that right?"

"Maybe it has a hive-mind," Cara says.

"Can the dragon talk to the Nimbus?" Ben asks.

"Yes, in a way, but it doesn't." She shakes her head again.

"How can we stop it?" Ronan asks the adults, but the dragon chooses to answer through Liv.

"It won't stop."

"Then what can we do?" Cara asks.

"Stop ships coming through the jump gates," Liv says.

"How the hell are we supposed to do that?" Ronan asks.

Ben wonders what Liv herself knows. "Time travel or not, she's from the future. Is it a version of the future? Can it be changed, or is it fixed?"

"Is it possible, Liv? Are there still jump gates?"

"I've never seen one."

"How do you get into foldspace?"

"The Dixie, of course."

"The Dixie, right." In Liv's future Gen flies the Dixie, but Liv doesn't know Ben or Cara or Ronan. Are they all dead? He does and doesn't want to ask—both at the same time. Would knowing the future change it?

"Oh, it's time to go," Liv says. "Good-bye, Daddy. I love y—"

The void dragon folds itself around her and they both disappear.

"Wait—" Gen calls out and reaches toward the older version of her daughter.

Max wraps his arms around Gen. "It'll bring her back. It's as good as said that both versions of Liv can't be in the same place."

"Why should it care?"

"If the older version of Liv is with you, she has to have grown up with you." He shakes his head. "I'm not sure what happens to me, though. She acted as if she hadn't seen me for a while? You're not planning to divorce me, are you?"

"I haven't married you yet."

"That's my Gen." He wipes the tears from her cheeks with his thumbs. "Ever practical. So you see, the void dragon is bound to bring her back. Any moment now." He glances across at Ben. "Please."

The tension is palpable. Ben glances around, absently rubbing his throbbing jaw. If hoping can make it happen, the whole flight deck is wishing the void dragon and baby Liv into existence for Gen and Max.

Then, as quickly as they vanished, the void dragon and baby Liv are back in their midst. Gen and Max fall on their daughter and draw her into the safety of their arms. None the worse for her experience, baby Liv reaches for the creature, who has now morphed into its dragon-shape again, or rather the shape of Liv's toy.

It nuzzles her hand and pulls away from Liv, growing to the size of a small horse.

"No, don't go." Tears well in Liv's eyes. "I don't want it to go. It's my friend."

Gen pushes the stuffed toy into Liv's hand. "Here's your dragon. You can talk to the other one again, when you're older."

"Promise?"

Ben sees Gen swallow hard. "Promise. I know you will. Now, say good-bye."

The void dragon whirls around the flight deck and, as Liv waves, it winks out of existence.

Liv begins to cry inconsolably.

Gen glares at Ben. "Now look what you've done."

◆ ◆ ◆

They move off the flight deck, Gwala leading the way, leaving Yan in charge and Naomi piloting *Solar Wind* safely to Crossways. Cara heads toward *Solar Wind*'s mess.

Gen immediately takes herself into a corner with Liv, now alternately crying and hiccupping. She rocks her gently, trying to lull her to sleep.

They strap in as Lynda broadcasts, *Realspace in three, two, one.*

"We're a hundred klicks from Crossways," Ben said. "With the docking tailback, we have an hour at least to work out what happened."

"Are you still here?" Cara said. "I thought Gwala and Hilde were locking you up."

She saw him wince and pushed home her advantage. "What's the Free Company going to say? Will there even be a Free Company this time tomorrow?"

He cleared his throat. "Wenna will keep it together. You and she—"

"Don't count on me for anything. Not after today."

"I'm sorry. I take full responsibility."

"Do you think that makes it better?" Would she have been happier if he'd tried to wriggle out of it? Probably not.

"You might not like what I did—hell, I don't like what I did—but it worked. Let's not lose the advantage it's given us."

"Ben's right." Ronan bent over to examine Max's hand, which was ballooning into a purple mess. "The end may not justify the means, but we can't ignore what we've discovered. That won't help anyone. Does that hurt?"

"Oww!" Max tried to drag his hand away, but Ronan kept hold of it. "Fourth metacarpal," he said. "Bar room fracture. Hold still, I'll get some ice."

"It's a numbers game," Ben said, massaging his jaw again. "Every time we send a ship through a jump gate, we're sending more recruits for the Nimbus army. It's been taking increasingly more. We don't know how many. I'm pretty sure the megacorps are hiding the real figures."

Though reluctant to join in with a conversation Ben was leading, Cara felt obliged to offer: "There are rumors on the tel-net. People talking. It's not easy to quantify, but I'd say the losses were way higher than the megacorps are admitting to."

"No ship is safe in the Folds," Ben said, "though jump-ships are probably safest because they appear randomly. Ships coming through the gates are predictable and easier to catch."

"So again, I ask how we can stop it," Ronan said as he brought ice from the drinks dispenser wrapped in a towel and gently applied it to Max's hand. "There has to be something we can do."

"I don't think we can," Ben said.

"But that thing can't invade realspace," Max said. "Can it?"

"Not by itself," Ben said. "Hence the human avatars. The only thing we can do is stop sending recruits, and stop letting the avatars into realspace. That's what Liv, or the dragon, said."

"Stop using the Folds?" Cara said.

"At least stop using the jump gates. And if our platinum is polluting foldspace to the extent that the one part per several billion is hurting the Nimbus, then do we have the right to destroy another creature's environment?"

"Are we talking morality?" Ronan asked.

"Possibly, but we're also talking practicality. We send people through the jump gates and there's a chance they become recruits for the Nimbus. The jump gates allow the avatars into realspace. The first few attacks were random, and ill conceived. The half-arsed way people with no idea about fighting might try to fight, but it's learning. There was the Agent Topax attack. It's using whatever we send it. If we give it troopships and weapons, we can expect it to use them. If we give it recruits with military training, we can expect to have them used against us."

"So closing the jump gates means denying the Nimbus assets?" Cara said.

Ben nodded. "Maybe I'm reading more into what Liv said, but she said she'd never seen a jump gate."

"There could be reasons for that," Ronan said, securing the towel filled with ice around Max's hand accompanied by Max's indrawn breath and a few choice curses.

"I'm willing to be convinced if there's another way," Ben said. "Gods! I hope there is. Closing the jump gates—even if everybody agrees to do it—is a paradigm shift." He sounded as though he was trying to convince himself, or maybe talk himself out of it. "I can't think of anything else that would ensure the attacks on colonies ended. At least until there's a technological breakthrough and we figure out how to stop platinum bleeding into the Folds with every jump."

"What about the colonies?" Cara said. "They're not all self-sufficient."

"They'll have to become self-sufficient," Ben said. "Or if they're not viable, they'll have to be evacuated."

"Without jump gates?"

"Jumpships can still risk foldspace. I admit the future for mankind in space looks bleak, but the question we have to ask is: is isolation better than annihilation?"

"What about the Nimbus' avatars, or drones, or whatever you want to call them?" Cara said. "Can they be rehabilitated?" She looked at Ronan. "What do you think?"

He shrugged. "We've got Kitty. We can try, but whatever we do is experimental."

Max glanced across at Gen and Liv. He looked as though he'd bitten into the soft heart of a fruit and found half a worm. "When Garrick collapsed after seeing Kitty, Liv ran off into the infirmary and we found her pressed up against the glass with Kitty on the other side."

"Max, don't you dare!" Gen said from the other side of the room. She had Liv asleep on her knee and didn't raise her voice, but she didn't need to.

"It might be important, Gen."

"This is our daughter you're talking about."

Max clamped his lips together on whatever he'd been going to say.

Chapter Forty-Three

SANCTUARY

ARRIVING BACK AT BLUE SEVEN, BEN DID THE walk of shame to his office—the longest walk of Ben's life. Gwala and Hilde walked slightly behind him, one to each side, and the parade of Cara, Ronan, Gen, Max, and little Liv followed about ten paces back.

He was conscious of the silence, not only verbal silence, but mental silence. Did they all know what he'd done? If they didn't now, they would soon.

He deserved whatever they thought of him.

Did he regret it?

Yes.

Would he do it again?

In a heartbeat.

At least they had an answer. It hadn't happened the way he'd expected it to happen, but taking Liv into foldspace had worked. He still wasn't sure why. Couldn't the void dragon have brought ten-year-old Liv to talk to them anytime? Obviously, not without baby Liv in exchange. Maybe it was something about balance.

Wenna's expression as he passed through her office to get to his own was the last straw. He was grateful to hear the door close behind him and lock firmly.

House arrest, Ronan had said, or rather, office arrest. His

office had everything he needed, including a small sleeping cubicle and washroom for those times when he'd had to stay ready, or had pulled an all-nighter.

He sank into his chair and covered his eyes with his right hand. His eyelids prickled, but tears weren't an option. He should be elated; he'd found out why the attacks were happening, but all he felt was hollow. The shell of Ben Benjamin was the only thing remaining. He'd scooped out everything else and thrown it away. Not only thrown it away but hurled it into a pit and heaped molten slag on top of it until it was irretrievable.

They hadn't insisted on a damping pin to cut him off from all communication, but he doubted anyone wanted to talk to him, and he didn't want to talk to anyone either. He was finished. It was up to the rest of them to take the new information and run with it.

He might even be relieved.

He let that thought sink in.

Maybe suddenly not being responsible for the livelihood and welfare of the Free Company was liberating. He'd been on the treadmill ever since Crowder had called him back to Chenon to head the Olyanda expedition. Lurching from one crisis to another took its toll. He opened a desk drawer and took out his own damping pin.

Time for a rest.

He stuck the pin in his collar, headed for the narrow cot, flopped down, and fell into a deep sleep. He didn't dream— not even of Cara.

◆ ◆ ◆

"I'm leaving," Gen said, stepping past Cara into the apartment. She had Liv on one hip and a small bag in her free hand.

"What, right now?" Cara almost squeaked. "That's the smallest traveling bag I've ever seen."

Gen's face cracked into a smile, though it was a sad one that barely reached her eyes. "No, these are Liv's toys. It saves her from pulling your stuff apart when she gets bored. I didn't want to stay in our apartment and I figured you'd be feeling all kinds of weird in yours, so we've come to cheer you up and say a proper thank you, and to ask for your help in getting out of here."

She put Liv down on the floor and gave her the bag. The first thing out was the dragon and Liv went running toward the garden door, whooshing for all she was worth.

Cara shrugged. "It was the right thing to do—though I don't know if it helped. Ben would have brought Liv back safely anyway, and the result would have been the same."

"Yes, but you stuck your neck out for us, you and Jake. And everyone is being super-nice since we arrived back."

"How's Max?"

Gen shrugged. "I don't get him. He slugged Benjamin and now he's saying it wasn't altogether a bad thing Liv spoke to the dragon, and he was pleased he met ten-year-old Liv. He thinks he's dead in that future. I mean—I know Liv acted like she hadn't seen him for a while, but there can be lots of reasons. . . ."

"Future Liv didn't know any of us," Cara said. "Are we all dead?"

Gen shook her head. "I've been thinking about that—"

"Good things can come from bad," Cara said. "I'm not making excuses for him, but I don't suppose Ben would have done what he did unless he thought he had absolutely no choice. I mean, would anything he said have persuaded you to let him take Liv into the Folds?"

Gen shook her head. "Not in a million years. Are you backtracking now?"

"No. He was wrong and he knows it. I don't know where everything goes from here. I suppose you have to make an official complaint."

"I'm not sticking around that long. Max can do it. I'm taking Liv and getting as far away as I can. I want Sanctuary."

"You do?"

"That's what it's for, isn't it? I want us to disappear where no one can ever find us again. That's the reason ten-year-old Liv doesn't know you all."

"It's so sudden." Cara swallowed hard. "I know you feel let down, but—"

"Betrayed. In the worst possible way."

Cara understood. What Ben did was so out of character. Even as she thought that, she realized how he did it was out of character, but what he did was probably not. He was still trying to save the world or — in this case — many worlds. She took a deep breath.

"All right, what can I do to help?"

"We'll need new idents, foolproof ones, and somewhere to go. Somewhere Ben can't ever find us. I've risked my life for Ben and the Free Company, but I won't risk my daughter's."

"What about Max?"

"You heard what I said. He thinks what Ben did will save millions of lives. He practically said Ben did the right thing."

"He didn't think so at the time."

She shrugged. "It's not been easy. I think Liv scares him. We'll be better off with just the two of us."

"I remember you and Max on Olyanda. You were so in love."

Gen swallowed hard. "That was then. This is now."

"Wherever you go, you're going to have to take her through the Folds again."

"I know. It's a risk if we go and an even bigger risk if we stay. It's obvious I take her into the Folds when she's older. We've both seen the older version of her. Believe me, I wouldn't be doing this if I thought there was any other way. The Free Company's like family."

"All right. Whatever you need, but . . . I'm going to miss you."

"Come with us."

For a brief moment the idea was so tempting.

"Come on, Cara, you and me and Liv, free as birds."

Was it Ben that held her back, or was it the commitment she'd made to the Free Company?

"I have to see this through, Gen, wherever it leads. Whatever I think of Ben personally, I'll stick with the Free Company until this is resolved. We have to get the word out there. They'll need a long-range Telepath more now than ever. After that, well, maybe. Don't forget. Wherever you end up, I can contact you mind-to-mind."

"But you won't, will you?"

Cara shook her head. "Not if you don't want me to."

"I need a clean break from all this. Even from you if you're staying."

"I get it. When do you want to leave?"

"As soon as possible."

"I think I have an idea about those jumps though fold-space. What if you had a jumpship? Liv said you traveled on the Dixie Flyer."

✦ ✦ ✦

Ben didn't know how long he'd been awake. At least the damping pin was protecting him from Garrick's dreams. He didn't need them right now. He had enough problems of his own.

Leaving the problems to others was so tempting, but his brain wouldn't stop churning.

Close down the jump gates.

Just like that.

Thousands of them.

And he was only one man. He couldn't decide the fate of the galaxy. Even if the Free Company backed him, they were still pissing in the wind. What they needed was the agreement and cooperation of every corporation, mega and otherwise, every planetary government, and every colony with its own fleet. How likely was that? The task was more than daunting.

How persuasive were the facts?

The illusions from foldspace were real. Creatures lived in the void. There was scientific proof, though even Doctor Beckham would admit this was only the beginning of her study, so the proof was thin as yet.

Of course, the megacorps already knew foldspace creatures were real. Otherwise, why would they try so hard to persuade all their pilots in training that they were illusions?

Void dragons were benign and might even prove to be friendly. Otter-kind were neutral, but hadn't done anything to harm humans as far as Ben knew. The Nimbus, which appeared to be a hive-mind, composite creature, was actively antagonistic, and retaliating for damage to its environment. Maybe without the pollution it would have ignored them—or continued to ignore them. It had taken hundreds of years of foldspace travel for this to come to a head. Maybe the Nimbus didn't experience linear time, or maybe it was a vast hive-mind intelligence that regarded a few hundred years as an eyeblink in its eternity.

He needed to talk to people to see if the idea of closing the jump gates made sense.

Ben had questions. The void dragons had answers. Olivia May Marling was the missing link, but he could forget any further help from that direction. He truly regretted what he'd done, but still couldn't see how he could have done anything different. He hoped, in time, Gen and Max would forgive him.

❖ ❖ ❖

Max awoke to silence.

He felt the other half of the bed. Empty.

That wasn't right. The apartment was rarely quiet. If Gen and Liv were up and about, there was usually music playing, voices chatting, and the clatter of plates at breakfast time.

"Gen?"

No answer.

Gen?

No answer.

He felt the first flush of unease, but went through the routine of dressing at his usual pace. They'd probably popped out to take a turn around Blue Seven, or gone to have breakfast somewhere. He looked at the time. It was early, though never too early for Ada Levenson to be serving breakfast. Sometime in the early hours of the station's official morning, supper seamlessly turned to breakfast on the food counter. He wandered down there, but though there were four groups of early breakfasters, Gen and Liv were not among them.

He walked up to the main office, but it was so early that even Wenna hadn't turned up for work yet. There were two of Tengue's guards sitting outside Ben's locked office door. He left them guarding. Ben wasn't about to break out. He appeared genuinely contrite and willing to comply with whatever the Free Company asked of him, up to and including, "Go float yourself out of the nearest airlock."

With Ben in lockup, perhaps Gen was with Cara. She'd visited a few times over the last couple of days. The two of them were slipping back into their old friendship. Was it too early to wake Cara?

He knocked on Cara's door, expecting to have to wait while she dragged herself out of bed, but she answered almost immediately, fully clothed and wide awake.

"Max, come in. I didn't expect you so soon."

"You were expecting me?"

"Well, yes, I figured . . ." She frowned at him. "You've not read her note, have you?"

"What note?"

"Damn, damn, and double damn. She said she'd leave you a note to explain . . . to say good-bye."

"Good-bye? What do you mean?"

"She's gone."

"Gone?" Max felt stupid repeating what Cara said, but he couldn't take it in. "You mean she's left me?"

"Come in. Don't stand there on the doorstep." Cara opened the door wide. "She's left all of us. She's taken Sanctuary and gone where none of us can follow."

"But . . . But . . . Why didn't she tell me she was going? Why didn't she ask me . . . ?"

"She thought you were coming around to Ben's way of thinking. Some people are."

"Never!" Max looked at the sausage-fingers and the yellowing bruise flowing out of the casing on his injured hand and knew it was true. "Oh, I don't deny the greater good, but Liv is my daughter. When I thought we'd lost her, I . . . well I didn't know what to do. I can't lose her again, and I can't lose Gen. How can I find her?"

"That's the point of Sanctuary. There's a network. The people we send down the line are passed on and on again from one cell to another."

"She's flying through the Folds on commercial ships? How do I know she's even safe?"

Cara smiled. "Not quite. I gave her Ben's Dixie Flyer. She's flying herself, quick jumps in and out, not even staying in there long enough to give the void dragon a chance to call. I figured Ben owed her."

"He loves that little ship."

"Yes." She grinned even wider. "Doesn't he?"

"So how can I catch up?"

"You can't bring her back."

"I'm not intending to. I'm going with her."

Cara looked at him, eyes wide. Then she simply nodded. "Mother Ramona's not going to like being woken at this time in the morning for a new ident."

"Don't worry her. I still have the one she did for me when I went to Chenon with Ben."

"Okay, then we need Jake again. Pack a bag. Bring whatever you need."

"Can you give me half an hour?"

"To pack a bag?"

"I need to stop at the office first."

He packed a bag in five minutes and then raced to the accounts office. Billy Naseby hadn't arrived yet. Good. He could hear Wenna in the office next door, and it sounded as if Ben's guards were changing shift. He sat down at his desk. Everything was in order, Billy would be able to pick up where Max left off. If Ben managed to close the jump gates, the price of platinum would plummet. He'd already converted some of their stockpile to credits so the Free Company would survive any financial slump, and he'd warned Garrick to do the same.

Then Max thought of a figure and doubled it, and moved the amount to a secure account he'd once set up using his other identity. He carefully entered it in the records as Max Constant and Gen Marling—severance pay. It was probably what the platinum investments would owe them over the next five years, if they all lived that long.

Then he mailed a note to Billy with a time stamp for twelve hours from now, grabbed his bag, and ran out to meet Cara.

"Are we going in the *Howling Wolf*?" he asked.

"No such luck. She belongs to the Olyanda fleet. Oleg Staple has already taken her. I'm afraid this will be third-class travel. We're going in the *Flint*."

"Is Jake flying her?"

"Yes."

"If I asked what could possibly go wrong would I be tempting fate?"

Cara laughed, but there wasn't much mirth in it.

The *Flint* was definitely third-class riding. She had two forward facing seats and a line of four seats on each side, facing inward. Aft of the entrance hatch was a galley, the tiniest washroom Max had ever seen, and a cabin with two bunks and barely room to climb in them.

"She's not much to look at," Cara said, "but she's retrofitted with a jump drive."

Jake climbed aboard, took one look at Max and then at Cara. "Not another kidnapping?"

"Not this time. A mercy dash."

Jake raised both eyebrows. "Where to?"

"I'll tell you when I know."

Jake raised the *Flint* on her antigravs and eased out of Port 46. Max saw Cara's eyes get the kind of glazed look he recognized. She was talking to someone. Jussaro, probably.

"Oh, great." Cara pulled a face at Jake. "Dounreay is your first stop."

"What's wrong with Dounreay?" Max asked.

"The first time you take a taste of osteena beer you'll know," Cara said.

"Why can't you reach out telepathically and tell her we're coming?"

"I promised I wouldn't."

"Did she particularly say she never wanted to see me again?"

"Like I said, she thought you were going to side with Ben."

"But I'm not. I haven't. I never would."

"You need to tell her yourself."

"I would if I could."

"You'll be able to on Dounreay."

"What if she leaves before we get there?"

"We'll get there. Trust me," Jake said. "Gen's going to be doing bodkin jumps in and out of the Folds. We'll go in and stay in."

"What about the void dragon?"

"What about it? Can't have it both ways."

Max has his eyes closed as they fly the Folds. He can't see the void dragon anyway. Does it matter if he looks for it? He hears Cara reacting to something.

"Otter-kind," she says. "No problem."

He doesn't fall for that. He keeps his eyes resolutely closed.

Then with a rush . . .

They emerged from the Folds close to Dounreay.

"I thought you said it was hard-baked mud," Max said as they came in to land.

"That's the dry season," Cara said. "This is the middle of the wet season on this continent. Osteena comes up like weeds and then fruits at the end of a two-month growth spurt."

"Can't they grow anything else?"

"On the other side of the continent, across the Great Irrigation Ditch, they harvest rain and use it for crop watering in the dry season. This side of the GID they don't have the resources. Not yet, but they'll get there. Another fifty years or so and this place will look civilized."

"Gen's not planning to stay here, is she?"

"I doubt it. It's one of the staging posts. From here, Jussaro's contact will give her another destination. Three or four jumps down the line and she'll be safe."

"What's to stop her taking off in the Dixie and going wherever she likes?"

Cara shrugged. "Nothing, Sanctuary is organized in cells. There are staging posts like stops on a version of the old Underground Railroad. There's someone to help settle you seamlessly into wherever you end up."

"Are we heading for Wonnick again?" Jake asked.

"I'm afraid we are."

Cara had described Wonnick in the dry season. In the wet season, it was nothing but a sea of mud with waving green fronds growing out of it. Jake had to flatten an osteena bed in order to land the *Flint* close to the Dixie Flyer.

The town gate opened and Zandra Hartwell strode out.

"State your business—oh, it's you."

Cara strode forward, leaving boot prints in the mud.

"You go ahead," Jake said. "I'll bide here a while. Good luck."

"Thanks, Jake—for everything," Max said.

Jake waved him off with one hand and Max followed Cara to the gate in time to hear a craggy woman in a long raincoat say, "She doesn't want to see anyone and she's not going back."

Max pointed through the gate to the third house on the left. "Tell her to tell me herself and I'll leave."

Gen, honey, Liv, it's me. He put all the emotion he could muster into that one thought and pushed it out as hard as he could.

Max. We're not going back.

Of course not. I'm coming with you. If you'll have me, that is.

The door opened and a buddysuited figure appeared on the step holding the hand of a toddler.

Daddy!

Max almost took a step back. Liv sounded pleased to see him. His daughter stumped toward him on strong little legs, slipped in the mud, sat down hard, and stood up again. His feet didn't ask permission, he ran toward her, scooped her up mud and all, and almost fell into Gen's waiting arms.

"You took your time, mister," she said when he came up for air. "I guess you are coming with us, after all."

"If you'll have me."

"Well, I can hardly leave you in Wonnick." She jerked her head up to where the *Flint* was merely a dot in the sky.

Chapter Forty-Four

PLANNING

CARA UNLOCKED BEN'S OFFICE DOOR, WALKED in, and dropped the override key on his desk. She felt slightly sick, as she had done since this whole thing blew up.

Ben stared at it, slightly puzzled, and then looked at the door.

"You're free to go." She shrugged. "Or stay."

"Until when?"

"Permanently. No one is pressing charges."

"Gen and Max?"

"Gone."

"Gone? How do you mean?"

"Gone. Left. Vanished. Fled."

Ben blinked twice. "Gone where?"

"Just gone. What part of gone is unclear? They've left, and they won't be coming back. Ever." She wiped her cheek with her fingers. They came away wet.

"How can they just—? I need to find them, to apologize. I'll make it right."

"There are some things that can't be made right, Ben. Not with words, not with actions, not with time."

"Are you talking about Gen and Max, or are you talking about us?"

"There is no us. Not anymore. I've moved my things out.

The apartment's all yours. I'll work with the Free Company until we've sent out the news about the Nimbus, then I'm going, too."

His mouth moved into a W shape. Where? When? Why? But the questions died on his lips.

"You know I never intended to let anything happen to Liv."

"I know you tried your damnedest to keep her safe, but you're not God, Ben. It could have gone to shit at any time. It almost did. We thought it had. The void dragons, the Nimbus. Foldspace itself. You know that. I know that. And Gen and Max know that. You can tell yourself you had no choice. You can tell yourself the results outweigh the damage, but that wasn't your choice to make."

His jaw tightened. "Yet here we are. We have an answer."

"Then we'd damn well better save the universe with it." Cara swiped her cheek with a closed fist. It came away wet. "Because any less than that and all this pain will have been for nothing. Gen left us a message. After everything that's happened, she still wanted to help."

Ben made a small choking noise. Cara considered it an invitation to continue. "She said Kitty Keely told Liv she wanted to kill everyone."

"Define everyone?"

"The whole human race."

"Oh, shit. She really is the Nimbus' avatar."

"I believe she is," Cara said, "and that might account for why David Cho offed himself if he was conflicted about it."

"And Kitty's not conflicted?"

"It doesn't sound like it. Not conflicted in the least. Make of that what you will."

❖ ❖ ❖

Wenna stood in Ben's office doorway. "Looks like you're staying."

"While I can be useful. You're in charge, though."

She gave a soft snort.

"I mean it, Wenna. You've always been the one who holds this place together. Ask anyone. I'm surplus to requirements now. Half the people want to get rid of me for what I did, and the other half—well—I'm not sure I agree with them."

"Have we time for philosophy? They'll all get over it."

"The idea that morality is about achieving the right consequences only works when it's not your friends and your friends' child that you're letting down. I didn't respect their rights, as parents, as friends, as human beings."

"That's your burden," Wenna said softly. "And I'm sorry for it. But your task is to make the most of what you've learned."

"I'm going to see Garrick, and then I need to talk to Jessop in the Monitors. I'll need a Telepath to work with. Maybe not Cara."

"She's the best we've got."

"I know, but—"

"She said she'd stay for as long as it took to get the word out."

He sighed. "All right. Ask her if she's available later this morning, please."

He noticed a slight softening of attitudes from the people he passed on the way out to the tub cabs. Not everyone met his eyes, but a few did. There were a few curious looks and some polite nods. Would they have changed their minds so readily if Gen and Max had still been here?

He collected Gwala and Hilde on the way. As they settled into the cab, he broke the awkward silence. "Are you two my guards or my bodyguards today?"

"Which would you like us to be?" Hilde asked.

"Does it make any difference?"

"We still have to prevent anyone from killing you," Gwala said.

"For what it's worth, we knew right from the beginning what you were up to," Hilde said. "There's no way the child's mother would have let you take her precious daughter without at least coming with you."

"You didn't try to stop me."

"We figured it was above our pay grade. Besides, you must have had a good reason."

"If it makes you feel any better," Gwala said, "if it had come down to a choice of saving you or saving the baby, we'd have chosen the baby."

"Quite right, too." Ben wanted to laugh for the first time since he'd squeezed the trigger on his stunner.

Gwala punched in the destination and the cab hurled itself into the traffic stream toward the Hub.

"You could have called ahead," Garrick said as Ben left Gwala and Hilde at the office door. "I might not have been here."

"But you are, and so am I. This can't wait."

Ben frowned at the fading bruises on Garrick's face from his fall. "Are you feeling any better?"

"I don't feel as bad as I look."

"That's good, because you look like hell. One thing you might like to know is that after you passed out, Liv Marling told her parents that Kitty Keely wants to kill everyone—not everyone on the station, but all of mankind."

"You believe the word of a baby?"

"In this instance, I do. Absolutely! About that and about other things, too. When she was born, the void dragon put something in her brain. They can communicate."

"I heard about your escapade, of course. I had a visit from Max. He told me about seeing the older Liv, and he said more besides."

"Whatever he said, I probably deserve it."

"From his point of view, I'm sure you do. I'm a bit of a consequentialist. I believe the end can justify the means, and sometimes good things come from bad actions. So . . . what exactly did you find out?"

Ben told him about how humans were poisoning the void with their platinum waste, which was what had prompted the retaliation.

"It's attacking us the only way it can," Ben said, "by using what we send through against us."

"The jump gates—"

"Are our weakness."

"Are you saying . . . ?"

"We close them. The void dragon suggested as much."

Garrick gave a low whistle.

"Yes, I know," Ben said. "Huge consequences, but if we don't . . ."

"Huge consequences."

"Precisely."

"So do you have a plan?" Garrick asked.

"We can't do this without the megacorporations."

"You, my friend, are probably not the best person to speak to them. Your grandmother, on the other hand—"

"Maybe."

"You kidnapped a baby and took it into foldspace. Don't tell me you don't want to put Louisa Benjamin at risk. She's old enough to decide for herself."

Ben nodded. "Yes, she is, but before then I think we should practice what we preach. We have to close down the gates close to all the Crossways Protectorate planets."

"They aren't going to like that."

"No one's going to like it. We can only soften the blow by providing their fleets with jumpships, or at least retrofit jump drives, as an interim measure. It's not a permanent solution, but it's better than doing nothing."

Garrick paced the length of his office and turned. "The scale is enormous, Ben. We're talking about hundreds of jump drives for the Protectorate planets. We've only produced them in small quantities so far. We'd need to draft all the skilled labor we could find and set up a plant on Olyanda, and also contract out to any of the planets with shipyards."

"Yes."

Garrick let out a long, slow, breath. "All right."

"Once we pass on the blueprints to shipyards, there's no guarantee the megacorps won't get hold of the plans."

"I know. One more hard decision."

Ben shrugged. "The jump drives may be short-lived anyway. Ultimately, we have to find a way of not polluting foldspace with platinum, or we need to stop flying the Folds."

"Is that possible?"

"Maybe not alone, but if all the megacorps committed their Research and Development divisions working together, we—mankind—might crack the problem. It's been a race before with enormous advantages for those who are first past the post, but what if we all held hands and crossed the finish line together?"

"Do you believe that could happen?" Garrick sounded skeptical.

"I'm not such an idealist that I believe they're suddenly going to put five hundred years of bitter rivalry behind them out of the goodness of their hearts, but if they get scared enough, they might."

"How scared do they need to be?"

"I'm going to talk to my contact in the Monitors to see if I can get an accurate figure on how many ships have been lost in the Folds. If it's as many as I think it is, sooner or later one of the inner planets will be hit with an infantry army of massive proportions. That thought alone should galvanize them."

Ben turned to go, but Garrick called him back. "You realize this means demand will drop, so the platinum on Olyanda will lose its value."

"I suppose it will. I figured that in general terms, but economics isn't my strong point."

"Max warned me."

"What?"

"Before he left, he sent a message and warned me the price of platinum might plunge. We've converted a proportion of our stockpiles to credits, though obviously the plant is still producing. We'll need platinum rods for our own ships."

"I guess the Free Company should sell excess stock, too."

Garrick laughed. "That man was more your friend than you realize. He set that in motion before he left, and helped himself to his fair share."

"I can't blame him for that."

◆ ◆ ◆

Cara was waiting in the comms chair for Ben. She could work from his office, but chose not to. The comms chair was in a cubicle that isolated the operator from what was going on outside. It was a nice, quiet, neutral environment. Normally, Cara didn't mind the background noise and Ben's steady presence.

Today wasn't normal.

Ready? Ben asked.

His touch was so familiar she wanted to burst into tears. One more advantage of being in the comms chair. No one could see her tear-streaked cheeks or hear her blubbing.

Ready. Who to first?

Jess Jessop.

Cara was familiar with Jessop now. She sent out a thought and was rewarded almost instantly with a handshake, implant to implant. *Prime Jessop, I have Ben Benjamin requesting contact. Is it convenient?*

Keep it formal, girl. It will help.

If waking me in the middle of the night is convenient, then, yes, put him through.

Cara connected Ben smoothly.

Jess, I have some new information about the colony attacks and ship disappearances, but first of all I need some information from you about the numbers of ship losses in the Folds. It's my guess the megacorps are playing it down.

I could lose my job over this, Ben, or worse.

I wouldn't ask if it wasn't important.

How important?

There's an entity in foldspace that would like to wipe out every single human being in the galaxy.

Jess was silent.

You know I'm not prone to flights of fancy, Jess.

I know, I know. It's just . . . a lot to take in.

I have a very well-respected professor of astrophysics on Crossways who can actually prove there's something there, but sending you her dissertation will take more time than I have. Please, Jess, you know what you found out about the returnees doesn't make sense unless there's something in the Folds. Get me those statistics, and I'll tell you exactly what it is, but you're not going to like it.

Jessop swore. *I don't need to look it up. I was curious enough to check. As far as I can work out, over the last five years almost seven thousand ships have gone missing.*

Cara felt Ben stop to take a deep breath. She held the communication steady even though she was reeling.

Seven thousand ships, and no one had joined the dots. Or, if they had, they weren't willing to reveal their findings because this was so massive it threatened everything the megacorporations held dear—namely profit, profit, and profit.

How many souls? Ben asked.

Nearly a million and a half—and that's only the last five years.

Are any of them military ships?

Some, and a few of ours—Monitor transports.

Shit!

Now you're worrying me, Ben. What do I need to know?

Ben told him about the Nimbus and what they'd found out about its reasons for wanting to wipe out humankind.

I'd ask if you're sure, but—

I'm sure. Whether I can get your bosses and the megacorps to believe me remains to be seen, but we're going to meet with the independents in the Crossways Protectorate and suggest closing down their jump gates before something comes through them.

Cara let the communication drop as Ben withdrew. Already she had an incipient headache, and this was just the first of many calls she was going to have to make.

Chapter Forty-Five

WARNINGS

ARE YOU OKAY? BEN ASKED CARA.

They'd made fifteen calls so far, which was exhausting for a Telepath, even one as strong as Cara.

Yes. Get on with it.

Short and snappy. She was tired, and she was still mad at him. He couldn't blame her for being mad, but he could do something about the tiredness.

I need a break even if you don't. Let's take an hour.

She pulled out of his head without any of the usual niceties. He took a deep breath. If that was the way she wanted to play it, then he'd oblige and keep everything between them strictly business.

Ben needed food. He still didn't feel like sauntering down to the canteen as if nothing had happened and contemplated sending out for a tray, but he had to face the Free Company sooner or later.

Ada Levenson and her team served up food at all hours, but there was always a crush at lunchtime. Ben had hoped to slink into a table by himself, but they were all occupied, though not all full. He spotted Ronan at the same time as Ronan spotted him. The medic jerked his head to the empty seat opposite him in invitation.

"Are you sure you don't mind eating with a pariah?" Ben asked.

"I doubt you're a pariah. Besides, I've done more idiotic things in the past than share lunch with someone who's out of favor, and will probably do so in the future. Not that I think it's a problem for most people. Sit down, Ben, before the rubbernecking couple behind you pull muscles and I have to fix them up. People aren't blaming you. They're relieved to have an answer. They may not like it, but it's better than not knowing what's going on."

Ben looked around. Most of the people were simply getting on with eating lunch. He wasn't drawing unwanted attention. Maybe Ronan was right.

"You're being hard on yourself," Ronan said. "Much harder than anyone else is going to be. Apart from all the guilt you've been wallowing in, how's it going?"

Ben took a mouthful of what might be vat protein in a sweet-and-sour sauce and then told him about Jessop's estimate of ship losses.

"That's not good." Ronan played with his fork, the remains of his lunch cooling on his plate.

"Understatement of the century. How's it going with Kitty Keely?"

"Trying deep regression. I haven't triggered anything monumental yet. I was hoping I might be able to find out what had happened to her, but she's resolute. Her story is real as far as she's concerned. Even telling her the date and proving how long she was missing doesn't stir anything. It's as if she simply slides away from inconvenient facts."

"Let me know if—"

"Of course. Syke is spending as much time with Kitty as he can. He says she hasn't changed, but I still have them separated by the clear wall."

"Do you think Kitty can communicate with the Nimbus?"

Ronan shrugged. "There's no indication either way. She still claims it doesn't exist."

"With Garrick's blessing, I'm calling all the heads of the Protectorate planets. As soon as we can provide them with jump drives, we intend to close down their gates."

"Have you enough pilots?"

"Not yet. We'll be running a crash course—no pun intended—for any of their pilots who show aptitude. Jake,

Naomi Patel, and the Magena twins will be tutors while Captain Dorinska takes the *Glory Road* to Vraxos to see if she can recruit a few more pilots who can see the dragon."

"This whole thing, closing the jump gates, will be a huge shift for humans in space. Are you sure it's necessary?"

"I'd be monumentally relieved if anyone could come up with another solution, but the jump gates are our weakness. The more gates we close, the more concentrated travel through the others will be, so any ships using them will be more vulnerable, and the colonies nearby will be the first targets for the returnees. Every gate we close pushes the risk further down the line until we close the last one."

"You say the jump gates are vulnerable, but we haven't lost any ships through the Crossways gate, have we?"

"I have a theory, though it's only a theory at this stage. If our ships and jump gates discharge platinum into the Folds, the highest concentrations will be where the most traffic is. The Crossways gate has only been in position for the last year, so there's not much buildup yet."

"Which surely means the large jump gate hubs are going to be the most vulnerable."

"I'm afraid so, but they are hugely profitable, so getting their owners to believe us is going to be difficult."

"Almost impossible, I should say, unless you can convince another organization to back you."

Ben scrubbed his forehead with his fingertips. "They might believe the Monitors."

"How will you convince the Monitors?"

"I'll offer them something they want."

"What would that be?"

"Me." He laughed at Ronan's expression. "I'd better get back." Ben left his sweet and sour half-eaten and strode toward his office.

Cara! Break's over. Are you okay to go again?

Ready when you are.

Get me Jessop again, please.

You want what? Jessop said.

Ben could tell Jessop had rolled out of bed and straight on to his feet.

I want to talk to Eve Moyo and Sebastian Rodriguez.

I haven't the authority . . .

Come off it, Jess., You have a hotline to the top when you need one. Go through Moyo if you have to.

Moyo trained you, didn't she?

She trains all the class one Navigators for the Monitors.

Will she remember you?

Oh, yes. Ben left it at that since it was Cara handling this call. He'd been a precocious student—in more ways than one. *If possible, I'd like to speak to Moyo and Rodriguez at the same time. She's responsible for feeding this foldspace illusion crap to a whole generation of Monitor Navigators.*

How am I going to do that?

Tell them I'm willing to give myself up.

✦ ✦ ✦

"Are you mad?" Cara stood, fists on hips, in Ben's office doorway. "You're willing to give yourself up?"

"To the Monitors, not the Trust."

"As if that makes any difference. How many crimes have they laid at your door? You'll be on a prison planet for the rest of your life—and that's only if Crowder doesn't manage to have you done away with while you're awaiting trial."

"I didn't know you cared."

"I don't." She was glad she'd been able to say that in words. It was much more difficult to lie mind-to-mind. "I don't, but you have a job to do, and you can't do it from inside a prison cell or incarcerated on a prison planet with your implant disabled."

"Don't tear yourself up about it. I said I'd give myself up. I didn't say when."

If Ben promised he'd do something, he'd do it.

"How long have you been planning this?"

He shrugged.

"Of all the blasted, stupid ... brainless ... you're punishing yourself for what happened with Liv, aren't you? We're not going to do it, so you'll make sure you get what's coming to you from the Monitors."

He looked her straight in the eyes, his face unreadable. "In the meantime, please can we continue to contact the Protectorate planets?"

She nodded. There wasn't much else she could do. Damned, bloody infuriating man!

Another three hours and eighteen more planets, and Cara was faltering.

Take a break. Get some sleep, Ben said. *Laurie Gilmartin can take a short shift.*

She nodded and realized he couldn't see her. *Thanks, I will. Call me if—*

There won't be anything that can't wait until morning.

Yeah, right, because I always get an unbroken night's sleep.

If it's any consolation, I don't sleep so well, either.

It isn't.

"Sleep," she said to Wenna as she emerged from the comms cubicle.

"Yeah, thanks for the reminder, I'll try it sometime," Wenna said. "How did it go?"

"Over half the colonies contacted."

"And?"

"They're not happy, but they know what happened on Butterstone and Jamundi, and they're not stupid. Ben's given them all the assurances he can. They'll have jump-ships and pilots to fly them on the understanding they'll be working toward self-sufficiency. A few have pointed out that once the Crossways fleet has a monopoly on transport, we can hike up the prices. Ben has assured them the jump-ships won't belong to Crossways, and it will be up to the colonies how they use them. I'm not sure he could do more than that."

"It sounds fair. It's a deal I'd take if I ran a colony—but then I know what it's like when death comes screaming out of the sky." Wenna massaged her elbow, even though it was entirely part of the prosthetic.

Cara thought about it on her way to her new apartment. It was a good deal, or at least it was better than annihilation by a horde of recently resurrected space zombies. She giggled, not that space zombies was a particularly appropriate description in this instance, but you had to get your laughs where you could in these dark times.

She was too tired to eat, but forced herself to chew down the sandwich Wenna had forced on her and drink a large glass of water before switching on a mindless entertainment channel. The program, some historical crime drama set on Earth, was interrupted by an advert for men and women with engineering and technical skills to apply to be part of an exciting new project on Olyanda. The ad offered good wages, productivity bonuses, and fast advancement for individuals with initiative. Accommodation provided for transferees from Crossways. It looked like Garrick was making a start on the production of jump drives.

She missed the rest of the show on account of falling asleep in her chair, waking only to go pee, strip off her clothes, and fall into her lonely bed.

Dammit! She should have set her damping pin if she wanted unbroken sleep. An incoming telepathic handshake roused her at what her handpad said was six a.m. but felt more like two. She didn't feel as though she'd had a full eight hours, but she had.

Who?

Jessop for Benjamin.

He's not here and... She reached out for Ben. *Dammit—I think he's wearing a damper. Long story, Jess. We've had someone on station dishing out dreams like they were peanuts at a cocktail party. Can you give me five minutes to get dressed and find him?*

I'm at Monitor HQ in Shield City, talking through one of their class one Telepaths. Both Mrs. Moyo and Commissioner Rodriguez want to talk to Ben urgently. Can you schedule a meeting in fifteen minutes?

Yes, I can do that.

She deliberately didn't ask any more questions with the Monitor Telepath listening in. Instead, she hauled herself out of bed and staggered into the shower, leaning against the massage wall for a bit of comfort. It wasn't a substitute for Ben.

Don't think about that now.

The outer office door read her handpad and opened. It was still too early for Wenna.

Ben's door wasn't locked.

"Ben!" She knocked anyway before going in.

He'd obviously been asleep, but had always had the ability to pass from sleep to wakefulness without the intermediate woolly stage. He met her at the door of his sleeping cubicle wearing nothing more than his skin.

"Where's the fire?"

"No fire, just a meeting in . . ." She checked her handpad.

"Four minutes from now. Ms. Moyo and Commissioner Rodriguez. Get dressed."

He glanced down. "Do I sound different without my clothes on?"

"No, but I do." She turned her back on him and walked out, knowing that whatever she felt about Ben Benjamin, it wasn't indifference.

He joined her in exactly three and a half minutes in Wenna's office, still fastening the cuffs on his buddysuit.

"Whenever you're ready."

"Ready." She sat in one of the visitor chairs. Ben took the other. She reached out for Jessop's mind and found him almost immediately. *Ready when you are, Captain Jessop. I have Commander Benjamin here with me.*

Allow me to introduce Telepath Sweeting who will be facilitating for Commissioner Rodriguez, and Telepath Stafford who will be facilitating for Professor Moyo.

Cara felt the handshakes from two powerful Telepaths and acknowledged them. She glanced at Ben. "Are you ready?"

"Ready."

Cara brought Ben in, then slipped into the background. She felt each of the other Telepaths do the same.

Reska Benjamin, Ben identified himself.

Eve Moyo.

Sebastian Rodriguez. What's all this about, Benjamin? You have a string of indictments against you as long as my arm. I'm only here because of a very strong representation from Prime Jessop and Professor Moyo.

I appreciate that. Thank you for your time, sir.

Hello, Ben.

Hello, Eve. It's been a while.

Yes, it has.

Cara hardly had time to wonder at their warm greeting.

Benjamin, Prime Jessop has given me a set of very worrying statistics that he's been working on. Ship losses. I gather you have information for us, Rodriguez said.

I do. Very disturbing information, and that's why I wanted Eve, Professor Moyo, here as well. She's no doubt told you she trained me to fly a jumpship.

Yes, she did. I believe you were a class one Navigator.

Still am, sir. Don't let the new implant fool you. Professor Moyo, at the time I did my training, it was the accepted wisdom to tell pilots and Navigators that anything they might see in the Folds was entirely imagined, and foldspace hallucinations were only to be expected.

Yes, Moyo said.

Even though you knew it wasn't true.

It keeps them safe.

Except they're not safe, are they? Ben said. *Not now.*

There was a silence during which Cara could imagine Moyo and Rodriguez looking at each other and wondering how much to admit to. Moyo did the mental equivalent of clearing her throat, stalling for time.

Cara glanced across at Ben, his face intent as he concentrated on the conversation.

How many ship losses that no one has admitted to? Ben asked, but no one answered. *Eve, I know you. You're too smart to close your mind to it, whatever the official line. How many separate life-forms have you found in foldspace so far?* Again that pause. *If you want to know what I know, you have to give me something in return.*

Two, Moyo said. *We think there are two distinct life-forms in the Folds.*

Ben glanced across at Cara and mouthed, "Two!"

She widened her eyes in reply.

Is one of your life-forms a black cloud that swallows ships whole? We call it the Nimbus. Ben asked.

No.

Then make that three. Tell me about yours and then I'll tell you about the Nimbus.

There's one that looks like a dragon, Moyo said.

With prehensile claws in its beard?

That's the one. It's telepathic, but it doesn't have language. We don't know if there's one or many.

Many, I think, Ben said. *but they may all be mentally connected. What one knows they all know, unless we've only ever been dealing with the same one. We're making a start on the language thing. More on that later.*

There are some smaller ones that nearly always appear in pairs and are quite playful.

They remind me of otters, though sometimes they're cigar-shaped, sometimes more snakelike?

Yes, those are the ones, Moyo said. *But what about your black cloud, the Nimbus?*

It wants to wipe us all out, like the plague we are, to keep us out of the Folds.

This time the silence was entirely understandable.

Ben continued. *It has good reason. The platinum we lose in the Folds is toxic to it. We're poisoning its environment.*

Ben went on to explain what they knew about the Nimbus and how they knew it. He spared no detail.

So we're closing down the jump gates within our, that's Crossways', jurisdiction to keep the independent colonies safe. In the interim, we'll be supplying them with as many retrofit jump drives as possible, especially to those colonies which still rely on imported goods for daily staples.

That's a drastic measure. Rodriguez' mental tone was still tinged with shock.

We've had colony attacks, too. We believe the only way to deal with this is to close all the gates. Every ship that enters the Folds through a gate is a potential target. And every one of them could come back to attack us. We think the hubs are likely to be a major target. With multiple gates, the platinum detritus will have built up in the corresponding regions of foldspace. Similarly, any planet with multiple gates, even Earth itself.

Cara couldn't sense how Ben's news had been received. That was often the case when working through a Telepath. You got a better idea of what the Telepaths were thinking than their clients. These two were worried. One was already planning to cancel his next off-world job. Wise move.

Ben didn't let up. *Check the figures of gate ships as opposed to jumpships that have been lost. Jumpships are safer, but they're only an interim measure. Ideally, we—that's mankind, sir, not just Crossways or the Monitors—have to solve the problem of platinum loss in the Folds. We're poisoning the environment, and we don't have a right to do that. Think of all the mistakes we made on Earth in the late twentieth and early twenty-first centuries.*

*The megacorporations . . . * Rodriguez left his thought half-finished.

That will be better coming from you than from Crossways, Ben said.

We know about Crossways and the megacorps.

*You may know some of it, but you don't know it all. I told Jess—Captain Jessop—I'd give myself up, and I will *when the time is right, but in the meantime, I'm happy to give you a sworn statement if you have someone who can take it down verbatim.*

Cara pushed down her surprise. He meant to go through with it. She couldn't let him do it alone. She didn't plan to give herself up to the law. If she did, she'd end up back with Alphacorp having her brain scrambled, but her story both supported and added to Ben's and the Free Company's.

If I may interrupt, Cara said. *Cara Carlinni, formerly of Alphacorp, lately of the Trust, and now with the Free Company on Crossways. If Ben is going to give you a sworn statement, I'd like to add mine to it.*

A statement taken telepathically was as good, if not better than, a verbal statement under oath. Lying mind-to-mind was next to impossible.

It took a while. Wenna arrived before it was over, and they moved into Ben's office, walking as if in a dream.

When it was done, Ben raised his eyes to Cara's. "You didn't need to do that."

"Yes, I did," she said. "Fair's fair. I'm not brave like you. I'm not going to go and throw myself on the mercy of the law because I think we already know the law has no mercy, but if my story backs up yours, then I'm happy to give it."

"Thank you."

Chapter Forty-Six

FAMILY

OVER THE NEXT FEW DAYS BEN TALKED TO all the Protectorate planets and all of them agreed to close their jump gates, though not without reservations.

Six colonies were nowhere near being able to become self-sufficient. Three were mining operations, one for gold and other precious metals, including modest amounts of platinum, and two for iron and industrial metals which were then processed and exported. One of them was Ironhold, which until recently had relied on Butterstone for food staples, being the next planet in the Onix System, but too far from the system's star for optimum crop production. Since Butterstone was still a ghost settlement, they'd had to import supplies from beyond the system.

Ben needed to call Nan back into service. She was a much better negotiator than he was.

"I'm going to Jamundi to talk to Nan," Ben told Cara in the office. "Do you want to come with me?"

He tried to keep the question light. Her attitude to him hadn't slipped, but she wasn't actively antagonistic. If she said yes, he'd know she was thawing slightly. He almost held his breath.

"No."

"We could go in the Dixie. It would be like old times." He tried not to sound as if he was pleading.

"No, we couldn't. You've been so busy you haven't been to Port 46 since Gen left. I gave her the Dixie with your compliments. It seemed only fair."

He swallowed hard. "Yes. Fair. When were you going to tell me?"

"I wasn't. I was going to let you find out for yourself. I'm not sorry."

"I don't expect you to be."

So in the end he took *Solar Wind*, which meant he had to take a crew. His first choice was always Yan Gwenn, but Yan declined. Garrick had approached him to help establish the factory on Olyanda. After all, Yan had been working alongside Dido Kennedy and knew more about the retrofit jump drives than anyone else except Kennedy herself.

"Garrick's offered me a permanent job, managing the factory, and has offered to set up a workshop for Dido, dirtside, and even said she can bring the feral kids with her. That was the clincher. I haven't accepted yet, but I'm seriously thinking about it."

"You should go for it, Yan. Dido's a good woman."

"She's a nutjob, but she's my kind of nutjob."

Ben laughed. "I wish you both well. Make lots of drives for us. We'll miss you, though."

"The old team's not what it was, is it?" Yan said. "Suzi and Serafin gone to Jamundi, Gen and Max gone, Cas and others killed in the battle, and that's not counting the losses on Olyanda in the first year. And you've as good as said you'll go when this is over. So has Cara. I think I'm taking the coward's way out and leaving while there's still something to leave. I can't fly a jumpship, so if you get your way, I'll be flying shuttles. It's time for a new career."

Ben couldn't think of an answer that didn't consist of platitudes, so he slapped Yan on the shoulder, wished him well, and walked away with a heavy heart.

In the end, his crew for Jamundi consisted of Dobson in engineering, Lynda Munene on comms and Naomi Patel as copilot. Ben did bodkin jumps in and out of the Folds, which took longer but was safer and kept the void dragon and the Nimbus at bay.

There was always a warm welcome on Jamundi. Ben wondered if it would have been as warm if they'd known about him kidnapping Gen's child—or perhaps they did. There was every chance the psi-techs on Jamundi had been in touch with friends on Crossways.

Whether they knew or not, they didn't let it show in their attitude. Ben left his crew amusing themselves visiting old friends or sampling the hospitality of the Ecolibrians. He borrowed a groundcar and headed for the Benjamin farm, unannounced.

Tam and Lol, Rion's two working dogs alternately barked and bounded around his vehicle in delight as he pulled up in the yard. Rion came out first to see what the noise was about, with Nan following close on his heels. They say home is the place where when you turn up on the doorstep, they have to take you in, but for Ben it wasn't the place, it was family. Their welcome humbled him.

At times like this, he wished he could stay and leave the big decisions to someone else.

There was always plenty of food on the table in the Benjamin household, mainly because Thea was eating for two and Kai and Ricky were trying to match her.

"We did it, Uncle Ben," Kai said. "We didn't want any fuss, so Thea and I snuck into town early last Friday and Director Lorient married us. Thea's a Benjamin now."

"Well, congratulations," Ben said and gave Thea a peck on the cheek as they milled around the table to sit down. "There, I've kissed the bride. Is that acceptable?"

Thea blushed while Kai helped to push her chair as close to the table as she could go with her pregnant belly. "Not long now," Thea said. "And the house is almost finished. Just a little bit of decorating left to do."

"Finished enough that we already moved in," Kai said.

Nan and Ricky ferried pots from the stove to the table while Rion hacked a fresh-baked loaf of bread into ragged slices. Chatter died while they addressed dinner. Ben tried to bring up the current situation while they were still eating, but Nan redirected the conversation elsewhere.

After dinner, she said. *There's time enough.*

Ben supposed there was, and settled down to enjoy a meal with his family.

"So, Reska . . ." Nan said after the pots had been washed

and put away. Kai and Thea had gone across to their own little house and Ricky had been sent to finish his homework. "Want to tell us what went wrong?"

They were sitting in front of the living room fire. The offcuts of timber from the new building crackled and snapped in the grate.

"Do I look as though my life collapsed around my ears?" Ben asked. "You always knew how to read me too well."

"You and me, both, brother." Rion rose from his chair to stir the fire and put another chunk of wood into the ash of the last one.

He told them everything, including kidnapping Liv and driving away Gen and Max, and outlined the threat that now faced them.

Neither Nan nor Rion responded immediately.

"Well, say something," Ben said.

"I finished my homework," Ricky's forlorn voice came from behind them. "And I heard all that. Can I come and join you, or do I have to pester everyone tomorrow to find out what's happening?"

Rion sucked his teeth and looked at Nan. She shrugged.

"Come in, sit down, and shut up," Rion said. "Any requests for an early implant will get you an early bedtime."

"I get it. I do."

Ben turned to his nephew. "Just for the record, Ricky, in future when I say: do as I say and not as I do, I want you to take note. I've messed up bigtime."

"Maybe," Nan said. "Why did you think the baby was the key to understanding the void dragon?"

"The dragon as good as told me so. In pictures, not in words. It gave something to Liv on the day she was born. She's uncannily advanced for her age. She's not only talking in sentences, she's naturally telepathic. Maybe that helped with language."

"Do you think the void dragon imparted any kind of compulsion to you? It wanted to see the child, and the child, by all accounts wanted to see the dragon."

"Truth is, I don't know, and I don't suppose I'll ever find out. I don't think I was acting under a compulsion. I won't use that as an excuse."

"Do you think the child and the dragon communicate across the dimensional barrier?"

"It's possible."

"And you learned things you wouldn't have been able to learn any other way?"

"Yes. I'm sure of that. We might have figured out what the Nimbus was up to eventually, but we'd never have known why."

"What good do you think you can do with that knowledge?"

"Closing the jump gate system will cut off the Nimbus altogether. It's the only way to protect ships and colonies. I can't wave a magic wand and do that, of course. The megacorps, the Five Power Alliance on Earth, and possibly the Monitors are the only ones who can do that successfully, and then only if they work together."

"What's the worst thing that can happen?"

"That people don't appreciate the danger and refuse to close down the jump gate system because they'll lose their profit. More and more ships disappear in the Folds and more colonies, and possibly the inner system planets are attacked by an increasingly large army with increasingly more resources."

"Can the Nimbus ever succeed in wiping out humans?"

"I don't see how it can, not if it continues to use other humans to do the job. It's self-defeating. But it can cause massive hurt and damage, not only now, but for as long as we keep sending it more ships. A long war of attrition could knock us back to the stone age."

"How much hurt and damage will closing the jump gates cause?"

"Some colonies aren't self-sufficient, but others will be fine. Yes, their economies will change, but they can feed, clothe, and shelter their people, and that's a start."

Nan gave him one of her hard stares. "Are you sure— very sure—you don't have an ulterior motive for closing down the gates? It's going to put a serious dent in the megacorporations. Wouldn't you like that?"

"You're a historian, Nan. Bubbles burst. The megacorporations don't need help from me to reach the natural end to their lifespan, whether it happens now or two hundred years in the future. They're already unwieldy. They've expanded beyond their ability to control and support what they've created. Otherwise, the independent colonies would never have been able to break away. Closing the jump gates may hasten some kind of radical reorganization, but I doubt it will destroy them. They may take a dip in profits, but with enough jumpships they could be back in business within a decade, and they'll be better off for the contraction. Or, better still, they can join together to solve the problem of platinum pollution in the Folds."

He felt Nan's look going straight through him, as it always had when he was a child. Eventually, she cleared her throat, or it might have been a noncommittal grunt. "So what do you want from me? Reassurance that you're doing the right thing?"

"No, Nan, I want you at the negotiating table."

She chuckled. "I wondered when you'd get around to that."

"Well?"

"I'll come when Thea's had her baby and we have a new generation of Benjamins. In the meantime, get those jump drives into production and watch your back in the Folds."

✦ ✦ ✦

Some days it was like old times, Cara thought, apart from the situation between her and Ben.

They saw each other for work and that was it. She missed his easy company in off-duty hours and his body in her bed, though technically speaking it was her body missing from his bed, since she was the one who'd moved out.

He was never anything but polite and considerate when they were working together, but otherwise he left her alone. Ronan had tried to make peace between them, but this wasn't anything that could be solved by a third party—even Ronan—though he'd taken great care to point out that by stunning her alongside Gen and Max, Ben had protected her from the fallout.

The Free Company got on with things in its usual professional manner. Within a few weeks of Yan and Dido taking up residence on Olyanda with a house full of adopted kids, jump drives started to come off the assembly line in the new plant. It wasn't working to capacity yet, of course, but that would come with time.

Captain Dorinska had recruited three more qualified jumpship pilots from Vraxos and signed up a further eight likely candidates who had seen the void dragon in fold-space. The colonies themselves were suddenly keen to iden-tify potential jumpship pilots now they were close to getting their own vessels.

That meant Ben, Jake, the Magena sisters, and Naomi Patel were taking it in turns to fly training runs while the three qualified pilots from Vraxos, all known to Jake, worked most of the regular runs, ferrying goods and passen-gers as required alongside Crossways' own jumpship pilots.

Lynda Munene, Issy Monaghan, and Corin Butterfield, together with J.P. and Pami Lister, had salvaged another three ships from those Eastin-Heigle had abandoned, add-ing to the pool of armed ships now available to protect Crossways, Olyanda, and any of the Protectorate planets that called for help.

Blacklock, as the first colony to sign up to the agreement with Crossways, took delivery of three jump drives and a party of psi-techs to retrofit them into existing freighters. Its heavily industrialized cities, nestling in productive farm-land, traded tech with its nearest neighbors and imported coffee and pharmaceuticals from Blue Mountain. With the delivery of those ships, Ben had sent a team of Psi-Mechs under Archie Tatum to decommission the Blacklock gate.

Blacklock was the first, Keynes the second, and Brazil Colony the third. They'd decommissioned seven gates al-ready and—so far—no more attacks on Protectorate planets.

That was good news, Cara thought. Crossways and the Free Company were trying to catch up while still waiting for news from the Monitors that they'd approached the megacorporations about closing the jump gates.

In this case, maybe no news was bad news.

◆ ◆ ◆

"Let's get down to business." Ben addressed the ten poten-tial jumpship pilots he'd agreed to train. The six women and four men had come from all over the galaxy and now gath-ered in *Solar Wind*'s mess. Three from Vraxos and seven from the Protectorate planets.

"How many of you were trained by one of the megacor-porations?" Ben asked.

Predictably, most were.

Two of the pilots from Vraxos, Caleb Morlen and Chloe

Durand, said they'd had their implants fitted on the black market from a shady dealer working with an Alphacorp runaway med-tech. They'd learned their trade from a pilot on Vraxos a couple of years apart.

"So the eight of you who have learned from megacorp instructors need to know that the most important thing your instructors never told you is that foldspace illusions are real."

The collected indrawn breaths were audible.

Ben turned to the Vraxos pilots. "What's your take on it?"

"Real," Durand said.

Morlen nodded. "Real, but if you ignore them, they'll ignore you."

"And how has that worked for you so far?"

"All right, mostly, though there was a time when one of those big ones touched me. That was tough to ignore."

"You mean the big ones that look like this?" Ben projected a drawing of the void dragon on to the wall.

"Yeah, that's the one."

Ben looked at his class. "Does anyone not recognize this?"

No one answered.

"Good. The other thing you need to know is that nothing we take in with us is real in foldspace. It's a different dimension. The laws of physics don't work." He let that sink in for a few moments. "If you believe you can breathe and survive in foldspace without an EVA suit, then you can. If you believe you can't, you won't. If you believe the walls of your ship are insubstantial, then they will be."

"That's nuts."

Ben glanced at his list to see who'd said that. "Dorman, isn't it?"

"Yes, sir, Lois Dorman. Previously of Alphacorp. Assigned to work the Blacklock run. When the colony went independent, they bought my contract."

"We'll be going into the Folds soon. Tell me if you still think it's nuts when we come back. You can all pilot a ship through the jump gate system and keep on track between gates, navigating by the beacons. Flying a jumpship is a sideways step from that. You won't be using beacons, you'll be using your own innate navigational talent to find the line to your destination. You guys have a head start. You're sensitive to the Folds and foldspace creatures. Once you've learned the trick of finding the line, you're going to be as safe as anyone can be in the Folds."

He explained his theory to them that the frequently used lines between jump gates had left a trail of platinum pollution which was deadly to the Nimbus, but also acted as a beacon for it. "Think of it as tracing a bad smell to its source."

"Sorry," Dorman said. "You're getting ahead of me. What's a nimbus?"

So he told them.

When he'd finished, all ten of them sat in stunned silence. "Questions?" he asked.

"So we're going to be flying into foldspace where a creature from another dimension waits to trap us, weaponize us, and send us back to wreak havoc?"

"Yes, exactly like it's always been, had you but known it. The difference this time is that you won't be using the jump gates, so the statistical chances of you ending up as Nimbus bait are much lower. Say right now if you want out. There are some jobs going in the platinum processing plant on Olyanda. If you want to continue to fly, this is your new reality. It's no different from your old reality except now you know about it."

He gave them a moment to let the facts sink in. "I can take five of you at a time on the flight deck." He looked at his list again. "Durand, Stratton, Knox, Badel, and Dorman. The rest of you will take a turn next time out. In the meantime, you'll be stationed at different points around the ship. You may or may not see anything. Your job is to look hard at whatever comes your way. If any of you spot a darkness developing, you don't go near it and you yell as loud and as long as you can. Understood?"

"What happens if we see it?" Morlen asked.

"We get out of foldspace as quickly as we can before it does any damage. It grows quite slowly at first, so speed is on our side. My guess is that it doesn't experience time in a linear way as we do. You can debate that at your leisure. Let's get started."

With Lynda Munene on comms, Ben sat at the systems station and let Dorman take *Solar Wind* out of Port 46. She was a competent pilot and at no time did he have the urge to toss her out of the command chair and take it himself. The look on her face told him all he needed to know. She loved having *Solar Wind* under her control.

Welcome to my world, he thought.

He let each pilot in turn take the helm and get a feel for the ship before taking over for the first jump into the Folds.

Lynda, can you please join us all in a gestalt?

Lynda didn't have the same sure touch that Cara did, but she did the job. Ben and his five students connected as he took over the pilot's chair and felt his way into the *Solar Wind*'s jump drive.

I'm going to take us into the Folds and straight out again. See if you can all follow me.

In and out again, like a needle stitching through fabric.

Are you all with me so far? Ben asked.

They all were.

Right. Again. Twice this time.

He repeated the dips in and out of foldspace several times.

Everyone good with that?

They were.

All right. One at a time. Try it for yourselves. Straight in and straight out again.

Dorman went first and, despite her skepticism, made a clean job of the entry and the exit. Badel faltered, but Ben gave her another chance and she did it successfully the second time. Stratton, Knox, and Durand completed the maneuver competently but without flair. That was okay. Competence was what he required.

Now we're going to stay in the Folds and learn to look for the line to where we need to be. In this case we'll be looking for the line to Crossways. From now on you can expect visitors: otter-kind, void dragons, or possibly both.

Not the Nimbus? Dorman asked.

I sincerely hope not.

With a rush Ben takes *Solar Wind* into foldspace. This time all that happens is that the flight deck light dips. Ben searches for the line to Crossways, finds it, and pops them out of the Folds at a distance of some five hundred klicks.

"Don't get too close," Ben said. "I have enough trouble with Crossways control without you all ruining my reputation as a teacher. Right, who wants to try that?"

This time Josette Badel volunteered and Ben relinquished *Solar Wind* to her. Linked to all of them once more by Lynda, Ben followed her thoughts as she took *Solar Wind* over the threshold.

This time the negative light effect fills the flight deck with reversed images in black and white. That's no problem. These guys are all used to the effects of the Folds. It's not as if they're inexperienced, even though they've only used jump gates up to now.

Ben follows Badel's thought patterns as she looks for the line to Crossways—looks but doesn't find. He gets a wave of panic from her.

"Two minutes." Lynda calls.

I should be able to— Badel's thoughts stall as the void dragon pushes its snout through the bulkhead.

OLIVIA MAY MARLING, it says.

Gone, Ben replies. They are still connected so all his students can follow the conversation.

MAAAXXX. MOMMM.

Gone. They've all gone. Ben puts the feeling of loss upfront.

NEED. TALK. LEARN.

Ben's already beginning to think it's learning more words. Perhaps Liv started the process. Now it has some words, it might be possible to teach it others.

Where's the bad thing, the Nimbus? Ben asks.

NIMBUS.

Yes, the bad thing. Shadow. Cloud.

OVER THERE.

It's a bit like a child's version of time being yesterday, today, and tomorrow for past, present, and future. Over there. In dragon-speak it means not here, but it doesn't mean a specific place. He hopes it means not here.

He tries an abstract question. *Bad thing. Nimbus, can you speak to it?*

BAD THING. NIMBUS. SILVER. HURT.

Yes. We didn't know. We know now. Can you speak to it?

The void dragon struggles with the concept.

TOYS, it says.

Now Ben is struggling with the concept until he remembers Liv likened the humans to toys controlled by the Nimbus. *Can the toys speak to the bad thing?*

TOYS SPEAK. YES.

Where are the toys? Where does the bad thing keep the toys?

HERE.

Here?

YES.

Now?

YESTERDAY. TOMORROW. NOW.

Time?

It asks, *?*

Ben tries to imagine a sequence of things happening one after the other. He imagines humans being born, growing up, growing old, dying. He imagines a star forming, shining brightly, swelling to become a red giant, dwindling to a black dwarf, or becoming a super-giant and exploding in a supernova as it collapses under its own weight.

Time. Things pass.

NO.

You mean there's no such thing as time?

It blinks at him as if some things are so obvious they don't need saying.

"Four minutes," Lynda calls.

"Okay. Let's get out of here. Badel, you can do this. Look for the line to Crossways. There, that's it."

As if falling down a rabbit hole, they tumble into real-space.

Ben looked at his students. Their faces revealed several different stages of shock and awe. "Questions?" he asked.

Chapter Forty-Seven

HUB

CARA WAS ON DUTY WHEN SHE PICKED UP news on the tel-net of a disaster at the Pinch Point Hub.

"No, no, no," she said, pushing open the cubicle door and finding Wenna at her desk. "Ben was right!"

"What? What's happened?" Wenna pushed her chair back.

"Pinch Point Hub." Cara's voice caught in her throat. "It's gone dark. No communications, telepathic or otherwise. It looks like it's been hit."

It took less than an hour for the news broadcasts to carry the story. The hub, an old toroidal station set between five jump gates had been destroyed by forces unknown according to the news broadcasts.

Ben was out on a training flight with his student pilots. Cara contacted him and told him the news.

It's begun, Ben said. *Can you connect me with Jessop?*

Of course.

Jessop was awake. Cara would like to bet every Monitor within reach of a news net was awake regardless of the hour.

I told you the hubs would be a target, Ben said. *What's happening, Jess?*

Right now, they're officially blaming pirates.

But it's not, is it?

*Not unless the pirates had access to a state-of-the-art

battleship belonging to the Dominion Group, lost in the Folds five years ago. The Star of India *is one of the most heavily armed ships in her class and Admiral Henney was on board—a master tactician. The attack on the hub was recognizably his style.**

Has Commissioner Rodriguez pressed this home with the megacorps? Has anyone even talked about closing the gates?

I'm not that high up, Ben. You can't expect—

But you haven't heard anything?

No. Sorry.

Let me know if you do.

Ben signed off.

Cara, can you trace Rodriguez's Telepath. Was it Sweeting?

Yes, I should be able to. Stand by.

She let her mind range out. Having contacted Rodriguez via Sweeting once before, it should be simple to do it again, but her implant refused to handshake with Sweeting's, possibly because he was working flat-out to keep Rodriguez abreast of the news as it came in from Pinch Point. She kept trying. Eventually, she made a solid contact and connected Ben with Commissioner Rodriguez.

Commissioner, I warned you. All the hubs are vulnerable, as are the busiest gates.

Benjamin, it's been suggested you've deliberately done this—attacked a hub—to give credence to your wild ideas.

Oh, right. I'm to blame now. According to Captain Jessop, a battleship belonging to the Dominion Group destroyed the station.

That ship went missing only five years ago. How do we know the pirates from Crossways weren't to blame?

It makes a neat story if you want to spin it that way, but Crossways would never have had the firepower to steal a battleship like the Star of India—destroy it, maybe, with a concerted effort and ten ships working together, but not steal it in a usable condition. Five years ago, Chaliss was in charge. Crossways didn't have big ideas, and I was still a loyal employee of the Trust. Have you sent investigators?**

One ship.

And?

We can't raise them.

*So you think the Star of India *is out there waiting to take out the investigators.**

And possibly any other ships that come through the gates.

Cara heard Ben swear, but he recovered quickly. *You need to close or destroy all five Pinch Point jump gates before more ships stumble through. It's likely the Nimbus is lying in wait for ships in foldspace, and the Star of India in realspace. Hold all traffic.*

We're doing that now, but there are three ships in foldspace with flight plans filed.

How long since they passed through an outward gate?- Ben asked.

An hour or more.

Then, I'm sorry, you've probably lost them.

They might yet—

What kind of firepower can you field?

Two battlewagons. They might not be enough.

Would the Howling Wolf help?

Certainly would.

Cara let the call drop. Before Ben could ask, she cut in. *I know. Contact Oleg Staple for the Howling Wolf.*

Thanks. I'm going to see what it will take to destroy those gates.

Cara's guts turned a lopsided somersault. Why couldn't Ben stay safe for a change?

With a crew of students? she said.

Qualified pilots and Navigators, just not converted to jumpships yet. They'll be fine. Have to learn sometime.

Just like Ben. Throw them in at the deep end!

✦   ✦   ✦

Ben quickly explained the situation to his pilots. He was grateful he had his advanced group which included both Vraxos pilots: Caleb Morlen and Chloe Durand, as well as Rory Stratton, Josette Badel, and Tamara Knox, who had proved to be a fast learner after a shaky start. Lynda Munene was on comms again—he wished it had been Cara, but Lynda was good at her job and unflappable. Ed Dobson was in engineering as usual.

"Caleb and Jo, man the tactical stations, please. Rory—systems. Tam—copilot."

"What about me?" Chloe asked.

"Watch for the Nimbus on all screens, internal and

external. Stay safe. If it all goes to shit, get the ship and the survivors home."

She swallowed hard and nodded.

"If we get through this, you've all graduated."

"You didn't tell us the final exam would be a practical one," Tam said.

"I like to spring surprises. Lynda, connect me with Cara, please."

Ben? Cara was in his head almost immediately. She took over the link, which made it private, and Lynda dropped out tactfully.

Going to take a look at Pinch Point from the foldspace side of the gates.

You know the Nimbus will be waiting.

Seems likely.

Howling Wolf has gone to assist the two Monitor battle-wagons.

Good.

Will it take three ships to contain the Star of India?

It could.

Are you going to make it four?

That's not my plan. There are three ships in the Folds on their way to Pinch Point. It's probably too late already, but I'm going to see if they're retrievable.

And also going to see if you can take out the jump gates.

Probably. We'll be out of touch as soon as we're in the Folds.

I know.

I wanted to say I wish you were here with me.

Oh, thanks, on a suicide mission.

That's not what I—

I know.

I'm glad you're safe, he said. *If something happens—*

It had better not. That's an order.

Yes, ma'am.

He pulled out of the conversation before he could start to babble about being sorry, and loving her, and all the stuff he should have said to her face. He wasn't sure he could keep his mental voice steady, so they hit the Folds without warning.

There's a faint greenish cast to foldspace this time and Ben is almost sure he can smell burning, but he checks the panel by his left hand and there are no warning lights. Okay, that's a win.

He finds the line to Pinch Point's nearest gate. From this side, it doesn't look like a gate. It looks like a potential rift in space and time. He can see a faint haze of silver. He's sure he shouldn't be able to see platinum in such minute concentrations, but he can not only see it, he can smell it. It smells like death.

"Oh, shit."

"What's up?" Chloe asks.

"Can you see that trail of pollution on the screen?"

"By the gate."

"That's the one. Are there any ships on the screens?"

"Negative," Rory says.

"Nothing." Chloe backs him up.

"Then let's close this gate down."

Ben brings *Solar Wind* out of the Folds barely a hundred meters from the active gate.

About two hundred klicks away the remains of Pinch Point Hub float serenely. They won't be so serene from closer up. He can see five ships where he only expected four. From this distance, the battle that's raging looks small.

We see you, Solar Wind, the Telepath from *Howling Wolf* broadcast.

Status, Howling Wolf, Lynda responded.

Monitor battlewagon, Georgia, has taken a hit to her starboard maneuvering thrusters. MB Washington is covering her six. Star of India has brought a plus one to the party via Jump Gate Three.

You want us to take out the gates or join in the scrap? Ben asked.

Gates, please. Stop any more ships from coming through.

There were two parts to a gate, the larger crew quarters, built around the control center, and the smaller impeller unit. The impeller orbited the gently rotating crew quarters, so every few minutes the gate, a hole in spacetime, came around to present a perfect oval of blackness, darker than the deepest black.

"Lynda, hail the crew."

There should have been a crew of six, but no one was replying.

"There's an active beacon," Lynda said. "The crew have abandoned the gate."

"That makes our job easier." Ben made a mental note to check for escape pod beacons as soon as he could. "Tactical one, target the impeller. Tactical two, impeller first, but when the impeller goes, you can blow the crew quarters for good measure."

Caleb didn't waste any time. He hit the impeller with a DEW, a directed energy weapon. There was no dramatic flare or explosion. The unmanned impeller didn't have atmosphere, so there was nothing to burn up, but what was solid and boxy suddenly wasn't there anymore. The debris field was spreading away from them. Jo followed with a DEW to the crew quarters. This time there was a brief flare as residual oxygen consumed itself.

One down. Four to go, Solar Wind,* *Howling Wolf's* Telepath said. *Thanks for that.*

"Incoming," Rory said, an edge to his voice but no panic. Two hard-shell missiles had locked on.

Foldspace, Ben said.

They are back in black, the missiles probably heading for deep space, suddenly bereft of a target. Ben finds the line to another gate. Until they arrive, he doesn't know whether it will be empty or the center of the Nimbus attack.

It's empty.

If they blow it from foldspace, they can't check for crew. Ben finds the line and they pop into realspace.

As before, the gate crew had already abandoned their positions. Ben gave Jo the first shot this time and she destroyed the impeller with one burst, leaving Caleb to blow the crew quarters. The gate was even more remote from the action. They slid into the Folds. The third gate was a repeat performance.

"I hope they're all as easy as that," Caleb says.

Ben winces. He's not superstitious, but it's probably better not to tempt providence. The line to the fourth gate is lit by platinum waste sparkling like tiny ice crystals in a mountain sunrise. Ben follows it and stays in the Folds.

"You shouldn't have spoken," Lynda tells Caleb.

"Shi-it . . ." Rory stares at the screen. "Is that what I think it is?"

The blackness roils around a ship that Ben recognizes from the flight plans the Monitors forwarded. It's one of the missing ships, a freighter carrying soy protein intended for the Pinch Point Station commissary. At least it's not equipped with weapons. There's not much the Nimbus can do with soy except feed them all to death. The ship has, or maybe by now "had," a crew of five.

Two ships are poised to exit foldspace via the gates.

"Chloe, can you—"

"Checking," Chloe says.

She has the master list of all ships ever reported lost in the Folds.

"The far one is the *Princess Elizabeth*, an Earth ship lost in the Folds eleven years ago. She's armed, but not heavily. The near one is the *Cotton*. There's no record of loss in the Folds."

"Oh, take my word for it, she was lost. We practically gave her to the Nimbus. Ilsa Marquat and James Beech on board. I never forget the name of murderers."

"Murderer?" Chloe asks.

"They killed an elderly lady called Ully. She was a class one, long-distance Telepath who worked with Mother Ramona Delgath. She was kidnapped when Garrick eliminated Roxburgh. Roxburgh had her taken care of."

"By Ilsa Marquat and James Beech?" Chloe asks.

Ben nods. "We didn't get much time to examine the ship, but she was one of Roxburgh's, so you can take nasty surprises for granted."

There's another ship caught in some kind of web. Strands of darkness wrap around it like bindweed and two smaller nimbuses hover to either side.

"It's one of the three that filed flight plans shortly before the attack," Chloe says. "Passenger vessel *Dog Rose*, carrying a change of crew for Pinch Point Station. A hundred and twenty on board. Technicians and their families."

"Damn. We can't just leave her and hit the gate," Ben says.

"Can we swing—oh!" Tam says as realization dawns. "You're *that* Benjamin, aren't you? The one the Benjamin Maneuver was named after."

"I doubt I was the first."

"Well, you're the one that stuck."

When Ben had accidentally dragged another ship into foldspace by making the jump when it was too close, he'd learned about dragging ships in and out of the Folds by swinging them through on his coattails. Get close enough, make the jump and you either did, or did not, have the other ship with you when you emerged. There was no second try. It was either total success, or the ship was lost forever. Someone had tried it, unsuccessfully, with one of the fleet ships stranded when Ben stole the jump gate. The result of that was one of the reasons why they were still making their way home the slow way.

The Nimbus moves on. There's a black-wrapped cocoon left behind.

"I guess that answers the question of what happens to them between being taken and reemerging," Ben says. "Some kind of suspended animation."

"The *Dog Rose* hasn't been processed yet." Chloe's knuckles have gone white as she grips the arms of her chair.

"No, it hasn't."

Ben edges the *Solar Wind* toward the Nimbuses. "A dragon told me there were many Nimbuses, but only one mind. I think it's a hive-mind creature. We need to keep it focused on the *Dog Rose* and not on us. Lynda, use mechanical comms to—"

"*Dog Rose*, this is *Solar Wind*, can you answer? Come in, *Dog Rose*." Lynda was ahead of him.

She repeated three times before the comm crackled to life. "*Solar Wind*. If you're still able, get out while the getting is good."

"Stand by, *Dog Rose*," Ben said. "Going to try and take you with us. Can you cause a distraction?"

"We're in chains here—or something very like."

"Try and buck your way out of them, forward and reverse, roll and spin. Be random. Make them work to keep you."

"Keeping us isn't a problem."

"It will be in a minute. Keep it up until you get my word, then close down all your drives."

Ben hopes the jump gate crew have abandoned their station like the others. He's going to have to destroy the gate from the inside before those two ships go through to support the *Star of India*. Potentially six people in the gate and a hundred and twenty on the *Dog Rose*. It's a numbers game, but still one he doesn't like playing.

"Caleb, Jo, on my mark, go for the jump gate with DEWs and with hard shells."

"Right, Boss," Caleb says.

Ben swoops *Solar Wind* from above the Nimbus, skims the edges of it and points his nose at the gate as if he's making a run for it, or perhaps aiming for the two ships waiting to go through. The *Princess Elizabeth* begins evasive action. The *Cotton*, smaller and more nimble, pulls up in a loop from a standing start and rolls out at the top.

"Mark."

The shots fly between the *Elizabeth* and the *Cotton*. The gate disintegrates. Ben activates the forward defense screen, good for maybe only one or two critical uses before it needs recharging, but if ever there's a time, it's now. He flies straight at the debris cloud that marks the remains of the gate. Luckily, most of it is traveling in the same direction, not coming at him and testing the ship's shields to the limit.

There's no up or down in space, but relative to *Solar Wind* the *Cotton* is above, probably priming weapons. Ben flies an evasive helix and pulls around into a barrel roll. The rules for aerial combat were laid down more than five hundred years ago, but in Earth's atmosphere where gravity, thrust-to-weight ratio, wing loading, and turn radius were all considerations. In space, the calculations are different, though the maneuvers might look similar. The objective is exactly the same, however. Shoot the bastard before he can shoot you. The best kills are the ones where your enemy doesn't even see you coming.

No chance of that with the *Cotton*. She's small and turns on a button. Her pilot, James Beech, is good. Ben leads her away from the Nimbus, puts on a burst of speed, pops out of foldspace and back in again, and he's on the *Cotton*'s tail.

"Mark."

The *Cotton* takes a DEW to her main drive and begins to spin.

"Finish her," Ben says. There isn't any alternative.

"Damage report," Lynda asks.

"Deflector screen down to twenty-five percent capacity," Dobson says.

"Can you eject platinum?" Ben asks.

"Yes. But . . ."

"How much do we have to spare and still get home?"

"Theoretically, we can get home on one rod, but if we keep two, we can lose four."

"Can you break up the rods and spray a wide swath?"

"How long have I got?" Dobson asked.

"Yesterday will do fine."

There's a pause. "I can mist it into the water tanks and jettison it. It's going to take a lot of cleaning out when we get home, though."

If we get home, Ben thinks. "Do it." The Nimbus is sensitive to it. It might give us an edge.

He sweeps *Solar Wind* around and dives for the Nimbus. "Ready, Dobson?"

"Ready, Boss."

"Let it go."

As *Solar Wind* flashes past the Nimbus, Dobson releases the platinum. The burst doesn't last long, but it's enough to cover the Nimbus itself and the last dregs of it sprinkle across the two smaller Nimbuses that have the creeper-vine things around *Dog Rose*, which has, true to instructions, been thrashing back and forth against its bonds.

The Nimbus contracts and stiffens.

"*Dog Rose*, desist now," Ben says. The transport stops thrashing around. Ben swings in close, then closer still, activates the jump drive, and swings the *Dog Rose* out of the Folds with the two small Nimbuses still attached.

Ben fancies he can hear an unearthly scream, but whether it's pain, anger, or frustration, he simply doesn't know.

They arrived in realspace exposed to crossfire. The Nimbuses didn't make the transition.

"The shield's down," Dobson said as *Solar Wind* caught the edge of a blow meant for the *Star of India*.

"Jeeze, Benjamin. Look out!"

"Sorry, *Howling Wolf*. We have a bit of a situation here. Can you take *Dog Rose* and keep her safe? One more gate to close down and we need to get to it before the Nimbus does."

"We have her," Washington said. "Thanks, Benjamin."

"Yes, thanks," *Dog Rose*'s comms guy said. "We owe you one."

Ben left Lynda to reply.

One more gate. He wanted to see how this would affect the *Star of India*. The Nimbus had been close. How close did it have to be? Was there any kind of telepathic link between the Nimbus and the crew? Would closing down the immediate jump gates break the connection?

"How are we doing, Rory?" Ben asked.

"Systems are functioning within normal parameters, considering we have no water on board, and we're down to one and a half platinum rods. She'll hold."

"Lynda?"

"Fine, Boss."

"Caleb? Jo?"

"Holding up, Boss," Jo said. "Though my gut is telling me to throw up."

"One more gate, and then you can throw up to your heart's content. You're doing well, all of you." He glanced at Tam and Chloe and nodded.

The last gate loomed before them, but *Star of India* had spotted their direction and had broken away from the *Howling Wolf* to follow. Ben flew evasive patterns, randomly twisting and turning to avoid DEWs, which flared past and were gone.

"Caleb, Jo, fire on the gate as your weapons come to bear. I'll give you as much stability as I can."

Ben saw two hard shells stream away in front of them. The gate boiled away into nothingness.

Something clipped them and sent them spinning, the spin fighting against their own grav. Connected into the ship's systems, Ben felt an almighty blow land inside his head and everything went black.

✦ ✦ ✦

Ben's hurt. Ben's hurt.

It was all Cara could think of as she rushed to the infirmary. She was relieved to find him sitting in a treatment chair while Ronan ran a portable scanner over his skull, then checked his eyes with a light.

She glanced at Ronan. *Is he all right?* she asked on a tight band.

Nothing that a good sleep won't cure, Ronan replied.

Ben looked from one to the other. "Are you two talking about me?"

"What gave you that idea?" Cara asked.

"You're here, for a start."

She frowned. Busted. "What happened?"

"Caught the edge of a DEW. The surge knocked me and Tamara out, but Chloe Durand flew us home. Keeping a pilot unconnected to anything except the straps in her chair is a good idea. Remind me to do it again if we ever have enough pilots to spare."

"Pinch Point?"

He shook his head and then winced. "Everyone lost. The *Star of India* was packing some serious weaponry, but we closed the gates to stop further losses."

"According to Oleg Staple, after you closed the last gate, *Star of India* wallowed for long enough for all three ships to get a lock on her. She's nothing but debris now."

"That's almost a shame," Ben said.

"How do you mean?"

"I thought she might lose her connection to the Nimbus completely. She might have, of course, but we'll never know."

"I guess no one could take that chance."

Ben eased himself out of the treatment chair. "Thanks, Ronan. Is Tamara all right?"

"Same as you. I've sent her to sleep it off. I suggest you do the same."

"I will." He rubbed his eyes.

"Don't stop to check messages on the way or take any calls from Garrick. Doctor's orders."

"Right."

"I mean it."

"Right. I said right, didn't I?"

Ronan looked at Cara who produced a damping pin. "What everyone needs for a good night's sleep."

Ben followed Cara out on to the concourse.

"One message I will give you," she said. "Kai sent to say congratulations you're a great-uncle. Thea has had a boy. Mother and baby both doing well, and they're calling him Robert, though both of them admit he's been Baby Bobby, so far."

Ben grinned. "Baby Bobby Benjamin. I like it. So does that mean Nan's available for negotiations?"

"It does. She says she has a contact on Earth. Do you

suppose that might be your grandfather she's talking about?"

"He's already keeping tabs on Crowder on our behalf. Did you see the way her eyes lit up when she talked about Grandfather?"

Cara smiled. "She still loves him after all these years."

"It's not something you can switch off at will, you know."

Cara did know. She cleared her throat and turned away so he wouldn't see the confusion in her eyes.

Chapter Forty-Eight

MEETING

THE BOARDROOM AT THE TOP OF THE TRUST
Tower was crammed with extra seats around the table.
Tori LeBon had called the meeting. She'd invited representatives from the Monitors, the Five Power Alliance on Earth,
and the Independent Protectorate of Planets. Crowder understood the IPP were more colloquially the Crossways Protectorate, which made his skin crawl.

He felt as though he had a target painted between his
shoulder blades. Bad blood didn't begin to cover it.

This was a civilized political meeting. The representative from Crossways would be a talker, not an assassin. Of
course, there was no reason why he couldn't be both. It
certainly wouldn't be Benjamin, now with all the charges
still to answer and the Monitors crawling all over the
place.

As his elevator reached the top of the tower, he could
see through the clear walls that a number of people were
gathered and milling around with refreshments. A young
African was standing in the lift lobby, handing out expensive looking conference packs with wafer screens and a
number of datacrystals as well as a scribble pad and stylus.

All the board members were here. Though called at
short notice, it had sounded urgent enough to bring Isaac

Whittle back from where he'd been vacationing in the ice fields of Venezuela.

The representatives were all on the far side of the room, talking to Tori Le Bon. Was that good or bad? He recognized the tall man as Commissioner Sebastian Rodriguez of the Monitors, but didn't know the woman who was with him.

Oh, shit! The FPA rep was Malusi Duma. For someone who was supposed to be retiring from politics, he was more active than ever before. Why did Crowder get the impression that whenever Duma had dealings with the Trust it was almost personal? There was a woman standing with her back to him: tall, straight, and gray-haired. She was comfortably close to Duma and their body language said they knew each other well. Maybe the FPA had sent two delegates and the Independent rep wasn't here yet.

He took the pack from the young man and was about to thread his way through the room to see if he could muscle in on Tori LeBon's conversation, when she clapped her hands and invited everyone to take their seats. Isaac Whittle made small talk on the way into the boardroom. When everyone had been seated, Crowder found himself staring into the eyes of Louisa Benjamin, three meters away across the round table.

He'd underestimated her before. The last time was when he'd imprisoned her on Chenon with her great-grandson, Ricky, keeping her sedated so she couldn't use her telepathy and empathy. She'd managed to get away, though she'd had help from Carlinni and Benjamin.

She inclined her head toward him and raised one eyebrow. She might as well have passed him a note saying: I haven't forgotten.

"I'd like to call the meeting to order, please." Tori LeBon was fond of subtle amplification, which added resonance and presence to her voice. "This special general meeting is to discuss developments in foldspace which could have serious consequences for our trade. I'd like to introduce our guests, today: Malusi Duma, outgoing president of Pan Africa, for the next two years adviser to the FPA treasury, and life-member of the second chamber of the Five Power Alliance. Next, we have Miss Louisa Benjamin, representing the Independent Planets Protectorate, which now has a

membership of sixty-five. And here as an independent voice
is Sebastian Rodriguez, Commissioner in Chief for the
Monitors. Commissioner Rodriguez has brought Professor
Eve Moyo, who will begin with a short presentation."

Moyo stood, and all their wafer pads activated.

"My department is responsible for training pilots for the
Monitors and coordinating cutting-edge foldspace research
at the University of Shield City. Some very disturbing developments, borne out by recent events, lead us to believe
we are on the cusp of enormous changes in the way we—
and by that, I mean all spacefaring corporations, planets,
and independent colonies—need to approach long-distance
travel in future. Though the Trust's figures are somewhat
opaque . . ." At this she looked around the table, but received only blank stares, Crowder's among them. He knew
when to keep his face straight.

Moyo glanced down at her own pad. "Though the Trust's
figures are as opaque as every megacorporation's, I've had
a team working to collate ship and colony losses over the
past ten years. The figures are cumulatively astounding,
though I'm sure not entirely a surprise to the people
around this table. The figures are on your wafer screens.
You may be surprised to see that your own losses are not
the greatest."

That did get a reaction, though only a low-level murmur.

"You will, by now, be aware of the loss of the Pinch Point
Hub. I can confirm our own ship, the *Washington*, sent a
small research craft into foldspace and observed what, for
want of a better term, has been called the Nimbus. We believe it's a foldspace entity of unknown size comprised of
many elements connected by a hive-mind. In other words,
it's not something we can simply eliminate, and neither can
we ignore it. We've taught our pilot-Navigators that foldspace visions are an illusion. We've actually known for some
years that they aren't, but since this method has worked on
a practical level until now, we've continued to teach it. With
the discovery of the Nimbus, that has to change. The Nimbus is most dangerous to vessels flying the Folds via the
jump gate system. We've been able to analyze samples recently collected, and we can confirm that platinum discharge is polluting foldspace, especially the frequently used
corridors between major gates and hubs. That pollution is

damaging the Nimbus and is what has triggered this retaliation."

She glanced sideways at Rodriguez, and he jerked his head in a barely perceptible nod.

As Moyo sat, Rodriguez stood.

"The loss of Pinch Point Hub cost the lives of three and a half thousand people—administrative, technical, support workers, and passengers unlucky enough to be in the wrong place at the wrong time. I need hardly tell you that this is a disaster. More to the point, the cumulative losses are unprecedented in the history of humanity in space. It has been suggested, and we concur, that the only way to prevent further losses is to close down the jump gate system."

He halted for the shock wave to penetrate and the exclamations to cease.

"Order, please." LeBon's sound enhancement cut through everything.

Crowder kept his lips pressed together. There was no point in arguing with the delegation. Crossways had a hand in this. They knew closing down the jump gate systems would cripple the Trust, which was exactly what they were after. He'd wait until the next meeting, the one that was bound to come as soon as their visitors had left. He had his own views and would make them known.

Rodriguez handed the meeting over to Louisa Benjamin. "The Independent Planets have considered the alternatives and have agreed to decommission their jump gates. We have begun this process."

"What about essential supplies?" Andile Zikhali asked.

"Those planets not self-sufficient are being supplied by ships retrofitted with jump drives, but measures to become self-sufficient are being explored even now. It is our sincere hope that within a decade, barring natural disasters, no planet will need subsistence supplies. We intend to cut interstellar travel to a minimum because—in case you didn't pick up on the other important thing here—we are polluting foldspace."

Adam Hyde, always too obvious, had the temerity to shrug. Ah, yes. Now Crowder remembered why Miss Benjamin's iron-gray hair and steel-blue eyes had once made him wonder whether she had metal in her bones.

"Mr. Hyde ..." She glowered at him. "I don't need to

remind you about climate change and what kind of a state the Earth was in by the middle of the twenty-first century, do I? We nearly wiped ourselves out before we managed to launch our first colony ships. Pollution is serious. Reversing it is way more difficult than not creating it in the first place."

Malusi Duma cleared his throat and Crowder saw him brush the back of her hand. She sat down and gave him the floor.

"If I may . . ." Duma said. His voice resonated without Tori LeBon's amplification. "When Commissioner Rodriguez first approached the Five Power Alliance about this matter, we were as skeptical as I can see some of you are. That was before the loss of the Pinch Point Hub. We have debated this extensively and the Five Power Alliance supports the closure of the jump gate system, and as an interim measure, the use of jumpships until we can crack the problem of platinum loss in foldspace. I urge you to consider giving over your Research and Development resources to solving the platinum problem, not in isolation, but sharing resources with all the other megacorporations, with the universities, with the independent planets, and with the Five Power Alliance. As a mark of our sincerity, we have made all our ongoing research available to the University of Shield City and through them to any megacorporation or organization that will also do the same."

Ha! Crowder would bet that if the FPA was willing to give away research, it was worthless.

✦ ✦ ✦

Garrick woke from another nightmare, the third in as many hours. He couldn't take much more of this. He'd left Mona in their bed and settled on the couch in his study after the second one so he wouldn't disturb her.

Or was it so she didn't see him pop a second bulb of detanine?

He needed to sleep. There was too much to do and not enough hours in the day to do it.

If he didn't get some sleep, he'd be useless tomorrow. He'd offered to meet with Fynan Sharputra at nine, and to entertain Nathalie Beauvais of House Indigo at lunch. Both of them were exploring ways their respective organizations could put their criminal skills to profitable and legal use on

Crossways. Garrick was willing to overlook a little free-trading off-station, but only if it was sheltered behind a legitimate business.

He lay on the couch, turning first one way and then the other, desperate for sleep, but petrified about what it would bring with it. When he was awake, he knew the nightmares weren't real, but his dream self didn't have that luxury.

"Dammit-all-to-hell!" He swung his legs off the couch, sat up and reached for the bulbs on the table. He popped one and looked at the last one with longing. Well, why not. He needed the sleep.

As the second dose took hold of him, he knew he'd gone too far. He looked at his handpad, trying to discern the time in the gloom. The figures zoomed in and out. He screwed up his eyes and tried to catch them on the rebound. Aww, hell, it wasn't even three, yet he'd taken three shots of detanine in under three hours. No! Four shots. That couldn't be good. He needed to get help. Tell Mona, at least.

He had the weirdest sensation that he was perfectly still, but the room was spinning around him faster and faster. He tried to get his legs underneath him, but suddenly the floor was rushing upward.

Oh, no. Not again, was his only thought before darkness took him.

Someone was shouting at him.

Oww! His cheek stung, but he couldn't do anything about it.

Then his other cheek.

"Garrick!" He heard a voice from a long way away. "Garrick! Wake up!"

He tried to say he was finding it hard to sleep with all that racket going on, but his tongue stuck to the roof of his mouth. Something shook him, and then there was another voice. A light flashed in his eyes, which was odd because he could have sworn they were closed. Then he was floating and wobbling and shaking. Somewhere he could hear a siren and there were pretty lights overhead, flashing through the thin skin of his eyelids as if they were flying past quickly. He tried to lift his arm to point to them, but someone pushed it firmly down by his side.

"Keep still, or you'll pull out the tubes," a voice said.

It sounded like Ronan Wolfe, but he must be dreaming.

Still, it was a better dream than the Nimbus swallowing him whole again.

"Mr. Garrick." The damned voice was insistent. He tried to ignore it. Sleep was what he needed.

"Mr. Garrick!"

"Yeah wha . . ." His voice sounded slurred, even to his own ears, but at least he'd managed a sound.

"We've got him." The voice sounded relieved. "Talk to him. Pull him out of it."

A cool hand touched his arm. "Garrick?"

Mona. He tried to say her name, but he could only manage the vowels and it came out as, "Oh-a."

"Yes, it's me. Can you say my name?"

With the greatest concentration he managed, "Ohna."

"Close enough. Do you know where you are?"

He wanted to say, I'm where you are, but all he managed was "Ooo-ah."

"You're in Blue Seven. The infirmary."

"Ah-ih."

"Infirmary. That's right. I think he understands me, Ronan."

"Keep talking to him. Don't let him slide away again."

"Garrick, Ronan's here and I'm here. Ben and Cara are waiting outside. Can you say something—anything?"

Because there were no hard consonants, he managed a creditable attempt at vocalizing, "Here."

"Yes, here." He felt her lips on his forehead. "Stay with me, Garrick. Make an effort. Don't die on me now."

Die? He wasn't intending to die for goodness sake.

"Not. Dying." He managed to enunciate the two words, complete with their consonants.

He heard her laugh and she kissed him again.

It was a long day. It might even have been two days before Garrick was sitting up in bed, eyes open, talking normally.

"You had us worried." Ben was his first visitor.

"Unnecessary effort. I'm fine." He was less than fine. The need for detanine was already gnawing at his gut. "Who knows about this?"

"No one. That's why Mother Ramona called us rather than Dockside Medical."

"Good." Garrick nodded. "It wouldn't do to . . ."

"Look weak?"

"Quite."

"Then you need to kick the habit for good. You can't go on like this."

"Like what?"

"Detanine."

He opened his mouth to say he wasn't addicted and then shut it again.

"You've had a wake-up call."

So many things tumbled through his mind. He could have died, and then what would happen to his lofty plans for Crossways? What would happen to Mona? She was tougher than she looked. No, she was as tough as she looked, and she looked plenty tough. Would Mona do it without him? Very likely. Did that mean he was surplus to requirements? Very likely. Hell, she wasn't getting away with that. Was he going mad? He wasn't processing this very well. Mona didn't want him dead. Stay with me, Garrick — that's what she'd said, and he'd heard the sincerity in her voice. The . . . love. He'd never expected to find love. It had crept up on him and now it was his. He didn't want to leave Mona.

He realized he was staring into space and managed a single nod in response to Benjamin's statement. He'd had a wake-up call, yes.

"Let Ronan help," Ben said.

"Cold turkey?"

"I believe there are other alternatives."

"Are you suggesting Amfital? That's the most addictive thing out there. It encourages you to sleep to death."

"But it clears everything else out of your system while it's doing it. In the right quantity, under medical supervision . . . Talk to Ronan."

Half an hour later, Ben had left and Ronan was standing by his bedside.

"Amfital?"

Garrick watched Ronan carefully, trying to assess his reaction to the suggestion.

"It's possible," Ronan said. "Though it may cure one addiction only to replace it with another."

"It's faster than cold turkey, though, right?"

"It'll clear your system, but it won't cure the psychological dependence. That's yours to work through."

Garrick nodded. "Let's do it."

✦ ✦ ✦

Ben sought out Cara. She was sitting on a bench in the garden staring at nothing in particular. She looked up when she saw him approaching, but didn't immediately leave. He took that as almost an invitation and sat on the far end of the bench. No touching.

"How's Garrick?" she asked.

"I think he's going to be all right. He's opted for Amfital, and Ronan's put him under now."

Cara shuddered. "I remember what it's like."

"It's three years ago."

"You don't forget. I wouldn't dare do it again. Once could easily form a habit if you let it. Will Garrick manage it successfully?"

"I'd like to think Garrick's learned his lesson from the detanine."

"I hope you're right."

"Any news from Nan yet?" he asked.

She shook her head. "Nothing positive. Neither the Trust nor Alphacorp nor Rodontee nor Ramsay-Shorre will commit without further talks. Eastin-Heigle is taking the threat seriously and has closed, but not destroyed the jump gates at all of its Mirrimar stations."

"Mirrimar-14. Takes me back." He smiled.

It was where they had met. So much had happened since then.

"Unwise sex with a stranger. I remember."

"We weren't strangers for long."

"No." Her voice was quiet. Reflective.

"We could—"

"No."

He took a deep breath. "Are we over?"

"I don't know. I thought I knew you."

"You do. This is me. What you see is what you get." He held his hands up, palms forward.

"Is it? We were talking about having children together."

"I'd like that. You know I would."

"Would you use our child like you used Gen's?"

In the same situation, would he? He wanted to say no, but he owed her the truth. He didn't know, so he couldn't answer.

She squeezed her lips together into a thin line. "Always the greater good, no matter what you have to sacrifice — or who."

"No, it's —" He stopped. Was she right? What would he pay to save lives? His own life? Yes, he'd put that on the line more than once, and not always for friends or even people he knew. Always working for the greater good.

He let his arms drop. Maybe he was better off on his own.

She went that peculiar kind of still which happened when she had someone in her head with a message she wasn't expecting.

"What is it?" Ben asked.

"Ronan would like us both to go and see Kitty."

"Kitty? I thought he was dealing with Garrick. What's the matter now?"

"Let's find out."

She stood up, and he fell into step beside her, walking without touching, their steps aligned.

"Garrick?" Ben said on seeing Ronan.

"He's deeply asleep, locked into the Amfital. No need to worry about him for at least twenty-four hours. In the meantime, there's Kitty."

"There's some change?"

"Change, but I'm not sure it's progress. At this rate, we're going to need a padded cell."

He led them through to Kitty's room, still divided by the glass-steel wall. Syke was on this side of it, Kitty on the other. The glass was smeared with blood and Kitty's fists were bruised and her knuckles bleeding. She was sitting on the floor, face pressed against the glass, hospital softsuit torn at the shoulder and hanging off to expose one breast.

Syke was as pale as Ben had ever seen him. "She threw herself at me — sexually, I mean. Not that I could do anything with this partition in the way. Not that I would. She's not herself."

Kitty looked up and focused on Syke as if there was no one else in the room. "Come on, Syke, you know you want me. Let me out of here and I'm yours. Anywhere, any way you want me. Unlock this cage, and we'll go all night. All day and all night if you can keep it up."

Cara knelt so her face was on a level with Kitty's. "He can't let you out, Kitty. You tried to hurt people."

"I did?"

"You did."

Kitty touched her raw knuckles to the glass and let the blood trickle down. "I thought he liked me."

"He does. He likes you a lot. He likes you so much that he doesn't want to see you hurt yourself, or hurt anyone else." She glanced up at Syke. "Isn't that so, Arran?"

Syke dropped to his knees beside Cara. "Yes, that's it. I don't want to see you get hurt. I lost you once and you've come back. I want to keep you safe."

❖ ❖ ❖

Ronan cleared his throat. "I wondered. I know it's a big ask, Cara, but I think you might be able to help me to break through to Kitty. You know about deep regression, and you have . . ." He hesitated. "You have unique skills."

"You're not suggesting I crack open her mind, are you?" Cara stiffened. "You know I said I'd never use it like that."

Yet she had, when the need arose. Had she enjoyed it, or did it still make her squirm?

"Not alone," Ronan said. "We could do it together. I'll supply the direction. You supply the push."

"You don't know what you're asking."

"I think I do."

"Ronan, if she says no, she means no," Ben said quietly.

Cara glanced at Ben. Who was he to say she shouldn't do it? She took a deep breath. She'd show Ben Benjamin what she could and couldn't do. "All right, Ronan. What do you want me to do?"

"Join with me. Follow my lead."

She licked her lips and nodded.

Ronan had a sure mind touch. He was an Empath like her and they'd come through many trials together. He'd been the one who helped her to unlock her own hidden memories when she'd escaped from Ari van Blaiden and Donida McLellan. He was a friend. She'd often wondered whether he could have been more than a friend if it hadn't been for the fact that he was certifiably gay and settled with his partner, Jon, and, of course, she'd met Ben first. Well, the jury was still out on that relationship.

Being linked to Ronan amplified her own natural Empathy. She felt Arran Syke's concern for Kitty rolling off him in waves. And Ben—a shock ran through her—Ben was all concern for her. Maybe their relationship wasn't irretrievable if she didn't want it to be.

And there was Kitty: miserable, conflicted, puzzled, and very frightened.

All right? Ronan asked her.

So far, so good.

She felt Ronan begin to soothe Kitty in a way that was gentle and loving, but not at all sexual. Kitty's thoughts were all on the surface. She was Kitty Keely, Alphacorp spy. No that's what she had been.

Ronan pushed the first layer aside gently.

She was Kitty Keely, beginning to feel at home in the Free Company.

Ronan peeled another layer away.

She was Kitty Keely in mourning for Wes Orton, her lover, killed doing his duty, guarding Bay 22. It was a relationship cruelly ended before it had begun.

That layer buckled, showing what was underneath.

She was Kitty Keely, and her mom was so sick. She needed specialist treatment, expensive specialist treatment. Miraculously, Alphacorp offered to pay for the private clinic, but Kitty had to earn the bounty. She had to assimilate into the free Company on Crossways. How hard could it be?

Below that layer was a door.

Are you still all right? Ronan asked.

You want that door opening?

That's the idea.

Right.

It was as if Ronan leaned against the barrier, pressing but not hard enough to move it.

She felt as though she was putting her shoulder to it and pushing. Still no movement. She tried again.

It won't work like this, Ronan. How desperately do you want to get through?

We need to know what happened to her.

Stand back.

Cara studied the door for a while. Then, without warning, she sent out a thought like a battering ram and down it went.

A black oily cloud billowed out from the door and Cara felt a deep murderous rage. She threw herself backward and snapped the connection closed, feeling strong arms around her. She bent over, retching.

Chapter Forty-Nine

CHENON

CARA FELT LIKE A RAG DOLL IN BEN'S ARMS.
"It's over now. You did it. It's all right."

He blessed Kitty if this was what it took to get Cara into his arms. But, of course, it was only temporary. She shuddered and took her own weight, standing with barely a wobble.

She swallowed hard and nodded. "Thank you."

So formal.

"You're welcome."

Cara turned to look at Kitty, her expression revealing nothing but pity.

Kitty was in tears, crouched on the floor. She stared at her own bloodied knuckles and then looked up to where Syke knelt against the glass.

"I'm not safe while I'm here. I want to go home."

"Back to your mother?" Syke asked.

She looked at him and frowned. "Of course not. Foldspace. I want to go back to foldspace before I kill someone. Before I kill everyone."

"What would happen if we let her?" Ben asked. "Do you think the Nimbus would come for her? It started to develop in *Solar Wind*, in sick bay where she and Cho were. Coincidence, or was it trying to reclaim its own?"

Ben crouched down with Cara and Syke. "Kitty, the Nimbus, the black cloud. Do you know what it is?"

"Nimbus." A small half smile played across her face. "That's a holy name. Not dark at all. I want to go back."

"Can you understand it? Does it speak to you? Can you speak to it?"

"It doesn't speak. It simply is."

"Does it understand?"

"It knows what I know. What we all know."

"Do you mean the people it's taken?"

"Taken?" She looked down at her knuckles. "It's set us free. Let me go back. Send me home. You can all come, too."

"We like it here," Ben said. "Is it angry with us?"

"Of course not."

"Why is it sending people to kill us?"

She frowned. "Because it has to."

"What if it didn't have to?"

She shrugged.

◆ ◆ ◆

Hooked into eighteen channels, Cara was the first to pick up the news.

There's an attack on Chenon! She broadcast it to the whole of the Free Company.

She'd not spent much time there; just a few months when she'd first joined Ben and the Trust, and had been preparing for the Olyanda mission. And then again when she'd gone back to rescue Nan and Ricky from Crowder. It wasn't a planet that was dear to her heart, but many of the Free Company regarded it as home, or at least as a home-away-from-home. A few of them still had families there—parents, siblings.

How the—

Ben came racing into the office and flung open the cubicle door. "Details."

"Two battleships came through Chenon's gates about six hours ago. They destroyed the defense grid on the first moon, and captured three jump gates. Since then, they've been bringing troop ships through. They've bombed Arkhad City from the air, taken the main spaceport, and their troops are landing. They're not all professional soldiers, but they've got the numbers."

A small knot of people waited in the outer office, all anxious to know what was happening. Some wanted to know if Cara could get messages through to their families. They'd stayed out of contact so as not to involve loved ones in the Free Company by association, but this was different.

I don't know more than that, Cara broadcast. *More as I find out.*

The rest of the morning saw the members of the Free Company mainly milling about in the canteen waiting for news, or simply waiting.

Cara drew together all the Telepaths capable of long-range comms, either solo or in pairs, and set them listening to the news channels on the tel-net. She contacted Saedi on Jamundi, and together they took turns to tie into the official and unofficial channels.

A force of fifty thousand Nimbus ground troops had ringed Arkhad City and were slaughtering anyone escaping the bombed-out remains. Chenon's own forces were countering. The Trust had sent a task force, much smaller in numbers, but with high-tech weaponry.

"What can we do?" Cara forgot herself and gripped Ben's hand as more information came in. Images would take a little longer, pinged through from gate to gate in information packets.

"We're two hundred against fifty thousand," he said bleakly. "We can't make much of a difference to the ground assault. Contact Rodriguez."

Benjamin, you've heard, Rodriguez said.

Yes. At least I've heard what's on the regular channels. Is there anything else I should know?

Arkhad City's under siege, and the Trust compound there is gone. As near gone as we can work out, anyway. It looks like the Nimbus has been learning battle tactics from some of the captured troops.

What about the south, Russolta?

We're trying to evacuate people from there. You know it?

I was born there.

Relatives?

We brought out my brother and his two sons last year. What can we do to help?

Unless you've an army tucked up your sleeve . . .

We can help with the evacuation. Are their troops

effective? The Nimbus used ordinary citizens on Butterstone and Jamundi.

They have some military types and, dammit, some Monitors, so they've learned a trick or two. Not sure how that happened, perhaps the hive-mind extends to their human avatars. The troops aren't all fully equipped, but even the civilians are behaving like soldiers. What one knows, all know.

I get it. Effective.

Effective enough. We're putting more troops on the ground now to supplement the Trust's forces. A joint effort between the megacorps, ourselves, and the Five Power Alliance.

You'll have every ship we can field for the evacuation.

Dunkirk.

You know your Earth history.

It was the first thing your grandmother said when we decided to evacuate Russolta.

Ben let the conversation drop.

"We're going to Chenon, I take it," Cara said.

"You don't have to come."

"Yes, I do."

Garrick arrived at Blue Seven with Mother Ramona, trailing a dozen of Syke's guards.

"It's not your problem," Ben said when Garrick offered to help. "The numbers are against us."

"It's not about numbers."

"Okay. Lend me every jumpship you've got."

"Yes, take them."

"And the ark."

Too big for everyday use, the ark, which had carried thirty thousand settlers racked in cryo pods could probably take ten thousand individuals crammed together in her hold.

"Of course."

"We'll need shuttles and pilots to fly them. It will leave Crossways light on pilots and vulnerable."

"We'll risk it. We're asking big things of the megacorps. Time to show we're public spirited as well."

Cara fielded messages and made sure everyone knew what their job was and where they were going.

For the evacuation, Ben put Jake in charge of the ark, complete with shuttles in her hold. He put Chloe Durand in charge of the *Bellatkin*.

Solar Wind was last to leave, but would certainly not be the last to arrive. Cara slid into the comms chair, Gwala and Hilde took the two tactical positions, Dobson in engineering, and Wenna, out from behind her desk, at the systems station. It felt like old times. They didn't have a copilot. Every available pilot had a ship of their own.

Cara glanced at Ben. There he was again, doing whatever he could for the greatest good.

❖ ❖ ❖

Evacuating people who didn't want to be evacuated, or perhaps hadn't even grasped the need for it, wasn't like taking a disciplined army off a beach. Civilians flapped. They wanted to bring their dogs, their mother's antique clock, their prize bull, a bag of books, a picnic basket. Or maybe Auntie was in town and they couldn't leave without her. The head of Constantine's School for young ladies couldn't possibly let his charges go without a note from a parent.

Strong words were said.

It proved that even the most settled of the inner system planets should have regular drills about what to do if and when invaders descended from space.

Ben could cram ninety in a space designed for thirty if he used the hold space and shoved twenty people in the mess and another ten in the corridors.

The ark stood by to receive refugees with every available shuttle doing trip after trip to and from the surface.

Whoever had initiated the evacuation had laid down a few ground rules. *Bring only food and water you can carry on your person or in a small bag, maybe a blanket if you can wrap it around yourself, but no picnic baskets, no mattresses, no clocks, no books, and certainly no prize bulls.* Ben made an exception for dogs small enough to be carried and then wished he hadn't as a determined teenage girl struggled under the weight of a mastiff with drooling jowls and a mean look in its eye.

They'd set up access tubes to transfer passengers to the ark's hold. These were gravity-free with handholds. Most of the passengers had never been in space before. Some threw up as soon as their feet lifted from the deck; others grasped the idea quickly and pulled their fellows along. The mastiff yowled like a baby.

Ronan administered antiemetics and sedatives to those who needed them, but stocks weren't bottomless, so mostly he smiled and told the unfortunates they'd be fine.

Cara tuned into the main Chenon news channel and also listened out for updates and instructions from Rodriguez, now installed on the *Worcester*, the Monitors' flagship. A hurried consultation had put Admiral Hawker, head of the FPA's fleet, in charge of the whole operation. Word filtered back that the Nimbus' strategy was remarkably like Admiral Henney's, so the Nimbus either still had the grand old man or had learned from him.

Ben hoped someone had the big picture, because he certainly didn't. All he could do was concentrate on getting as many people as possible out of the vulnerable area around Corrigar Spaceport. *Solar Wind* was only one tiny part of a huge effort. For half a day they ferried confused, frightened people from the spaceport in Russolta to the belly of the ark. Then Rodriguez warned them the Nimbus army was on the move and the battleships were closing fast. Ben knew it would be his last trip, so he crammed in an extra ten people into the suit room and onto the flight deck, took off vertically, and disgorged another hundred into the ark's hold.

"I can be more use on the ark than here," Ronan said.

"Good luck." Ben slapped him on the shoulder as he launched into the tube to follow the last of the passengers across.

"Ask Rodriguez if we have time for another load," Ben said. "There will still be people on isolated farms. If this had happened when Rion was still on the farm, he wouldn't have been able to get to Russolta in time."

"But he would have known the country well enough to find somewhere to hunker down," Cara said.

As the last access tube detached, thankfully scoured clean by exposure to space, Jake took charge of the ark and pulled away.

Benjamin, we've had a request from the Trust, Rodriguez said via his telepath. *There's an evacuation request from an island called Norro.*

I know it, Ben said, a knot in his stomach. *Crowder's ex-wife.*

That's right?

Did he ask for me?

I believe he said you'd know the north end of the island.

Oh, yes. Ben's jaw tightened and he looked at Cara.
"Don't do it," she said.

Ben huffed out a breath. "Damn Crowder. He knows I
wouldn't leave his family behind no matter what I think of
him."

How long have we got?

*It's hard to tell. Norro isn't on the direct flightpath from
Arkhad City to Corrigar. You might be lucky.*

Yeah, right. *Okay, Rodriguez. If the island isn't in flames
already, we'll see what we can do.*

❖ ❖ ❖

Crowder finished the call to Rodriguez and smiled to himself. He knew Ben would take the bait. If anyone could
snatch Agnetha Sigurdsdottir from the jaws of death, it was
Benjamin. Success wouldn't hurt Crowder's standing with
his daughters. Failure would at least show he'd tried, and
had the added advantage that this Nimbus army would rid
him of Benjamin and Carlinni permanently.

Thank goodness his daughters had moved off Chenon.
He'd been devastated at the time, but now all he felt was
relief.

As for the rest of planet, it was a travesty, a tragedy. He
marshaled the words he'd need for the press interviews. He
would be called upon; after all, he'd lived on Chenon. Could
he manage that catch in his voice when he talked about all
his friends? The press didn't need to know he'd never made
friends.

Aggie had always been the one for making friends. He'd
coasted behind her social skills, too intent on his job. If he'd
missed her for anything after she left him, it was for the
impeccable way she kept his social diary. He sighed. That
and the sex, of course.

This was not the time to think about sex.

Everybody he'd worked with at Colony Ops was probably dead already. The Trust compound had been one of the
first targets. Lawrence Archer, who had been acting head of
department since Crowder moved to Earth, had died in the
first wave. He was no great loss. However, if the enemy fleet
had targeted the servers on both moons, they might have

destroyed colony records, which would be much more difficult to replace than personnel.

Crowder examined his feelings and found he didn't have any. Oh, it was a tragedy and all that, but Chenon didn't touch him on a personal level. Stefan had family, though. He must remember to be solicitous to the young man. His neural reconditioning hadn't stripped him of his feelings toward his family. It had obviously been an excellent job. An operative with a very light touch had left Stefan appearing absolutely normal. Was it worth reminding the boy that he would have died alongside his parents and siblings had Crowder not brought him to Earth?

Maybe if the Trust had closed their three jump gates, the Chenon attack wouldn't have happened. Maybe. Crowder wasn't entirely convinced that he believed the spiel Eve Moyo had given them. Benjamin was behind all this, he was sure—Benjamin, Crossways, and those independent planets, some of which had once been profitable colonies for the Trust.

Close the jump gates? Not likely. It would have to be the last possible choice from a series of bad ones. Much as he hated to admit it, solving the platinum problem once and for all was the best solution all round. He'd already suggested as much to Yolanda Chang. He knew Chang had been closeted with Tori LeBon all day yesterday, and they'd put several calls through to Eve Moyo.

It was hardly surprising everyone was focused on Chenon and the Nimbus today. They'd all be talking about repelling the attack and disaster relief. He could go and be solicitous, or he could think outside the rather small box everyone else's mind was trapped in right now.

He called up the distribution of Trust resources at any one time. It showed which ships were where. He needed a small fleet of decently armed ships. The Trust sometimes worked with independent contractors. Yes, all right, mercenaries. With the right crew, he should be able to take what he wanted from Crossways via the backdoor while everyone else was focusing on the wrong thing.

"Stefan!"

There was no answer. Oh, Damn. He'd already forgotten his secretary was with everyone else up on the ground floor, watching the big screens and waiting for news as it unfolded.

He activated his desk pad, a little slow because he was too used to having someone do this for him. Pav Danniri had moved to Earth after she left him high and dry on Chenon. She'd been a good bodyguard; a better tactical thinker than her brother Tom, who'd managed to get himself killed by Benjamin in a fair fight. Crowder had directed Pav's thirst for revenge, until she'd discovered for herself that Ben hadn't actually murdered Tom in cold blood. That little misjudgment on Crowder's part had been the end of a good working relationship, but he'd kept tabs on her. She'd gone independent; she might be looking for some work.

Ah, there she was.

Crowder thumbed the index.

"Well, well, Mr. Crowder," Pav answered his call on her handpad. "Just one moment, please." He could see as her hand moved. She'd been driving. She set the groundcar to auto and pushed her seat back to stretch out her legs.

"I have a job for you, Pav."

"I don't work for you anymore."

"I thought you might if the price was right."

"That depends. I'm not going after Benjamin again."

"That's not the job. In fact, since he's on Chenon, that might have been taken care of by now."

"Yeah, Chenon. Bad break. This call's coming from Earth, though, so you're obviously not on Chenon anymore."

"Luckily, no."

"So what's the job?"

"Crossways."

"I told you I'm not going after Benjamin. That goes for his crew, too. The Free Company, or whatever they're calling themselves now."

"That's the beauty of it. They're all on Chenon, or in orbit around it. Crossways should be wide open."

"Should be."

He shrugged. "I'll find you a few battleships as a distraction, and you can slip in quietly while everyone's concentrating on a bigger threat. There's something I need you to get for me. I'll be sending a tech team with you. Retrieval specialists. All you have to do is get them to the right place. They'll do the rest."

She snorted and said something Crowder didn't quite catch, but then she flashed up a series of numbers. "My bank account," she said. "Make the transfer."

"I take it that's a yes, then?"

A few calls later, Crowder had everything in place without worrying anyone else about the details. He'd found Jack Damary, who liked to think of himself as an admiral, but in reality was a man who had built a mercenary fleet, and by some instinct for when and where to deploy, had managed to keep most of it intact. Crowder had hired Damary before, a long time ago, for a job on Hera-3 which hadn't gone entirely to plan, but that hadn't been Damary's fault. If Ari van Blaiden hadn't jumped the gun . . .

He sat back, anticipating the congratulations when he delivered the jump drive plans to the Trust. Garrick was overdue—long overdue—for some payback. The blueprints were the main objective. Blowing a hole in Crossways would be a bonus, and he had the perfect man for that, someone he'd been cultivating against the day he could be used to good effect.

Crowder had two more calls to make. He didn't expect a response, but he'd leave messages anyway. His daughters hadn't spoken to him since he'd accidentally led Benjamin to the island of Norro where their mother was living. He'd tried to tell them it hadn't been deliberate, but they'd not chosen to believe him.

Ingrid first. It was no surprise when she didn't take his call, but he left a message anyway to say he'd requested extra assistance to get their mother airlifted off Norro before the Nimbus army arrived.

Then Tamsin. Again, he left a message in the hope that she would get back to him, or at least understand he'd done everything he could.

Almost immediately his comm beeped.

His daughter's tear-streaked face appeared on his screen.

"Inga, sweetheart, it's so good to see you again." And it was, even though she'd obviously been weeping for her mother. Her eyes were heavy and red-rimmed, her lovely face blotchy. That was understandable. Aggie could be the bitch from hell to him, but never as far as her daughters were concerned.

"Poppa." She hadn't called him that since she'd hit her teen years. "Poppa, it's Tamsin."

"I left her a message. I've sent someone for your mother." He needn't tell either of them it was Benjamin.

"She won't get it, Poppa. She's taken Nini to visit Mom. That's what I mean. She's on Chenon."

Crowder felt as if he'd been doused in ice water. Sending Benjamin after Aggie on Norro had been win-win, whichever way it had worked out, but now that had changed. His daughter and granddaughter . . . Oh, gods! Tamsin and little Nini. He should have asked for a full troop of special forces. Instead, he'd sent his worst enemy to rescue all that was precious to him.

Chapter Fifty

NORRO

"**S**TATUS?" BEN SWEPT *SOLAR WIND* LOW OVER the Calman Sea toward the island of Norro. Last time they'd been here, Crowder had almost killed Cara and Ben had fired three anesthetic darts into Crowder. They should have killed him. Cara had been out of it, but she knew the story.

She checked the relative positions of the invaders and the resistance. The ships were decimating the Nimbus fleet, but every time they shot one down, another two appeared.

"They're defending the gates," she told Ben. "Keeping them open. Pouring more ships through and landing ground forces. It's a ragtag army, but there are so many of them, and they're throwing everything they've got at the assault. It doesn't matter how many they lose, they keep right on coming."

Ben swore. He'd warned them, yet they'd done nothing. Cara could almost see steam coming out of his ears he was so angry.

She knew how he felt—literally. Being an Empath meant she felt it all, the anger, the frustration. Ben was usually good at keeping his feelings to himself, but there was a limit and he'd reached it.

Cara's screen beeped. She checked the message. "The Nimbus has landed a secondary force at the Corrigar Spaceport."

Ben's eyes narrowed. "Did they get all the transports away in time?"

"Yes, but they didn't get all the refugees onto the transports, and the last ship was hit by the incoming enemy fleet. No survivors."

He swore again. "What about Norro?"

"Still clear. Maybe it's too small for them to bother with."

He shook his head. "If they make a push for Ganya, Norro will be in their way. They don't even need to land forces; a couple of well-placed bombs will do the trick, or maybe they have more stocks of Agent Topax or something equally deadly."

"There's a ship ahead," Wenna said. "It looks like a Monitor vessel, but the Nimbus has some of them, too."

"Hail it, Cara," Ben said.

She did. "It's Jessop." She felt the rush of relief right down to her toes.

"Put it on speaker." Ben flipped his throat mic into position.

"Jess?"

"I've got your six, Benjamin. I'll take the south of the island. You take the north. There's a surge of Nimbus ships heading this way."

"How long have we got?"

"Twenty minutes, tops."

"You can't evacuate half an island in twenty minutes," Cara said.

"I can try."

Agnetha Sugurdsdottir had her home in a large walled compound on the northern tip of Norro. Cara remembered it from last year, a cliff-top approach, a high wall, and within it an elegant house and sculpted gardens. They'd rebuilt the wall since last year's confrontation.

"No time to knock first," Ben said and landed *Solar Wind* inside the wall.

As soon as they touched down, Cara activated external speakers.

"Agnetha Sugurdsdottir, we're your evacuation transport.

Please make your way to the hatch and board in an orderly manner."

Agnetha Sigurdsdottir, a smart woman in her mid-fifties, appeared on the terrace carrying a high-powered rifle and flanked by what must be her new security team. They were probably putting a dent in the Trust's budget. Cara didn't blame her after what had happened last year. *Solar Wind* was the last ship she'd want to see.

"We can look after ourselves," she yelled, waving her arms in the universal signal for go-away-move-along.

"What the hell does she think she's doing?" Ben leaped out of the nav chair. "Does she know what's heading her way?"

"Maybe not entirely," Cara said. "No one wants the population so panicked they can't think straight."

Ben hit the access tube from the flight deck and Cara slid down after him. The hatch was already open and the ramp extended.

"Let me go first," Cara said. "She'll shoot you as soon as she recognizes you. Maybe that's what Crowder intended."

"Whatever he intended, he knew I wouldn't leave her behind."

"Yeah, he knows your fatal flaw—White Knight Syndrome."

"So I'm not letting you go first."

"We'll go together." Cara grabbed his hand and stepped onto the ramp. "Agnetha—Mrs. Crowder. Can we talk?" she yelled. "Close up? Civilized? All this shouting's bad for your throat." She coughed. "And mine," she said softly. "Charm offensive, Ben."

"Right. Hard when she's pointing a gun at your belly. At least, I think it's my belly, but her aim's a little low for comfort."

The gun stayed steady, and Agnetha and her crew didn't step out from the shelter of the porch.

"I thought it was you," Agnetha said.

"I think your ex is hoping you'll kill me," Ben said. "He's tried a couple of times, but I'm not all that easy to get rid of."

"My team is quite proficient," she said. "I upgraded since our last encounter."

"I apologize for the last intrusion. We used Norro as a rendezvous because I figured it was the last place Crowder would be. He obviously had the same idea. Unfortunate."

"Is that all you thought it was?"

"We haven't time to argue, Mrs. Crowder," Cara said.

"Don't call me that."

"I'll call you the Queen of Heaven if you'll move yourself and your staff to the safety of the *Solar Wind*," Ben said.

"Young man, there's no need to be ru—"

"There's every need. Within ten minutes this island's going to be overrun, probably bombed from the air."

"Make that five minutes." Cara picked up a signal from Wenna. "Incoming."

"Momma, we should go. I'll get Nini." A young woman stepped forward from behind Agnetha. Cara hadn't taken much notice of her, but now she looked, she could see the echoes of Crowder in the girl's face. This must be one of his daughters.

"Just bring what you have with you," Ben snapped.

The young woman looked at him, eyes wide. "Nini's my daughter. She's asleep in the house."

"Oh, shit!" Ben said. "Cara, get them all aboard. You—" He turned to the woman. "Let's get the child. Run."

He headed for the house with the young woman.

"Quick, to the *Solar Wind*!" Cara waved Agnetha, her guards and all household staff forward. She ran after them, chivvying the slowest and grabbing Agnetha by the arm and dragging her along when she slowed to look behind her.

"Ben will get your granddaughter," Cara said. "Just get into the ship and strap in for takeoff."

✦ ✦ ✦

Why did they always have to tuck children away in the quiet corners of big houses? Ben ran after the young woman, who must be Tamsin Crowder, as she wove her way through corridors and up staircases. He remembered Crowder's delight at the birth of his first grandchild, Nini. It had to be at least six years ago.

"Up there." Tamsin launched herself up another stair to a bedroom at the top.

"Nini, sweetheart, wake up." Tamsin sat on the edge of the bed and gently touched the little girl's arm.

The child woke, took one look at Ben, and started to wail.

"We have to go, now," Tamsin said.

"Don't want to go. Want to stay with Grandma."

"Grandma's going, too. Hurry we have to catch up."

Instead of instilling a sense of urgency, Tamsin's agitation transferred itself and Ben could see a tantrum developing.

Three minutes, Ben, Cara said.

Tamsin swept Nini out of the bed, but the child, at six was too big for her to carry, especially while wriggling and screaming.

"Bring a blanket," Ben said, and lifted the kicking child from her mother's arms. "We go now."

He ran out of the door and down the stairs, trusting that Tamsin wouldn't let him out of her sight as long as he had her daughter. He retraced the route to the ground floor and out through the garden doors at a flat run, Nini still screaming in his left ear.

One minute.

"We should lock up," Tamsin said.

"Not unless you want to die right here." Ben half-turned, grabbed Tamsin's hand and dragged her toward *Solar Wind*.

An ominous whistling in the air, high-pitched but on a descending scale was exactly what Ben didn't want to hear. He let go of the mother and put his hand over the back of the child's head, drawing her closer to protect her as much as possible with his body.

A huge whump, a missile strike from the south end of the island, shook the ground. Ben angled himself to be between the child and the blast, felt the heat, and saw a column of smoke and flames rise to their left. The only good thing was that it shocked Nini out of the screams, though if ever there was a time to yell, it was now.

He could hear the *Solar Wind*'s drive rising in pitch and see Cara standing in the open hatch. She didn't need to urge him onward. His legs pumped, his muscles ached. And he knew he was leaving Tamsin behind.

One thing at a time. Get the child to safety.

He almost threw Nini up the ramp to Cara, then turned to see Tamsin about twenty paces behind. Ten paces to grab her hand as she pounded toward him, and ten more paces to drag her to the ramp which began to retract as they made a leap for it.

Another descending whistle.

Ben shoved Tamsin through the hatch. A whump behind

him knocked him forward. The house disappeared in a cloud of ash and debris and he felt as if someone had hit him from behind with a club. For a moment, his brain didn't register that he was on the floor, his cheek on the metal grill. The ramp retracted and the hatch closed. A weight pressed him into the deck as *Solar Wind* rose vertically. Who the hell was flying the bus?

Cara had Tamsin and Nini under control, and had wisely sat them down before they fell down and was holding onto both of them.

Ben struggled to his knees and then his feet and lunged for the access tube to the bridge. Wenna was in the pilot's chair, hands steady on the controls, face a mask of concentration. As he lurched forward, she scooted out of the way.

"I didn't know you could fly," he said.

"I can't," she said. "I was banking on you getting here before I needed to do anything except hit the lift controls."

Ben changed *Solar Wind*'s incline. "You just won a course of flying lessons if we manage to get out of this."

"Make sure we do. I want to live to collect."

"Incoming," Gwala shouted from tactical.

Ben glanced at the screen. They were going to have to punch a hole through the oncoming Nimbus fleet.

"Hilde, Gwala, hit them with everything we've got."

He highlighted coordinates, and the two mercs fired a continuous stream. A small ship flamed and went down, leaving a gap.

"Well done. Again."

They aimed at the cruiser that had targeted them. Hilde's shot damaged its engines, and Gwala's shot smashed its forward weapons array.

A third ship took a hit and skewed out of place.

You're welcome, Jessop said from the *Carylan*. *Let's get out of here.*

Ben aimed *Solar Wind*'s nose at the gap and they punched through. None of the Nimbus fleet broke away to follow them.

❖ ❖ ❖

"Hold on," Cara said to Tamsin and Nini. "Going to be a rocky ride." She felt the whole ship reverberate as the torpedoes fired. "Are you hurt?"

Tamsin stared, wild eyed, then started to laugh. "I wanted to take time to lock the doors. We would have been so—" She began to sniffle. "So dead." She pulled Nini toward her and held on to the child as if she were going to evaporate.

Cara heard firing, but didn't like to say they weren't safe yet.

Gravity pushed them down and down. There was a blip as they reached the outer atmosphere and artificial gravity cut in. She hoped they'd cut through the invading fleet. She risked standing.

"Everyone's in there." She pointed Tamsin to the mess. "Go and tell your mother you're all right. Find a seat. Get settled."

"Where are we going?"

"The refugees from Russolta are being sent to Earth, at least for the time being."

"Dad's on Earth."

"Yes."

"He said Mom was never in any danger from Ben Benjamin. He was right, wasn't he?"

"Mostly. Sometimes good people get hurt, but Ben would never have hurt your mom on purpose." She resisted saying: unlike your dad, but Tamsin was ahead of her.

"My dad. Those things he's supposed to have done . . ."

"All true, I'm afraid. All for platinum."

"But he's not a greedy man."

"It wasn't for himself, it was for the Trust. I don't know if that makes it better or worse. Do you?"

Tamsin shook her head. "He's always wanted a seat on the board. Said it was his right. Our ancestor, you see, Anne DiDoren, ran the Trust for fifty years. At least, that's what he always said, but I checked our family history. I wanted to know where the connection was . . ." She sniffed and wiped her nose on the back of her hand. "I couldn't find anything in the records. Why would Dad say we're related to Anne DiDoren if it's a lie? He always said it like he believed it. Like he had a right to be chairman of the board because of it. I think . . ." Her voice dropped to a whisper. "Mom says he's out of control, and I think she might be right."

"Tammy?" Agnetha opened the mess door and leaned against the frame. "Nini? I was so scared."

"We're all right, Mum. Ben Benjamin saved us. After

everything Dad's done." She took her daughter's hand and led the child to her grandmother's embrace.

Cara headed for the access tube to the flight deck. *Ben Benjamin saved us,* echoed round her head. Of course, he did. That's what Ben Benjamin did. Couldn't she forgive him one lapse? Was it even a lapse? He'd done a bad thing, but only for what he understood to be the greater good. And no one had been hurt—physically, at least. Gen and Max might never stop looking over their shoulder, but they had plenty of credits and a good ship. They'd make a life for themselves.

She swallowed down a lump in her throat as she emerged on to the flight deck.

"Are they all right?" Ben asked.

"Yes. Shaken but not injured."

"You're bleeding."

"Am I?"

He touched his right cheek. "Here."

"Rubble from the explosion. I never even noticed."

She slid into the comms chair and dabbed her cheek with a fingertip. If that was the worst that happened on this trip, she'd escaped lightly.

Solar Wind, come in.

Cara recognized Mother Ramona's telepathic voice filtered through Phoebe Tilston.

Here, Cara said. *What's wrong?*

Something was wrong; she was sure of it.

We're under attack.

And with every spare jumpship taking part in the evacuation, they were vulnerable.

"Tell them we're on our way," he said.

"What about the refugees?"

"We don't have time to take them anywhere. For now, they're ballast."

Chapter Fifty-One

BLOCKADE

BEN HEARD CARA WARNING THEIR PASSEN-
gers to prepare for foldspace. They entered with a rush.

Wenna calls fifteen seconds and they're out again.
    Rinse and repeat.
    Bouncing in and out like a stone skipping over a pond.

It took four jumps to exit the Folds in Olyanda space. When
they did, an amazing sight met them. A fleet of ships bristling with armaments hung in space. Between them and
Crossways Station, a hundred unarmed civilian jumpships
blocked the way, some of them shuttles, some of them
freighters. Five from Blacklock, sixteen from Cotille. He
lost count as they changed positions, flying a protective net
pattern. There were ships from Keynes, from Prairie, from
Blue Mountain, and from Cranford; in fact, from all over
the independent planets.

"That's what the Crossways Protectorate is all about,"
Cara said as another two ships popped into being from the
Folds and joined the blockade.

Ben took up a defensive position.

"What's happening?" Agnetha Sigurdsdottir emerged
onto the flight deck without permission.

"Someone is taking advantage of the situation to attack Crossways while her fleet is helping with the evacuation," Cara said.

"I wonder who that could be," she said, heading for one of the bucket seats and parking herself there. "Would you like to hazard a guess? And if you did, would my ex-husband be somewhere near the top of your list?"

Ben nodded. "I'd come to the same conclusion."

Close by, a ship solidified out of the Folds.

"Monitors," Wenna said, and magnified the image of the cruiser.

"It's Jessop," Ben said. "Can you connect us, Cara?"

What are you doing here, Jess?

I thought you might need some help.

You're willing to go up against these guys?

It might not come to that if I'm here as your independent observer.

Stand by, Jess.

"Cara, can you connect me with that fleet and link it with Crossways and with Jessop?"

"Sure can."

It took Cara less than half a minute to connect everyone on audio.

"Benjamin to armed fleet. Please stand down."

No response.

"Benjamin to armed fleet, please respond."

Nothing. But they didn't fire their weapons, and neither did Crossways.

Ben looked at Cara. "They're a decoy. Someone's already on the station."

Cara connected to Mother Ramona through Phoebe. *We think this fleet is a decoy. What's your situation?*

Everything's quiet—or as quiet as Crossways usually is. Let's call it normal, though the guys in Crossways Control might need a change of trousers. When that fleet turned up, they thought it was all kicking off again. Did you see the Protectorate ships out there? Like terriers driving off a bear.

Have you had any kind of message or demand?

Nothing.

I don't like it. Alert Syke. Put the station on lockdown. Coming in. He switched focus. *Jess?*

Standing by as requested, Jessop said.

Please back up this blockade.

Ben eased *Solar Wind* toward Port 46 while Cara alerted all the Free Company still on-station. With a population of half a million people, they were unlikely to be able to identify intruders until something kicked off, but when it did, they'd be ready. He hoped whatever kicked off didn't involve the station exploding or massive loss of life.

They slid into Port 46 and powered down.

"Noncombatants stay put," Ben said. He turned to Agnetha. "That includes you and your family. We'll get you to Earth as soon as we can."

"You can borrow my guards. They're good and they take orders."

He weighed up their lack of local knowledge against ten extra bodies on the ground. "Right now, they're more use here. This port could be one of the targets. Tell them to report to Franny Fowler. She's in charge of port security. Whatever she says goes."

"No problem. Commander Benjamin . . ."

"Yes?"

"I apologize for my ex-husband."

"No need. You're not responsible for him, but thank you, anyway."

The flashing red lights and droning alarms of station lockdown were muted inside Port 46, but out on the concourse the full effect hit them like an avalanche.

No one's going to be able to ignore that. Cara screwed up her face as if that would help.

Let's hope not. Anyone moving around the station had better be Garrick's or ours.

Wenna set off for Blue Seven to organize the remains of the Free Company into search teams. Gwala and Hilde stayed with Ben and Cara as they grabbed a cab.

"Doesn't Tengue need you two?" Ben asked.

"He needs us to guard you," Gwala said. "Shall I drive?"

The cab had an override, which Gwala used. With their own screamer clearing everything from the roadway ahead of them, they made it to the hub in less than five minutes.

A team of guards parted for them to run into the office complex beneath the Mansion House. Garrick and Mother Ramona were ensconced in a room full of screens that covered all the major thoroughfares. Every few minutes the image flipped to another length of corridor, plaza, or public space. The parameters were set to jump immediately to any eyes that spotted movement or anything out of place. The search teams cropped up regularly, but each had an electronic signal to identify them on the system.

The eyes, some static and some mobile, flicked up image after image with nothing out of place. Their own security teams, made up of Syke's militia, Tengue's mercenaries, and Free Company, showed up regularly, but so far they'd found nothing untoward.

A screen flashed red and drew their attention, but it was a couple of scrawny kids from Red One playing chicken with a drone eye, pulling faces, then laughing and running away.

"Bloody hooligans," Garrick said. "Since Kennedy moved to Olyanda, the little bastards have been running riot. I never realized how much influence she had or how much we should have thanked her for. She took a dozen with her. These are the ones who weren't officially part of her feral pack, but I'm thinking of rounding them up and sending them down anyway."

An adult hand snaked out, grabbed one of the kids round the waist, and yanked him back. Another hand took the second boy's arm and pulled. Ben's immediate thought was that their parents had taken control and dragged them off to safety. With any luck, the kids would get a blistering telling off and learn from their mistakes, but then his mind replayed the scene. The arms that had dragged the kids back were buddysuited.

"Can you follow the kids with that eye?" Ben asked. "Their parents could never afford buddysuits."

The operator, one of the station's Psi-Mechs, flew a drone eye into the corridor where the kids had been but found nothing. No children, no parents. Nothing to show their passing.

"They cleared off pretty quickly," Cara said. Even for inhabitants of Red One who were professionals when it came to avoiding station eyes. "Check the side—"

"Corridors. Got it," the operative said.

The little eye flew into the head of the first corridor, a dead end and completely empty. The second corridor was longer, but the operator abandoned it. "Got a fixed eye. We'd have seen them on Screen Fifteen if they'd gone that way."

The third opening was a narrow maintenance shaft.

"Oh, shit!" Ben said softly.

Two heaps of ragged clothes with a foot sticking out of one and the back of a head visible behind an outthrust arm told their own story, as did the blood spatters up the wall.

"Syke, two teams to Red One," Garrick hit the comm. "Corridor 38. Two children down. Service vent—" He looked at the screen. "Eighteen-D. Proceed with caution. Intruders, but we don't know how many or where they're going."

"But we do know they'll kill children who look like they're attracting attention," Ben said.

"Why Red One?" Mother Ramona asked. "There's nothing there except the station's underbelly. What are they looking for?"

"Dido Kennedy," Cara said.

"She's on Olyanda."

"Maybe their information is out of date. Maybe they're not looking for Kennedy herself but access to her files, details of the retrofit drive."

"And once they've found it, what then?" Ben asked. "How much damage would a bomb do in Red One?"

Mother Ramona's white marbled face flushed pink with anger. "It's close to the bottom of the core. If they blew the power plant . . ."

"Wait until I'm through and then close all the blast doors," Ben said, checking the pulse pistol at his side. Fully charged. Good.

"You're not going on your own," Cara said.

He didn't know whether to be macho and tell her she had to stay behind in relative safety or to let her do what she was good at. He simply nodded.

Hilde sighed. "Well that's it, then. If you two are going, we're coming, too."

"You don't have to," Ben said.

"Yes, we do." Gwala levered himself up from the wall he'd been leaning against. "Can you imagine trying to explain to Tengue that we lost you two?"

"Tengue scares you more than the idea of a bomb?"

Gwala glanced at Hilde and Hilde raised one eyebrow.
"What do you think?"

✦ ✦ ✦

Cara ran for the elevator half a pace behind Ben, with Hilde
and Gwala barely a pace behind her. Something at the back
of her mind said, "Oh no, not again," but she couldn't
choose her battles; only fight them when they came along.
She'd said she'd stay until the jump gate issue was solved,
but it might never be solved, not completely. Even if all the
gates closed, there would still be some traffic through the
Folds.

An elevator stood waiting for them, doors open. Ben
waved toward the camera eye and they all piled into it, feeling it plummet like a stone until it slowed, gravity pushing
them against the floor plates. They came out into a lobby.
Above them, they could hear the clang of blast doors dropping.

They changed elevators again. This time, the journey
down the core of the station was slower. Cara wanted to
stamp her feet to speed it up, the way she had done as a
child. Not that it had worked then, either.

"Don't be impatient to find danger," Gwala said. "It will
find you soon enough."

She had a sick fear that it would. Every time she took
chances, the odds shortened that this would be the time she
wouldn't get away with it.

And neither would Ben.

They all set their retractable lobstered helms and faceplates.

The elevator ground to a halt and the doors opened. The
lobby was clear, but the red lights still flashed and the sirens
still moaned. Ben gave her the universal cut-it-off sign and
she passed the message on via Phoebe. The siren stopped.
The red light blinked once and then was replaced with a
calm white.

Syke? Cara sought him out.

Corridor 31. Vent 18D Two dead children as reported.

She felt the emotion behind his bald statement. For all
his veneer of formality and professionalism, Syke abhorred
cruelty and needless death. She thought of his patience with
Kitty, visiting every day, letting her talk. Listening.

We have a Finder, Syke said. *One team is trying to track them from the traces left on the bodies, the other is scouting the main thoroughfare.*

We think they might be going to Dido Kennedy's workshop. Meet you there.

The four of them jogged along the corridor, keeping contact with Phoebe in the screen room so they knew the way ahead was clear. Cara wished they had a Finder with them—specifically Max. She missed Gen and Max. They'd been closer than family.

Ben halted everyone on the edge of the open square outside Dido's former workshop.

The last time they'd come here there was a stall busy serving food to the locals. Dido had fed them all, buying ingredients for her famous "Don't Ask" stew, which, as far as Cara could discern, contained nothing identifiable except for its genuine vitamin supplements. Garrick had paid Dido for the patent on her retrofit jump drive, but rather than showing in her own lifestyle, the bonus had shown in better ingredients for the Don't Ask, and stockpiles of food and medicine left with trusted friends in Red One.

Cara checked the eyes again via Phoebe, and searched ahead with her Empathy to see if there was a flicker of emotion that would indicate intruders in the workshop.

There's no camera eye in Dido's place, Phoebe said. *Shall we send you a drone eye?*

"She wouldn't have a camera, and we don't have time to wait for a drone." Ben was listening in. "We'll have to go in blind. When Dido first hooked up with Yan, they made home an apartment above the workshop. There has to be a tube entrance from up there. Yan wouldn't have missed a trick like that."

"There's someone in there," Cara said. "I'm getting a mix of fear, tension, and excitement all mixed up. I can't tell how many but definitely more than two."

Cara passed the information to Syke who passed it to his second team. Syke's own team came at the square from the opposite side.

Everyone's in place, Benjamin, Syke said. *On your mark.*

Ben looked around to make sure they were all ready. *Let's go. Mark!*

Pulse pistol drawn, Ben barreled through the main entrance, bent double to present a smaller target. Cara, Hilde, and Gwala followed close behind, with Syke's team after them. At the same time, Syke's second team dropped down the access tube which put them behind four buddysuited figures standing by a bank of computers.

The four figures crouched behind the machines while death blasted out from guns positioned in the workshop's four corners. The first two out of the tube made it to safety, but the second pair took two consecutive hits and fell close together.

Cara tucked in behind a solid bench, Hilde to her left and Gwala to her right. Ben and Syke had taken shelter behind a hefty looking cabinet. Another of Syke's men went down behind the first two, but he was conscious and using the bodies as a shield. From that angle, he fired off two quick shots and one of the intruders fell in the far corner.

"No need for anyone else to get hurt," Ben shouted. "You're outnumbered."

A fusillade of shots answered. Pity they wanted to play it that way. Cara felt at the edges of the room to pick up ambient emotions. There was better definition now. Fear, naturally enough, determination, anxiety, and—worryingly—someone was getting a real kick out of the situation.

Syke, do you have an Empath with you? Cara kept the communication tight, not knowing whether the intruders were psi-techs.

Negative. I have five Telepaths and one Finder. The others all have receiving implants.

Any one of yours likely to be getting a high from this?

I doubt it.

Ben frowned at her from behind his cabinet, knowing something was going on, but not what it was.

Someone's loving this, Cara said. *A real loose cannon. Thinks he knows something we don't.*

Explosives, do you think?

That would be my guess. Or maybe they have reinforcements around the corner.

How many of the intruders are psi-techs?

Hard to tell. All of them, I think. I'm still trying to sort them all out from each other without giving anything away.

One of the intruders rolled forward out of his corner,

obviously trying to change the status quo. He hurled a canister, Cara ducked one way, Ben the other, but instead of an explosion, there was the hiss of gas. He wasn't going to get far with that. They all had helms and breathing tubes. But gassing them hadn't been his intention. As she came upright, Cara saw they'd changed position. There were now four of them behind the terminals.

I'd bet my breakfast that's Pav Danniri behind the terminal, Ben said. *Something about the way she moves.*

Mother Ramona hailed Cara. *There's an attempt to hack into our systems from Red One. We have J.P. Lister here. As fast as they're breaking down barriers, he's building them. He's damn good, but if you can stop them, that would be excellent.*

Are they looking for Dido's files?

If they are, they won't find them. Dido keeps all her work close. None of it is on the station's system. I think most of it is in her head.*

Good to know, Cara said. *We've trapped them. They're outnumbered, but they're not giving in. I hope you've sealed those blast doors down tight.*

Don't worry about us. You all stay safe.

That was easy to say, but not so easy to do. Cara picked up that someone was highly amused, but radiating tension and anticipation.

Is Pav Danniri the hacker? Cara asked Ben.

I doubt it. Strictly the physical type. She'll be the hacker's minder.

Activate your sound baffles and visors, Syke said.

Cara did.

Syke threw two screamers into the far corners of the workshop. Without sound baffles, Cara would have been reeling from the noise and blinking from the ultra-bright light. Even if the intruders had baffles and goggles, it would have taken them precious seconds to activate them.

Ben must have thought the same. He surged forward, Gwala and Hilde right behind him. Ballistic weapons cracked and pulse pistols whumped and whined, whumped and whined.

The intruders were distracted enough for Cara to crack the wall of mental silence around them. She identified Pav

Danniri, obviously in charge, but she wasn't the one whose excitement and delight had been bleeding through. That was coming from someone at the console. He was excited because ... Cara couldn't quite get the detail, but it involved an explosive device no one else knew about—one that would rip the station apart from the inside. All he had to do was to wait for the download to finish, bounce the information straight off to the ships out on the station's perimeter and—boom.

Cara felt like insects were crawling down her spine.

Suicide bomber, Ben. I think he's wearing it. Or it could be small enough to fit in his pocket.

You couldn't reason with someone who was willing to give his life to blow you up. But why? Maybe he was unbalanced and suggestible, or maybe he was the victim of illegal neural reconditioning. It had happened to Cara once—not to the extent that she would have blown herself up, but it was easy to see how it could. She guessed the rest of the crew didn't know they were on a suicide mission.

"Pav Danniri, is that you?"

"Benjamin? You're supposed to be off rescuing folks from Chenon."

"Sorry to disappoint. You working with a new crew?"

"A girl's got to eat."

"No, not ever again. Eat, I mean. You brought a suicide bomber with you. A present from Crowder, I believe."

Cara felt a jolt from the bomber. In a panic he checked the download, but it hadn't completed. She could see one of the figures crouched behind the console was struggling to rise. His fingers were fumbling for something. She didn't have time to worry about it. She reached into his mind and without knocking him unconscious—which might have detonated the device—held him still.

"Suggest you take his fingers off the trigger very carefully, Danniri," Cara called. "And do it now. I'm not sure how long I can hold him."

"Got it. Get out of his head." Danniri's voice was accompanied by a whump and a whine. Somewhere behind the console a body slumped to the floor. Thank goodness she'd given warning. Being attached to a person as they died could seriously hurt—or worse.

"Still want this job?" Ben called. "That's twice Crowder's been economical with the truth. Want to give him a third chance?"

"Are you offering a deal?"

"Maybe. Are you likely to take it if I do?"

"Maybe."

Chapter Fifty-Two

MKHULU

"ARE YOU SURE ABOUT THIS?" JESS JESSOP asked as Ben held out his wrists for shackles. "Surely there's no need for—"

"If we're going to do it, let's do it properly, Jess. I said I'd give myself up to answer charges, and I will. You tell me Rodriguez is a man of his word, and since you are, too, that's all I need. What's left of Chenon is safe now. Just some mopping up to do, but the Nimbus may strike again, anywhere, anytime."

It had taken a massive air and ground offensive to stop the Nimbus' attack on Chenon. It would take some time to sort out everything, especially considering they'd taken some of the Nimbus' troops alive and were now trying to solve the problem of what to do with them.

Jess ran a hand through thinning hair. "You know I'll do my best, but Crowder and the Trust—"

"I know, but I've given myself up to the Monitors. The Trust can bring charges, but unless they jump through judicial hoops, they can't take me into their custody."

"Your witnesses—"

"Following under their own steam as we agreed. You've made all the arrangements?"

"Rodriguez has. He was somewhat intrigued by the list."

"They've all taken part in this convoluted series of events."

"I never thought you'd get a sworn statement from the Lorients with Jack Mario to deliver it. They must owe you big-time."

"Their story will come out, and Jack is as good a man as any to state the case without revealing anything that isn't relevant."

"Such as their current location."

"Exactly." Ben smiled. "Jamundi is off the map, and we all intend to keep it that way. It's already been threatened by the Nimbus. I don't want any more trouble for them. They deserve their happy ever after."

The Nimbus forces on Chenon had been defeated by the megacorporations and the Five Power Alliance throwing ships and troops at it on a scale unprecedented in galactic history. That kind of help wouldn't be available for Jamundi, so it was better to keep it hidden from view.

Jess nodded. "I understand. Is everything else sorted out?"

"I hope I've thought of everything." Ben grinned. "That usually means I haven't, but I hope there's nothing big enough to bite me in the butt."

Jake was bringing Ben's witnesses to Earth in *Solar Wind*, people who could tell the story of treachery and deceit going right back to Hera-3 when Gabrius Crowder and Ari van Blaiden combined forces to bring a new platinum-producing colony under the sole control of the Trust. Wenna's testimony would help with that.

Jack Mario and the Lorients' sworn statements should cover Olyanda. Morton Tengue had stepped up to relate the story of Ari van Blaiden's involvement, and wherever Tengue went, Gwala and Hilde weren't far behind.

There was Jake, himself, who had played his own part in losing the ark carrying thirty thousand settlers in foldspace, and then rescuing it again with Ben and Cara.

Mother Ramona had actually volunteered to come, too. He would never have asked her in a million years, and had hoped for nothing more than a sworn statement from herself and Garrick, but her willingness to appear personally spoke volumes about friendship and loyalty.

Then there was Cara, of course. He hadn't asked her to come, but she was coming anyway. Dare he hope she'd forgiven him? Or if not entirely forgiven him, perhaps she understood that taking Liv into space had been the least bad option. Her story was so deeply intertwined with his that it would be sure to come out, and she was better off telling it herself. He'd made sure that as a major witness, she was safe from arrest on her own account.

Clearing Ben would exonerate the whole of the Free Company.

A public trial would drag the Trust and Alphacorp through the mud. Ben hoped to avoid it. All the charges had been brought by the Trust. He hoped he could persuade the board that dropping them would be in their own best interests.

Malusi Duma, the grandfather he didn't remember, had brokered a meeting with the joint Trust and Alphacorp boards, presided over by Vetta Babajack, the current European prime minister, and president elect of the Five Power Alliance. It would be Ben's best chance to persuade them to close down the jump gate system. If he had to risk his own freedom to do that, then so be it.

Following Ben's advice, Jess instructed his crew to punch in and out of foldspace in a series of short jumps, finally reaching Earth and taking a shuttle down to Shield City, a domed habitation on the northwestern shore of Hudson Bay.

Ben had visited the Monitor headquarters on Earth twice when he'd been a new recruit, but he wasn't particularly familiar with it. He certainly wasn't familiar with the cells which, though fitted with all modern conveniences, still smelled of desperation. Being here by choice helped, but not much.

First, they took his buddysuit and gave him gray fatigues with no pockets and no metal fittings. They took images and scans and processed him, allocating a number to his name. Then they had a physician give him a checkup and a clean bill of health. After that, he spent two hours going over the statement he'd given previously, confirming that it was a true transcription, not given under duress. He signed and thumbprinted it.

He was a model prisoner: no aggression, all cooperation.

His cell was fitted with a damper, which, he supposed, was marginally better than being drugged on reisercaine to prevent him from contacting, or being contacted by, undesirables.

That meant Cara, who was very desirable as far as Ben was concerned, couldn't contact him. They'd known this would be the case beforehand and made plans accordingly.

Meals arrived regularly, and the food was decent. He had a few unread books on his handpad, had he been in the mood to read them, and there was a wall screen with a limited choice of entertainment channels. He scanned for documentaries on the colonies or space travel, but it was mostly Earth related, which was logical. Having been brought up on Chenon, with its predominantly pink foliage, the innate green of Earth on the screen felt alien to him. He'd long since become habituated to a twenty-four hour day, though, because it was the norm out in space, so his body clock wasn't as messed up as he'd thought it might be.

It was still a long and largely sleepless first night, but in the morning, along with his breakfast, came a message that his lawyer and a representative from the Five Power Alliance had arranged to see him at ten. Good. It was starting at last.

They came for him on the dot of ten, guards he didn't know, who insisted he stand facing the back wall of his cell while they entered. While one kept a stunner handy, he turned for the other to put on shackles. He couldn't blame them. His charge sheet was impressive and his dossier testament to his resourcefulness. He took deep breaths and reminded himself that it was by no means certain this was how it was going to be for the rest of his life. Even so, the atmosphere of desperation undermined the confidence he'd brought with him to this place.

He followed one guard down a long corridor. The second one followed behind with a stunner. Ben didn't need to be an Empath to know he was jumpy, so he was careful to move slowly and deliberately and not give him any reason to react. Being stunned wasn't Ben's favorite pastime.

They took him up what appeared to be three levels in a steel box elevator and delivered him to a plain white interview room where the light was too bright and the walls too clean. A faint smell of disinfectant lingered. There was a metal table bolted to the floor and a single metal chair on one side of it. His guards had him sit and then they bolted his wrist shackles to the table. He didn't object. There wasn't much point.

A few minutes later a different pair of guards brought in two more comfortable looking chairs which they placed opposite. He heard voices in the corridor and the door opened again.

Two men entered, one elderly and brown with a wiry cap of salt-and-pepper curls, the other middle-aged and of Chinese descent with black hair tied in a ponytail. Both wore smart suits which made Ben's gray fatigues feel even more like pajamas.

Ben smothered a laugh and started to stand before realizing his shackles wouldn't let him. He smiled instead. "Hello, Grandfather. You're the representative from the Five Power Alliance. I should have guessed. Not the way I'd hoped we'd meet."

"Reska, good to see you. We have met before, but you were a baby and I don't expect you to remember."

"Please, call me Ben. Only Nan calls me Reska."

"She can be a remarkably formal woman on occasions." He smiled. "Ben, then. And you may call me Mkhulu when no one is listening. It's Zulu for grandfather. How are they treating you?"

"Well enough, since I'm classified as dangerous." He rattled his shackles. "I have no complaints."

"Your grandmother sends her love and says to tell you that you are an idiot. I'm not entirely sure you are, but I think you like to live dangerously."

Ben shrugged. "Tell Nan I'm sorry. I needed a way to speak to the Trust and Alphacorp boards. This is it."

"You'll get your chance. I've set a date, three days from now."

"Thank you."

"This is Charles Wong, your lawyer."

Ben dipped his head in acknowledgment while asking, "Do I need a lawyer?"

"You most certainly do, Mr. Benjamin," Wong said. "You admitted to killing Ari van Blaiden, for a start."

"Self-defense." Ben would do it again in a heartbeat to protect Cara.

"And attempting to kill Gabrius Crowder."

"Self-defense again, or at least, defending someone else, but I admit I made a botch of it. Otherwise, I suspect we might not be having this conversation since Crowder is behind all the charges. Don't we have enough proof against him?"

"What you have is hearsay and witnesses, all of whom back you without exception, even Miss Danniri who possibly counts as a hostile witness. But proving Gabrius Crowder is guilty of criminal acts is not the same as proving you, and the Free Company by association, are innocent."

"Isn't discrediting him and proving that we had just cause enough?"

"I rather think it all comes down to whether the Trust and Alphacorp continue to press charges when they've heard what you have to say. If they do, you could be looking at a very long time on a prison planet and, by that, I mean the rest of your life."

"And what would that mean for Cara and the Free Company?"

"The charges against them would stand."

"What about the ones who've come here as witnesses?"

"They came under amnesty." His grandfather leaned forward. "You have my personal guarantee they will be allowed to leave."

Ben huffed out a relieved breath. "That's what matters. Thank you."

His grandfather chuckled. "I've been talking to your witnesses. I think I have a better idea of the kind of man my grandson is, now. Your . . . err . . . Cara is a delightful young woman. If I were sixty years younger, I'd be fighting you for her attention."

"Nan might have something to say about that."

"Ah, yes, very probably. Your grandmother is a strong woman."

"I know."

"So now we have to plan for the board meeting. They requested we all meet in holographic space, but I've persuaded them a physical meeting is required. It will take place at the Trust Tower in KwaZulu Natal."

"On Trust territory."

"In a way, yes, but the Trust Tower was built over the bones of Umlazi Township. Your ancestors came from there. Remember, you have as much right to that space as the Trust has. You are descended from a long line of Duma warriors."

Ben smiled. "I hope one day we'll have the opportunity to discuss my ancestors, but in the meantime, what do I need to know about the boards?"

Chapter Fifty-Three

AMBUSH

CARA HAD BEEN ON EDGE SINCE ARRIVING IN Durban with Jake and the other witnesses. They'd all been cooped up in a hotel together with every luxury, but with limited freedom. There was an unobtrusive but effective guard, partly, they said, for their own protection. Ben's grandfather, Malusi Duma, had visited with Nan, and they'd all, one by one, told him their individual stories, even Jake, who was understandably embarrassed by being duped into almost killing thirty thousand people by dumping their ark ship into foldspace while they were all in cryo. He'd redeemed himself several times over, but Jake still had to be convinced he was forgiven.

So much had happened. So many deaths could be laid at Crowder's feet. Pity he wasn't the one who would be on trial.

Yet all that counted for nothing when compared to the danger from foldspace. They probably weren't the first to encounter the Nimbus, but they were the first to survive and spread the news.

Cara spent hours with Nan and Malusi Duma, hoping for the best, but planning for the worst.

"Don't worry," Nan told her. "The person who controls the options controls the situation."

"Do we have options?"

"Malusi can't interfere with the proceedings, but he's been finding excuses all year to get under Crowder's skin and some of it may have come good. Vetta Babajack is chairing the whole thing. He's a friend of Malusi's. Reska will get a hearing—a fair one."

After an eternity of waiting the day came for the board meeting.

Cara knew Jessop had brought Ben to Durban the day before, but she wasn't allowed to visit. Again, no surprise.

All the witnesses assembled in a room off the hotel lobby.

"Are you all right?" Ronan asked. She shouldn't be surprised he'd picked up her agitation. His Empathy was partly what made him so good at his job. "I thought you and Ben were over."

She gave him a look which he interpreted correctly and then laughed.

"Do you think you should tell Ben?"

"Maybe. Someday. Just because I love him doesn't mean I don't hate what he did."

"I know you have issues with trust."

Did she?

"I had issues with Ari van Blaiden and Alphacorp. I always thought I could trust Ben."

"You can always trust him to do what he thinks is right."

"But taking Gen's baby into a dangerous situation . . . Why didn't he tell me?"

"He didn't tell you because he knew you'd be conflicted. He didn't give you any choice about which side to be on."

"And now he thinks the right thing to do is to risk his freedom for the sake of getting the truth out there."

Ronan merely cocked his head to one side. She'd answered her own question.

"If he gets out of this alive, remind me to kill him," Cara said. "The only thing worse than living with a man with no honor is living with one who has too much."

For an answer, Ronan simply pulled her into his arms and gave her a fierce hug. "If he ends up on a prison planet, you don't think for one minute we'd leave him there, do you?"

"That's good to know. I wouldn't want to have to break him out all by myself."

"Is everyone ready?" Nan arrived in the doorway with Malusi Duma. Cara noticed they'd been holding hands and didn't let go fast enough. Had they finally decided to get together? They'd waited long enough.

They all filed out of the hotel to the transport, following Malusi and Nan: Cara, Ronan, Wenna, Hilde, Gwala, Tengue, Jake, Jack Mario, Mother Ramona, and Pav Danniri. There were twenty seats on the bus, ten singles, facing forward down each side of an aisle. Their Monitor guards arrived, two officers and eight constables, each armored and carrying a heavy-duty weapon. Cara wasn't sure why they should be carrying Newtons unless they were expecting trouble. It certainly wasn't in Crowder's best interests to allow the witnesses to testify. Maybe they were worried there might be an ambush between the hotel and the Trust Tower, twenty klicks south. Cara would have felt better if she'd been allowed to pack her derri. It wasn't much of a weapon, but she felt better knowing it was in her thigh pocket.

The driver climbed into the cab. The door shushed closed and the armored windows darkened. The vehicle rose on its antigravs and began to glide forward. At the end of the hotel's driveway, she felt the bus turn left when she'd been expecting it to turn right. Probably something to do with the city's road system. All the same, though she was no Navigator, she was sure the bus was heading north rather than south. Their guards were all buddysuited up to the eyeballs with face shields that hid their expressions. Cara reached out with her talent for Empathy and found nothing. The guards were all wearing dampers. Ten dampers on a small vehicle interfered with her own ability. It felt like she was swimming through soup to contact Ronan who was sitting right in front of her.

Ronan? Can you feel it?

What?

Nothing. That's what I mean. Seen those Newtons? Why would guys on our side need their weapons prepped while on the inside of the bus?

And you said you don't have trust issues.

It's not my issue if someone's trying to kill me. Help me to get through to the others.

Ronan lent his power.

Be aware. Cara sent out a tight broadcast. *Look at those weapons. I think these guys aren't our friends.* Malusi Duma, Jack Mario, and Pav Danniri were the only deadheads. Cara saw Nan lean across and say something to Malusi, her face fixed in a disarming smile.

The bus's engine coughed and died.

"Technical trouble," the driver said over the comm. "Nothing to worry about."

Yeah, right, Wenna said. *I trust your instincts, Cara. Plans?*

It's close to even numbers.

Unless you count the bloody big Newtons and their sidearms as well, Jake said.

The driver made a couple of halfhearted attempts to restart the drive. "Sorry, folks. I've sent for a replacement vehicle, but we're out of the city now, so it will take half an hour to reach us. I'm not going to be able to keep the climate control operating, so it will be hotter than hell in here inside five minutes. You might want to wait outside where there's a bit of a breeze coming in from the sea."

"You heard," the Monitor officer said. "Everyone off."

The bus had settled low to the ground.

This is it, Cara said. *The plan is to fight for your lives.*

She saw a look pass among Tengue, Gwala, and Hilde.

Cara shuffled next to Jack Mario and squeezed his hand.

"These aren't real Monitors, are they?" he asked in a low voice.

"I very much doubt it," she said, smiling through clenched teeth. "When the rumpus starts, get down and stay down."

She was horrified to see that Nan and Malusi were going to be the first off the bus behind eight guards. If those guards were going to be waiting with weapons drawn, that was the most vulnerable position. But as Nan stepped on to the roadway, she stumbled, going down and taking Malusi with her. They rolled to the side, leaving the way clear for Tengue, Gwala, and Hilde to leap out of the door, splitting up, darting, diving.

Unable to see out of the darkened windows, the two guards at the back were slow to react when the rumpus kicked off at the front of the bus. Ronan went for one and Cara hopped onto her seat and launched herself at the other.

Jack Mario had crouched between the seats. Good. That took him out of harm's way. It was doubtful he had much unarmed combat experience. That thought was fleeting. Grappling with an armed guard took all her attention.

She didn't feel pain at the gun butt against her cheekbone. It was more like a kinetic shove. She shoved back, not letting him point the muzzle of the Newton in her direction. He kicked out at close quarters and tangled his foot in hers. They went down in the aisle. All she could concentrate on was holding the damn gun while trying to get her feet under her. Suddenly an arm snaked out from under the seat and locked itself around the guard's head. Thank you, Jack. She grabbed the Newton, turned it around, and drove the stock into the vulnerable space between the bottom of the man's face guard and the collar of his buddysuit.

He gurgled and choked. She didn't know how much damage she'd done, but she couldn't leave him to recover behind her. She turned the Newton again and fired at point-blank range at the exact same spot she'd pounded. The report was deafening in the close confines of the bus. Blood sprayed in an arc. At that range, she'd probably taken his head off.

She scrambled to her feet, gun in hand, at the same time as Ronan.

It had taken seconds.

Wenna had crouched down inside the doorway when it all kicked off outside, and then she'd flung herself at the driver in his cab.

Ronan ran to the front of the bus. Cara paused to rip the sidearm out of the holster of the downed guard.

"Get whatever weapons you can find, Jack," she said, and ran after Ronan.

The yellow African sun caused her to blink and screw up her eyes. They were on a quiet stretch of road, certainly not the main highway, with sparse grass growing on the sandy verge and the azure sea not a hundred meters away beyond rolling dunes. A good place to bury bodies.

It took three seconds to extend the lobstered helm of her buddysuit and click the visor into place. Gwala had downed a man and was in the process of rising to his feet.

"Manny!" she yelled, and tossed the Newton to him. It would do more good in his hands than hers.

There were bodies. Pav Danniri lay still in the roadside dust. Nan and Malusi were two shapes in the shelter of the bus' skirt, but Cara didn't have time to check for injuries. There were still four guards standing, or rather crouching and taking aim.

Gwala took two of them with the same burst of fire. Tengue tackled one from behind and the trail of shots arced upward. Ronan hit the fourth squarely across the back of both knees, cutting his legs from beneath him, whereupon Jake grabbed the man's gun, yanked off his helmet, and held the muzzle to his head.

It was over.

Wenna emerged from the bus holding her right arm, now detached, in her left hand and using it as a club against the driver who looked dazed.

"Bastard grabbed me by the wrong arm."

"The right arm, I'd say," Jake said.

Suddenly, Wenna began to giggle. She pushed the driver toward Tengue and Gwala who had rounded up the surviving guards.

Ronan checked everyone for injury. "That's going to hurt in the morning." He touched Cara's face where her cheekbone and the gun butt had collided.

"It's superficial. Check the others."

She knelt beside Nan. "Are you hurt?"

"Only my pride. Malusi's taken a straight-through slug in the leg. I've got a compress on it. No arterial bleeding, and I don't think it's caught the bone."

"That's good."

"Not from where I am, young lady." He scowled at her.

"You know what I mean."

Pav Danniri was dead, a small hole between her eyes, a large one in the back of her head. Hilde had taken three shots to her shoulder and upper arm, but her buddysuit had turned two more potentially fatal ones to her chest, which had left her bruised and gasping for breath. Gwala, bleeding from a gash to his jaw, wouldn't leave her side.

"Where's Jack?" Cara peered into the bus.

Jack was still on the floor. "Did we win?"

"We did. Thank you for your help. You can come out now."

"I'd love to, but I might need a bit of help. I felt

something tear in my knee. Not sure if I can even get up. How do you hardy types manage to take a beating and bounce back as if nothing had happened? Gods, your face looks awful."

"Thank you, kind sir. A lady always appreciates a compliment."

"Does it hurt?"

She touched her cheekbone. "I think it's going to."

Chapter Fifty-Four

BOARD

THEY ALLOWED BEN HIS BUDDYSUIT FOR THE board meeting, though they checked it thoroughly for hidden weapons first, and he had to wear a damping pin. He felt more like himself as he waited in an anteroom five floors below the boardroom. He was accompanied by three guards, and they'd put on the damned shackles again. He smiled at them and settled down to wait. It wasn't as if he was going anywhere. His whole purpose in surrendering was to get to this moment.

A light knock on the door. One of his guards answered it, and Jess Jessop entered.

"Jess, I didn't expect you to be here."

"I'm a character witness."

"For me?"

"And against Sergei Alexandrov. Though I'm not sure that's quite what Alphacorp's lawyer expects. I'll tell it the way I saw it, and remind people how many you rescued from Chenon, including Crowder's family."

"Thanks, Jess. Much appreciated."

"Your other witnesses haven't arrived yet. Are they usually late?"

"No. Aren't your guys supposed to be transporting them? Should I worry?"

"I doubt it, but I'll see what I can find out."

Of course, that meant he did worry. Sitting high in the Trust Tower, he felt disconnected from the real world far below. He went to the window, fancy glass-steel that was as invisible as air, and peered out. The main arterial road ran north to south with intersections that spilled traffic onto local roads.

A public road-train ran alongside the arterial, dipping under the access ramps and serving the busy station built especially for the Trust Tower. In the distance, the rolling parkland had swallowed up all signs of Umlazi Township. All that remained was the name and a life-size bronze sculpture in the lobby depicting a people fierce and proud. Malusi Duma's people. Should he feel they were his people, too? That South Africa was long gone. Africa was prosperous, now, and the south doubly so with its platinum.

A bus pulled off the arterial and swung in through the gates, past the checkpoint, without stopping, and right up to the front entrance. Even from this height he could recognize Cara, Ronan, Wenna, Tengue, Gwala. They were his people. There was some kind of fuss going on, security being called, a gurney being summoned. Who was that? He couldn't tell who the figures were under their emergency medical blankets, but some of them were covered head-to-toe. What the hell had happened? Who was dead?

Dammit! The damping pin prevented him from connecting with Cara even though he could see her three hundred meters below.

"What's happening down there?" he asked his guards, but they didn't know and wouldn't ask.

Time slowed, but eventually Jess returned, his face creased in a frown. "Someone was trying to make sure your witnesses didn't testify. Impostors with a duplicate bus while the real transport was snarled in a traffic jam."

"There were corpses down there."

"Mostly the would-be assassins. Your guys are good."

"Mostly?"

"Pav Danniri."

Ben hardly knew the woman, and she'd spent part of last year trying to kill him, but she'd done the decent thing and exchanged her testimony for a free passage out to the Rim.

"Casualties?"

"Hildstrom, bullets to arm and shoulder, but she's stable. Ex-president Duma, bullet to the leg, also stable, and Mr. Mario, torn knee ligaments. He's cursing like a regular trooper, but otherwise unharmed. Cara took a gun butt to the face, so some bruising. Don't panic when you see her. It's spectacular, but not dangerous. You should have seen the other fellow. He was one of the ones under a blanket."

Ben took a deep breath. "Glad you warned me."

"She says to tell you they'll all still be testifying, and not to worry about your grandfather." Jess frowned. "Your grandfather is here? I didn't know you had family on Earth."

Ben smiled.

"We can go up, now," Jess said. "I'm afraid you still get your guard."

"Hey, everyone has a job to do. For all I know, they've saved me from assassins already, simply by being there." He turned to the guards. "Gentlemen, I can assure you you'll get no trouble from me. Shall we go?"

Jess led the way to an empty elevator shaft. Ben was about to grab him by the shoulders when he realized there was a floor mat lying in midair. "Glass-steel," Jess said. "Can't see the point myself unless you're being architecturally pretentious."

"Glad they decided to put a telltale mat on the floor."

"I asked the receptionist." Jess chuckled. "She said no one would use it until they did. Sometimes they take it out to tease newcomers to the place, or to impress important visitors that they don't like very much."

As the elevator rose to the top of the tower, Ben began to see the point. The unobstructed view was magnificent from up here.

The board meeting started two hours late, everyone agreeing to wait while the witnesses received medical attention. It wasn't a judicial trial, so the witnesses were allowed into the meeting and given a bank of seats with room for two float chairs on the front row. Jack Mario was in one, and Malusi Duma in the other, sitting next to Nan. She'd shuffled her chair close enough for their arms to touch. On his grandfather's other side was Charles Wong. Ben didn't know whether to be grateful his lawyer was there or worried because his grandfather believed it might be necessary for him to have legal support even in this preliminary meeting.

He caught Cara's glance, glad Jess had warned him about the bruise on her face. "All right?" he mouthed.

She answered with a slight raise of one shoulder and a twitch of her lips.

Ben recognized some of the Trust board. He knew of Tori Le Bon, of course, though he'd never met her. He had met Isaac Whittle, the vice-chair, who had been in charge of the Hera-3 inquiry. He knew Yolanda Chang, head of Research and Development, by reputation. She was a scientist and might be one of the people he could appeal to.

Crowder wore a blank expression and had a damper pinned to his collar. Had the bastard ordered this morning's attack? Probably, but Ben figured he wasn't the only one on the Trust board who would like to see them all vanish in a puff of smoke. Alphacorp, too. They'd certainly like to keep Ari van Blaiden's crimes covered up.

Akiko Yamada headed the Alphacorp board. Ari van Blaiden had been on the board, of course, until his unfortunate demise, which they'd covered up by saying he'd been lost in the Folds.

Vetta Babajack, European Prime Minister and president elect of the Five Power Alliance, had agreed to chair the meeting.

"Gentlefem and gentlemen of the boards," Babajack began. "Rarely do corporations and governments have the opportunity to clean house in private, but under the terms of this agreement that is what we have today. Mr. Benjamin has offered testimony and has brought witnesses to things past and things to come. He has proposals which I will ask you to consider and vote on at the end of this session. You've all read the transcript of his statement and may ask questions as you see fit. As you all know, this session is being monitored by four independent Empaths to ensure the truth at all times from all parties."

And so it began. It was up to Ben to frame his story in the way the board members would find acceptable, and even to elicit sympathy. Sure, Crowder had overstepped the mark when he'd orchestrated the attack to destroy the colony on Hera-3, so the Trust could waltz in and take control of the platinum, but Ben would be an idiot if he thought the Trust's board completely innocent.

Crowder had made two mistakes. The first of these was

starting this whole thing in the first place. The second was leaving Ben alive to finish it.

Ben answered questions from several members of the board without looking at Crowder. He figured the Empaths in the room would be having a party with the emotions washing from that direction.

They called Cara next.

A great red-and-purple welt splashed across her cheekbone and the bruising had spread down to her jaw. He knew by the way she held herself that she was in pain, but she spoke clearly and succinctly about Ari van Blaiden's attempt to crush her mentally as well as physically, using the unique talents of Donida McLellan in charge of the neural reconditioning unit on Sentier-4.

Ronan backed up her story, Wenna backed up Ben's.

Then Ben turned his story around. "At this point, please don't forget we were all loyal employees of the Trust—and would still have been if we hadn't had to choose between living and dying."

Jack Mario gave an insight from the colonists' point of view. Jack might be taken for nondescript at first glance, especially when sitting in a float chair like an invalid, but he was blessed with liberal quantities of common sense and a powerful intellect. He was also a very good speaker, striking a balance between fact and emotion.

Ben eyed the two sets of board members. He didn't want to stretch this out beyond their tolerance to listen. "I put it to you, gentlefem and gentlemen, that Gabrius Crowder is out of control. That all our actions subsequent to finding the platinum on Olyanda were reactions forced on us by Crowder and van Blaiden working in partnership." He paused for effect and took in each member of his audience with a sweeping gaze. "And now you're all wondering what will happen when this story gets out as it surely will. No, this is not an attempt to blackmail you. It's a plea to your intelligence and better nature. History spins on the point of today because everything we've told you means next to nothing alongside the new discoveries in foldspace."

He felt the shift in the atmosphere in the room.

"Commissioner Rodriguez has already given you the facts about the Nimbus. You haven't failed to notice that you are losing so many ships and colonies that your profit margins are shrinking. Your accountants are probably already weighing the cost of defending Chenon from a vast, if unskilled army. You have now defeated them, but not without throwing massive resources at the problem, and you're probably wondering where they'll strike next.

"There is only one solution: close the jump gate system." He waited for the muttering to die down. "When the Trust and Alphacorp take this problem seriously, the smaller corporations will follow." That's it, butter them up. "We've already decommissioned all the jump gates close to the Independent Planets that have signed up to ally with Crossways. Since then—not one further attack. The attack on Chenon was initially successful because Chenon's three jump gates allowed their battleships and troop carriers through three times as quickly."

He turned to the four hitherto silent Empaths. "Come on, guys, help me out here. Am I lying about this?"

"No, you believe everything you say," one of them said.

"I've seen the Nimbus," Ronan spoke up. "Tiny as it was when I saw it—or I wouldn't be here to speak to you now— it was utterly terrifying because it was the very definition of nothing. It was as if it sucked up your right to life."

"My husband saw the Nimbus a year ago," Mother Ramona spoke. "There is not one night when it doesn't visit his dreams. He wakes screaming."

"I could take you into foldspace," Ben said, "and prove it to you, but you didn't attain your current positions by reckless adventuring."

"Aren't you currently under arrest?" Crowder said.

"Thank you for the reminder, Mr. Crowder." Charles Wong stepped forward. "Charles Wong, gentlefem and gentlemen." He half bowed. "Legal counsel for Mr. Benjamin and the Free Company. I propose that the joint boards put forward a motion to drop all charges against Reska Benjamin, Cara Carlinni, and members of the Free Company, since it must be clear that these charges would be thrown out of a judicial court and fresh charges made against Mr. Crowder." He looked around and paused as if enjoying the moment. "And possibly jointly with your good selves who supported his endeavors, including Mr. Crowder's most recent raid on Crossways to steal the blueprints for the retrofit jump drive. Though Miss Pav Danniri was killed in this morning's attempt on the lives and liberty of the witnesses, we do have her sworn and witnessed video statement clearly stating she was hired by Gabrius Crowder for the express purpose of stealing the blueprints."

He didn't mention that one of her team had a device to blow a big hole in Crossways and eradicate the whole team. Dead men—and women—tell no tales. He didn't need to push the point home; it was all in the transcripts.

Ben didn't even look at his old boss. He wanted to convey that Crowder was beneath concern and contempt. He did, however, see glances from members of both boards in Crowder's direction.

Mother Ramona spoke up. "I have full authorization to make you all an offer. Closing the jump gates will irreparably damage the trade of the megacorporations; we know this. However, losing ships and colonies at this rate will damage them even more. If Alphacorp and the Trust will commit to closing their jump gates with immediate effect, we will release the blueprints and technical details for the new retrofit jump drives completely free of charge." She looked at Miss Yamada when she said it and nodded. "Furthermore, we will not make the plans available to the other megacorps for a period of ninety days, which should give you a head start on the technology. This, however, is dependent upon the free flow of information between the respective R and D divisions of all the megacorps, the FPA, and ourselves in order to finally solve the platinum problem. We all know Earth's history. Even before the meteorite, the planet was nearly lost in the twenty-first century due to catastrophic climate change caused by man-made pollution. We cannot continue to pollute foldspace if we intend to be among the stars for centuries to come. Think about it. It's the best offer you're going to get."

Ben couldn't add to that, so he sat down and shot a sideways glance at Cara.

Chapter Fifty-Five

GLASS

CROWDER WAS SURE HE HAD SUPPORT FROM at least half the board, so he forced himself to sit through Benjamin's testimony with a blank and—he hoped—innocent expression on his face.

Tori LeBon said she'd back him, for a consideration, of course. She was as good as her word as long as he delivered. Isaac Whittle was on his side; he owed Crowder a favor having been tipped off to buy Hera-3 shares at rock-bottom prices before the platinum news broke. Yolanda Chang would do whatever Tori told her, and Adam Hyde always went with the majority. The problems would be Beth Vanders, Sophie Wiseman, and Andile Zikhali.

Vanders and Hyde might not be lovers now, but they had always retained a deep affection for each other. That might influence her. Wiseman was a wild card, easily swayed by rhetoric and ruled by her heart. Zikhali was ruled by his head, cool and logical and always looking at the bottom line.

Crowder figured that when the dust cleared, he should still have his seat on the board. They might not like what he did, but they'd accept it. He'd always been faithful to the Trust. It wasn't as if his motivation had been personal profit, like van Blaiden. The Alphacorp board was lucky the problem of van Blaiden had been taken care of. He knew he hadn't handled this well. He should never have let things drag on after Hera-3. He'd been soft. He'd still thought of Ben as a friend. Dammit, he'd tried to protect Ben and all his psi-techs by recalling them as soon as he realized Ari van Blaiden had jumped the gun and attacked early.

If only Benjamin had obeyed orders, but leaving a colony under attack had not been his style.

He supposed he should be grateful for Benjamin's sense of honor, misplaced as it sometimes was. The man had rescued his daughter and granddaughter from Chenon—and Aggie, too, of course, though he was ambivalent about her survival. He didn't actively wish his ex-wife harm, but she'd made it clear she stood between him and their daughters.

But he did wish Benjamin harm. Last time they'd come face-to-face, Benjamin had almost killed him. Moreover, he was a danger to the Trust. Crowder was confident he had Benjamin this time. He'd made plans, plans that were about to come to fruition right ... about ... now.... He tried not to smile. It was a bold move, but would ultimately benefit the Trust. And as they always did after all his other actions, they would take advantage.

Vetta Babajack asked the witnesses to leave the meeting room as the white-skinned woman with the strange blue hair, Mother Ramona, laid out her offer in more detail. The board members listened attentively. He wished he'd foreseen this development. He'd never have sent Pav Danniri into Crossways. He could simply have waited, and the plans would have fallen into the Trust's lap anyway. Or maybe he could argue that Crossways was only offering now because they realized they couldn't hold on to the plans forever. Someone would snatch them, whether it was the Trust, Alphacorp, or some third-party opportunist.

Throughout the negotiations, Mother Ramona never asked for a pardon for Benjamin and the Free Company. That was encouraging. Crossways was playing its own game.

When the two boards split up to consider their options, Crowder rose to follow, but Tori LeBon nodded to the others to go ahead and turned to him.

"Perhaps you should wait outside, Gabrius. For the sake of propriety, you know."

Nonononono ... This was not how it was supposed to go.

"But I can answer any questions you might have."

"I think we have all we need." She dropped her voice so only Crowder could hear. "You know I have your back."

He nodded. He hoped so.

Vetta Babajack moved over to talk quietly with Ben's grandmother and Malusi Duma. How had the wily old man managed to get in on this decision? It was as if he'd been dogging Crowder's footsteps for the whole year. First the endless meetings over the Trust's local tax liabilities and now this.

Louisa Benjamin looked up. "Do you have somewhere else to be, Mr. Crowder? We have some private business to discuss."

He didn't, but he could take a hint, especially when it was delivered with a sledgehammer. He rose from his chair, resisting the urge to rub the painfully numb patch on his thigh. Dipping his head, he headed for the hallway, letting the door close behind him.

He could see some movement in the elevator lobby. Something was happening. He looked again.

Oh, of course. Perfect timing.

◆ ◆ ◆

Vetta Babajack motioned for them all to wait outside. It was the first time Ben had had the opportunity to see Cara in over a week. His minders tried to edge him out into the elevator lobby, but Jess pulled rank and told them to wait and give Ben a moment.

Ben thanked everyone. Coming to Cara last, he pulled her into his arms. The bruise on her face looked painful.

"Is Ronan taking care of that?"

She nodded. "Nothing's broken."

"Am I forgiven?"

She sighed. "For Gen and Max, and little Liv? Forgiven? I don't know, but I understand what you did, even though I wish you hadn't done it."

"Are we still . . . us?"

She closed her eyes, her lashes beaded with moisture, and touched his cheek. "Presuming you don't end up on a prison planet."

"If I do—"

"You know I'll come and get you." Her eyes crinkled into a smile.

He hadn't known until that moment, but he felt as though a huge weight slid from his shoulders. It hadn't mattered that he'd put his own liberty in jeopardy if Cara wasn't in his future. Running the Free Company without her would be simply going through the motions. When had she become the fulcrum on which his life balanced? If he was honest with himself, he'd fallen hard right at the beginning, though he knew it hadn't been the same for her. He'd had to win her trust—and his recent actions had almost lost it again.

"I love you," he said.

"I never doubted it, you maddening man. I love you, too."

A pointed throat-clearing drew Ben's attention to one of his guards waiting in the doorway. It was a new one. There must have been a shift-change.

"I think my moment is up. I'd better wait with the guards."

"How long do you think they'll take to make up their minds?" She jerked her head toward where the two boards were meeting.

"I don't know. Nan and Grandfather can be quite persuasive, and Mother Ramona is still in there. It's a good offer, considering things can't stay the way they are."

"But it might not save you. Pardoning you and the Free Company wasn't part of Mother Ramona's offer."

The officer coughed again.

Ben glanced up and nodded. "I hope they're sorting that out as well."

He followed the guard out to the elevator lobby where there was a magnificent view of his ancestral homelands through the glass-steel walls. He took it all in, glad he didn't suffer from vertigo. The elevator controls, showing the doors were open, appeared to float in front of him. He could understand why people had refused to ride in there until they put a telltale mat on the floor.

He glanced down.

No telltale.

The doors were open, but the elevator wasn't there.

He looked up and saw the floor of the elevator from the underside. This was the top floor, but there must be a maintenance level at the top of the shaft. At the same time as he took all this in, the three guards moved toward him, backing him toward the elevator shaft.

Crowder again.

"Come on, guys, don't you think this is a bit obvious?"

He still had the damping pin. He couldn't call for help even though he could see Ronan, Wenna and Cara turning toward Mother Ramona as she made a stately entrance. The sound baffles made for excellent privacy, but a marching band could strike up in the lobby without disturbing the meeting rooms.

His guards weren't talking. That was a bad sign. Professionals. He wondered what had happened to his real guards. Three against one. He could possibly manage two, but not with his wrists shackled. He doubted he could take all three, but it wouldn't stop him from trying. At least he could make enough of a commotion to attract attention. Where the hell was Jess? Ben refused to believe he had anything to do with this. These were not Monitors.

He'd barely run the options through his brain when one of the guards jumped forward. Ben dived for the space he created, but it brought him closer to the gaping maw of the elevator and a fast drop to oblivion. He pivoted, swept his feet around, and caught the back of one guard's knees and sent him flying. The second guard put a boot into his ribs while Ben was down, but he sprang up, trying to breathe away the pain, and shouldered him backward. The elevator shaft beckoned, but the guard caught himself on the wall by the control and bounced back toward Ben. The third guard grabbed him from behind. He pushed backward and elbowed him in the gut, but it didn't dislodge him. The other two closed in.

Ben twisted, overbalanced, and took the third guard with him, lashing out at the second with both feet. He couldn't escape a stunner, but if they wanted this to look like an accident or possibly suicide, they couldn't use anything but brute strength. Everyone would know, of course, but it still gave them plausible deniability.

There was a fourth pair of feet. He hoped it was Jess, but

he knew from the shape and the cut of the boots that it wasn't.

Crowder.

He wasn't yelling for help or telling the guards to stop. That pretty much clinched matters. These were Crowder's goons. He couldn't bear to leave it unfinished between them.

Out of control.

And now, so was Ben.

He shoved with his hands and pulled his feet beneath him, coming upright under the chin of the first guard who'd moved in too close. Delivering his own kick to the side of guard number three's head, he launched himself at Crowder with a two-fisted punch to the gut. Crowder staggered back with an audible "Ooof."

"Bastard!" Ben said through his teeth.

Crowder opened his mouth to reply, but he could barely make a sound. The two guards still on their feet came at Ben from either side and effectively pinned him.

"You gave it your best shot, Benjamin." Crowder's breath came in ragged wheezes as he fought for control of his diaphragm. "But I win in the end."

"I don't think so." Tori LeBon's voice cut through his words.

The whole of the Trust board had poured out of their meeting and into the elevator lobby.

His would-be assassins had frozen at the sight of Jess Jessop's stunner. He fired anyway. Three times. The two at Ben's elbows dropped to the floor, the one already down twitched and lay still.

The Free Company came charging out into the lobby, too, forcing the board members closer to Crowder.

"That was ill done," Tori LeBon said. "I think you'd better offer your resignation, Gabrius."

"Seconded." Whittle took another pace forward.

"I would have seconded the motion if he hadn't." Hyde joined him.

"Me, too," Beth Vanders said, taking another pace forward.

"I've never wanted anything for myself," Crowder yelled. "The rest of you have skimmed profits where you could and built your own fortunes. All I've ever done is work for the Trust. I've been faithful. I've no more credits in the bank now than when I took on this job. My ancestor Anne Di-Doran—"

LeBon laughed. "Oh, Gabrius, you were such an easy convert. You spent hardly any time at all in Neural Readjustment as a new recruit, yet you came out believing you had a direct connection to Anne DiDoran. The Trust is your whole life! Of course, it is. My predecessor ensured it. I've known your history since I became chair of the board."

Crowder's expression passed through shock and disbelief to realization and anger.

Of course . . .

Ben's face may have mirrored Crowder's as he took in the information. He thought of the decisions Crowder had made. Yes, always doing the best he could for the Trust, sometimes at the expense of ordinary people. The man had never been his own master. Maybe the friendship he'd once offered Ben was a mark of the man he might have been. Ben didn't know whether to feel angry or sorry for him.

"But sometimes things work too well." LeBon stepped forward. "You've become a liability, an embarrassment."

Sweat beaded on Crowder's forehead. He stepped toward the gaping hole where the elevator should be. His left arm flailed as he reached out to slap the control and summon it, not once, but three times. The panel gave a jaunty ping.

Ben glanced upward. The elevator hadn't moved.

"I guess this is unanimous," Zikhali stepped forward. "We've heard enough today."

LeBon smiled, with lips and teeth only. "The best thing you can do for the Trust now, Gabrius, is to resign. Your final act of true loyalty."

Crowder searched the faces of his fellow board members. His gaze came to rest on a young man who slid through the crowd to stand beside him. "Stefan, I knew I could rely on you."

"Why? Because you sent me to have my mind altered? Didn't think I knew? My loyalty lies with the lady who let me out of there whole." He glanced sideways to LeBon. "Who do you think I've been reporting to?"

She nodded back. "You know what to do, Stefan."

Stefan's foot snaked out. Crowder tried to keep his balance and staggered into the elevator that wasn't there.

"Resignation accepted," LeBon said.

For a moment Crowder teetered on the edge, realizing what he'd done. He reached out toward Ben.

He was close enough to touch.

Ben could have grabbed him.

But he didn't.

Crowder fell without a sound.

✦ ✦ ✦

"Ben!"

Cara's knees felt like jelly, but she elbowed through the crowd and stood between Ben and Tori LeBon in case she felt like getting rid of another inconvenience. Ronan followed, then Wenna and Jake. Tengue and Gwala dragged the unconscious guards out of the way and stepped over them. Jack drove his float chair forward, too.

She glanced backward at the elevator shaft. Damn silly conceit to have an invisible elevator. Surely, there should have been a fail-safe. She took in the three downed guards . . . unless they'd already overridden it and set it up for Ben to be the one to take the fall.

How close had she come to losing him?

LeBon stepped back. "The Trust board has unanimously agreed to accept the offer on the table. We will close our jump gates in stages, beginning immediately, allowing essential supplies through only. Once we retrofit our ships, we'll destroy the gates in a phased operation."

"As will we." Akiko Yamada stepped forward, peered over the edge of the elevator shaft and shrugged. "Waste of a good brain. Suicide, of course."

"No doubt about that," LeBon said. "It's a hell of a way to resign. So sad. He will be missed." She held out her hand to Yamada. "Here's to a successful project to solve the platinum problem once and for all. I suggest we set up a joint research facility."

"Your place or ours?" Yamada jerked her head toward the building surrounding them.

"How about Chenon? They'll need help regenerating infrastructure after the attack."

"As long as we remove those three jump gates with immediate effect."

"Agreed."

They shook on it.

LeBon turned to Ben and all the Free Company members. "The charges against all of you were instigated by the dear departed Mr. Crowder. Without him, we find that there isn't enough evidence for the Trust to press any kind of case."

"Ditto Alphacorp," Yamada added. "Of course, there will be conditions."

"Our lips are sealed," Ben said.

"Minds, too," Cara said.

With that, Jessop stepped forward and unlocked Ben's shackles.

Chapter Fifty-Six

NIMBUS

"HOW LONG DO YOU THINK IT WILL TAKE them to realize their access to foldspace will be limited not by their ships, but by the pilots who can fly them?" Cara asked.

"Not long," Ben said. "Eve Moyo already knows, but she didn't see fit to point it out, so there's no reason we should. But by the time they realize not every pilot can be retrained, it will be too late. The jump gate network will be broken, the hubs turned into staging posts servicing a smaller number of jumpships, no doubt, but still in business—most of them anyway."

They were back at the hotel lobby in Durban, preparing to leave. *Solar Wind* waited for them at the spaceport.

Malusi Duma, arm still around Nan's waist, came and offered his hand to Ben.

"Thank you for all your help, sir," Ben said, "and thank you for employing Mr. Wong on my behalf."

"Don't forget to call me Mkhulu. All my other grandchildren do."

"Are there a lot of us?"

His grandfather smiled. "Oh, yes. I have been married four times. I have nine children and twenty-eight grandchildren. There are great-grandchildren as well, but I've lost count."

"But you're not married right now." Ben looked pointedly at his grandfather's arm, suddenly feeling protective of Nan, her heart if not her virtue.

Nan laughed. "That horse bolted the stable a long time ago. I'm going to stick around on Earth for a while, Reska. Tell Rion and the boys I'll be home before harvest."

She stepped forward and kissed his cheek.

His grandfather, Mkhulu, watched her fondly. "You should come and spend some time with us as well, Ben, and meet your family. It would be good to get to know you better."

"One day I will."

"But you still have things to do, places to go, promises to keep. Is that right?"

Ben smiled. "Closing the jump gates is going to be a huge change. We'll need to train jumpship pilots, and set up emergency supply routes for those colonies that still rely on imports. Until we solve the platinum problem, we're still going to be polluting foldspace, though not as much as we do now. We've made a start, but there's still plenty to take care of."

The loose ends could keep him busy for a lifetime. Pilot training was only the start. There were still questions about foldspace. Could the Nimbus' human avatars be rehabilitated? That wasn't Ben's problem now. There were captives from Chenon, so the megacorps and the FPA would have to work on it, too.

Nan raised one eyebrow. "Don't take it all on your own shoulders. Share the load."

"He will." Cara had slipped up to his side.

Nan looked at them both and smiled.

The journey home had a celebratory air. The flight deck was full of laughter and relief. Jake cracked jokes, and even Hilde laughed, bandaged and sitting next to Ronan in the bucket seats.

Ben didn't worry about the dips into and out of foldspace. They were so brief that encountering the Nimbus was unlikely. Maybe when the easy fodder from the jump gates disappeared, that would change. The Nimbus could become a wilier predator. He wondered whether it would be possible to send a message to it. Tell it they would prevent fur-

ther incursions into realspace and defend their ships and
settlements with vigor. But also could they tell it that they
hadn't known about the pollution, or at least not about its
effects, and they would be seeking an effective solution.
Was it even possible to explain such human concepts to an
entity with no shared language?

What are you thinking? Cara asked.

That there's one more thing.

Why am I not surprised? It's the Nimbus, isn't it?

*We've done it a great disservice. Yes, it's terrifying, but it
didn't start trying to kill us until we started to fill its home
with deadly platinum.*

What are you thinking?

Kitty Keely. She wants to go back to the Nimbus. Why?

Cara shrugged. *Let's ask her.*

On Crossways, the Free Company came together to ex-
claim and congratulate. They were truly free at last, no longer wanted criminals. For some of them, it meant being able
to contact their families again and either return to them or
bring them to Crossways. They all had choices now, and not
all of them would stay. But for some of them, the Free Company was their family. Yan Gwenn had been wrong; they
would not simply drift apart.

Jussaro had hitched a ride from Olyanda to offer his congratulations in person and to report on the progress of
Sanctuary.

Garrick came by Blue Seven to collect Mother Ramona.

"You did the right thing to offer the jump drives to the
megacorps," Ben said. "It's what clinched the deal."

"Sometimes you have to give to receive," Garrick said.

"How are the dreams?" Cara asked.

Garrick lifted one shoulder in a shrug. "I'm learning to
live with them. Sometimes that's all you can do. At least
with the damping pin Mona is getting a good night's sleep,
and I hope you are, too."

"Much better."

"Good."

"And how shall we sleep tonight?" Ben lowered his lips
to the side of Cara's neck and whispered.

"Is that an invitation?"

"Only if you want it to be."

"I do."

"Do you suppose we could sneak off now without anyone noticing?"

"I'm sure they'll notice. Does it bother you?"

"Not in the slightest."

"Let's go, then." She took his hand.

❖ ❖ ❖

Cara stretched in bed. Her world was coming right again. Ben was a warm mound beside her, still sleeping soundly after a glorious night. They should fall out more often if reunions were always so good.

Her mind turned to breakfast and then beyond.

Kitty Keely. Did she truly want to return to the Nimbus?

Ben turned in bed, and Cara knew he was awake. "I don't suppose I could talk you into taking the day off?"

He groaned. "Don't tempt me. Let's get this last thing over."

"Kitty."

"Yes. We need to talk to Ronan, and to Syke, too. He's the only one who can stand as an advocate for her."

"Breakfast first."

"I think we can take time for that."

They breakfasted in the canteen alongside a dozen other late risers, receiving knowing looks from some, which Ben answered with a grin.

"I sent a message for Syke to join us. I hope you don't mind," Ben said.

"Better to get the Kitty thing over with."

"I thought so."

Syke arrived as they were finishing up. Ben explained his thoughts about Kitty and the Nimbus.

For the longest time Syke didn't say a word, then he nodded. "She talks to me, but she's not happy. She's placid and then she turns into something wild, without any reason or explanation. She's becoming more and more divorced from her former life, less and less like herself. There's not much of Kitty left, the Kitty I knew, I mean. She looks like Kitty, but that's all. She keeps asking to go home and she means back to the Nimbus."

"I'm sorry," Cara said. "I know you cared for her."

"I still do, but you know what they say: if you love someone, let them go."

Ben nodded. "If we take her into foldspace, do you want to come with us?"

"Yes. You will give her a choice, right?"

"Of course."

Ronan admitted none of his regression therapy had penetrated the shell she wore. Kitty was most relaxed when talking to Syke, but even that was failing lately. She alternated between bouts of violence and sullen depression.

"I've tried everything," Ronan said. "At this rate, she'll end up in an institution for the violently insane. None of us wants that, but she's dangerous to others, and probably to herself as well. The Nimbus started all this. Maybe the Nimbus can finish it, one way or another."

"You realize she might not come back?"

"Give her a choice. When she's not actively trying to kill someone, she's as rational as anyone."

So Cara, Ben, Ronan, and Syke confronted Kitty through her glass window.

"This looks serious," Kitty said. "A delegation. For me. Should I be flattered?"

"We've come to see what you want to do," Cara said. "You keep saying you want to go home, but where is home? Do you want to go back to your mother?"

"My mother?"

"You used to be terribly worried about her."

"Did I?"

"Kitty," Syke said. "Look at me."

She did.

He put his right hand on to the glass and she pressed her own against it from the other side.

"I care for you, Kitty. But I want you to be happy. Do you truly want to go back to the Nimbus?"

She took a deep breath. "More than anything."

"Ask her if she can take a message?" Ben whispered.

"I heard that," Kitty said. "What do you want it to know?"

"We didn't know about the platinum pollution. Now we know, we're working hard to solve the problem. In the interim, we'll be closing all the gates. There will be far fewer ships, less pollution, and eventually no pollution at all."

She nodded.

"Once the gates are closed, the Nimbus won't be able to send its armies. It won't need all those people. Can it send them home, not to kill, but to take up where they left off?"

"I don't know."

"Can you ask?"

"Are you asking me to speak for humankind?"

"I am."

"That's a big ask. I'm not even sure if I'm hu—"

"Can you do it?"

"I believe so."

✦ ✦ ✦

Garrick's hand tightened on Mona's as he listened to Ben Benjamin's plan. Eventually, she winced and pulled her fingers free.

"When are you going?" Garrick asked.

"Now. No point waiting," Ben said.

"Do you think—"

"I have no idea. It's worth a try, though."

"We left Kitty behind once," Garrick said. "Will we have to do it again?"

"I don't know."

"You said 'we,'" Mona said.

"I did, didn't I? I think I have to go, too. Kitty said the Nimbus sang to her. It sang to me, as well, but I didn't hear the end of the song."

"Do you want to go?"

Did he? He shook his head. "I don't, but I might have to. Maybe if I face the Nimbus down, I won't be so scared of it anymore."

"And what if you don't come back?"

"Then I certainly won't be scared of it anymore."

His laugh sounded hollow, even to himself.

"I'm coming, too," Mona said.

He didn't even argue, but took her hand again, this time being careful not to crush her fingers.

✦ ✦ ✦

There were too many ways this could go wrong. Ben suited up, wishing he could have persuaded Cara to stay behind.

Tough, she told him, picking up his thought.

They walked to the office hand in hand.

Wenna fussed around them, brushing a bit of nonexistent lint from Ben's shoulder. "You two take care of each other."

"Remember what I said about keeping the Free Company together," Ben said.

"You know I will."

"And keep a look out for Sanctuary as well," Cara added.

"Jussaro's a big boy. He can look after himself." Her face softened. "You know I'll do that, too."

"I know."

"Not that I'll have to."

"Of course not," Ben said. "We'll be back by suppertime."

"You'd better be."

Jake joined them, and finally Ronan and Syke with Kitty. She didn't appear to be in homicidal maniac mode, which could only be good. Perhaps now she was finally getting her wish, she had decided to cooperate.

They met Garrick and Mother Ramona in Port 46. Ben guessed Garrick would have preferred Mother Ramona to remain safe at home, too, but there was little chance of that. Sometimes you had to roll with people's choices.

Climbing up to the flight deck, he was surprised to find Gwala already at the main tactical station.

"Hilde's as mad as blazes that she's not fit enough for duty yet," Gwala said.

"How is she?" Ben asked.

"She says her wounds itch, which is a good sign, and she's cranky."

"That's a good sign, too."

"I hope so. I'm not sure how much more crank I can take."

"As much as she needs you to, I guess. Thanks for coming, Gwala."

"All part of the job."

They all fit somehow: Cara on comms, Jake on systems, Mother Ramona in the spare tactical seat, with strict instructions from Gwala not to touch anything; Garrick in the little-used engineering station—little-used because Dobson was, as usual, down in engineering, preferring the hands-on approach. Ronan and Kitty took the two bucket seats. Syke settled on the floor next to her.

Ben slid into the pilot's chair, placed his hands on the controls, and linked into the ship's navigation systems. *Solar Wind* lifted on her antigravs and slid gracefully away, down the glideway into space. On precisely the hundred-klick mark, Ben popped them into the Folds.

"What now?" Garrick asks. "How do we find the Nimbus?"

"With Kitty on board, I think it will find us," Ben says.

"One minute," Jake calls.

"Is that all?" Cara says. "It feels like hours already."

A form swirls through the bulkhead.

"There's a void dragon here," Ronan says for everyone who can't see it.

The void dragon curls its sinewy shape around the pilot's chair and concentrates on Ben.

OLIVIA MAY MARLING, it says.

"Not this time," Ben tells it.

EXPLOSION.

"I hope not. We're going to talk to the Nimbus."

NIMBUS.

The void dragon shudders, but it doesn't disappear. Instead, it shrinks down to the size of a large dog and curls up at Ben's feet. It's coming along for the ride. That's unusual. In the past, it's always preferred to stay away from the Nimbus.

"Two minutes," Jake calls.

"I can hear it singing." Kitty closes her eyes. "It's beautiful."

"Oh!" Garrick says. "That's it. I can hear it, too."

Mother Ramona stands and crosses over to him, both her hands resting on his shoulders as if she can hold him into his seat.

"Screens," Ben says.

Jake spins the screens through all the available angles and then settles on one that has a darker shade of blackness. "Is that it?"

"Oh, yes," Kitty almost breathes the words. "I should go." She turns to Syke. "For what it's worth, thank you."

"You don't have to go. Stay with me." Syke's voice comes

out in a choking sob, but he swallows down the emotion.
Though Ben sees his hand twitch toward Kitty, he doesn't
grab her.

She looks at him, face full of regret, maybe for something that might have been.

"Remember the message," Ben says.

Kitty nods, bends her knees, and springs for the ceiling,
floating as if there's no gravity. She goes straight through.
Everyone looks to the screen as her small form crosses foldspace. The Nimbus swells toward her and draws her into
itself tenderly, like a lover.

"Is that all?" Syke asks.

"I don't know whether we can expect more," Ben says.
"Kitty's got what she wanted."

Suddenly a tendril shoots out from the Nimbus faster
than Ben would have believed possible and twists itself
around *Solar Wind*.

"Oh, shit!" Jake speaks for all of them.

"No, no, no," Garrick says.

Ben rolls the ship from side to side, up and down, back
and forth like a bucking bronco trying to dislodge a rider.

Mother Ramona staggers and falls against Garrick who
grabs her and drags her on to his knee. Syke drops into Kitty's vacant seat.

Another tendril wraps around and joins the first. It
catches *Solar Wind* and holds her tight. Her desperate
movement slows. A darkness begins to form in the center of
the flight deck, small as an eyeball at first, but growing until
it's the size of a human head.

Garrick sets Mother Ramona to one side and stands up.

"You. Have. No. Hold. Over. Me!"

She grabs his hand and pulls him back.

From being a formless blob, the shadow begins to shape
itself until it's a human head with a recognizable face.

Kitty.

WE UNDERSTAND.

The voice isn't exactly Kitty's, but it's close enough.

WE WILL RETURN THEM.

The void dragon swirls around the space, grows to fit the
flight deck and raises its head on its long neck and stares
directly into the Nimbus' eyes. It says nothing, but the

Nimbus fades. In an instant the void dragon swells, bursts out of the flight deck into foldspace, coils around *Solar Wind*, and pulls her free of the Nimbus' black tendrils.

GO, it says.

Ben doesn't need telling twice. He finds the line and hits realspace. Glad to be alive.

Chapter Fifty-Seven

AFTERWORD

THE NIMBUS WAS AS GOOD AS ITS WORD.

One year and four months later, when most of the jump gates had been destroyed and levels of pollution in foldspace were beginning to fall, a ship came through one of the last remaining gates. The Monitors might have destroyed it out of hand, but it simply hung there, not making any attempt to evade them or to bring its weapons online. The comms operator identified the ship as the *Konstantin* and said they'd had a little trouble in the Folds.

Figuring this might be another ploy like the original refugee ships, the Monitors directed them to land on Butterstone, now deserted but still with all its facilities in place. Records showed the *Konstantin* to have been lost in the Folds fifty-six years earlier. Her passenger list of six hundred tallied exactly with the records on file. The pilot thought they'd had a rough crossing which had taken almost a day instead of the expected few minutes. He was astounded to discover they'd lost fifty-six years.

Though the passengers were in shock, they didn't appear to be homicidal. These returnees didn't have odd gaps in their memories, and after a suitable quarantine period, showed no signs of violent intent.

The *Konstantin* was soon joined by the *Chandler*, the

Finton, the *Ashelle,* and the *Gwillam*. And that was only the start of it. There were civilian transports, military ones, cargo ships with their goods as fresh as if they'd never gone missing.

The task of sorting out the returnees fell to the Monitors. They headed a combined task force drawn from all the megacorps. Checking to see if the returnees had living relatives who were willing to take them in, or restore property and funds which had been distributed according to their wills, was a massive and ongoing task. The legal hot mess looked likely to keep a brigade of lawyers in work for decades.

Cara divided her time between comms duties for the Free Company and the new facility on Olyanda, which housed not only Sanctuary, but also the flight training school which had outgrown Crossways.

Ben spent about half his time on Olyanda and half on Blue Seven, not always coinciding with Cara, as their duties sometimes dragged them in different directions, but they managed about two thirds of their time together. This was a good thing since they were now a family of four, the twins, Duncan and Kaitlin, having been born six months earlier.

Jake's cousin Dree had inserted herself into the family as nanny, secretary, and trainee identity forger.

Ben concentrated on the Free Company, still resisting Garrick's persistent attempts to inveigle him onto taking a more active role in the governance of Crossways. Their fleet of jumpships had grown and much of the Free Company work involved transporting goods and people between colonies, and assisting in task-force projects.

Ricky had his implant and was showing every sign of becoming a Navigator like his Uncle Ben. His father had given up trying to hold on to his strings and had willingly consigned him to Ben's care for a three-year course at the University of Crossways on condition he returned to Jamundi for the long holidays. Nan always tried to make her visits coincide, but since Malusi had finally reduced his duties as outgoing president, they'd been making up for lost time visiting relatives, and finally managing to see the Ice Falls of Venezuela.

Dido Kennedy and Yan Gwenn hadn't managed to solve the platinum problem, but Dido had added a component to the Mark III jump drive that reduced platinum emissions, coughing the residue into realspace after the jump instead of into foldspace, where at least there were no creatures—to their knowledge—allergic to it. She was now working on a method of catching and recycling it.

Everything was as it should be.

And then Cara received a call from Jess Jessop.

She was down on Olyanda, helping Jussaro with half a dozen psi-techs who'd found their way from one staging post to another, until they'd been picked up by Ben in *Solar Wind* and brought to Sanctuary.

She'd just completed a delicate alteration to a woman's handpad to give her a new identity, when she felt a telepathic handshake she recognized.

Hey, Cara, is Ben with you?

He's up on Crossways, Jess. Are you coming to visit? We haven't seen you since before the twins were born.

This is official business.

Should I be worried?

Not exactly. Jess paused. *We've processed a new batch of returnees. Robert and Anju Benjamin, lately of Chenon, were on the passenger list. Would they happen to be any relation?*

We're on our way, Jess. See you soon.

Cara could hardly believe it. Ben's dream of rescuing his parents from the Folds had come true, if only by a roundabout route. It was . . . She took several deep breaths. Stupendous. Momentous. All those things and more.

Ben would be . . . what? Elated. Ecstatic . . . and probably scared shitless. Two people who'd meant so much, but whom he'd never known except as the perfect parents of his own personal legend.

The Benjamins would be expecting to find two children waiting for them. How would they take the news that they now had adults? Not only that, but they had grandchildren. Hell, they had great-grandchildren with Kai's two, a girl, little Anju, having followed Baby Bobby Benjamin barely a year later. And both of Kai's kids were named after the returnees. That could get confusing.

Cara swallowed hard. Names were going to be the least of their troubles. What if they didn't get on? What if Robert and Anju Benjamin couldn't readjust?

Ben. Come and pick us up, Cara said. *We need to get to Butterstone. Quickly! And send someone to Jamundi for Rion, Ricky, Kai and the family. Your parents have come back.*

She should have been able to sense what Ben was feeling, but he clamped down on his emotions. He arrived on the landing field, dropping Solar Wind neatly on her antigravs. Cara scooped up the twins, one in each arm, and hurried across.

Ben came down the ramp. He wasn't hiding anything from her right now. Cara felt the full wash of hope, fear, excitement. She didn't hesitate but ran toward him. He enfolded all three of them in his arms. She buried her face in his neck, and he hugged them all, laughing.

Ben took Kaitlin and settled her in one of the baby seats that had temporarily replaced the bucket seats. Cara strapped Duncan into the second one. They'd already decided to ignore the perceived wisdom about taking babies through the Folds, it being preferable to leaving them behind. Ben was always careful to do shallow, short jumps, however, to avoid unwise meetings with the void dragons. That would happen eventually, but not yet.

"Aren't you scared?" Cara asked him as Solar Wind rose on her antigravs and then pointed her nose to the clouds and surged forward. "I'm petrified, and they're not even my parents."

"Is that why I feel as though I'm about to have a heart attack?" He laughed. "Yes, scared and delighted in equal measure. All sorts of things are churning through my mind. I'm older than my own father by a couple of years. And Rion is almost old enough to be his father. I don't know how that will sit with my dad at all."

"Nan will be the only one who relates to your parents in the same way. She'll remember them both at the age they are now."

"It's all so complicated. I won't blame them one bit for having a hard time adjusting."

"How old were you when they were lost?"

"Rion was nine, I was six. He'll have better memories than me. I'm not sure what I remember. Maybe my memories are only photographs mixed up with what Nan told me about them."

He slipped into a silent reverie, but Cara wasn't fooled. Although he looked calm, she could tell his thoughts were still churning.

Eventually, he took a deep breath. "Let's take it as it comes. If they want to go back to the farm on Chenon, it's vacant. And I checked, it wasn't damaged in the Nimbus attack. Too far out of the way, I guess. Or if they prefer, there's plenty of land on Jamundi and a whole family to help them break the ground."

"What if they decide to have more children?"

His jaw dropped and his eyes widened.

"You said they're still young."

"Dad's thirty-three and Mom's thirty-one. They might want more children. Yes, why not? They've lost the two they had. Even though we're not dead, we're certainly not their boys anymore. How strange it will be." He laughed. "Yes, I think we definitely need to take it as it comes."

Cara fed the twins and changed their nappies while Ben made the approach to Butterstone. Then she strapped them in again for the actual landing.

Ben brought *Solar Wind* down on a new landing pad a few miles outside of Rhyber City. The Crossways Protectorate had sanctioned the empty colony's use as one of the new staging points for returnees. Though many of the bewildered people were going back to their families or their original home planets, some had been cut adrift by time and were settling on Butterstone, taking advantage of the infrastructure already in place, though conscious of the reason it was a ghost town.

"I think they all know it could have been them sent to fight," Jess said when he picked them all up from *Solar Wind* in a groundcar. Cara bundled the twins into the back and hooked their flight harnesses into the safety restraints before squeezing herself between them. Duncan beamed beatifically while Kaitlin wriggled and fussed, so Cara only had half her attention on the conversation between Ben and Jess.

"Are we sure it wasn't?" Ben asked. "Some of the attackers found their way back to the Nimbus through the Folds."

"If it was, their memories have been wiped very thoroughly. I think most of these returnees were in some sort of long-term storage for later use. None of them remembers anything after entering foldspace until they reappeared a short time ago. Some have been missing for less than a year. It's the long-term ones we're worried for."

"Like my parents."

Cara saw Jess' shoulders rise and fall. "They've all had the lectures, a reorientation course, and a session with a psychiatrist and a psychologist, but it won't hit them until they see their families again—or not, as some of their families are long gone. Yours are lucky—well—for a certain definition of lucky, I guess. Here we are."

Jess rolled the groundcar to a stop outside a modest house on the outskirts of town. "Just give me a call if you need a lift back to your ship."

"I'm expecting Rion and the family sometime soon. Jake's bringing them. I don't know how long it will take Nan and Mkhulu to arrive."

"Mkhulu?"

"Zulu for Grandfather. Malusi Duma."

"Malusi Duma is your grandfather?"

Ben grinned. "I guess I didn't make that clear."

"No wonder— Oh, well played."

"Make no mistake, he wouldn't have backed me about closing the jump gates if he'd thought I was making a mistake, but he did know all of the details of Crowder's dirty dealing, so he was already on my side when it came to the Trust. In fact, he'd been after them for tax evasion on behalf of the FPA for years. He's retired now—officially—which means he's enjoying sticking his nose into all sorts of dark corners and shining a little light where it's needed."

"And your Nan?"

"Still with him. They say they're thinking of getting married. It's only taken them most of a lifetime to get around to it."

"Well, good for them."

"I think we're expected." Cara interrupted. "I saw someone at the window. Here, Ben, take Kait. She's being a little wrigglebottom."

Cara handed Kait into Ben's waiting arms and climbed out of the groundcar, reaching in for Duncan who waved his arms around and made experimental singing noises.

The front door opened, to reveal a couple standing in the doorway, hesitant smiles on their faces. Cara would have rec-

ognized Robert for a Benjamin anywhere. He was lighter-
skinned than either Ben or Rion, but he had the same
broad-shouldered, slim-hipped build and he still looked fit
and outdoorsy. Well, that was only logical. According to his
timeline he'd been heaving bales of hay around on the farm
less than a couple of weeks ago. He looked like Malusi, she
realized.

Ben's mother was petite and slim, with altogether more
delicate features, but much darker skin. Ben had once told
Cara that though her family had been on Chenon for over
two centuries, they still referred to northern India as the
home country.

She looked up as they approached, her expression hopeful.

"Rion?" she asked.

"No, Mom. Reska, though these days everyone except
Nan calls me Ben."

"Reska. My little boy." She put one hand to his cheek.

Cara stepped forward and took Kait in her other arm as
Anju hugged her little boy and he hugged her back.

"I'll get my turn next." Robert smiled at Cara. "You look
to have your hands full. May I help?"

"These are your grandchildren. The smiley one is Duncan and the little madam is Kaitlin. I'm afraid she needs
changing again. There's only so much that self-cleaning fabric will take."

"Nappies hold no fears for me. Give me the smelly one
and come inside. We have the kettle boiling. I'll make tea.
You must be Cara. Prime Jessop told me about you."

"Only the good bits, I hope. Pleased to meet you," she
said. "And you don't know how much I mean that."

Tea. Suddenly the Benjamins felt like family. It was easy
to see both Malusi and Nan in Robert, and Robert in Ben,
while Ben's finer features, straight hair, and inherent grace
came from Anju.

By the time they had exchanged hugs all around, dealt
with the twins, and been furnished with tea in sensible ceramic mugs, two groundcars had pulled up outside. Cara
peered out of the window.

"It's Rion and Kai and family, and—oh, fantastic—Nan
and Malusi as well. They must have arrived at the same
time." She turned to Robert and Anju. "Prepare to be overwhelmed."

While Nan reacquainted herself with her son, and Robert and Anju met their family, Cara left the twins on the rug with Kai's little ones and slipped into the kitchen area to wash mugs and make more tea.

Thea followed her in to help. "It's all a bit overwhelming, isn't it?"

"For them," Cara said. "They had two descendants when they left and now they have eight—and that's not counting us."

"Are you hiding away?" Robert grabbed a drying cloth.

"Of course not," Cara said. "We're just talking about you."

He laughed. "Are we what you expected?"

"I don't know what I expected. I thought you'd be overwhelmed, sad to have missed your boys growing up, uncomfortable because they're older than you."

"Yes, all of that." His face was suddenly serious, but he forced a smile. "It's going to take a while to get used to the idea, to hear all of your stories, to decide on our next move." He tilted his head to one side, a gesture she'd seen Ben do a thousand times, and never taken any notice of until she saw it mirrored by his father. "But I think of it this way—no one has ever figured out how to time travel and this is like time traveling for us. We've come fifty years into the future. We get to see what our sons have become, and though we didn't have as much of a hand in that as we'd have liked, it seems as they are both fine men."

"Yes." Cara grinned. "They are. Ben and I have both time traveled. Cryo—like Nan."

"I think I'll throw away all clocks until I get used to it."

Ben joined them, putting his arm around his father's shoulder. "There's plenty of time to get used to everything. We're happy to have you both back."

"A toast," Rion called as Cara handed out refreshed mugs of tea. "To the Benjamin family and all who sail in her."

"Benjamins," Cara echoed and grinned at Ben.

He winked back.

Yes, plenty of time.

Lisanne Norman

The *Sholan Alliance* Series

"This is fun escapist fare, entertaining..."   —*Locus*

"Will hold you spellbound."
—*Romantic Times*

To Order Call: 1-800-788-6262
www.dawbooks.com

Jacey Bedford
The Psi-Tech Novels

"Space opera isn't dead; instead, delightfully, it has grown up."   —Jaine Fenn,
author of *Principles of Angels*

"A well-defined and intriguing tale set in the not-too-distant future.... Everything is undeniably creative and colorful, from the technology to foreign planets to the human (and humanoid) characters."
—*RT Book Reviews*

"Bedford mixes romance and intrigue in this promising debut.... Readers who crave high adventure and tense plots will enjoy this voyage into the future."
—*Publishers Weekly*

Empire of Dust
978-0-7564-1016-2

Crossways
978-0-7564-1017-9

Nimbus
978-0-7564-1189-3

To Order Call: 1-800-788-6262
www.dawbooks.com

Jacey Bedford

The Rowankind Series

"A finely crafted and well-researched plunge into swashbuckling, sorcery, shape-shifting, and the Fae!"
—Elizabeth Ann Scarborough,
author of *The Healer's War*

"Bedford crafts emotionally complex relationships and interesting secondary characters while carefully building an innovative yet familiar world."
—*RT Reviews*

"Swashbuckling adventure collides with mystical mayhem on land and at sea in this rousing historical fantasy series...set in a magic-infused England in 1800." —*Publishers Weekly*

Winterwood
978-0-7564-1015-5

Silverwolf
978-0-7564-1191-6

To Order Call: 1-800-788-6262
www.dawbooks.com